The
GOLDEN HORSESHOES
MURDERS

A Nora Duffy Mystery

august 2022

To: Gary and Karen,

   Happy reading. Thanks for your
friendship!

         Love,

      Babs L. Murphy

Babs L. Murphy
(Barbara M. Croker)

NEWMAN SPRINGS PUBLISHING
320 Broad Street
Red Bank, NJ 07701

First originally published by Newman Springs Publishing 2020

ISBN 978-1-64801-900-5 (Paperback)
ISBN 978-1-64801-901-2 (Digital)

Printed in the United States of America

For Don, my brave hero

Hope is not optimism, which expects things to turn
out well, but something rooted in the conviction
that there is good worth working for.

—Seamus Heaney, Irish poet and playwright (1939–2013)

ACKNOWLEDGMENTS

My thanks to Peg and to all the storytellers everywhere who help us to dream about endless possibilities.

CHAPTER

1

Monday, June 10
Sneem, Ireland; 1:00 a.m., IST

Nora's usual positive and happy disposition was countered tonight by a premonition that something evil was imminent and nearby. These feelings came to her unbidden but undeniable and had often proven to be accurate. Tommy called these her *fairy fey* moments and was convinced that she shared an unbroken link to the mystics that litter Irish history. Nora must have inherited this dubious ability from a long-dead grandmother. Sometimes, these warnings frittered away like the wind, but they were not going away tonight, and she was wary.

The rising fury of the roiling ocean not far from the castle's walls matched Nora's increasing sense of foreboding and reminded her of the witches in *Macbeth*, hard at work stirring up their potent brew:

> *Double, double toil and trouble;*
> *Fire burn and caldron bubble...*
> *Like a hell-broth boil and bubble...*

From the huge windows in her round tower bedroom at the castle, she had a view of the sea and the "greatest show on earth," sunrise and sunset. Back home in Chicago, Nora often barely noticed the sky's transitions, but here on the southwestern coast of Ireland, it was almost impossible to ignore the sun slowly sinking into the ocean at dusk, the gradual twinkling of a zillion stars, and then the first red and golden rays of the dawn.

She was becoming more familiar with the various sea sounds that reminded her of the eternal breathings of a great beast like *Smaug* in *The Hobbit*, sometimes just quiet and rhythmic but now roaring and uncontrollable. Huge waves and spray were slamming into the rocks at the cove, and she could only imagine how noisy it must be for the inhabitants of the few old thatched cottages on the hill that faced the beach. Through the pounding rain, she could see the lights of a large ship in the distance that was probably headed for Cork Harbour, and she hoped that those brave sailors who consistently put themselves in harm's way would be safe.

A streak of lightning directed her eyes to a streetlight in the parking lot and a person who was running through the downpour. No one should be out in this storm, and she wondered who it might be.

Nora's two big dogs, Liam, the very tall and white wolfhound, and Bran, the graceful Irish setter, were usually sound sleepers, but they had sensed Nora's distress and came to share it with her as she peered out the window. She could feel them shaking underneath her touch, and she was chilly too. It was only 1:00 a.m., so Nora sent the dogs back to their sheepskin rugs by the fireplace. Liam didn't realize how big he was and had tried a few times to curl up next to Nora, but Tommy had discouraged the sharing of their bed by the immense dog that was twice as big as his mistress.

Nora crept back to bed and attempted to get a few more hours of sleep. She dozed for a while and dreamt of trying to fight off something that was dragging her into the ocean. Nora was a moderate swimmer at best, and the thought of those powerful waves closing over her head forced her to wake up a few hours later with a yelp and a headache. *Wow,* she thought, *something surely has me spooked today.*

She reached over to Tommy's side of the bed and then remembered that he had stayed in Dublin last night after his meeting. They had only been married for a few months, and she disliked these separations, no matter how brief. He often complained to her that these meet-and-greet sessions with international lawyers were boring, so she hoped he would be better pleased this time.

Nora felt covered with love as she huddled under the colorful new quilt that she had received in the mail from Grandma Dee yesterday. She could picture her grandmother and her longtime friends hand sewing the oversized green and gold quilt pieces patterned with many Celtic symbols and backed with dark green velvet. They loved doing this with their arthritic fingers, but she doubted that she would have had the patience to sit still as long as it must have taken them to complete this masterpiece. It was so beautiful; she probably should have just hung it on the wall, but she knew they had made it to keep them warm and comfortable, and it was certainly accomplishing its intended purpose.

She tried to shake off her negative feelings, since morning was her favorite time of day. She believed in her family's motto: "You'll have a long time to sleep after you're dead," so she wasted no more time than necessary to begin her energizing routine. A host of concerns and schedules immediately vied for her attention, but she held them in abeyance while she lay still for a few minutes and thanked God for the new day and all its possibilities.

She often woke up with a song going through her head, and today, she found herself humming "We'll Meet Again," the nostalgic and hopeful tune from World War II days made famous by Dame Vera Lynn during Britain's "Darkest Hour."

> We'll meet again,
> Don't know where,
> Don't know when
> But I know we'll meet again some sunny day
>
> Keep smiling through,
> Just like you always do
> 'Til the blue skies drive the dark clouds far away
>
> So will you please say "Hello"
> To the folks that I know?
> Tell them I won't be long
> They'll be happy to know

That as you saw me go
I was singing this song.

So many people had never returned from the war, but the ones who
made it back said this song had given them hope that they would
meet their loved ones again.

Nora had been fascinated by the brain since childhood, and the
impulse to sing these tunes was just another example of the mysterious powers exerted on us by the supercomputer that each of us has in
our heads. She had not thought about or heard that song for years, so
why was it so "top of mind" today? *Did the brain maintain a playlist
of all the songs we hear over the years? Did some cause or another make it
select "play" for a certain song on a certain day?* These were unanswer-
able questions, but she had learned not to take these occurrences for
granted. Perhaps she would be meeting someone again today whom
she had not seen for a long time.

She listened to a raucous chorus of birdsong from the chittering
flocks that made their nests in the towering oak trees that sheltered
the castle. Enticing smells of lavender and roses were wafting through
the garden window that was protected from the elements, as well as
the tang of salty air from the nearby ocean. Embers from the remains
of the peat fire filled the room with that distinctive smell. Ducks
and geese were looking for their breakfast and calling to one another
in the lake, and she could hear soft whinnies from the grazing bog
ponies. *What a spectacularly beautiful place this is*, she reminded herself for the umpteenth time.

At the nearby Franciscan monastery, the monks would be singing the prayers and psalms for matins as another day began, and
Nora joined them in spirit as she asked God to send blessings to all
the people in the world who would be most in need and to keep her
family and friends safe and well.

Her musings were interrupted by Harrigan, the large red and
white rooster who lived in the chicken enclosure far away in the
backyard. His impressive cock-a-doodle-dooing carried for a long
distance and eliminated the need to be reminded that it was time to
get up and moving.

Liam and Bran sensed that Nora was awake and trotted over to her, whining and waiting for her to tousle their ears. They barked a morning hello to her, and she petted their sweet heads and greeted them with her usual song, "Good Morning, Glories." She then stretched for a few minutes, jumped out of bed, and filled the dogs' bowls with Mrs. O'Hara's homemade dog food, which they quickly gobbled up.

Tinker Bell, the calico kitten they had adopted last month from the shelter, had her own little bed, but she had taken to sleeping in the curve of Liam's stomach, which the huge dog seemed to like. Nora had taken a number of pictures of them sleeping together, which her friends found unusual, at best. She played with the bouncy little fur ball for a minute, fed her some of the kitty chow she liked, and put her into her habitat with her toys. Tink pitifully meowed since she hated being separated from Nora, but a long walk was beyond the capabilities of the kitty just yet.

Nora then hopped into the recently rehabbed shower and once again admired the patterned cobalt blue and white tiles that Mr. McGovern and his talented team had used to replace the ancient and crumbling cement in the old bathroom. It was a pleasure now to have a safe and pretty floor and full water pressure as she warbled Violetta's magnificent "Sempre libera" from *La traviata*. Reaching for those high notes forced her to open her eyes as well as her diaphragm, and it was fun pretending that she was Renée Fleming. They had seen her sing *Traviata* at Covent Garden last year and had joined the audience in showering this amazing woman with deafening applause, flowers, and shouts of *brava*.

Nora was gradually using the many wedding presents they had received from the castle's staff, and today, she enjoyed drying herself with the extrathick white cotton towels that sat on the bathroom shelves. One of these days, she might think about getting her long mop of red hair cut, which would make everything easier, but after using a generous amount of the castle's own lavender shampoo on her curls, she settled for a towel dry and ponytail.

The extralarge bathroom contained a sizeable vanity, and she sat down to prepare for the day. Her nod to beauty at this early hour was to cover her face and hands with a thin layer of Carol Cleary's magical skin cream, apply a dab of her favorite honeysuckle rose lipstick, and squirt *Harvesty* perfume on her neck and wrists. She silently thanked Aunt Vinnie for developing these fragrant products, dressed in her comfortable pale pink running gear and chartreuse Skechers and was ready to go.

Her mother had taught her to make her bed right away long ago, but today, Nora settled for pulling up the new quilt and fluffing up the pillows. *I'll give it a lick and a promise*, she thought to herself. *What does that really mean?* She loved all those old sayings that expressed so much wit and wisdom that people had accumulated just by living.

There was always a chance for rain on the Kerry coast, especially after a night storm, so she tied her silver North Face jacket around her waist, just in case. She used her phone's flashlight to look at the thermometer outside the bedroom window and was pleased to see that the moderate temperatures were holding. The waves at the beach seemed to be subsiding, and the morning fog appeared to be minimal. She was slowly getting used to thinking in Celsius terms and knew that the twelve she saw on the gauge equaled about fifty degrees Fahrenheit.

She checked her phone calendar and remembered that Mr. McGovern the architect and Mr. Carmody the construction superintendent were due at 4:00 p.m. for another meeting about the construction dig that was to take place in about a month, as well as the plans to excavate the old part of the castle that had collapsed in on itself hundreds of years ago.

Uncle Cy told me they'd never bothered to explore the ruins, but he thought it possible that it could contain some lost treasures, she thought to herself. There was always something to look forward to here, but the anticipation of what they might find under the enormous pile of bricks was exciting.

She snapped on the dogs' green, white, and orange leashes; grabbed her small backpack; and filled it with her phone, towel, bottled water, and collapsible bowls for the pets. "Well, boys," she addressed her loyal companions, "Tommy's in Dublin and Mrs.

O'Hara is visiting her sister in Limerick, so we won't have to worry about offending her by not eating one of her delicious breakfasts. Let's take the long walk today."

The dogs readily agreed, and she let them lead the way down the inner filigree staircase, their nails clacking on the white and gray marble. They had the feeling that Nora was going to have an adventure today, and they wanted a part in whatever that was going to be. Their ears were up and alert, and their tails were wagging back and forth like metronomes set to *presto* time.

It was too early for Enda Feeney, the delightful receptionist to be on duty, but Nora waved to the security camera and pointed to 4:30 a.m. on her Fitbit watch. The staff at Duffy Hall Castle had become accustomed to the castle's new owner taking early morning runs, so they would not be too surprised, although Chief Herlihy, who was supposed to be responsible for her safety, would not be best pleased.

She then trotted down the twenty-eight exterior steps and used her flashlight to lighten her path. She waved to Uncle Cy's silver leprechaun statue and noticed sadly that the abundant rose bushes lining the path had lost many of their lustrous petals during the storm. She took some breaths of the delicious Kerry air and began to run west toward the Atlantic Ocean and the Coral Beach.

Nora had come to love the surrounding scenery on this run toward Gleesk Pier that refurbished her spirit. It was still dark enough to behold the awesome power of the Milky Way and its incredible number of stars. Chicagoans like herself were used to the fact that only a few handfuls of the very brightest stars could twinkle their way through her giant city's light pollution gloom, so she appreciated the dark sky here all the more.

Some sheep were already rooting around the stone pier in front of her, and she petted a few of the adorable lambs and waved to Mick, their watchful shepherd. She could hear bells tinkling that were tied to the masts of a few colorful small boats that were rocking back and forth at anchor. When the sun came up, the light gray hue of the algae-encrusted Coral Beach against the blue of the sky and the brilliant green of the surrounding trees would be so pretty; this view was the subject of many postcards. She ran down the grassy path that was bordered by tall rocks, and she was suddenly at the beach, a sight that never grew old.

No matter how many times Nora beheld the Atlantic Ocean at close range, she always found herself surprised at its power and dangerous potential. It was a fearsome thought that the next land to be encountered on this huge expanse of water was thousands of miles away. She always remembered this whenever she got too close to the sea and was careful to keep her distance from the currents that could easily carry her past the safety point. Tommy had been wanting to go kayaking here, but Nora was waiting for a calm day on the sea before she would try it.

Each of the excited dogs outweighed her, and they were running faster than her short legs could carry her, so Nora pulled on their leashes to slow them down. Their noses were practically rotating as they sniffed delicious odors coming from a pile of driftwood or the shells of sea anemones and shellfish that enticingly lay on the beach after the tides and the storm had done their work. Nora pulled out the dogs' collapsible bowls and filled them with bottled water, which they quickly slurped up. She unhooked their leashes and let them run into the beckoning waves.

There were a few other stalwart joggers that Nora recognized, and she waved to them and gave them the Irish greeting for good morning, *Maidin mhaith*, or the English pronunciation, *mod-jin wot*. She stopped to chat with Mr. Boyle, one of her tenant farmers, who grew such delicious vegetables on the Duffy estate. He was likely her grandparents' age, but he was a kindred spirit, who could always be found up early walking Flossie, his ancient collie with the sweet face and the game leg. Liam and Bran came running back to Nora and barked hello to Flossie, who returned their greeting. "I wonder what they're saying to each other?" Nora asked herself.

John Boyle removed his gray tweed cap and asked Nora how long she would be staying at the castle this time. That obsequious gesture of taking off his hat as he spoke to her annoyed Nora since the class system was hopefully gone in Ireland, but she also treasured these old customs of loyalty and respect that were fast disappearing now.

I should make more effort to get to know these fine farmers better, Nora thought to herself. *I don't even know if John has a family to notify if anything should happen to him. I'm going to ask Kitty to arrange a special meeting with the farmers when we return in a month.*

She had to speak loudly for the short man with the permanently squinted eyes and sunburned face to hear her over the din of the wind and waves. She told him that she had come for a meeting with her Board of Directors for Duffy Medical, Ltd., but that was finished now. She and her husband, Tommy, would be heading back to Chicago on Saturday.

"I don't know how you do all that traveling back and forth," said Mr. Boyle with a smile, "but I wish you the best of luck with your new building. I saw the news about it in our local newspaper. You're about to start on it soon, aren't you?"

"Yes," responded Nora, "and I hope you will come for the dig that is scheduled for a month from now. We are hoping to have quite a party that day as we begin construction of the Duffy Medical Research Center, where doctors and scientists can hopefully find some clues to counteract rare diseases and help many desperate people. One of my friends in Chicago had a young child die from Tay-Sachs disease, so that is one thing we'll be specializing in."

Just then, Nora heard frantic barks from both of her dogs and Flossie. They were running back and forth in a circle around a clump of large rhododendrons that was also surrounded by squawking birds. She excused herself from Mr. Boyle and ran over to the shiny-leafed plants as fast as she could to see what had them so agitated.

Bran grabbed onto her jacket and nudged her around to the other side of the abundantly blooming rhododendrons covered with purple flowers, and then she realized why the dogs were barking so much. The leaves and flowers were partially hiding what at first glance could have been a wax statue of a nude very pale young woman lying on her back, but this was a person who was now definitely dead.

Nora flinched as she saw small crabs crawling all over the pale body, and bugs emerged from a wide-open blue eye. She'd heard that dogs had been known to eat corpses, but Liam and Bran wanted nothing to do with this smelly thing and were whining and backing away.

Nora shooed off some of the crawling crabs from the woman's body with her backpack and shivered as a drawing above the woman's breasts was gradually revealed of two interlocking golden horseshoes embellished with green shamrocks and all crossed out by a jagged red X.

Nora's earlier concerns about something bad happening today had been confirmed, and then some. She suppressed her tears while gathering her dogs to her, told Mr. Boyle to take Flossie home, and walked far enough away from the body so the unmistakable putrid and fruity smell was less powerful. Then she pulled out her phone and called her old friend Chief Jack Brennan of the Killarney Garda and told him of her grim discovery.

Nora then turned her attention back to the blond young woman and recalled the sobering words of the Anglican burial service: "In the midst of life, we are in death." She was sure this girl hadn't been thinking along those lines when she'd had a recent mani-pedi with cherry red gel nail polish, the only thing she was wearing at the moment.

CHAPTER

2

Monday, June 10
Sneem, Ireland; 5:30 a.m., IST

Chief Brennan had been an enormous help to them at the castle last year when they had been menaced by a crazed killer, and he would know what to do. She recalled wondering about the "We'll Meet Again" song she'd been humming this morning. The chief must be the person she was destined to meet today.

Chief Brennan answered on her first ring, said hello, and asked what she was doing back in Ireland. Nora gave him a brief explanation about finding the dead body on the beach, and she could tell that she had his undivided attention. He almost asked her what she was doing on the beach at this early hour but then remembered Nora's morning energy. He assured her that he would be there as soon as possible and reminded her not to contaminate the scene and to keep anyone else away until he and his team arrived. He said he would set the wheels in motion for the local garda and the coroner to get involved. It was too bad that the body was naked since it would make identification harder for them. He also reminded Nora to be watchful in case a killer could still be lurking nearby.

Death stinks in so many ways. The terrible smells emanating from the body of the young woman came from the release of urine and feces as well as the gases produced by her inner bacteria. The odor was mercifully lessened due to its beach setting and last night's storm but was still nauseating.

Nora was used to seeing dead bodies since she was a doctor at her Chicago hospital, but she usually encountered them after they had been sanitized. She knew it was all part of nature's work for the trillions of bacteria in our gut to start their effective work of eating the body from the inside out within minutes after death, but she had never gotten used to it.

Ravens and seagulls were circling and squawking and had also discovered the dead flesh, and she saw many spots that indicated they had already taken some bites. Nora first said her usual prayer for the dead, "May the angels lead you into paradise," and then she looked closer at the corpse. With her long and straight blond hair, the young woman reminded her of her sister Maureen, who was twenty-two and weighed about 110 pounds. She noticed that there were no obvious cuts or bullet holes or strangulation marks on the front of the body, although a huge purple bump covered most of her forehead. Nora saw no rough skin on her elbows, knees, or feet, so this was a girl who had taken good care of herself. Nora was tempted to cover up at least that poor battered face, but she knew the police would object to that.

Nora's active mind asked herself a number of questions. *Who was this girl, and why was she here? Where were her clothes and her purse? Maybe she liked to swim in the nude and had come out here at night? Maybe she'd come here to have sex with her boyfriend, and an argument ensued? There could be so many maybes—drugs or gambling debts or a prostitution meeting that had gone awry?*

And what about those golden horseshoes and the red X picture over her breasts? The colors were vivid, and if they had been placed there by a killer, how did he do it? Were the horseshoes a clue that she had some connection to horses or just a sign that her luck had run out?

Nora had read a book about the psychology of murder after the violence at the castle last year. She knew that in the US, murder was so common as to be almost unremarkable, occurring somewhere about every half an hour. The root cause of the murder might be sex or money or revenge or just a desire to dominate another person. But whether premeditated or sudden impulse, the murderer at some point lost all self-control and—*bam*—the deed was done and so was the victim. Then it was a struggle by the authorities to find the killer and bring him or her to justice. Sometimes, the killer won, but Nora intended to do what she could to make sure that would not happen.

Sherlock Holmes, when starting a new case, would say, "The game is afoot." Sir Arthur Conan Doyle had adopted this phrase from Shakespeare to indicate that something exciting was about to commence, but as she stared at the grisly apparition so close to her, "game" hardly seemed fitting. Nora thought that anyone who could kill so cruelly would be a deadly serious adversary.

Nora also realized that whoever had treated this young woman in such a vicious fashion could make short work of her with her four-foot-five frame and seventy-five pounds. She had developed a habit of choosing music for any occasion, and she could almost hear the menacing background notes from the movie *Bullitt*. The Coral Beach was relatively small, but in the dim light, it was looking huge and the path back to the castle seemed far away. She whipped her head from side to side searching the surrounding trees and rocks for signs that anyone could be watching her. The moon was waning, and she struggled to see through the fog that seemed thicker now.

There was an abandoned building in the distance, which would make a good hiding place. If the killer were smart, he or she would be long gone by now, but she had heard that sometimes violent per-petrators liked to see what happened once the body was discovered. She saw nothing unusual at first as she scanned the few people on the beach, but there was a man with a large body shape standing next to a yellow boat. *Was he a fisherman or someone more sinister? Was she just imagining it, or was that a dim light flickering in the abandoned building?*

Her trip to the beach that had seemed so attractive had sud-denly lost its allure, and she fervently wished that she were back in bed under Grandma Dee's quilt. She told herself to stop being so jumpy and turned her attention again to the girl's body.

The coroner would have to confirm Nora's guess, but a glance at the decomposition of the body indicated to her that rigor mortis had already set in. The woman must have been killed last night about the time that Nora had been peering out the window at the storm.

It hardly seemed likely that even the killer would have wanted to be out in the midst of that wind and rain. She recalled seeing that person running across the castle's parking lot and wondered if he had anything to do with the murder.

She still considered herself a land lubber from Chicago and had acquired only rudimentary knowledge about the ocean and its changeability, but she was pretty sure that a body found on an Irish beach would likely have been affected by the high or low tides that happened twice a day. Whether the woman had been a victim of drowning was still to be determined, but parts of the body appeared to be pruney and wrinkled.

Nora recalled that Ireland has a plethora of myths that reflect the fact that its inhabitants live on an island. One of the most popular stories is about a fisherman who finds a "selkie," a beautiful woman hidden within the skin of a seal. He removed her seal skin and hid it, brought her home, and married her and had children, but she constantly wanted to return to the sea. One day, this impulse was so overwhelming for her that she searched far and wide until she found her former skin, changed back into a seal, and was never seen again as a woman. Looking at the mournful and piercing eyes of the seals on the beach gave rise to such stories in folklore and in haunting movies like *The Secret of Roan Inish.*

Nora briefly looked around the murder site for any clues, being careful not to walk around too much. There were pieces of driftwood in various places, and any of them could have been used to bludgeon the girl. She saw some cans and plastic bags among the detritus of objects on the beach after the outgoing tide but did not spot anything that looked like it could have been a murder weapon.

Nora saw the dogs rooting around in the algae, and Bran came trotting over to her with something very shiny dangling from his mouth. Nora thanked the affectionate mahogany-colored dog for his help, and she retrieved a most impressive diamond bracelet from him, which she placed in a plastic bag she had in her backpack. It had likely belonged to the dead girl. The coroner's team would be able to determine more about it, but Nora noticed a red welt on the girl's left wrist, so perhaps the bracelet had been ripped off during the death struggle.

Nora sat down away from the body to wait, waving off the predatory birds who were anxiously waiting too. She grabbed some stones from the beach, which she could use to throw at the gulls. She had always thought that gulls were pretty as they floated aloft, but at close range, she could see that their yellow beaks and claws were very pointed and sharp. Ocean gulls were decidedly bigger than those she was used to seeing in Chicago squawking around garbage dumps. These birds provided a service similar to vultures in keeping the beaches clean, but Nora tried not to think too much about what they would do to the body if she wasn't there.

She first called her solicitor at the castle Fiona Finnegan and gave her a brief description of what she had found. Nora could tell that she'd wakened Fiona from a sound sleep, but her brilliant solicitor was always ready for any event. She told Nora that she would likely be asked to make a statement to the garda when they arrived, so she would get dressed and would be with her as soon as she could. Nora asked her to let Sean and Kitty Duffy, the castle caretakers, know where she was, and Fiona agreed that she would.

"Please call Chief Herlihy too," she asked Fiona. "He will not be happy that I've put myself in possible danger. And ask Micheál to come and collect the dogs who won't want to stay around here for hours more."

She next called Tommy in Dublin, who had also been asleep. "Sorry, mate, but I've once again found a way to put myself in the middle of a possible murder," Nora told him. She described the horrible discovery of a beautiful and naked young woman on the Coral Beach.

Tommy didn't waste time commiserating but focused on the most important thing to him. "Bitsy, you're big in spirit but small in body. Keep the dogs right next to you until the garda arrive," ordered Tommy. "The killer might still be there somewhere."

He assured her that he would drive back to the castle, but that would take about four hours. "Let's go to Dan Murphy's Bar for dinner tonight, and you can tell me more about it all. Love you, and give my regards to Chief Brennan."

Nora responded to her sweet husband that she always appreciated his good advice, and she wished he were here with her now. "Of course, you're right," she said. "I suppose I should be keeping Liam and Bran right next to me. It would be a bold and foolish person who would argue with an angry wolfhound of extraordinary size like Liam. If he thought someone was planning to hurt me, the ancient instincts that wolfhounds were bred for when they hunted wolves might return. Please hurry back as soon as you can."

Nora chuckled as she pondered what she had just said about Liam having the potential to be so ferocious. Yesterday, they had encountered a gray squirrel in the woods, and when it jumped closer to them, her gentle giant Liam had yelped and tried to hide his huge head behind Nora's legs. *Oh well,* she thought, *his size alone should be some deterrent to keep an evil doer away, and he is a good growler.*

It would be close to midnight in Chicago, and if her parents had an early morning operation to attend to, they would likely be in bed already. Her father was Doctor Michael Duffy, chief of Cardiology at Holy Savior Hospital, and her mother, Eileen, was his head nurse. Nora settled for sending them a text in case they saw something about the girl on the beach on the Irish news channel. Ireland time was six hours ahead of Chicago, and they often had the television tuned to the Irish news, especially when Nora was there. Her parents had gotten used to seeing Nora's face on television during the last year, but a gossipy story about what she might be spending money on now was very different from seeing their darling daughter being involved with a murder.

It wasn't long before she had a return call from her dad. He had learned to sleep fitfully as an intern many years ago and never got out of the habit. "Bitsy," her father always called her by her nickname. "Yes, we have a triple bypass this morning—young woman, only forty-five years old, but a heavy smoker and drinker. How do you get yourself into these things? I'm sorry that you're going through this alone in that beautiful place. Tell me a little more about the condition of the body."

Nora explained the little she could tell by just looking at the front of the body, and her father said it did seem as though perhaps it was the blow to the head that had killed her, although the paleness of the body could be from blood loss.

"You'll have to see what the woman's backside reveals when the coroner gets there. Look around for anything that could have been the murder weapon. And please call us back later so you can talk to your mother. You know how she worries about you. She'll not be happy to hear that you and homicide are linked up again."

Nora assured him she was fine, with fingers crossed, and promised to call them back with a later update. She also called John O'Malley, the CEO of Duffy Medical, to give him a brief rundown of what had transpired. As far as she knew, Duffy Medical was not involved at all, but she didn't want him or the other members of the board to hear secondhand about her finding the young woman on the beach. A few of the dedicated Irish board members were still getting used to the fact that a young American woman was now the chairman of the board for their large company, and she tried hard not to offend them.

Nora called up Facebook on her phone and looked for news from family members on their site named "Buffy Duffy." She rarely entered a post herself, but she tried to check the latest entries every few days. Today, she saw that her sister Siobhan's boyfriend, Mick, had posted a picture and a warning about a coyote boldly walking on the sidewalk in front of their house. These animals were being seen more frequently even in very populated areas, but this was too close to home. If they were hungry, coyotes could be a menace to anything small or weak, pets or people. She also saw a note from Sister Mary Alice, Grandma Marie's oldest sister, a Dominican nun who lived in Philadelphia. The octogenarian was asking for prayers since she had tripped over a broom and broken her ankle. Nora glanced through the twenty-eight comments this news had elicited so far, and she thought that Sister Alice would be comforted by this outpouring of support.

Nora reflected that there were some aspects of Facebook that probably needed to be curbed, but she was grateful for the instantaneous news and the easiness of two-way communication, no matter one's age. She sent a few responses and then noticed that the weather seemed to be deteriorating again.

As she continued to wait for people to arrive, Nora thought about the events of the past year that had brought her to this place in time.

CHAPTER

3

Monday, June 10
Sneem, Ireland; 6:30 a.m., IST

It was almost a year ago that she had received the phone call from her cousin Sean Duffy and his future wife, Kitty Lloyd, telling her they were in Chicago and wanted to visit them. They told Nora that her uncle Cyrus had died unexpectedly at his castle in Sneem, and they wanted to make sure that Nora and her parents would come to Ireland for the reading of the will and the funeral.

Cyrus had been one of her favorite people, and he was her father's uncle and her grandfather's brother, so she and her parents had dropped everything and got an Aer Lingus flight the next day to Dublin. Uncle Cyrus's chauffer, Old Tim McMahon, had picked them up and drove them west across the island to Sneem, where she had met up with Uncle Cy's sister Aunt Lavinia, the officers of Duffy Medical, and many others she didn't know.

Nora had visited her aunt and uncle at least once a year—and sometimes more often—since she was five years old, and she had always been met at the castle by Uncle Cy's smile and bear hug. It had been difficult to remain composed as she realized she would never experience that welcome again.

She had given little thought to how Uncle Cy had decided to divide up his estate, but the next day, when the will was read, she was amazed to discover that her old friend considered her to be the daughter he'd never had and had left her an enormous fortune. He'd also made her the owner of Duffy Hall Castle, which she had first fallen in love with as a little girl, as well as designating her the Chairman of the Board of Directors for his company Duffy Medical, Ltd., one of the premier medical supply firms in the world.

Nora, Tommy, and the family had been in grave danger from a deranged killer all during this period. Nora still bore the physical scars on her body of several bullets that had fortunately only grazed her scalp and arm and given her a headache, but the emotional scars would take longer to go away.

They were assisted during this ordeal by the resident good ghost of Duffy Hall Castle, whom they thought was likely Bridie Fitzpatrick, whose picture as a young beauty from two hundred years ago hung in one of the bedrooms. Bridie had been the daughter of a long-ago owner of the castle. Once the killer was disposed of and all the danger had passed for the Duffy's, no one had experienced the whispered warnings of the good ghost nor had they smelled her honeysuckle perfume. Nora hoped that something good had happened to Bridie, since she had helped to save them all.

Chief Brennan had been a huge help to them then, as had her Chicago police friends Lt. Matt Braxton and Sergeant Laura Belsky. Nora tried not to think too often about the killer, and the damage that had been done to her and to the castle, but the remnants of those frantic days often came back to her in her dreams.

Nora had been shocked at her inheritance and was still getting used to the fact that she was a very wealthy person. It made her uncomfortable initially, but she had gradually developed coping skills, formed charitable Duffy Foundations in Chicago and in Ireland, and had been trying to use the money wisely. She had discovered that it was difficult to do, and too many people wanted a share of it.

There were definitely some positive things about it. Her younger siblings could now attend any university in the world, and she could easily pay for it, and she was supporting so many charities through her foundations. It had been a balancing act to give her family money, but not too much so they wouldn't become spoiled and unwilling to work as hard as they could. One of the worst things about it was that there was no longer such a thing as being anonymous. She had always taken it for granted that she could travel where she wished without being recognized, but that had gone by the wayside because of her worldwide popularity as the "Mighty Rich Midget."

Nora and Tommy had their fairy tale wedding in Chicago about three months ago on March 17, St. Patrick's Day. They had considered beautiful places around the world as a destination for their honeymoon but had decided on Dingle Town on the tip of the Dingle Peninsula, mostly for its beauty and engaging people but also in the hopes of avoiding the media. They had a marvelous time there and promised to return, but they had been too busy recently.

When they had returned to Chicago, they moved into their spacious new home. It had been designed by a renowned architect, Mr. Jack Kamin, and had been built by Nora's uncle Joe Flaherty and his fellow union workers. The home had turned out to be even better than they had expected, and they were hopeful that someday soon they would be welcoming a baby to the nursery.

Nora had finished medical school and was now a pediatric oncologist surgeon, and Tommy was an international lawyer for his firm in downtown Chicago. Their lives were so busy but were very much intertwined with their large families. Nora had nine siblings—four brothers and five sisters. Tommy had seven siblings—three brothers and four sisters. All of their parents and grandparents were still alive and relatively healthy, and they were fortunate to interact with many other relatives and friends.

Nora and Tommy spent some of their free time as runners and musicians, and they loved ballroom dancing when they could find an orchestra in town. Tommy was a born athlete and belonged to several seasonal sports teams. He had received many awards for his abilities as a rugby player in high school, but he did not want to risk the injuries now that could result from playing that violent sport. As it was, he had to wear a false front tooth from his hockey playing days. Nora tried to keep up with her Irish dancing skills by joining her young sisters when they practiced. However, she had discovered that the addition of a few extra years and lack of daily focus prevented her body from doing the kicks and leaps she had done so easily not long ago.

The couple used to make the trip across the pond several times a year, but with Nora's new responsibilities at Duffy Medical, there was usually something that brought her here now about once a month. She often hankered for the days when she could just go sightseeing and not have to worry about being recognized or have duties that needed her attention.

Nora forced her mind to come back to the present and hoped that everyone would get to the beach soon. She was still nervous about the whereabouts of the killer and was getting tired of chasing away the aggressive birds. The earlier promise of some sunshine was suddenly obliterated as the "Irish mist" turned into a steady rain. Nora was glad she had brought along her waterproof jacket, and she hastily put it on and tied the hood under her chin.

Death stops all our normal human inclinations, Nora mused. *I feel as though I should try to keep the young woman's body protected from the rain, but there's no longer a need for that.* Nora thought this girl must have relatives who were worried about her, and she murmured a prayer for them and what they would soon be facing.

Fiona Finnegan, Nora's friend and solicitor, was an expert in Irish and British law and could converse easily with Enda in the Irish. Fiona arrived shortly looking marvelous, as usual, with her flawless makeup and chiseled ebony hair. She wore a deceptively casual outfit in a lovely shade of teal blue with a matching jacket. Nora loved shoes and admired her friend's cordovan Doc Martens boots. Fiona gave Nora a reassuring hug and got out her umbrella that was, of course, color coordinated to her outfit. Fiona had her notebook ready, but she also had taken the time to bring along a pistol in case anyone was still threatening Nora. Fiona looked fragile, but she was a confident and crack shot. She also never appeared to be in a hurry and always turned all her attention to the problem at hand.

Chief Herlihy and Johnny Moreland, the security people from the castle also arrived, and they did not look happy that Nora had left the castle and gone to such a deserted place without telling them. They were responsible for her safety since she was Duffy Medical's chairman of the board. Sean and Kitty Duffy, the castle caretakers, arrived with a thermos of hot tea for Nora and wearing expressions of concern. Micheál McCann also came running over to them and said he would be glad to bring the dogs back to the castle for their breakfast. Nora assured her trusty canine companions that it was all right for them to leave, and they pulled Micheál faster than he had anticipated as they headed back east.

The arrival of the An Garda Síochána and Chief Brennan at the beach was announced by the wail of sirens and the glow of many blue lights. Nora was always reassured by Chief Brennan's stolid and confident nature. He was just turning the corner as to seeing some gray hairs among the brown, but he was still as vibrant as ever. He gave Nora a hug, and they each wondered how they came to be involved in this sad business too often. He was accompanied by a crew of gardai and crime scene fingerprint analysts and photographers dressed in protective white coveralls.

Nora brought him over to the young woman under the plant, and after a brief glance at the body and surrounding area, Chief Brennan directed his experienced team to get to work. The chief asked Nora for her first impressions about the case. She handed him the plastic bag containing the diamond bracelet the dogs had found.

"The girl must have been lying on the beach for a number of hours when I found her since the crabs pretty much covered her. My Irish setter spotted the diamond bracelet among the algae on the beach. I noticed a red welt on the girl's left wrist," Nora recounted, "so the bracelet might have been torn off during a struggle. I think I saw a dim light in the nearby abandoned building, so I wonder if someone could have been hiding in there. I also saw someone running through the rain during the night in our parking lot. I looked at the clock, and it was 1:00 a.m."

A silvery blue sports car pulling into the castle parking lot told Nora and the chief that Lucy Sullivan, the coroner, had arrived. Nora had met Lucy last year at an event at the castle, and she had been impressed by her BBC London accent and knowledge about her position. Everything around Lucy had an air of glamor, and she did not fit the usual image of a coroner. She was tall and thin with chestnut curls and wore stylish clothing that made her look more like a film star.

Lucy had told Nora then that she had been blessed with good parents and a happy childhood and had married her childhood sweetheart, Rogan Sullivan. Unfortunately, Rogan had died some years ago of an unexpected massive stroke. After that, she had spent five years working in London, where she had acquired her British accent. She'd been busy and fairly happy in London, but Lucy had returned home last year and moved in with her sister Jemma in her restored ancient cottage in Killarney.

Jemma also had a degree in forensic science and sometimes accompanied Lucy on her assignments. She greeted Nora today with a hug and told her she was sorry about the circumstances that had drawn them together. Jemma had told Nora that after some exposure to dead bodies, she'd realized that her interest in the forensic profession was more academic than something she'd want to do on a regular basis. Jemma looked a lot like Lucy but was much shorter and dressed more casually. The two sisters had been best pals as children, and they were happy to be back together again.

Gemma had told Nora that she had married Mac Doherty after university but realized soon enough that monogamy was not for him. After she had seen Mac coming out of Dillon's Pub while kissing first Mary Ann Dennehy and then Patty Gordon, she decided that she'd had enough. In her mother's time, women just endured men like Mac, but Jemma had no intention of waiting for his wastrel ways to change. She had divorced him last year and joined the sisterhood of women who pretend they don't care and can get along on their own. Gemma had become a librarian, and she supplemented her income well by painting attractive pictures of homes and portraits of the owners. Nora had asked Gemma to paint Duffy Hall Castle, and that had gone well and was almost finished.

Nora gave the sisters a brief update about finding the body on the beach, and then the chief directed the experienced coroners to do a preliminary examination. Lucy found it easier to deal with her difficult job if the dead person had at least some kind of identification, so she named the unfortunate girl Blondie. Once Blondie's body was turned over, Lucy discovered that there was a wide and deep incision on the left side of her back, which had likely punctured her lung and her heart.

She told the garda that they should look for any long, pointed knife or similar instrument. She confirmed that rigor mortis had set in, so Blondie would have been killed about midnight, although it could have been even earlier since the cold temperatures at the beach would have slowed down the deterioration of the body.

Lucy explained that they would send the body to the morgue in Killarney for more tests. They would find out more about the head wound and the gash in her back, look for any signs of drugs or alcohol, what her last meal had consisted of, and if she had signs of recent sexual activity. Lucy was especially interested to know more about the golden horseshoes with the jagged red slash, but she did not want to disturb the picture for now. Bud Crotty and other crime scene photographers took pictures of the body from every angle, and then the young woman was loaded into the waiting ambulance and sent on its way.

Chief Brennan introduced Nora to Declan Fortier, the local representative of the garda. Declan was one of those Irishmen with a baby face, but when he said hello and shook Nora's hand, he had a vibrant voice and personality to match. She thought that he would be a good help in the case since he knew the Sneem area well.

Chief Brennan sent out a request on the National Police Service radio and asked if any other cases similar to this one with the golden horseshoes marks had been discovered. He also asked for a report on recent missing young women in the area.

The gardai continued to search the beach for any other signs of weapons or clothing but to no avail. Declan said he used to play in the abandoned building as a child and knew it well. He led a contingent of gardai to the ruins to do a thorough search, and they did find the remains of a fire and the butts of several Marlboro cigarettes. They packaged up the cigarette pieces and gave them to the coroner, who might be able to find some DNA evidence on them.

Someone must have contacted the media, and they soon arrived, bearing all the paraphernalia of their trade. "Oh no," wailed Nora when she saw them. She had a good idea of what to expect after her experiences with them during the past year. The reporters wanted to talk to Nora since she was the one to discover the body. Once they saw her signature curly red hair and small size, they quickly recognized her as Nora Duffy, now one of the richest women in the world.

The media members had spent a lot of time covering her last year, and they now called their news directors to tell them to hold the front page since this was going to be a bigger story than they first thought. Fiona Finnegan told them it was too early for any statements, but she and Nora knew that the media would be pursuing them relentlessly.

The media people said they could put out a request for information about the missing girl. They could photoshop the picture of her face so the gash across her forehead was covered up, and they would ask anyone who knew her to step forward. That would probably help with the girl's identification, so Chief Brennan agreed. He was going to need all the help he could get to find out more about the unfortunate girl and begin to search for her killer.

CHAPTER

4

Monday, June 10
Sneem, Ireland; 11:00 a.m., IST

Some hours later, after the initial investigation and removal of the girl's body, the Duffy Hall Castle crew was finally able to head back to the castle. Fiona said she had business in Galway today but promised to call Nora later. Chief Herlihy, the security director for the castle, was waiting for them. He asked to speak to Nora privately, and she could tell that he was upset with her.

"Miss Nora," Chief Herlihy began, "you keep telling me that you have acquired street smarts since you're from a big city like Chicago, but to me, you're being as foolish as could be prancing around in the dark just so you can see the stars. It seems to me that you and your family live in a rosy-colored world where you assume that most people are good, work hard, and follow the law. I worked in London before I came here, and let me tell you that all over the world, there are lots of people whose only interest is living well but on other people's money. They have no qualms at all about engaging in criminal behavior, including murder. I've encountered guys who would cut your heart out for a few quid. What do you think they would do to you with all your money and your small size? I know you want to continue to live like a regular person, but you lost that type of privacy when you received your inheritance from your uncle.

"At the least, you could let me know when you leave the estate. You've been shot at not far from here, so you should know better. Your big dogs love you, but they would be no match for someone

33

with a firearm. I gave you a gun, but you evidently are not going to use it. We've all grown fond of you, and your uncle Cyrus would not be happy with me if I didn't warn you to be more careful."

The chief looked stern, but Nora could tell that he had been genuinely worried about her. She knew how loyal he had been to Uncle Cy and that he still missed him terribly.

Nora thanked her trusted employee for his wise advice and said she knew he was right. She still had the gun he had given her months ago, and she would talk to Tommy about it. Guns scared her, and she had not wanted to think about carrying one, but she knew she would have to give it more thought now. She gave the chief a hug and sent him on his way.

She said hello to Enda at the reception desk and admired the brilliant green and orange outfit she'd chosen for today. Enda's vibrant clothes matched her ebullient personality, and it was always a surprise to see how she would arrange her blond curls. Nora remembered that the pretty receptionist was supposed to have been taking today off, but Enda said she would like to take tomorrow off instead.

She explained that she and boyfriend, Bill Callahan, were going to go shopping in Galway today, but he had found out that he had an unexpected appointment to do a tourist's portrait. Bill was a talented local artist who had the rare gift of being able to accurately draw anything he looked at. He supplemented his carpenter's salary by painting beautiful pictures of Sneem and the people who visited there. He got paid well for these portrait sittings, so he did not want to pass them up when they came knocking at his door.

Nora said that would be fine, and she realized that she was pretty hungry by now. She promised to tell Enda about the recent excitement after she had made lunch for both of them, and then she headed to the kitchen. Nora was a passable cook, but this was one time when she wished that she could see Mrs. O'Hara bobbing about in her kitchen kingdom and producing something warm and delicious. She would be very glad when Mrs. O'Hara returned from her sister's in Limerick. Nora looked over the leftovers in the huge refrigerator and decided to settle for meat loaf sandwiches heated up in the microwave with Tayto chips, accompanied by her usual hot

Barry's tea with lemon. She brought a sandwich and Diet Coke to Enda and told her of her gruesome discovery on the beach.

Enda made an excellent receptionist since she made it her business to know everyone in the company and in the surrounding villages. The official language of the Republic of Ireland was Irish or Gaelic, and Enda had grown up in a Gaeltacht village. She was invaluable when they received communications in Irish since she could proficiently read and write this language that had so many consonants, very few vowels, and looked and sounded nothing like English. Nora was gradually learning Gaelic just by listening to Enda switch so effortlessly between the two languages. If one wanted to know the Irish for a swear word or the best theatres or places to eat or gamble or a less popular request, where to go to church, Enda was your gal. Nora had often heard Enda tell questioners that the location they were seeking was "just ten minutes away, a good stretch of the legs."

Enda's whole face reflected her interest in the conversation. Her bright blue eyes opened wider and wider, and she chewed her sandwich faster and faster as she heard the details about the beautiful body on the beach with the tantalizing mystery of the golden horseshoes that had been slashed through with a jagged red line.

"OMG! Nothing much sensational happens in Sneem," Enda gasped, "so this is pretty amazing. I could accept that she wouldn't mind shedding her clothes, but no self-respecting girl would be without her purse. I wonder what happened to it? My friend Kathie in Cork tells me that people come west looking for cheap drugs. I'll just bet that's what this is all about. I can also ask Ellen at the tattoo shop if she's heard anything about a horseshoes tattoo."

Nora asked her not to publicize the story yet, but with her love for gossip, she was sure that Enda would be sharing the story and adding her own spin to the details within the hour.

By now, the media likely had most of the details with accompanying pictures too. Nora had neglected to share the part about the girl being stabbed in the back, and she hoped the media hadn't received that detail yet.

Just then, Enda heard the phone ringing, and she answered a caller who wanted to know if it were true that Nora Duffy had found a dead body on the beach. The experienced receptionist told the caller that she should call the local garda and ask for more information. She suspected that many people would be making such inquiries today, so she girded herself and tried to be prepared. Nora thanked her for her discreet handing of the call and asked her to give a similar answer to any other questioners.

"Oh, my goodness," Nora shouted, realizing that she sounded like Shirley Temple, as she saw her phone light up with an amazing number of incoming calls and texts. "The media must have wasted no time publicizing the story of me and the dead body." She looked at some of the incoming numbers and recognized family members and friends, as well as news agencies wanting her to do an interview. She decided not to answer anyone yet and jogged over to the horse stables.

Her old pal Finnbar, the giant ebony racehorse, whinnied a greeting when he saw her, and Nora gave him a hug, which he returned with a lick of his long tongue. Tim Taylor, the stables director, helped her to put on the special saddle he had made for Nora to accommodate her short legs. He had also heard the news and told Nora he was sorry she had stepped into the middle of things again. Nora thanked him for his concern and wondered how he had heard about everything already. "Small village," Tim acknowledged. Nora said hello to the other horses and gave them an apple. Then she mounted Finn and they went for a leisurely canter.

Finnbar had become even more powerful than he was last year as their horse trainer Frank Donovan had prepared him for the Galway Races this summer, and Nora found herself increasing her grip on his reins. Finn had run in a trio of races, had won two, and placed second in the other. His usual jockey Tim Giblin was sick for that third race; otherwise, he thought he would have won that too. Nora had donated all the money they'd won to St. Brigid's Orphanage that Uncle Cy had supported for so many years. She thought that Uncle Cyrus would be pleased that she had grown to love his "Black Beauty."

Nora continued to ride Finn as they passed Bambi and his friends in the red deer enclosure that were nibbling at some leaves from the willow trees. Then she stopped at the tombstones for Uncle Cy, Aunt Emily, Aunt Vinnie, and Mort O'Brien. She said a prayer for them before returning Finn to the stables so she could jog back to the castle.

She'd hoped that keeping busy with a lot of activities would prevent her from thinking about the murdered girl, but the images of Blondie's battered forehead and the golden horseshoes covered with crawling crabs were too powerful and kept appearing whenever she closed her eyes.

Nora knew that evil could happen everywhere, but it somehow seemed to her that the beautiful Coral Beach should be a protected place. Maybe Blondie had thought that too, much to her regret.

CHAPTER

5

Nora was getting tired out about now, so she ran up the castle steps to her bedroom for a hot bath and a few minutes of relaxation so she could read more of her Maeve Binchy book on her Kindle. She then changed into her favorite blue daytime dress, got out her violin, and played and sang a few verses of "Somewhere Over the Rainbow." Whenever she was sad or confused, playing some of her old favorites on her violin helped her to think.

As she looked out the window, she saw the happy coincidence of a vibrant rainbow that ringed the countryside with its many colors. Legend had it that leprechauns were laughing as they guarded their pot o' gold at the end of the rainbow, and she thought of the big silver leprechaun statue that Uncle Cy had sculpted himself and placed at the entrance to the castle.

Mr. McGovern the architect and Mr. Carmody the construction head arrived just on time at 4:00 p.m., and they talked for an hour or more as they discussed final plans for the building of the Duffy Medical Research Center. Then they switched gears and talked about the possible plans for excavating the collapsed part of the old castle. That would take a lot of finesse and experience since the ruins were adjacent to the working castle.

They had done some initial exploration and measurements and brought along an expert, Doctor Alice McGillicuddy, who said she thought the ruins appeared to be from the 1500s. They would not speculate as to what lay underneath the collapsed stones and roof, but it often happened that these old buildings contained valuable antiques.

After the building people left, Nora called the Children's Cancer Clinic at Holy Savior Hospital in Chicago and talked to Therese Cummings, who gave her an update on the patients and doctors. Therese said they had a few kids that they were pretty concerned about, but no one was critical at the moment. She hoped that Nora would get back soon since Doctor Whiteside had been in a bad mood lately. She said she thought it had something to do with the recent finance meetings at the hospital and the constant pressure to reduce expenditures.

"You always exert a positive influence on our hardworking boss," Therese explained, "and then he's more positive with all of us."

Nora assured her that she should be back home in a few days. Once Therese saw the news about the body on the beach, Nora knew that her friend would want to know every detail about it all.

Nora had called Tommy earlier and told him there was no rush for him to get back to the castle since Chief Brennan had things well in hand. He said he would stop on the way back from Dublin to get some parts for his car and have fish and chips at one of his favorite Old Head eating spots. He said he should be back in time for them to go for an early dinner.

Nora took another quick shower and changed into her black flowered dress with the satin trim, added her rings and diamond pendant, put on her black strappy Louboutin sandals, and waited for Tommy to arrive. She heard the powerful engine of his vintage stainless steel DeLorean sports car about 5:00 p.m. Nora smiled when she recalled how happy he was on the day they bought his dream car. For Nora, the main attributes of a car were safety and efficiency. She could explain all the workings of the human body, but she didn't much care about the innards of a car. She appreciated the complexity of it all, but she just wanted her car to get her where she wanted to go without any worries about its reliability. She liked having a nice paint job, but the brand didn't matter too much to her.

For Tommy, and she suspected for many men, the style and beauty of a car were most important, and the stainless steel DeLorean with its upward opening gull wing doors and panache as the time machine car of *Back to the Future* had plenty of that.

Nora smiled as she thought about that engaging movie with Michael J. Fox and the professor traveling back and forth between decades in that elegant car. Little did that talented young actor, who ran and jumped with such ease when the movie was made, know that he would soon be remembered for a very different reason, as the champion of people with Parkinson's disease.

Tommy ran up the stairs and called to her with his usual happy greeting, "Fee, Fie, Foe, Fum, here I come." They embraced and laughed for a long time and then talked about where they should go for dinner. Rather than going to Dan Murphy's Bar in Sneem, where she would immediately be recognized, Tommy suggested that they drive to one of their favorite restaurants they had found on their honeymoon on the Dingle Peninsula, or Corca Dhuibhne. The Boatyard Restaurant & Bar was across from the marina, and the Oceanworld Aquarium was nearby. They had not yet had a chance to visit that interesting place and hoped to do so soon, but they would probably wait until some of their younger siblings were around.

Any hopes of being incognito were quickly dashed as the Boatyard's owner recognized them from their several visits during their honeymoon. He shook his head and told Nora he was sorry that she was going through such an ordeal, an indication that just about everyone in Ireland would have seen the news about this morning's gruesome discovery by now. Several patrons also smiled at them, and a boisterous woman asked to take a selfie with them on her phone.

As they waited to be seated, Tommy knew that when Nora was upset, she preferred to listen while he talked. He proceeded to explain that while many of these lawyer meetings he attended about international cooperation were boring, this one in Dublin had been worth the time and money. He had received many valid insights, and he thought that his boss Mr. Kornan would agree. He had met a lot of new people, and he had run into Matt Conway from Australia again, and they'd had lunch.

"Matt invited us both to his wedding this spring to his fiancée, Madeline, a professional violinist, so you'd have something in common with her. I'd love to see Sydney, wouldn't you? I've already looked up the season at the Sydney Opera House, and one of their features will be *Figaro*."

Nora mumbled a "yes," and *The Marriage of Figaro* was one of her favorites, but she realized that Tommy's question was an attempt to get her to begin talking about her morning's ordeal.

Just then, they were seated and given menus that illustrated the restaurant's delicious offerings. Tommy ordered a glass of Sauvignon blanc, and Nora asked for lemon water. They loved seafood, and Nora ordered the seafood chowder and mussels while Tommy asked for the very substantial seafood platter that was so artfully prepared. They chitchatted through dinner and shared happy memories of their honeymoon in Dingle. Nora never ate very much, but Tommy could see that she was barely touching her delicious food.

Finally, Tommy asked Nora to tell him more about what had happened on the Coral Beach. Nora presented a rock-solid exterior, but she had to wipe away tears as she proceeded to tell him about finding the dead girl in such a terrible condition. "She has to be pretty close to our age, Tommy, and I can't stop thinking about what she must have gone through before she died.

"You remember Lucy Sullivan, the coroner we met a few months ago at the art fair? She is going to be doing a thorough examination of the girl, whom she's nicknamed Blondie. She'll find out more about the golden horseshoes that were crossed out with a red slash and if they were drawn above her breasts by a killer. Blondie had a huge gash on her forehead and a deep cut on her back, so Lucy will make the determination as to which wound killed her. I thought I'd recovered from the violent doings at the castle last year, but this brought it all back to me so vividly."

Tommy held Nora's hands tightly as she relayed more details, and she gradually stopped shaking. He told Nora to give up on eating her food, but he suggested that they could share the sticky toffee pudding with butterscotch sauce. They ordered the rich dessert with an extra plate and added a pot of tea. The sweetness and the tea did help Nora's stomach and her mental outlook, and she began to feel better. On the way out, she looked for the owner in the kitchen and thanked him for his food and for his good wishes and promised they would be back the next time they were in Ireland.

CHAPTER

Monday, June 10
Sneem, Ireland; 8:00 p.m., IST

On the way back to the castle in their powerful car, Nora decided she needed some inspiring music. She found the video of Mozart's *Magic Flute* on her phone and played the incredible "Queen of the Night" aria at full volume. She recalled the vivid scene in *Amadeus* where the coloratura soprano in the beautiful blue dress sang this so impressively. She remembered that Mozart said that "music is not in the notes but in the silence between the notes." Some people, like the Emperor in *Amadeus*, would say that Mozart's music had too many notes, so there wasn't much time to hear that silence. Others, like Sir Georg Solti, said that "Mozart makes you believe in God," and Nora agreed.

It was kind of God to provide the human race with geniuses like Wolfgang Amadeus Mozart, and kudos also had to be extended to the people around him who nurtured his talent like his knowledgeable but domineering father, Leopold Mozart. Wolfgang Mozart died when he was only thirty-five, and every music lover wondered what else he might have added to his incredible accomplishments had he lived longer.

Tommy had become more of an opera fan in the last few years, but Nora could see that the Mozart piece was a bit too much for him. She looked up one of his old favorites by the British rock band Coldplay, and he nodded his gratitude to her as they sang along to "Viva La Vida." She thought that Mozart would approve of this well-crafted music, and she wondered what he would have produced if he lived in our times.

They then called their respective parents in Chicago to give them an update. Nora's mom, Eileen, teared up when she heard Nora's voice. "Are you okay, Bitsy, a stor?"

Nora loved hearing her mother's voice and the "a stor" greeting, which meant "my treasure."

"We saw the news about you and the murdered girl on the Irish RTÉ News, and tonight it was on our local news channels too, since you were involved. It sounds terrible, and I'm sure it must have been such a shock for you. I'm glad you're getting out of there on Saturday."

Nora assured her that it had been just as horrible as she had imagined, but now that Tommy was with her, she was feeling better. She asked about the family and Jesse, their beloved housekeeper. Her mother gave her updates on her nine siblings and their many activities.

"The twins will be so glad that you'll be home by the weekend since they both have science fairs coming up for their summer programs. Molly has been working on the effects of music on the human psyche, and Caity's is on the history of communicable diseases.

"We're all pretty concerned about Grandpa Conor. Your father thinks he is showing some signs of heart disease, so we are keeping a close watch on him. Jim told us that he and Trish have finally gotten around to settling on a date for their wedding, May 2. I'm pretty sure that Jack and Sally are getting closer to declaring their formal engagement. I think they want to go to Hawaii for their honeymoon. Jesse is doing fine, but she is so worried about you after hearing the news that you found a dead body. You know that she thinks of you as her little girl. Father Ahearn and so many neighbors have been stopping in since they heard the news, and we have had dozens of calls. Aunt Janet from Sonoma wanted to know if she should come out here to see you. The sooner you get home, the better!"

Tommy called his parents at Barry's Irish Pub and had a similar conversation with his parents, and they passed along their good wishes to Nora. Mr. Barry reminded him that the big party was a week from Wednesday at their pub, and they were both expected to perform. The Barrys rarely interfered with their children's activities, but tonight, Mrs. Barry said she wished that both of them would stop traveling so far from home.

Tommy and Nora decided to go to bed early, but just as they were about to go upstairs, Nora had a call from Lucy Sullivan, the coroner.

"I hope you're feeling better by now, Nora. I could tell that you were awfully upset, and I was too curious myself, so Gemma helped me to do the autopsy on Blondie this afternoon. I'm putting together a more detailed report, but briefly, her last meal consisted of beans and bread, and there were some signs of sexual activity. I couldn't tell you if that was consensual, but there were black and blue marks on her arms and legs.

"The body had become pruney from being at least partially covered in water, but she must have been dead already, so she didn't drown. That large bump on her head would have bled a lot originally and stunned her, but the cause of death was exsanguination from the sharp instrument wound to her back that had penetrated her lung and her heart. The golden horseshoes picture above her breasts was drawn there with permanent markers. An aside observation is that the image was done by someone skilled in artwork.

"You were right about the wound on her wrist, and that would probably have caused considerable pain. She had an old scar on her left side from an appendicitis operation and multiple old stitches on her right leg from some kind of injury. I can't really say if she was killed elsewhere. I'll give the report to Chief Brennan tomorrow. What a shame for this beautiful girl that she came to such an end. It's most definitely a case of murder."

Nora thanked Lucy for her prompt work and the call and asked her to also thank Gemma. Lucy's report left her feeling anxious and apprehensive for all the females in the vicinity. She would talk to Chief Brennan tomorrow and ask him to alert the general public that a monster was in their midst.

In the meantime, she opened up her laptop and prepared an urgent warning note for all the women who worked at Duffy Hall Castle, as well as those in the surrounding estate buildings. She also forwarded the note to all the administrative offices of the eleven towns on the Ring of Kerry. She printed it out; made copies on bright pink paper; and went downstairs and put the notes at the entrance hall, in the kitchen, and on all the cork boards. By the time she was finished, it was nearly bedtime.

Nora went upstairs with two small bowls of popcorn, and she called to Tommy who turned on the television and came across *Dancing with the Stars—Ireland.* They always enjoyed this show in Chicago, and it was fun trying to guess which couples would continue to be successful until the next week. Some of the contestants were real beginners at ballroom dancing, but others were experienced dancers or athletes who could be expected to do well. Nora and Tommy were disappointed at the end of the show when their favorite couple dressed in blue sequins, who had done so well with the fox-trot, discovered that they'd been eliminated. They found it interesting that this show that had begun in the UK was now part of life in more than forty countries.

Nora then washed up and got ready for bed and changed into her pretty turquoise nightgown and snuggled with Tommy in their big bed. He was properly amazed at the gorgeous quilt they had received from Grandma Dee and enjoyed trying to figure out the various Celtic symbols. They didn't have much time to spend alone, so they talked for a long time and said a prayer for their families and the girl on the beach.

They were still in honeymoon mode and thought that each other's bodies were beautiful and inviting. They forgot about their troubles as they joyfully made love and looked forward to a happy future.

Nora often wondered what a baby of theirs would look like. She was so small all over and so short, while Tommy was six feet two and wore size 13 shoes. Her face was milky white with some freckles, and she had green eyes while Tom's skin was darker and his eyes were bright blue. Her hair was red and curly while his straight dark brown hair had just a little waviness in the front. Most of the Duffy children had long second toes, which was a help to Nora for her Irish dancing. Tommy and four of his siblings were "double-jointed," which really meant that their bones were hypermobile and could account for Tommy's being adept at almost any sport. The main hope for any baby was good health, but it was fun imagining what a future child would look like as she attempted to combine all these traits.

Tommy fell asleep almost immediately, but Nora enjoyed looking at the vast expanse of the night sky with its minimum of one hundred billion (!) or more stars with an even larger number of accompanying planets. The composition of the universe seemed to her to be one of the most compelling reasons to believe in God since the very largest as well as the very smallest entities have such order to them. She fell asleep humming the old Bing Crosby tune, one of her grandmother's favorites that she had used as a lullaby for the babies, "Swinging on a Star."

CHAPTER

7

Two others were also watching the events that had occurred on the Coral Beach with great interest. Ralph and Hitch were the resident ghosts at Duffy Hall Castle, but they spent most of their time in the cellar of the Two Squares Pub, hoping to get more beer and whiskey. They were the stooges of ghostdom and were constantly getting themselves into trouble.

"I told you we should have left here early last night," complained Ralph, "but you insisted on sticking around because you couldn't get the lids off of Mr. Foote's new barrels of Guinness."

"Don't blame me," retorted Hitch. "You had way too many Jameson's to navigate in that storm last night. Now we missed the whole thing, and we have no idea who was so cruel to that poor girl out there on the beach. We'll have to ask Bridie for help again, and she's not going to be best pleased one bit."

Hitch kicked one of the Guinness barrels, stubbed his toe, and put his head down in pain and shame. Bridie Fitzpatrick had been the good ghost at Duffy Hall Castle, but she had achieved angel status last year, so they didn't see her very often now. She kept watch over them when she was not singing with the angelic choir.

Ralph and Hitch had been responsible for impaling Bridie and her boyfriend, Brendan, with their longbow arrows two hundred years ago. They didn't want to do it, but Bridie's cruel father, Rupert Fitzpatrick, told them that if they saw the young couple trying to flee the castle,

48

they must kill them with their arrows, or else he would do the same to them. The two ghosts had been feeling bad about it ever since.

Lord Fitzpatrick was always finding ways to kill people, and Ralph and Hitch found out the hard way that he meant what he said, and they too died under a barrage of arrows. They discovered the pain that Bridie and Brendan had undergone soon enough, and they joined her in the belfry of the castle. She had been trying to civilize them ever since, but they seemed impervious to good influences.

Last year, Bridie had helped the young new mistress of the castle, Nora Duffy, to escape the clutches of a murderer, and the pretty ghost had been rewarded by Angel Christopher with a fancy gold sash over her white silk gown trimmed with Irish lace and membership in the angelic choir. Ralph and Hitch were happy for her, but they doubted they would be joining her. They were enjoying the nastiness that ghosts were entitled to too much.

"Stop looking at me like that, Ralph," said Hitch. "I know we should get back to the castle, but you know when I get frustrated, I have to make myself feel better by causing a little mischief."

No sooner had Hitch said this than he swooped over to the boxes of pub glasses that sat on the shelf, and he pushed them all onto the floor, where they broke with the most satisfying sound of shattering. Then he found several bottles of honey and poured them all very slowly on top of the glass shards while shrieking wildly. "That will show Mr. Foote that he shouldn't make those lids so tight on the Guinness barrels," laughed Hitch.

"What it will do is to make sure we won't be getting any points toward angel status any time soon," responded Ralph. "Hand me that broom and I'll at least move this mess away from the stairs so that Mr. Foote doesn't cut himself if he comes down here in the dark. Bridie won't have anything to do with us otherwise."

As their parting gift to Mr. Foote, they filled the basement with the powerful smell of sewer gas. Bridie used to be able to emit the pleasant smell of honeysuckle, but Ralph and Hitch had never learned how to do that, nor did they want to. It was more fun watching the people they haunted trying not to vomit after they had been visited by the ghostly pair.

Ralph and Hitch took a few more swigs of their drinks to keep themselves fortified, and then they swooped as fast as they could back to their belfry in the castle. They weren't sure what they could do to help Miss Nora, but they intended to listen closely and watch for anyone who might be threatening her. Ralph sent out a message to Bridie to come and see them when she could, and then they settled down for a long, cold night.

The Duffy Hall ravens and pigeons made a racket in the belfry, where they had taken refuge from the storm, and they covered the two miserable ghosts while they were resting with their droppings. The birds had seen this hapless pair here before, and they enjoyed spreading around some nastiness themselves.

CHAPTER

8

Tuesday, June 11
Sneem, Ireland; 7:00 a.m., IST

Nora woke up at her usual early time the next day but decided not to go to the Coral Beach, where she could be a target. She and Tommy stayed in bed a little longer than usual and checked their phones for messages and the news and answered texts and e-mails. The story about the nude girl on the beach seemed to have received only small interest on the Internet so far, so that was good. The media had used a doctored-up picture of the pretty girl's face in their news stories, and Nora hoped that someone would recognize her and contact the garda.

They dressed in their business casual outfits and then went to the kitchen where Mrs. O'Hara heard them. The indefatigable cook gave Nora a bear hug and never stopped talking.

"I told my sister that I can't leave the house without you getting into trouble. I believe I told you, Miss Nora, that you should not be going down to that beach at such an early hour, did I not? Sure, and it's pretty there, but it's just too dark to be safe. I ask Saint Brigid to protect you every day, but she can only do so much. When I saw the picture of that girl's face on the telly, I could not stop crying when I thought that it could have been you. You take too many chances. Sit down here, please, and I'll make you some of my maple pancakes and syrup with smoked bacon," Mrs. O'Hara said as she wiped away her tears.

After giving her another hug, the middle-aged woman with the titian curly hair and piercing green eyes turned her attention to the stove. Nora assured Mrs. O'Hara how much they had missed her, and Tommy said she was the best cook anywhere, and that finally got the sweet woman to smile. Mrs. O'Hara was right about how much they enjoyed the breakfast, and then they decided to go for a walk.

They were just about to run out the back door of the castle when their neighbor Mick Fergus, the shepherd of the Duffy Hall flocks, was pounding on the door. He frantically yelled out to them that Jenny had been killed.

Tommy took hold of Mick's hands and ushered him into the kitchen, but he also had to ask, "Who is Jenny?"

"Oh, I'm sorry. I give names to all the new lambs. Jenny is only two days old, and I found her this morning outside the barn with her throat cut. Her mother was cryin' terrible. You should come with me to the front doors of the castle," pleaded Mick. "I spotted something horrible on them as I was coming over here."

They all ran out to the front doors, and they saw that two horse-shoes had been painted with sparkly gold paint, the tips were deco-rated with green shamrocks, and they were hanging from the door knockers. Something red had been splattered over the horseshoes, and they realized it was likely Jenny's blood that was dripping down in rivulets and pooling in the Celtic carvings on the tall bronze doors. A hand-painted sign also hung down from the door knockers and proclaimed in capital letters, "YOU'RE NEXT!"

Nora gulped and wondered if the warning was for the castle in general or for her. Tommy pulled Nora close to him but didn't know how to reassure her. Mick's tears finally overflowed, and he just kept repeating how sorry he was that he couldn't stop this terrible person, whoever he was.

Nora and Tommy consoled Mick and gave him a hug. This ten-der man was grieving for a little lamb while some monster was loose and had killed a young woman so easily. And who knew what he had planned for her? Nora asked Mick to stick around for a while so he could talk to the garda.

Nora thought about the powerful scene in *The Ten Commandments* where the people had painted their doors with lamb's blood to save them from the curse of having their firstborn die. She was the Duffy's firstborn, but it was doubtful that Jenny's blood was going to help her very much.

She called Chief Herlihy and Chief Brennan and asked them to meet them at the front doors right away. The two policemen were shocked at this latest development and told Nora and Tommy that they would work on this right away. They took notes after talking with Mick and then sent him on his way. They assured him that they would post a guard at the barn, and that relieved Mick's fears somewhat. They walked over to the barn to see where Jenny had been killed, and they found Mick still shaking with grief and fear as he held Jenny's mother in his arms, who pitifully baaed.

They called the fingerprint analyst and the photographer Bud Crotty. They asked the fingerprint expert to see if there was anything he could identify, but he told them the lamb's blood had probably made everything too wet. He and his team would try, but it was likely that too many other fingerprints would be found on the large doors.

The chiefs then told Nora and Tommy that they would gather up the mess from the front doors, package it up, and send it to their lab. Chief Herlihy said he would notify Sean Duffy about the cleanup needed for the front doors. The Celtic door carvings were old and fragile, and Sean would make sure to hire the best experts for the job. The two policemen were concerned about Nora and the others at the castle, but it seemed as though there was nothing more to be done today, so they left.

Nora and Tommy gathered Liam and Bran and took a tour of the grounds, especially around the back of the castle where they were going to dig the foundation for the Duffy Medical Research Center. They also looked at the exterior of the ruined part of the castle that had yet to be explored. Excavating that caved in structure would be the next project they would tackle once the research center was well on its way.

Nora had been told that it was dangerous to try to enter that old section, but she was so curious as to what they would find in there.

She poked at a few of the loose bricks, but they fell down too easily, so she decided to wait until the expert demolition and reconstruction people could do things properly.

They also looked at the new shop on the edge of the parking lot that was due to be operational in time for Christmas. The architects had made it look like a large thatched-roof cottage with black shutters aside the many windows and with emerald green doors. The shop would sell produce from the tenant farmers like fruits and vegetables; cheeses; and casseroles such as shepherd's pies and salmon pasta; honey; lavender; bouquets of flowers; and St. Bridget crosses, seasonal ornaments, and calendars. The farmers also had plans, depending on how the first season's sales were, to add meats and fish.

According to Enda's reports, people from the surrounding villages were anxious to come and shop. That meant they had to be prepared with adequate security and bathroom facilities, and those necessaries were in the process of being ready. Nora was sure the shop would be a big hit.

Early on, Nora had called a meeting of the mayors and councilmen from the towns on the Ring of Kerry and received their suggestions so that Duffy Hall Castle's shop would encourage tourists to visit the other towns for certain goods that would not be available here. That sense of cooperation relieved the other towns' worries that their stores would get overlooked. Notices were posted inside and outside the Duffy shop, explaining the various goods that tourists could find in each of the other towns.

Tommy had an important conference call with his home office today, so he said goodbye to Nora for now and returned to the castle. Nora was shaken by the morning's events, but she decided that today was the day that she was going to see relatives in Ireland that she had not gotten around to visiting yet. Her aunt Tilda ran a thriving bed-and-breakfast outside of Cork and said she would be delighted to have Nora come to see her.

CHAPTER

9

Aunt Tilda warmly welcomed her little niece to her story-book-pretty red and white home surrounded by flowers, and they shared stories and scones for several hours. She was happy to hear that her sister, Nora's grandma Marie, was doing well. Tilda had been a widow for a long time, and her only daughter, Marie, now lived in London, and she rarely saw her, so Tilda had been lonely. She said she had always intended to come to Chicago for a visit, but her business kept her so busy, she never had the time to get away. Nora asked her to please come to the construction dig for the Duffy Medical Research Center next month, and she said she would.

Their conversation was interrupted by a guest who wanted to check out, so they exchanged hugs, and then Nora headed to her next stop, her father's two cousins who lived outside of Killarney. George and Harry Duffy were part of the busy trade that catered to tourists who came to Ireland. George was a gregarious tour bus driver who ferried people around the 111 miles of the Ring of Kerry towns, and Harry conducted tours of Muckross House and Gardens. There was an impressive mansion built in 1843, and the surrounding lands were all part of Killarney National Park.

Nora met them at George's home outside of Killarney, and she was welcomed by George's wife, Portia, and their two children, Kat and Jack. They were so excited to see her, and they appreciated the fact that she had taken the time from her busy schedule to visit them.

Harry had never married, but one of his passions was cooking. He had provided the dinner, which looked delicious and consisted of vegetable soup, salmon, risotto, green beans, and strawberry mousse.

They talked and laughed and caught up on family news, and the two children entertained Nora with a rendition of the "Star Spangled Banner" that they had been practicing on their violins. They also gave Nora a picture they had painted of her standing in front of the castle. Nora praised the children for their work and thanked the family profusely for the wonderful afternoon, and then told them she had to return home. She hoped they would come to the construction dig for the medical research center next month. She took pictures of them all, gave hugs all around, and drove back to the castle.

When she entered the back door, it was obvious by the delicious smells that Mrs. O'Hara must have been hard at work preparing something good for their dinner. She peeked into the kitchen and realized that she was fixing one of Tommy's favorites, round steak with bacon and onions. It smelled so good, but Nora wouldn't eat too much of it. She knew that Tommy would be happy though, since he didn't get that when she cooked.

Nora had been trying to ignore Liam and Bran, but the two big dogs almost knocked her down with their boisterous welcome. She ran up the stairs to her bedroom and greeted Tinker Bell, the kitty, with her string toys. Tommy had left her a note, saying that he had gone into the village to get some treats for the dogs and Tink and said he'd return shortly. Nora took a shower after her busy day and dressed in her old jeans and black T-shirt with the picture of her and Tommy at their wedding.

She turned on the television to the news, and there was a story about the mysterious girl on the Coral Beach. Her picture had been edited so the wound to her forehead wasn't visible. The media had done a good job of explaining that they needed the public's help to identify her. Nora hoped that this appeal would get some response so they could find out who the unfortunate young woman was.

They enjoyed eating the perfectly cooked dinner that Mrs. O'Hara had prepared, and Tommy gave the blushing cook a box of chocolates he had picked up in town. He told her he'd never had such a delicious meal, and the little woman was thrilled with his praise.

They were just about to enjoy a tempting fruit tart with their tea when both their phones started ringing. Kitty Lloyd alerted them that the alarm on the back fence of the estate had gone off. Nora and Tom ran over to the chain-link fence and discovered that it had been cleanly cut. Nora didn't hesitate and immediately called Chief Brennan of the garda and Chief Herlihy again to let them know of the break in.

Kitty had started calling all the people who lived on the castle estate, and everyone, except Farmer John Boyle, had responded that they were fine. Nora and Tommy ran over to Farmer Boyle's attractive little cottage under the copse of willow trees and realized she would not have to worry about his future anymore.

The front door was open, and they found the dear man on the floor quite dead with his throat cut. How could there be so much blood from such a small man? His beloved collie Flossie was lying prone, whimpering nearby, and blood was dribbling from her mouth. Nora gathered Flossie into her arms and called Father Lanigan from the village to come and give Mr. Boyle the last rites.

Chief Herlihy came running through the door and was horrified to find his old companion covered in blood. He said he would look in the other rooms and the cellar to ensure that no one was hiding. Nora knelt down and cried over Jack's body and gave him the traditional Irish send-off: "May the road rise to meet you and the wind be always at your back."

Nora called Sean Duffy and asked him to bring her the estate file on Jack Boyle. Tommy called Tim Taylor and asked him to come and take a look at the injured dog.

At that point, Nora saw that the sweet farmer had written a message with his own blood: "BILL C," and then it trailed off. There were many "Bills" in this neck of the woods, but the first one with a "C" surname that came to mind was Enda's Bill Callahan. Surely, that funny and kind man would not have done anything so violent, but Nora knew that anyone with the name of William or Bill would be questioned.

Nora forced herself to look more carefully at Mr. Boyle's body, and she noticed that his right hand appeared to be clutching something very tightly. She was tempted to pry his fingers apart to see what that might be, but she knew that Chief Brennan and his Garda team would want to do that.

Jack's body lay next to his bookshelf, and she was surprised at some of the titles. There were some well-thumbed novels but also books like "Paradise Lost," *On the Origin of Species, The Rise and Fall of the Roman Empire, A History of the English-Speaking Peoples*, and several about the history of Ireland and the Irish Republican Army. A small black Bible sat on the table next to his well-worn chair, and there was also an oversized green leather volume of Shakespeare's plays.

A plaque on the wall above his little table contained a quotation from the famous Roman orator Marcus Tullius Cicero from more than two thousand years ago:

> Six mistakes mankind keeps making century after century: Believing that personal gain is made by crushing others; Worrying about things that cannot be changed or corrected; Insisting that a thing is impossible because we cannot accomplish it; Refusing to set aside trivial preferences; Neglecting development and refinement of the mind; Attempting to compel others to believe and live as we do.

Obviously, there was much more to know about Jack Boyle than the image he had presented as just a jovial farmer, whose only social activities appeared to be going for long walks and having a pint at the local pub with his friends.

Nora wondered what the assailant had been looking for when he had trashed Jack's neat little home and if he had found it. On top of a pile of books, she spotted a pair of horseshoes that had been painted gold. Did this mean there was some connection to the girl who had been found on the Coral Beach?

Nora was about to stand up when her surgeon's eye caught the glint of a small pin under the table with a picture of an Easter lily, which she knew was the emblem that commemorated all those who had died during the 1916 Rising during Easter week, an attempt to end British rule in Ireland and establish an independent Ireland. Did the pin belong to Jack or to the man who had killed him? Things were getting "curiouser and curiouser."

The grounds were soon filled with flashing blue lights, and blue uniforms as the garda fanned out across the Duffy estate looking for any clues. Nora took Chief Brennan aside and showed him the pin under the table and mentioned her suspicion that Jack must be holding something in his hand. The chief said that he would wait for the crime scene people to open his hand and see what it was. Nora had seen a documentary about the IRA, the Irish Republican Army, on her last trip to Ireland, and she started to wonder if they could be involved. Supposedly, the violent group had been disbanded with the 1998 peace accords.

Fingerprint analysts and photographers did their work, and the coroners Lucy and Gemma were called again and asked to come and look at Jack's body. They discovered that the farmer must have torn off a gold button from his assailant's jacket and was tightly clutching it in his hand. A more surprising find was that the beautiful volume of Shakespeare was hollowed out and held an antique revolver. Perhaps Jack knew that he was being hunted and he kept the old gun handy.

It took hours before Jack's body was removed to the morgue, and the grounds were searched and cleared. Nora reflected that the old saying "life is what happens when you're making other plans" was all too true. She so wished that she could have asked Jack more about his eclectic collection of books and more about his surprising life. She would miss seeing him and Flossie on the beach.

Chief Brennan and his crew also were investigating the entire house since someone had been doing a thorough search looking for something. Jack's small but tidy cottage was a wreck with furniture and pictures slashed and drawers emptied and overturned. Even the floorboards were pried up in places. Chief Brennan asked if Nora thought the unassuming farmer might have had a hidden fortune that no one knew about, but she assured him that she doubted that was the case since he seemed to live so frugally.

Tim Taylor said he was hopeful that Flossie had only suffered some broken ribs, and it seemed as though she would survive, but tears kept leaking from her sad eyes, and she was obviously in pain when she moved. Tim said he would keep her with him at his home and tend to her whenever she needed it. They both agreed that the person who had done this to the sweet dog and his loving master was a monster and should be caught as soon as possible.

Tommy and Nora said goodnight to the chiefs and then headed back to the castle to try to get some sleep.

CHAPTER

10

Tuesday, June 11
Sneem, Ireland; 10:00 p.m., IST

Ralph and Hitch were greeted in the belfry of the castle by the pleasant smell of honeysuckle flowers and Bridie, the former good ghost of the castle and now a member of the angelic choir. Bridie was not smiling as she said that Angel Christopher had received many complaints that Ralph and Hitch had gone beyond the causing mischief stage to just being malicious. She told them their appearance was a disgrace, and they smelled horrible too, covered with bird droppings. The two ghosts hadn't realized what the birds had done to them and yelled out that they would put poison in their seeds.

Bridie said she would love to see these two in the heavenly choir, but she saw no hope of that happening as long as they continued on their destructive paths. However, Angel Christopher was personally requesting their help in scoping out the castle grounds to see who was causing mayhem like hanging golden horseshoes covered in a lamb's blood on the front doors of the castle. Worst of all was the sign that accompanied the horseshoes, threatening Nora and those at Duffy Hall Castle. Now, one of Nora's good friends had been violently murdered too.

"Don't you want to become angels, you two?" asked Bridie. "You're never going to make it if you continue with your bad behavior, and you could do a lot of good here."

Ralph was the more sentimental of the pair, and he said he found it terrible that a cute little lamb who had only had a few days of life had been so horribly killed. Even though Mr. Jack had many days of life, the fact that his throat had been cut too was even worse. He asked Bridie what Angel Christopher would like them to do.

"Stop hiding out in this belfry or going down into Mr. Foote's cellar," commanded Bridie. You could easily fly back and forth over the area and watch what everyone is doing here. You could use your ghostly GPS system and look for the people who are causing all this violence and death."

The two ghosts could usually be swayed by Bridie's pleas, at least for a while, and they said they would help, but they weren't too anxious to join the heavenly choir since they hated to sing. Bridie said they should begin their mission, and perhaps Angel Christopher could find something for them to do that they would like better.

She said that the garda appeared to be stymied at the moment, and if they helped them to find the killers, they might also receive their own garda stars. That provided the incentive the two ghosts needed, and they first cleaned themselves up and said they would get started right away.

CHAPTER

11

Wednesday, June 12
Sneem, Ireland; 9:00 a.m., IST

The next morning, Chief Herlihy went house to house, asking questions of every resident on the Duffy estate about their whereabouts and activities last night. After a few hours, they realized that no one seemed to have heard or seen anything unusual near Farmer Boyle's cottage. Mrs. Wittington from the laundry building did think that her dog had let out a few anxious howls about 9:00 p.m., and they were following up on that.

Jack's dog Flossie seemed to be holding her own. Even though she was so weak, she kept struggling to walk back to the cottage and her beloved master. Tim Taylor told Nora that the poor dog was shivering so much, so she raced over to the stables and held Flossie in her arms until she quieted down. Nora gave her teaspoons of water, and Flossie seemed to be able to keep that down. She brought Liam and Bran over to the stable and the dogs licked their old friend's sores and lay on either side of her. Flossie gradually seemed more comfortable and she finally fell asleep.

Nora loved dogs so much, and she thought that a person's humanity might be reflected in the way they treated these beautiful animals. When they finally caught the perpetrator, she would be tempted to kick him like he had kicked Flossie. She realized that she was using male pronouns and that it might easily also be a woman, although she hated to think of that.

The media was swarming over the estate and wanted a statement from Nora about this latest violence. She could truthfully tell them that she had no idea why Mr. Boyle had been attacked, so she was not going to speculate as to who might have done this. Even the most hardened reporter could tell that Nora was so sad about her old friend, so they left after she assured them that they would receive notification if any more news emerged.

Enda called Nora and said there had been a call for her from a young woman, who said she would like to talk to her about the girl who had been found on the beach. She told her that she had seen the pictures on the television, and she thought it might be her sister.

"OMG," cried Enda when she reported this to Nora, "what is happening to our peaceful village?"

Nora called the number back and talked to the young woman. "I'd like to come and talk to you, Miss Nora," said the girl. "I saw the news this morning, and I'm afraid that the girl you found might be my sister. My name is Carol Dillon, and my sister's name is Dotty Dillon. I'm too scared to talk to the garda, but I'd like to hear about it from you. Can I come and talk to you?"

Nora assured her that would be fine, and the girl said that she would be coming from Cork, so it would take a while for her to get there. Nora explained that the garda would have to be involved eventually, but this afternoon, they could just have a conversation. Nora noticed that Carol had a heavy brogue when she spoke English, and she asked if she would be more comfortable if her receptionist Enda was there, who was fluent in the Irish. Carol said that would be fine and she would be leaving now.

Nora gave her some driving directions for the best way to approach the castle, and she asked Enda to meet the girl when she arrived. She also asked Mrs. O'Hara to make some of her famous herbed tomato soup and grilled cheese sandwiches with chamomile tea, a meal that usually worked like a comforting and soporific tonic.

Tommy had to do some work online, but he assured Nora that he would be on hand if the girl sounded as though she needed legal help. Nora didn't know what to expect of Carol when she arrived, but she hoped that she could make her feel comfortable enough so that she could give them more information about her sister. She also called Chief Brennan and gave him a heads up about the girl who was coming to talk to her.

Enda kept an eye out for Carol's arrival and guided the frightened-looking girl through the castle and to the patio outside the back door. Carol shook Nora's hand, and Nora noticed that everything from her faded jeans and pink long-sleeved T-shirt to her speech marked Carol as a pretty ordinary girl. Her nails were nicely trimmed, but there was no cherry red nail polish for her. She wasn't crying and seemed fairly composed, which was a good sign.

Mrs. O'Hara brought out some of her famous brown bread with the tomato soup, and as Nora hoped, the grilled four-cheese sandwiches were so tasty that Carol ate most of what was on her plate. The sunny weather contributed to their easy conversation, but it was clear that Carol felt more at home speaking in the Irish. Enda was able to assist several times as Carol tried to tell her story. After they were finished with lunch, Nora asked Carol to tell her more about her family and her sister.

Carol began, "You'll probably want to know that I'll be seventeen next month, and Dotty is twenty. I'll be graduating from secondary school next summer. Dotty is smart and could have gone to university, but she was never interested in pursuing more education. We live on a farm outside of Cork with my mam and da. I've always loved everything about the farm, and Dotty has always hated it. She said that she would be moving to a big city the first chance she got. The one thing she did like was that we had a few horses, but they were just workhorses. She said she'd like to have a beautiful racehorse, and she knew she'd need money to get it.

"She was always one to make goo-goo eyes at almost any boy who seemed interested in her. Recently, I knew there was somebody more important than the usual guys she had been seeing, but she never told me his name. She just said that we would all be surprised about him. The last thing she said to me was that she was going to be seeing 'Frank.' I doubt whether that was really his name, and she asked me not to say anything to our da about it. I always wanted her to like me more, but it didn't seem like that would happen. Da always said you can't change the course of a river, and Dotty was like a force of nature when she'd made up her mind."

"Was your father abusive to Dotty?" Nora felt she had to ask.

Carol negated that question with a firm shake of her head. "My father is a quiet but firm person who believes that there's a right and wrong way to do everything, with very few grey areas. That has been fine for me, but with Dotty, there needed to be 101 grey areas. I think that Da knew that Dotty wanted to get away from him as soon as possible, but he kept trying to get through to her because he loved her so much.

"I knew he had always loved her a little more than me, but I didn't mind, since I was sure that she'd be leaving soon. He never raised a hand to her, but he made it very plain that he did not approve of her clothing or going out with so many boys. He and Mam kept pushing our neighbor at her. Dick Cassidy is a good farmer and a good man, and they went out on a few dates, but I knew he was about the last guy she would be really interested in. He's too nice and too ordinary, and he doesn't have much money to buy her the nice things she likes.

"The last time I saw Dotty, she'd put on her new purple dress with the low-cut top. She worked at the beauty shop in town and saved a little money here and there so she could afford to buy some pretty things and have her hair and nails done. I knew she was going to meet the guy that our parents would not approve of, but I didn't even try to stop her. I was tired of trying."

A few tears ran down Carol's cheeks as she realized what she had just said. Nora told Carol that she would need the name and location of the beauty shop Dotty had worked at so they could talk to them. She also asked if there was anyone that Carol thought might look on Dotty as an enemy. After thinking for a few minutes, Carol responded that she could think of several people.

"Almost all the girls at school didn't like Dotty much, since most of the boys pivoted toward her. Maude Mitchell especially seemed to hate Dotty. My mother was always suspicious that Maude had begun life as a Michael. She was twice as broad as Dotty and very strong.

She was especially upset that her brother Dylan seemed attracted to Dotty and was always warning my sister to stay away from him."

Carol continued, "Bill Allen had it in for Dotty ever since she threw him over for another boy. He has a rough and tough exterior and a personality to match. I was always afraid of him, but Dotty insisted she could handle him. He came from the Travellers people that live just over the hill behind our house. My da was glad when she broke up with him because he never trusted 'the tinkers,' as he called them. Another Travellers boy, Guy Smith, had a habit of giving Dotty gifts, but she wanted no part of him. She only seemed interested in a boy if he projected a 'bad boy' image. I tried to tell her not to play with fire, but she never listened to a thing I said."

"Was there anyone at school who tried to help Dotty?" Nora asked.

"Our principal, Mrs. Meachem, is pretty strict, but she seems to really care about us. She has been very nice to me and my family. I believe she has a husband, but I've never seen him. We have a teacher who is supposed to act as our counselor, Miss O'Dea, but I could not see Dotty opening up to her at all.

"I'm in my last year, and we have a very smart history teacher, Doctor Allenby, who seems to know a lot about Irish history in general and the Travellers people. Some of the kids feel comfortable talking to him about their problems because he seems like he understands us. My friend Erin said he seems shy, but he gave her good advice when she was falling behind in her studies, and now, she is doing very well. Dotty never mentioned that she talked to Doctor Allenby, and he does seem like the kind of man who would only be interested in academics. Our gym teacher, Miss O'Neill, tried to help Dotty, but I think Dotty was jealous of her because she's so pretty.

"I couldn't tell you much about my sister's life away from our home or the school, but the chances are that Dotty kept up the same bad habits wherever she was."

After Carol stopped talking, she was visibly shaking, and her tears started to flow. She sobbed out that would like to see her sister's body now. Nora called in Chief Brennan and introduced him to Carol. The chief assured Carol that the garda needed to be involved if she was officially going to identify her sister. Carol had thought she would be afraid of him, but she found Chief Brennan to be as supportive as Nora had described him.

Nora called Tommy to help with the driving, and they drove Carol to the morgue in Killarney. Carol seemed composed enough until they were about to pull out Dotty's body from the refrigerators. Nora warned Tommy and the chief to keep hold of her, and she moaned in pain, "Oh, Dotty," and then started to faint. "Yes, that's her. That's my sister Dorothy Jean Dillon or Dotty."

Afterward, Tommy drove Carol home in her car, Nora followed in their Ford Escape, and Chief Brennan drove his squad car. They talked to Carol's parents and explained that their youngest daughter had just identified the dead girl from the beach as their daughter Dotty. Mr. Dillon assumed a hardened face and said he might have expected as much, but Mrs. Dillon began sobbing her heart out and calling out for her baby. Carol kept rubbing her mam's hands and tried to comfort her.

Chief Brennan said they would like permission to search Dotty's bedroom to see if they could find any information about the man she had been seeing. They didn't find anything at first and were about to give up, but Carol remembered there was a loose floorboard where they used to hide things when they were kids. They pried it up and discovered an address book with a name and phone number Carol did not recognize, nor did the parents.

Dotty's parents gave permission to the chief to take Dotty's book with him, and Nora, Tommy, and Chief Brennan decided to leave. Nora assured Carol that she could call her at any time if she wanted to talk. She gave the shattered girl a hug and bid them farewell, but she was sure that no one in that house was going to be having a good night for a long time to come.

CHAPTER

12

Wednesday, June 12
Cork, Ireland; 5:00 p.m., IST

A fter they left Carol, Tommy and Nora decided to stop for dinner at a place that Nora's aunt Tilda had recommended to them
outside of Cork, Bunnyconnellan's or Bunny's, "The Cottage on the
Rocks." They called the restaurant and were told they would accept
their reservation so they should come ahead.

What a pretty place the large white building was—and hardly
a cottage—perched on the hills above Cork and overlooking the
Atlantic Ocean. Tommy parked his DeLorean in the farthest spot he
could find in the parking lot. He was always concerned about others
wanting to get a better look at his unusual car and putting dings on
his doors.

They were a little early for their reservation time, so they walked
about the hills surrounding the restaurant and admired the majestic
views of the ocean. They both agreed that when they were stressed
out, as they were after spending time with Carol Dillon and her family, it helped their spirits to spend time with nature.

Tommy looked up the history of the building, which had been
built in 1824. The O'Brien family had taken it over about forty years
ago, and it was now an attractive modern restaurant with a well-
stocked kitchen and appealing menu.

They asked to be seated outside since the weather was fair, and
they had their jackets with them. Jerry, their friendly waiter, showed
them to a table with an excellent view of the ocean and the sur-

rounding hillsides and gave them a menu. Tommy noticed that all the wines sounded delicious. Most were from European countries, a few were from South America, and several were from Australia or New Zealand. There was just a single wine from California, a bourbon barrel Zinfandel, among them. He ordered a bottle of that, while Nora ordered her usual lemon-flavored mineral water.

They decided on their food orders when Tim returned. Nora ordered Bunny's Creamy Seafood Chowder, which contained a variety of fish and was accompanied by brown bread, Nora's favorite. Tommy thought the Scallops and Monkfish Gratin sounded delicious.

While they were waiting for their soups, they spent some time talking about the morning they had spent with the Dillon's and Chief Brennan. Nora reflected that policemen had such a difficult, although necessary, way of making a living, and she was glad she didn't have to be involved with his way of life all the time.

Nora knew that most people who had left Ireland to emigrate to the US, Australia, or other countries had boarded ships in Cork Harbour, and she wondered what they must have been thinking as they glanced out over the huge expanse of water. Their families had likely had an "American wake" for them since they knew they would probably never see them again.

The soups lived up to their delicious descriptions and whetted their appetites for the entrees to come. Tommy ordered the Surf and Turf offering, a combination of steak and prawns. Nora had filled herself up quite a bit already, so she ordered the Puff Pastry Parcel, a dish filled with squash, cheese, and nuts.

They finished off their meal with lemon sherbet and Barry's tea and agreed that they had thoroughly enjoyed the ambience and the food at Bunny's. Jerry gave them their bill and asked if they would mind if he asked for their autograph. He saw a bunch of enthusiastic young faces peeking out from the kitchen, and he and Nora signed autographs for all of them, as well as giving each of them a generous tip. It was interesting to see how their fame sometimes caused them to have uncomfortable times, but at other times, like today, they realized that they could bring joy to people's lives in unexpected ways.

It would take about an hour and a half to get back to Sneem, so even though they would have liked to linger more at this attractive place, they headed out on the highway so they could get home before it was pitch dark. Tommy told her more about his most recent lawyers' conference. People from all over the world had similar problems, and it helped a lot to hear the solutions that bright minds from other countries came up with. Tommy showed her a chart that he had typed up as he listened to the men and women attendees and what they thought was important.

One speaker who was interesting to him suggested that some solutions seemed to mirror their countries' national characters. People from Germany and Russia, whose social constructs are so organized, preferred perfecting technology to solve most problems, while those from sunny places like Spain and Brazil seemed to put more emphasis on helping the people who were the users of the technology.

Matt Conway from Australia asked Tommy if social mores were really valid as a way of analyzing a country's use of technology, and they had spent a few heated moments of discussion about this with their friend from Leeds, Malcolm Hicks.

Nora said she knew that Tommy was such a people person, and she was sure these exchanges were interesting for him. She liked the sound of making plans to attend Matt Conway's wedding in the spring in Australia, but she reminded him of the many things that were scheduled for their calendars about that time.

They were so busy chatting that neither one of them had paid much attention to the traffic. Tommy suddenly pulled on Nora's jacket and asked her to look behind them at the car that was close on their tail. Tommy told her he noticed the car as soon as they had left Cork and was now getting suspicious as to why it was following them so closely. Nora realized that the car's headlights were very bright now and shining directly into their car.

She didn't hesitate at all and called Chief Brennan and told him what was going on and asked him for help. He said he would call the garda in Cork and alert them to the situation. In the meantime, Tommy wondered if he should stay on the main road. He would be very unhappy if anything happened to his silver car or to them.

It wasn't long before they heard the sirens and saw the blue lights of many Garda cars in the rearview mirror. The black car behind them suddenly made an exit at Kenmare, and Tommy pulled his DeLorean off to the side of the road so he could wait for the gardai to catch up with them. It was frightening to think they were apparently being stalked by someone without any understanding of their motive.

The Cork Garda soon reported that they were unable to locate the black car, so they were not sure what the driver's intentions had been. They said they would keep an eye out for it.

When they talked to Chief Brennan, he asked if they could give him a little more information about the car that had been following them. Unfortunately, it was almost dark when they had first noticed the car, which appeared to be pretty ordinary and black. Since they had just seen it out of the rearview mirror, they had not even seen any numbers of its license plate.

After talking more with the garda, Nora and Tommy headed home, grateful that neither their car nor themselves had suffered any more damage than stress. Tommy pointed his powerful car in the right direction, and they were soon near Duffy Hall Castle.

As they pulled up to the back door of the castle, they saw that Tim Taylor, the stable director, was waiting for them. Nora could see that he looked as though he was in some difficulty. She told Tommy to go ahead and get started while she talked to Tim.

Now what? Nora thought. Time was getting short for them to do all the things needed before they could leave for Chicago in a few days, so she hoped there were no major problems with the animals.

"Miss Nora," Tim began, "would you have a few minutes of your time? I need to talk to you."

Nora didn't know Tim too well, but she thought he looked "sad and sorrowful." She encouraged him to come into the kitchen for a few minutes. Tim had taken off his brown cap and was twisting it nonstop between his two large hands.

"I'm in trouble," Miss Nora, "and I need your help and advice. I believe that you have met my girlfriend, Betsy Reilly. I decided a few weeks ago that I was going to propose marriage to her, and I planned to do that on her birthday next week."

"That's wonderful news, Tim," Nora responded. "Betsy seems like a very nice girl, the kind that would make you very happy."

"She is wonderful," said Tim, "but I've done something very foolish that might jeopardize our happiness and even my very life."

"Tell me," enjoined Nora with her usual brusque directions.

By this time, Tim was almost gasping for breath, but he continued, "My Duffy salary is generous, but I decided I wanted to buy a new home for Betsy and give her a really nice engagement ring. No matter how I juggled the numbers, I knew that I did not have enough money for anything near that.

"I know a guy who gambles for a living, and he told me that I could make a lot of money very quickly if I just invested one thousand euros in his establishment. Of course, I lost the one thousand right away, but I kept hoping that the next toss of the dice would be the winner. Now I owe this fellow one hundred thousand euros, and I only have three days to come up with it or he said he would tell Betsy and you about it all. He's also threatened to break both my legs," Tim tearfully cried out. "I just don't know what to do."

Nora sat quietly as Tim poured out this story and marveled at the many ways that people could get themselves into trouble when they tried to take the easy way out.

"Well, Tim, as I said I'm in a hurry right now, and this is going to take some time to process so that it gets dealt with properly. I suspect that you also told me about this ahead of time hoping that I would just pay off this fellow with the one hundred thousand euros. I might do that, but just off the top of my head, I have some questions. Is Duffy Medical or my family at risk for any resulting gossip about this whole thing? Did any of this gambling take place on Duffy Medical's property?

"No," Tim said, "I always went to Joe's building outside of town, although I wouldn't be surprised if Joe tried to drag your name into things. I never realized what a cruel person he is."

"Here's what we're going to do to start with, Tim," directed Nora. I'm going to get Fiona Finnegan, my solicitor, involved in this whole situation. If she seems satisfied with what you have to say, she will give the money you promised to this gambler. We will talk later about what you can do to help pay me back. I also want you to repeat your story to Chief Brennan of the garda, so he can see if 'Joe' has done something that could result in his arrest and being put out of business. I'm going to call him right now and ask him to talk to you.

"I also want you to talk to Betsy so that you can tell her the whole story. She has the right to know what you have done and to make up her mind as to whether she wants to commit her life to you. It sounds as though she would accept you with your promise never to try gambling again. But to back up that promise, I want you to call Gamblers Anonymous and follow their instructions for attending their regular meetings. You can promise all you want, but if you managed to get in the hole for one hundred thousand euros, you must have more of a problem than you thought. Fiona will be able to tell you who to talk to at Gambler's Anonymous."

"Thanks, Miss Nora. I'm afraid to tell Betsy what I've done, but I'll accept your terms, and I thank you more than I can say. I'll be sure to take good care of your animals while you're gone."

Nora called Chief Brennan and asked him to come to the castle and talk to her groom Tim Taylor. She also called her solicitor Fiona, gave her a brief description of Tim's problems, and asked her to be present for the meeting between Tim and Chief Brennan, which Fiona agreed to.

Nora then ushered Tim out and started to climb the stairs to her bedroom. She was tired after her long day, and she was anxious to share Tim's story with Tommy.

CHAPTER

13

Wednesday, June 12
Sneem, Ireland; 10:00 p.m., IST

Nora had only gotten about halfway up the steps when she received a phone call from Carol Dillon, saying that she had come across a hidden note in her jewelry box from her sister, which she had just found. Carol explained to Nora, "Dotty almost never called me Robin anymore, but that was her pet name for me when we were little and she was still nice. Here's what the note has to say:

> Dear Robin,
>
> I know you don't wear much jewelry, so I'm not sure when you'll find this note, but I'm going out tonight with that guy I was telling you about, "Frank." I don't think that really is his name, but that's what he calls himself. He seems pretty sophisticated. So far, he's only asked me for a few kisses, but I sense that if he wanted more, he would be pretty aggressive. Just in case, I'm leaving you his name and information in my blue purse with the gold clasp. I may be exaggerating his intentions, but I'm not stupid, and I want somebody to know about this in case things turn ugly.

I know I haven't been very nice to you lately, but I think you're a good sister and a good friend, and I wish you all the best in life.

Take care of yourself,
Dotty

By the time Carol finished reading the note, she was openly sobbing. Nora asked Carol if she knew where the blue purse was that Dotty had mentioned. Carol said she remembered when Dotty bought it, and she had looked all over the house for it but had not been able to find it. Nora told her to call Chief Brennan and set up a time for him to come and talk to the family again. Nora also sent Chief Brennan a text just to be sure that he heard this news in case Carol forgot to call him.

Chief Brennan answered her text by saying that he would call her shortly. Nora answered his call on the first ring, and he said that he had received the autopsy report on Dotty Dillon from Coroner Lucy Sullivan. It left him with more questions than answers, although it did seem that the deep stab wound to her back was the cause of death.

He told Nora that they were going to start interviewing people outside of Dotty's family who had known her to see if they could shed more light on where she'd been and who she'd been with before she had gone to the beach. He planned to start with the beauty shop where Dotty had worked, as well as other nearby shops. Then he would go to Dotty's old school and interview teachers to see if they could give him more information. He would also be talking to the Travellers people, who currently were settled near Mount Finnaragh outside of Sneem, since Carol Dillon had told them that several of their young men had seemed interested in Dotty.

The chief told Nora that he had instructed the media when talking about the golden horseshoes drawing to not mention the two small green four-leaf clovers that were drawn at the tips of each of the horseshoes. It sometimes happened in a murder investigation that the killer trapped himself by revealing that he knew details that had not been publicized. Nora agreed that it was a wise precaution. She bade the chief a good night, and then she dragged herself up the stairs to go to bed.

The chief detailed the little they had discovered so far. He and his assistant Molly Norris began their investigation into Dotty Dillon's murder by interviewing the proprietor of the Pearl's Curls beauty shop just outside of Sneem. Pearl Reardon said that she had been expecting their visit ever since she'd heard about Dotty's murder.

Chief Brennan asked Pearl the usual questions about how long Dotty had worked at her establishment, whether she was reliable, and anything else she could tell them. Pearl began, "I believe it's just about six months since Dotty started here. I wasn't too sure how reliable she would be when I first hired her, but we became pretty good friends. I've heard the gossip about Dotty by some of the old hens around here, but she wasn't really a bad girl. She was just mixed up. I told her several times that she should leave Sneem and go to a bigger city like Cork or even Dublin. She stood out too much here with her appearance and her ideas.

"She was a big help to my business, and I'm going to miss her. She usually dressed like she was going to a rock concert, but she kept up with the latest hairstyle trends. She also brought in flavored coffees and scones for the customers. Some of the younger women from the surrounding towns suddenly discovered us, and I was glad about that."

Pearl continued, "You know that hairdressers can be a substitute for a doctor's couch or a priest's confessional. You would be surprised at the private details the customers share with us. The young ones are trying hard not to get old, and the old ones are desperately trying to turn back time and hang on to memories of their happier days."

Chief Brennan asked if she knew who the man was that Dotty had been seeing, but she said she did not. Molly asked her if she remembered what Dotty had been wearing when she left there and said they were particularly interested in finding a blue purse with a golden ornamental closure. Pearl said she had been upset with Dotty when she left and she hadn't paid too much attention to her clothes, but she remembered that she had a big black purse with her since that was where she put her paycheck.

The chief and Molly gave Pearl their cards and asked her to call them if she remembered any other details about Dotty that could help them. As they were leaving the beauty shop, they spotted an elderly woman sweeping the sidewalk outside a cafe. They introduced themselves and she said she was Mrs. Beth Gorman. They showed her Dotty's picture and asked if she knew anything about her.

"Of course, I know about her. We all do. I used to wish her bad cess for the sorrow and shame she was bringing to her family, and it was no surprise to me to hear what happened to her."

Garda Molly asked Mrs. Gorman if she had seen her yesterday before she disappeared. Mrs. Gorman said she had not seen her, but she called her daughter out of the shop and asked if she had seen Dotty Dillon yesterday.

Mary Gorman said that she had seen the chief and Molly from the window and had known just why they were there. "Yes," Mary said, "Dotty said she was going on a date last night, and she asked me if I would hold on to her blue purse until today. I told her I would, but then she left right away, and I have no idea where she went."

The chief and Molly hid their excitement that Mary had the missing blue purse, and they asked her if she would please go and get it since Dotty's sister Carol said there might be something in there that would give a clue as to her whereabouts. Mary said she had the purse in her room, and she went upstairs to get it. She returned shortly with the blue purse, and there was the golden closure piece, and sure enough, there was a note with the name of Frank and a phone number in one of the small inner pockets.

Chief Brennan said, "Mary, we're going to have to take the purse with us for evidence."

Mary nodded her head in agreement and said she hoped that it would be helpful in finding out who had killed Dotty.

Chief Brennan and Molly went back to their car and called the phone number shown on the piece of paper. There was no answer, but they decided to bring it back to the station and work with the phone company to get a reverse lookup for the associated address with the phone number.

Unfortunately, the address turned out to be the aquarium outside of Dingle. They tried again to call the home of many beautiful sea creatures but were told that they had no employee named Frank. Chief Brennan and Molly could only assume that "Frank" gave Dotty the wrong phone number to deliberately mislead her should she ever call it.

This investigation was not going smoothly at all so far, and they had not yet had a chance to talk to the school that Dotty had attended nor talk to the Travellers people to find the young men who had liked Dotty.

Nora thanked the chief for the update, said goodnight, and wished him good luck with the rest of the investigation.

CHAPTER

14

Thursday, June 13
Sneem, Ireland; 9:00 a.m., IST

After hearing the disappointing report from Chief Brennan last night, Nora had an idea. She called Pearl's Curls and asked if they would have an opening for her in a few hours for a haircut and mani-pedi with gel nail polish. Pearl sounded surprised but said she could see her at 2:00 p.m.

Nora didn't really feel like spending several hours in the small shop, but she thought she might be able to wrest more information about Dotty from Pearl than the police had been able to do so far. Nora knew that most beauty shop owners learned that they got better tips if they conversed with their customers, and Pearl would likely talk more to a potential big tipper like Nora.

Nora arrived at Pearl's a few minutes before 2:00 p.m. The shop's gray exterior looked old and tired, and the interior didn't look much better. The walls had needed a new coat of paint quite a few years ago, and there were only three hair cutting stations. She was a little apprehensive about having work done here, but what was the worst that could happen? Her hair grew fast, and she could always have it cut shorter when she got home if she didn't like what Pearl did to it.

It was obvious that Pearl was apprehensive too as to why this famous person was in her shop, and she appeared to be all business as she asked Nora how she wanted her hair done. Nora asked her to just trim it about an inch all around and pay special attention to the bangs area that always grew so fast. Nora asked her to wash her hair gently since the bullet grazes on her scalp from last year were still tender. Pearl suggested that she could tame Nora's curls if she used the broad curlers she had in back, and Nora agreed with her suggestion just to keep things going as long as possible.

Nora tried to think of some subject that would encourage Pearl to talk to her, so she told the beautician that she was fortunate to have such a good view of the Sneem River. That didn't work very well since Pearl agreed but said she'd stopped looking at the scenery many years ago since she was always so busy. Nora didn't see any other customers at the moment, but she supposed that did happen occasionally.

Next, Nora complimented her on her pretty daughter who was waiting to do the work on Nora's nails. That train of thought was more successful, and Nora realized that this woman thought the world of her daughter Mary. The dam of conversation opened up, and Nora learned more about Mary than she had hoped for.

After that, Pearl seemed more comfortable, and Nora thought she had better strike while the iron was hot. She said she had heard about the death of her assistant Dotty, and she was sorry to hear it. She continued by saying that she'd heard that Dotty was quite a handful. Pearl defended her and said that people around here were too critical of a young woman trying to make her way through a sea of traditional prejudice. The vehemence of Pearl's response led Nora to think that Pearl herself had gone through a similar situation herself when she was younger.

After a few more exchanges, while watching carefully as Pearl kept hacking away at her hair, Nora felt comfortable asking the question she was really interested in. "It must have been hard for a girl like Dotty to find the kind of men she'd be interested in among the few young males in your village," said Nora. "I would think she would have wanted someone who had money and would be able to take her out of your rural environment. I wonder if the man who killed her was someone completely unknown to the locals?"

"Well," answered Pearl, "I thought the same thing, and I think she had already found someone she thought could be her ticket out of here. She told me that his name was Frank, that he was older and had money, and that he was going to give her a special gift the night she disappeared. I tried to warn her about getting too friendly with older men, but she just laughed and told me to stop sounding like her mother."

Pearl's daughter Mary told Nora to move over to the pedicure station while she was waiting for her hair to dry. Mary asked her what color nail polish she wanted, and Nora picked out the bottle of blackberry plum. Pearl went into the back of the shop, and Nora could tell that Mary was impressed that Nora was there, and she had a feeling she knew more than she had told the garda.

"Mary, I'm sorry about your friend Dotty. I'm sure you must miss her," Nora said. She thought that Mary would notice that she'd had a pedicure just before coming back to Ireland, but the preoccupied girl didn't mention it.

"She was never my friend," responded Mary hotly, "but my mother liked having her here, so I had no choice. I used to think that my mother liked Dotty better than me, even though I had helped out in the shop since I was five years old."

Nora responded to Mary that she was sure that wasn't the case, but here was another person who was just glad that the controversial Dotty was no longer around.

Mary continued, "I saw this Frank once when he came to pick her up, and he looked like my father, God rest his soul."

Nora pretended to be shocked that she had seen Frank and asked what he looked like, but Mary said she had only seen him sitting in his big black car, and she hadn't seen his face clearly. She said nothing would induce her to go out with some old guy just because he had money.

Nora asked what kind of car Frank had, but just then, Pearl returned and took the curlers out of her hair. Pearl had overheard them and said that she recognized the car as a Mercedes S-Class. She hadn't seen Frank's face either, but she thought his hair was dark brown.

Nora was excited about this information but tried not to show it. Pearl worked on her hair some more, and Nora had to admit that it looked better than it had in some time. She told Pearl she was pleased, and the woman blushed with pride.

Mary finished up Nora's nails with the blackberry plum gel polish, and she did a good job of it. Nora told Mary she thought it surprising that a little shop like theirs used gel nail polish, and Mary told Nora that Dotty had been responsible for bringing it in and getting training for them to learn how to use it.

Nora left them both generous tips and was glad to leave the depressing little shop so she could tell Chief Brennan what she had discovered. Nora told the chief the few new details she had found out. The man's presumed name was Frank, and he must be middle-aged with dark brown hair and drove a black Mercedes S-Class. There probably were not too many of those vehicles around in their small town.

"That's more than we were able to find out. I may have to be in touch with you if I need more details after you've gone back home," said Chief Brennan.

Nora agreed that he could call her at any time and then she said goodbye to the dear man and wished him good luck.

The castle's security officer, Chief Michael Herlihy, also called Nora and said they had been looking into Farmer Jack Boyle's background, and they had not been able to find any living relatives. He had been born in Belfast seventy-five years ago, but he had lived in Sneem most of his life and was one of the first farmers Uncle Cy had hired when he purchased Duffy Hall Castle. Jack had never married, but the landlord at the Two Squares Pub said everyone knew Jack and Biddy Flanagan had been best friends for years, and they flung up their heels in the ceili dances on Friday nights. Biddy had died last year of pneumonia, and people at the pub had seen a noticeable decline in Jack's usual happy good humor since then.

He had always seemed to be in such good health, but his friend Jim Quinn said Jack had recently been talking about retiring. No one they talked to could think of a bad word to say about him, and the villagers theorized that it must have been a malicious outsider who had killed him. They doubted that he had much money around the house, so motives were in short supply. His friends were contributing to a collection for a memorial stone for him to be placed on the Coral Beach that he loved so much.

Nora called Father Lanigan at St. Mary's in Sneem and made arrangements for Farmer Jack Boyle's funeral and burial in the churchyard cemetery, and she made a generous donation to the memorial stone fund. She was sorry she would not be able to attend his funeral, but she asked St. Mary's to make his final services as nice as possible and to invite everyone in the surrounding villages to a luncheon at the Sneem Hotel, which she would pay for.

Jack's poor dog Flossie had mostly physically recovered from her assault, but she was still exhibiting signs of emotional trauma and was shivering and whining when she wasn't being held. Nora directed Tim Taylor to take special care of Flossie and to let her spend time with her old friends Liam and Bran while she was gone.

Nora had a meeting with John O'Malley the CEO of Duffy Medical and Duncan Lloyd the chief solicitor, and they had reviewed the schedule of board agenda items for the next few months. Duncan reminded her that there had been some financial problems with their offices in Germany, so he was sending George Keller there to investigate.

Duncan said he realized that former company officers Fred Carroll, chief accountant, and Ben Jordan, treasurer, had been dismissed last year after they had foolishly tried to implicate Nora and Aunt Lavinia in a plot to undermine the company, but he missed their counsel and expertise. Nora said that perhaps they should look closer at that situation. She had always liked both men, but they had let their intemperate wives lead them astray. She asked Duncan to find out what both men were doing now and to see if it would be feasible and wise to reinstate them at Duffy Medical.

Nora had organized a hasty memorial service for Jack Boyle and invited Duffy Medical members who lived nearby, the castle staff, and everyone who worked on the castle grounds to come for a brief goodbye ceremony. She had Kitty Lloyd find a good picture of Jack with his trusty pet Flossie, and she enlarged the photo and placed it on the antique table in front of the stained-glass window in the great hall dining room.

The evening shadows falling upon the high walls and distant roof timbers, lit only by dozens of candles, provided a somber backdrop for the service. Nora began by reminding the group that there would be a wake and funeral for Jack after the police were finished with their investigation where his body would be present. She hoped they would invite as many people as possible to attend. Since she and Tommy would be leaving soon and would not be able to attend those services, she wanted to honor "one of their own" by having this gathering tonight.

The beautiful golden harp from the minstrels' gallery had been carefully carried down the stairs and now sat next to the table, holding Jack's picture. This lovely instrument had survived many difficult situations in the past, and Nora started thrumming the strings to Aaron Copland's "Appalachian Spring," one of her favorites that always had a calming effect on her spirit. It was no wonder that the harp was seen in so many places in Ireland, including on its flag and on glasses of Guinness. The harp was the symbol of the immortality of the soul and was the perfect instrument for conveying every emotion.

Liam and Bran, the castle's faithful dogs, knew that something unusual was happening, and they added an occasional sad howl, which heightened the rueful spirit in the room. Jack's beloved Flossie was still in the infirmary at the stables, but she was present in their imaginations.

One thing the garda had discovered when they searched Jack's cottage was that he was very knowledgeable about the beginnings of the Irish independence movement since his grandfather had been killed on that fateful Easter day so long ago and yet so near in Jack's heart.

Ed Simon, whose cottage sat the closest to Jack's, read a portion of William Butler Yeats's famous poem about the Easter 1916 "Rising."

> *Too long a sacrifice*
> *Can make a stone of the heart.*
> *O when may it suffice?*

That is Heaven's part, our part
To murmur name upon name,
As a mother names her child
When sleep at last has come
On limbs that had run wild.
What is it but nightfall?
No, no, not night but death;
Was it needless death after all?
For England may keep faith
For all that is done and said.
We know their dream; enough
To know they dreamed and are dead;
And what if excess of love
Bewildered them till they died?
I write it out in a verse—
MacDonagh and MacBride
And Connolly and Pearse
Now and in time to be,
Wherever green is worn,
Are changed, changed utterly:
A terrible beauty is born.

There was a moment of silence as the mourners contemplated the master poet's words and Jack Boyle's life and tried to make sense of it all. Jack had been "changed utterly," but could his violent death bring about a renewal of the "terrible beauty?"

Kitty Duffy, who had known Jack since she was a little girl, used his own ancient Bible they'd found on the table next to his bed and read the inspiring words from Timothy that seemed to fit him so well: "I have fought the good fight, I have finished the race, I have kept the faith." Father Lanigan from the village told the group that they probably were not aware of this, but Jack made it a point to visit the pensioners who lived at the nearby Happy Glen home every week and bought them little gifts. He was the epitome of a dedicated servant whose good deeds were only known by God.

Tommy used his baritone voice to intone the hymn "Johnny I Hardly Knew Ye," which they all sang, and then Sean Lloyd ended the service by playing "Amazing Grace" on his bagpipes. Mrs. O'Hara provided Jack's favorite strawberry tarts with chamomile tea for all. Nora encouraged everyone to be sure to attend the actual wake and funeral for Jack, and then they said a sad goodnight and went their separate ways.

Nora and Tommy held on to each other tightly as they went upstairs for the night. The mournful spirit of the last two hours was hard to shake off, but they put the pets to bed and climbed into their own. They contemplated the eternal movement of the stars and listened to the ebb and flow of the ocean's waves and were just about to fall asleep when she saw a call coming in on her phone from Chief Brennan.

CHAPTER

15

Thursday, June 13
Sneem, Ireland; 11:00 p.m., IST

C hief Brennan began the call by saying that they had barely started to work on the Dotty Dillon investigation when he had received a response to his request for more information about recent murders in Ireland. He had been flabbergasted to hear that another nude body of a young woman had been found on the famous Ballybunion Golf Club a while ago, not too far away from the castle in Sneem. The description of the corpse sounded similar to the girl found on the Coral Beach, and there was again another drawing of two interlocking golden horseshoes with the red slash through them above the young woman's breasts. Two violent killings of two young women with the golden horseshoes markings certainly seemed as though they could be the work of a serial killer and much too close to home.

Chief Brennan said that the second girl had been found in one of the many deep bunkers on the famous golf course. Nora told Chief Brennan that this was incredible. She wondered if there could be a connection between the two girls being killed to Jack Boyle's violent death. The chief gave her a brief description of what he knew so far about the second murdered girl.

The chief had received the initial call from the manager of the golf course, who said one of the young men who had been clearing golf balls from the bunkers had discovered the dead girl. They had had a break with this girl's identity since the traumatized lad who found her was a former schoolmate of hers. The chief and his garda colleagues had driven to the golf course, which had been closed off, and after looking back at the photos of Dotty Dillon, he quickly confirmed that the size of the girl, the damage that had been done to her, and the appearance of the golden horseshoes with the red slash were almost exactly alike.

It was a small leap to make the connection that the killer of both girls might be one and the same. They had looked at shoe prints, but unfortunately, there were too many of them, and the ground around the bunker had been trampled too much to give up any useful clues.

Sgt. Molly Norris briefly went back to the golf course, remembering the plots of many television show murders and possible clues to the murderer. She looked for a missing button, a cigarette butt, or a piece of paper that could lead to the discovery of who had committed the crime, but the killer must have watched those same shows because there was nothing unusual to be found.

They had started to interview some of the people that Carol Dillon and her family had mentioned, but they now would have to turn their attention to discovering who had killed this girl as well as continuing to search for more information about who could have killed Jack Boyle so violently. The last few days must have set a sad record for violence in their usual peaceful corner of the world.

The chief explained to Nora that the unfortunate young man who found this latest girl had appeared in the golf club's office and hysterically informed them that he had found the body of Annie Matthews, a former school friend of his, whose family lived in a village just outside of Killarney.

So far they'd discovered that Annie Matthews was an eighteen-year-old girl who was a merit scholar and the pride of the household. Annie had been helping out at a senior citizen home. She had gone to take out the garbage and never returned, and they suspected that she must have been kidnapped.

Her siblings were a sister who was fifteen and two brothers, ages nine and five. The father was a stock trader, and the mother worked part-time at a solicitor's office. Their house is middle class but neat and surrounded by plants and flowers. When it was confirmed that the body was their daughter, the disconsolate parents were quickly surrounded by family, friends, and priests.

The chief said they asked if it were possible that Annie was not kidnapped but had gone to meet someone. That didn't seem likely since she often warned her younger sister about being too friendly with strangers. Annie was supposed to have had a piano recital playing Mozart's "Lacrimosa" portion of his *Requiem in D Minor* the next day, and she was so excited about it. She had gone shopping with her mother to Harper's in Galway for a new blue recital dress and couldn't wait to wear it. Obviously, she had every intention of being at home and no intention of running away or committing suicide.

When they arrived at the Matthews's home, Annie's parents tearfully gave permission for Chief Brennan to search the girl's room. They had temporarily sent their younger children to stay with Mrs. Matthews's brother and his wife.

They sadly but proudly told them that Annie had written a long piece on the place of women in the myths of Ireland and had submitted it to Trinity College in Dublin a few months ago. Just two days ago, the college had written back and offered her a full scholarship.

They found a notebook that the girl had written that highlighted some of the most famous women in Irish myths. She had cited author Morgan Llywelyn as one of her sources, a favorite author of Nora's. Anne had written an inspiring paper on one of Nora's favorite ancient stories and had added her own thoughts about it:

> Macha was forced to run a race against the King of Ulster's chariot horses, even though she was heavily pregnant. She resisted but was forced to do it. She won the race but collapsed and gave birth to twin boys, Fedach and Fomfor. With her dying breath, Macha cursed the men of Ulster so that they would suffer the pangs of childbirth before they could ride into future battles.

Annie had written that she thought that sounded like the ultimate female curse, and Nora agreed. Another version of the story said that Macha lived another twenty-five years and had become the high queen of Ireland.

The "curse of the pangs of childbirth" had a disastrous result for the Ulstermen in stories like The Cattle Raid of Cooley.

> The King of Connaught, Ailell, and the Queen, Maeve, were comparing their wealth and after enumerating various possessions realized that they were about equal, except that Ailell owned the enormous white bull, so that put him ahead. Maeve made up her mind to acquire the famous brown bull of Cooley in Ulster that was even bigger than the white bull.

Much of the story revolves around Cú Chulainn, the Hercules—like warrior of Ulster, who was immune to the battle curse. Eventually, Maeve succeeded in obtaining the brown bull, and peace was finally made.

Annie also wrote about the supposed first people of Ireland, the Tuatha Dé Danann, or in Gaelic, "People of the Goddess Danu." In Celtic mythology, they were a race inhabiting Ireland before the arrival of the Milesians, the ancestors of the modern Irish. The Tuatha Dé Danann were said to have been skilled in magic, and the earliest reference to them relates that, after they were banished from heaven because of their knowledge, they descended on Ireland in a cloud of mist.

Garda Molly Norris told Nora that Annie also summarized the collected folklore and poetry that had been gathered from the Irish people in the 1800s and written down by Thomas Crofton Croker, a renowned historian. Annie's observations on all this history and allegory continued for many pages, and she added one of her own poems:

"Boomerang"

I aimed for the stars' light
Tried to get the trajectory right
But shot myself in the foot when
I forgot to first count to ten—again.

It's an ill wind that blows nobody good
So I'll give myself a push—again
And maybe this time my arrow could
Find the sweet spot.

Nora was curious as to what the poem's words meant to Annie, but she was sure that had she been allowed to live, this intelligent and observant girl would have had a bright personal and academic future.

As the chief and Molly described the scene so well, Nora couldn't help but notice the wide difference in the families' expectations of the two murdered girls. Dotty Dillon's family didn't seem to be very surprised that Dotty would someday be murdered because she took such risks. She seemed to be headed in a dangerous direction, no matter how much her family and friends tried to stop her. They were sad that she was gone, but quite frankly, some of them admitted they were relieved that they would not have to worry about her anymore.

Annie Matthews's family had expected continued excellence from their beautiful and hardworking daughter. It seemed almost impossible that Annie had been deprived of her birthright. The parents were devastated and barely able to function enough to take care of the rest of their children. It was clear that everyone thought her death had deprived the world of a great talent.

In terms of the mores of society, Dotty had done almost everything wrong, and Annie had done almost everything right, but the end result was the same. Both of them had died long before they normally would have and in a terrible fashion.

Lucy Sullivan and her sister Gemma conducted an autopsy on Annie Matthews body, and she said that it was likely that the blow to her head had killed her. There was the stab wound to her back, but it had not resulted in exsanguination.

Chief Brennan said that he had given the release for both families to proceed with having a funeral for their daughters now that the autopsies had been completed. He and his team were determined to find the killer of the two girls, and they were still investigating the death of Farmer Jack Boyle. They had talked to anyone they thought might have some knowledge about him, but so far, they had not turned up any new information. He said good night to Nora, and she wished him good luck.

The media had been drawn to their small town like flies to honey, and they were still trying to interview anyone they could find who knew something about these murders. They produced lurid headlines with accompanying lurid stories, but they hadn't resulted in any more answers as to who the killer might be. They were disappointed that they couldn't seem to discover more information since this was the home of Nora Duffy.

Nora heard her distinctive phone ring with the Irish jig and looked at the number that was calling her. She recognized her best friend from babyhood's number Connie Carroll and promptly answered it with joy that it was Connie but apprehension that it was Connie since she almost never called her when she was out of the country.

She could tell by the tearful sounds in Connie's voice that something was very wrong. "Tell me," directed Nora. They knew each other's moods so well that no more words were needed.

"I hope you're coming home soon, Bits," responded Connie in a shaky voice. "I'm at Holy Savior's Emergency Room. I decided to take the subway to Barry's Pub, and I was shot on the platform at State and Jackson. Your mom and dad have both been here, and they're both working with Doctor Boyd. The bullet seems to be close to my spine, and they're not sure what to do about it yet. My family are all here, but I wish I could see you. Oh, I have to go. They're coming for more blood."

Nora realized that she had two incoming calls, most likely from people in her family letting her know about Connie. One benefit from being part of a big family was that Nora had learned long ago to adapt and change on the spur of the moment.

"Connie, dear, I'll change my flight, and I'll be there by tomorrow. God bless and *semper fi.*"

Connie's dad had been in the marines, and her family's motto matched that of the US Marine Corps. They were always faithful and ready for anything. Nora's assurances made Connie relax more, and Nora asked to talk to Eileen, Connie's mother.

"Oh, Bitsy," Eileen Carroll cried into the phone, "I'm so scared right now. Your dad assures me that he'll stay with us until the doctors decide the best course of action, and he'll assist Doctor Boyd, the spine surgeon. What is this world coming to that a young woman can't go down to the subway for fear of her life? Dan is so mad about the whole thing and we're all feeling so helpless."

"Mrs. Carroll, I just told Connie that I've changed my plans, and I'll be there by tomorrow afternoon. In the meantime, hang onto each other and to my parents for strength. They are good at figuring out how to help people in the best way. Tommy and I are adding our prayers to the many that I know are being offered up for Connie right now." Nora ended with, "I love you all."

Nora stopped for a moment to say a prayer for her dear friend and to give the doctors and nurses strength and wisdom. She was glad that Stan Boyd was going to do the surgery. He lacked a bedside manner, but he was one of the best spine surgeons in the country. He only accepted cases where he thought there was a degree of hope for recovery, so that was encouraging.

Nora explained this latest development to Chief Brennan, and he said he was so sorry, and he understood that she would be leaving Ireland right away. He told her that he would keep her informed since these murder cases seemed to somehow be related to her.

Nora gave Tommy this latest update about Connie, and they both agreed that they would take the next nonstop flights out of Dublin, which would be tomorrow morning, just a few hours from now. She called Old Tim McMahon, told him there had been a change of plans, and asked him to pick them up at 5:30 a.m. They kept their suitcases at the ready, so they hurriedly threw clothes and shoes together.

They had both been scheduled to fly to Boston on Saturday to see Tommy's younger sister Maeve make her debut dancing with the Boston Ballet Company on Sunday. Nora told Tommy she thought he should still go to Boston a day earlier than originally planned since this was such an important event in Maeve's life, while she would go to Chicago to be with Connie and her family.

Nora called her secretary Kitty at the castle, gave her a brief update, and told her to get her on tomorrow morning's flight to Chicago and Tommy on the flight to Boston. She realized that her hands were shaking as she tried to navigate her phone and that she was more upset by Connie's condition than she originally thought.

Just then, she saw that her mother was calling her. "I know about Connie. Tell me," directed Nora, and Eileen Duffy gave her the good news that Connie appeared to be out of danger, although she'd lost a lot of blood. Doctor Boyd, Nora's dad, and other doctors were still analyzing how to safely remove the bullet. The Carroll family were all there and Michael and Eileen were doing their best to keep them calm.

Nora told her mother, "I've changed my flight plans, and I'll be home by tomorrow afternoon. Tommy is still going to go to Boston to see Maeve dance. Tell Jim to pick me up at O'Hare tomorrow afternoon and ask Jesse to double up her prayers to St. Brigid. Spine surgery is always risky."

Nora's mom assured her she would take care of things on her end, and she'd be so glad to have her home.

Nora saw another number appear on her phone and said hello to her Chicago Police Department friend, Lt. Matt Braxton. "Hi, Bitsy," he began. "I'm sure you've heard about your friend Connie by now, and I wanted to assure you that we're doing everything we can to track down the thugs who were involved in the shooting. It sounds as though Connie got caught in the crossfire between two rival gangs. I'm really sorry this happened, and Laura sends you her love."

Laura Belsky had been a police person last year during their scare at the castle, and she had a major part to play in bringing it to a successful conclusion. Afterward, Laura had decided she had had enough of police work, and she was now a paralegal at Tommy's law firm and liked it very much. Matt and Laura were scheduled to be married in September in Chicago.

Nora tearfully thanked Matt for his call and said she was glad he was involved. She told him she would be back home by tomorrow afternoon, and she would appreciate anything he could do to expedite finding out who did this to her dear friend. "Matt, this is terrible for Connie and only adds to people's fears about feeling safe in the busier parts of Chicago. Do what you can."

She also told him about the second murdered girl she'd encountered today, and he said it sounded like she should get home to Chicago where there might not be any more violence than what she'd encountered there in the last few days.

Tommy talked to the various castle staff and answered their questions as best as he could while they prepared to leave. The staff members all said they were sorry to see them go, and they were told that they could call them on their cell phones whenever they would like. Tommy reminded them all to be especially vigilant for their safety and anyone who would be visiting since no one knew who the killer might be. He handed out cards that contained Chief Brennan's phone number and said they should call him if they thought of any information that might be helpful to the case.

In the morning, Nora contented herself with a very brief run, and they both enjoyed some breakfast treats that Mrs. O'Hara had left for them. They made sure to do one last check of everything they would need for their trips and dressed comfortably. Tommy carried their suitcases down to the front hall, and Tim McMahon arrived promptly at 5:30 a.m. to drive them to Dublin Airport. They gave hugs all around to Enda, Sean, and Kitty; petted the dogs while transferring their leashes to Tim Taylor; and then they were off. Tommy told Tim that they were worn out and would try to sleep in the car for a few hours.

CHAPTER

16

Friday, June 14
Dublin, Ireland; 8:30 a.m., IST

Tim McMahon stopped the car about an hour from Dublin so they could walk around and stretch their legs. It was encouraging to see that the good weather was holding, and the threatened rain might wait until after they had taken off. As they got closer to Dublin Airport, they could see the traffic was stopped for an accident involving two trucks, so it was good that they had left early. They finally arrived at the airport and checked in their luggage.

Before Nora and Tommy could separate and go to their respective gates, they spotted a number of reporters waiting for them. Someone must have spilled the beans that they would be traveling. Nora was glad to see that one of them was her old friend, who had been so helpful to her last year, Ann O'Shea of the *Ennis Tribune*. As usual, Ann was dressed fashionably, and Nora admired her peaches-and-cream outfit with matching shoes. They greeted each other cordially, but Ann was hoping to get a statement for her paper. She asked Nora if she could share anything more about the murders that had taken place near her home, but Nora told her they still didn't know very much, and she would send her an e-mail since she was in a hurry today.

Nora asked the media folks to let them go with a minimum of fuss today since she was in a hurry to get home to Chicago to see her friend Connie Carroll, who had been shot and was about to have surgery. The murders near Duffy Hall Castle were still being investigated, and she had nothing new to report to them. Tommy told them he was on his way to Boston for his sister's debut with the Boston Ballet. The media was obliging today and let them go with a few pictures. Ann told Nora that she hoped her friend would recover soon, and they left with hugs.

Tommy gave Nora a kiss and then went to his gate for the trip to Boston. He would be happy to see his sister begin her career with the Boston Ballet, but he also felt as though he should be going with Nora who was so concerned about Connie who was like one of her sisters.

They were reluctant to let go of each other, but they finally did, and Nora jogged over to the Chicago departure gate. A cute little girl recognized Nora's signature curly red hair and came over to say hello to her. Nora chatted with Mia and her mother, Amy, until their flight was called, and they started to board.

One of the friendly stewardesses who helped Nora with her boarding pass looked familiar, and she recognized a few of the others of the flight crew from her last trip back to Chicago and chatted with them before taking her seat. She always preferred to sit next to the window, and the aisle seat was taken by a young boy who was traveling by himself. He seemed nervous and unwilling to talk to anyone. Nora didn't press him, and she could imagine that he would be scared to be taking this long trip alone, but she hoped to find a way to help him feel more comfortable as the flight got underway.

Nora was always fascinated by the sight of the submerged islands that lay under the Atlantic as the plane left Ireland. She said a fond goodbye to the Land of Saints and Scholars and looked forward to arriving in Chicago, just 3,664 miles or 5,896 kilometers away. It was a blessing to live in the days of air travel and get home in less than half a day rather than the ten days it used to take by ship.

She was soon told that they could start using their electronic devices, and Nora checked her many e-mails and prepared a report for the hospital. She saw an e-mail from Chief Brennan and was curious to see what he had to tell her. She could not have been more surprised at what his note said.

From what they had been able to glean so far, Jack Boyle had been born in Belfast and had apparently been a member of the IRA. However, one of his old pals at the Two Squares Pub said that most of them knew about Jack's past, but it was his brother who had participated in blowing up a British fort, and Jack had nothing to do with it. Jack decided then that he wanted no part of violence on either side. He had learned to be a farmer from his father, so he left Belfast and went as far away as he could to their village of Sneem and began his life as a tenant farmer growing vegetables. They were still following many paths of inquiry, including the gun hidden in the Shakespeare volume and the pin with the picture of the Easter lily as well as the gold button he'd had in his hand.

The friendly stewardess Mary Lou offered them a choice for lunch, but Nora's stomach was queasy since she was still so concerned about Connie and what she would find when she got to Chicago, so she settled for a cheese omelet and lemon water. The young boy in the aisle seat was having trouble getting his tray table to open properly, and when Nora offered to help him, he told her that his name was Finn Doyle, and he was headed home to his mother and his sister. He said his father worked in Ireland as a steelworker, and he had been to see him in Cork. Nora was happy that Finn didn't seem to have heard of her fame, and they had a pleasant conversation. She gave him the chocolate chip cookies that had come with her lunch, and he seemed much more at ease.

Nora started to doze after lunch and thought about the violent events they had experienced over the last few days. She wondered if Chief Brennan had time to make any progress with interviewing people who knew Dotty Dillon. She felt bad for Dotty, although she appeared to be one of those unfortunate people who was so intent on following her own way that she completely ignored the advice of anyone else. The evident pain in Annie Matthews's family deserved some immediate attention, but so far, they had been unable to discover anything more that could be helpful.

Nora realized how glad she would be to see her family. She thought about her dad and how much she owed to him. As they were growing up, Doctor Duffy would often call all the kids together for "the talk." This did not happen on a regular basis but rather when he had time to spend with them, which was often on a holiday. He would remind them that part of becoming a fully developed human being was to figure out what your principles were and how to articulate them. He said it was important to develop your language skills, but the most important thing was for each of them to decide what they believed in and how to talk about it in an intelligent manner. Nora had often thought that if he had not become a surgeon, her dad would have made a great teacher. He was a master at getting his audience's attention by getting them involved in the conversation.

She especially recalled one such session at a birthday dinner where he got her brother Jim to talk about why he had a very black and blue eye. At first, Jim resisted, but he eventually relayed that Eddie Johnson had said that his father was a doctor, so he had killed people. "I was so mad at him, so I just tried to sock him, but he's so much bigger than me, and he knocked me down," Jim explained. "You're always busy saving people's lives, not killing them."

"Well," Michael Duffy asked his other children, "who do you think was right in this situation?" Her dad was always so good at this and helped the children make good moral decisions by getting them to think about the right thing to do rather than telling them what he thought that was. Most of the children agreed with their brother, although Mary Ann, the thinker, said that her father had probably killed a few people inadvertently when they were too sick to survive a heart operation. Michael said that was true, but the most important lesson he wanted them all to learn was that they had to be able to articulate what they were thinking and not just keep it within themselves. As to the knocking down part, some people like Eddie, who was always so mean, might deserve it, but it was always better to try to avoid violence if they could.

After many such sessions over the years, each one of the Duffy children was good at telling people what they thought and the reasons for it. People might not agree with them, but the Duffy children rarely lost an argument, and most of them had become members of their schools' debate teams. As they matured, they also realized that they at least had to listen carefully to what other people's points of view were.

Nora then switched to thinking about her mother, Eileen, and she would be so glad to give this beautiful and talented woman a big hug. She knew that many people didn't seem to like their parents much as they aged, but Nora admired her mother more than anyone else she knew. She worked hard at everything she did, and that included being a wonderful wife and mother, as well as a talented head nurse while maintaining her health and her beauty. She'd had ten children and done a very good job with each one.

Nora chuckled to herself as she recalled one of her less-stellar moments as a young girl. She had stood Mark Calloway's teasing as long as she could about her curly red hair until one day, she'd bopped him in the nose and then run away. Mrs. Calloway then marched over to the Duffy's house and confronted Eileen about her uncontrollable daughter. Eileen had calmed the neighbor down but mentioned that it was rude of her son to criticize someone because of their physical appearance. She assured her that Nora would receive a good talk about it. Nora and her mother had quite a long conversation about being proud of the looks that God had given us but also about the best way to go about personal attacks. Nora had never let herself be put in that situation again.

Eileen Duffy's parting words to her children as they left the house each morning was to remember that they were Duffys, and that involved bringing honor to their family name wherever they were. More than once that wise advice had prevented Nora and her siblings from getting involved in petty quarrels with other people.

Nora smiled as she thought about the importance given to sex education today and how well her parents had taken care of that subject. In a house with many children, new babies, and few bathrooms, the Duffy children had seen the attributes of both the male and female bodies many times as they were growing up. Michael and Eileen Duffy had engaged in what they called life education at many points along the way. The anatomy of the human body and how smart God was to make it that way was just part of the lessons they had absorbed, like toast soaking up butter. Knowledge is power, and the Duffy children were well prepared for the challenges of sex and relationships at appropriate times before they were teenagers.

Eileen Duffy had a host of acquaintances and a core group of good friends who had shared their joys and sorrows over many years. They gathered often to celebrate birthdays and holidays and to listen to each other's family stories. They played cards, shared recipes, belonged to church groups, played golf, and attended lectures and concerts. Often, their husbands attended events with them, but they sometimes just enjoyed the company of other women.

Now that their children were older, they had branched out to take advantage of learning about new things, and Eileen and three friends had taken a few classes that taught them how to draw and paint. One of her more successful attempts at painting their summer garden in oils now hung in their bedroom. *Not bad*, thought Eileen as she gazed at her colorful painting, but the next visit to the Art Institute of Chicago made her appreciate all the more the planning and execution it would have taken for these geniuses to produce these masterpieces.

Eileen had told Nora that on this trip she was especially struck by the huge painting of *The Crucifixion* by the Spanish painter Zurbarán in 1627. Eileen tried to separate any religious feeling it invoked in her and concentrated on what seemed to her an impossible task of keeping the large black background separate from the brown cross and then the incredible anatomical details of Christ's body while doing it all so well in oil paints. *Where was the light coming from? How did this man know how to measure things so well all those years ago? How long would it have taken to complete this masterpiece?* Eileen knew that she could never hope to achieve anything approaching this level of painting, but she determined to take more classes about how to paint in oils.

The Duffy children thought of their mother's friends more like fond aunts, and they were friends with their children. Unfortunately, one of the drawbacks of getting older was that two of the ladies were now widows, but "the gals," as Doctor Duffy called them, were always there for each other.

Nora also thought about her siblings and reflected that, while it was inevitable that in a group of ten people occasional arguments were to be expected, they usually got along well. When people asked her about her nine brothers and sisters, she told them that she was the eldest, and then there were two boys, three girls, two boys, and two more girls. Jim and Jack were just a year apart. Jim was a tech person while Jack was a stock trader. They were both engaged to gals that Nora already thought of as sisters, Trish and Sally. Mary Ann had married her childhood sweetheart somewhat early, but she was a brilliant mathematician and a high school teacher. She and Al already had a beautiful baby boy, and Nora wouldn't be surprised if they told them she was pregnant again. Maureen was going to be a nurse, and Siobhan was a musician and aspiring actress. Kevin and Brian were dedicated students as well as soccer and rugby players. The youngest members of the family were identical twin girls, Molly and Caitlan, and they had just finished their freshman year in their high schools.

Nora's plane touched down a little early about 3:00 p.m. at Chicago's O'Hare Airport. Jim and Trish and Jack and Sally were waiting for her in the baggage area, but the media had heard that Nora was coming home and were also waiting for pictures and answers to a few questions. Nora explained to the waiting reporters and television crews that she was on her way to the hospital to see how her friend Connie Carroll was doing after being shot.

This revelation was like throwing red meat to the media since they had still been trying to find out about the shooting but hadn't realized that the girl was Nora's good friend. They tried to press Nora for more information, but Jim had become quite an expert at defusing these situations, and they let Nora and the family leave after just snapping a few photos and the information that Nora and Connie Carroll had been next door neighbors since they were born.

Nora called her dad at Holy Savior Hospital to see how Connie was doing. He was cautiously optimistic about her chances for a full recovery and said the operation to remove the bullet had gone well. Nora said they would be coming to the hospital soon, but she was going to stop home first to freshen up.

The traffic on the expressways was busy today, but Jim managed to get Nora home in about an hour. Nora thanked her family for picking her up and said she would be ready to go to the hospital after she took a shower. Nora always found it thrilling to be back at their recently built home. Their dogs Satin and Clancy had been staying with Jesse, the housekeeper at the elder Duffy's home, but she would see them later.

She recalled that their architect, Mr. Jack Kamin, had asked them a number of questions about the kind of home they wanted him to design before he would even begin to think about sketching out a plan. How did they envision the appearance of the home, inside and out? What would make their usual routines easier? Who would be the frequent visitors they could expect? What features would they want to add to maximize the experience for the youngest and eldest members of their large family? Water features would look pretty and make attractive sounds, but they might not consider them safe around young children. The resulting home was a mix of traditional and contemporary features and had met all their expectations and then some.

Nora emerged from her shower and change of wardrobe, and they left right away. They arrived at Holy Savior, and Nora used her surgeon's pass to take the elevator up to Connie's room. Her dear friend was still sleepy after the anesthetic, but Nora talked to her mom and dad, who said that the doctors were hopeful that they were able to remove the bullet without doing any further damage to her spine. They thanked Nora for coming home early and said they knew that Connie was counting on seeing her.

While they waited to be able to talk to Connie, Nora went up to the cancer clinic to visit with her friends and say hello to her boss Dr. Carson Whiteside. This brilliant man had been waging war against children's cancers for twenty-nine years and had seen at least some progress in areas like leukemia. They were able to keep more children alive longer now, but despite money and time and effort, they appeared to be far from the goal of eliminating the ancient foe. Nora was amazed that this gaunt man with the sad brown eyes appeared to be eternally optimistic that we would someday be able to look back on cancer as we do now on polio. His outlook inspired his staff to keep going no matter how hopeless things seemed. Doctor Whiteside was happy to see Nora back where she belonged and said he would like to chat longer, but he was due at another finance meeting shortly. Finances seemed to be the driver of everything for hospitals these days, and he got very tired of trying to defend the need for all the equipment they needed to run the tests to keep his patients alive. Nora said she would like to set up an appointment with him tomorrow to see if there was anything she could do to help, and he was delighted. He asked her to see his secretary Maude and get that on his calendar.

Nora asked him how he was feeling, and he admitted to being very tired and having trouble sleeping. Nora didn't like the looks of the bags under his eyes and asked him if he'd had a checkup lately, but he protested that he did not have time. She thought she would work on him some more tomorrow to get this done. It would not do for the department to lose their valuable leader to illness or worse. Nora stopped to say hello to Maude, the secretary, and asked her to put her on the boss's calendar for tomorrow.

She also got updated on current kids' cancer cases and reviewed the notes for the brain surgery that she was to assist with tomorrow morning for an eight-year-old boy, Clete Clement. He had been diagnosed about two years ago and had not been having many symptoms, but in the last month, he appeared to have gone downhill and was now having trouble talking.

Nora went back to the ICU and was told that Connie had shown more signs of being awake. Her mother asked Nora to come and hold Connie's hand and tell her she was there. Nora and Connie had lived next door to each other as they were growing up, and their birthdays were just a month apart. They had done everything together as kids, and they were still like two peas in a pod. Connie was lying in an uncomfortable position since she couldn't lay on her back, but Nora asked Connie to tell her their secret password, and Connie immediately answered, "Jolly Ranchers." That was an excellent sign and gave Nora more encouragement about her dear friend's mental acuity. Nora told Connie that she would be around whenever she needed her, and then she made way for Connie's family to rejoice that she was conscious and talking.

After spending a little time with her parents, Nora and her siblings drove back to her house. She confirmed with Father Ahearn, Monsignor Callahan, and Matt Braxton and Laura Belsky that she was still on for having them over for dinner. She called the local diner Swanson's and ordered some of their excellent soup, entrées, and desserts, and then she took a brief nap.

Before her guests arrived, Nora called Tommy and they exchanged news about their plane trips and Connie's prognosis. Tom said he was staying at a trendy hotel in downtown Boston and was just about to go to dinner with his family, who were all so excited about his sister Maeve making her debut with the Boston Ballet tomorrow. They said goodbye with their usual line: "Life is just a bowl of cherries."

Nora's guests arrived for dinner and all went well, but she realized that jet lag was setting in. It had probably not been a wise decision to host a dinner when she had traveled from Ireland just this morning. The six-hour time difference meant that it would now be 4:00 a.m. in Sneem, so she had been up for about twenty-four hours. Her guests noticed that she could hardly keep her eyes open, so they left, and Nora dragged herself up the stairs to bed.

CHAPTER

17

Saturday, June 15
Chicago, Illinois; 8:00 a.m., CDT

Doctor Whiteside himself decided to operate on Clete Clement's brain that had been invaded by a tumor, and Nora was one of his assistants. Clete had started out having some of the classic signs of a brain tumor with headaches, nausea and vomiting, and sleepiness. Those symptoms could be signs of a number of other problems, but as time went on, he began to develop seizures and experienced vision problems, some hearing loss, and he was now searching for words as he tried to speak. More testing confirmed that the tumor was growing, and it was decided to operate immediately.

The long surgery itself seemed to be a success, and they now had to wait to see how Clete would be in the near future. Clete would be seeing a lot of doctors for the rest of his life, which they hoped had just been lengthened after their work.

Nora had a positive response to how she had performed during the surgery, and she felt that her training had prepared her well to interact with these children and their families. Seeing the nerve center of the human person's brain unearthed from its home inside Clete's skull was thrilling but sobering, and she prayed for this little person's future.

Clete was small for his eight years, and he looked very vulnerable under all the bandages. Nora assured the family that they could talk to him as soon as he came out of recovery, and they thought that Clete had done well during the surgery. The parents had undergone so much stress during the past year, and Nora asked God to give them some relief over the next months. Doctors know a lot about the brain now and which areas control the various actions of a person, but there is much more to learn. Even a nonmalignant brain tumor can be troublesome if it grows and presses on a sensitive area near the brain and can require surgery.

In the afternoon, Nora spent time with Connie Carroll and her family. She had been moved from ICU to a room, but the number of visitors was limited. Nora was encouraged that her dear friend's coloring had improved substantially, and Connie was able to talk to her in complete sentences. Nora had talked to the spine surgeon Dr. Stan Boyd, who said he thought Connie was making good progress. Tomorrow, the physical therapy department was going to get her up and walking with a walker, and then they would see what next steps they would recommend.

The hospital social worker asked if the family wanted her moved to a rehabilitation center for recovery, but the Carrolls said that they had plenty of family members who could care for Connie when it was time for her to come home. That wouldn't be soon enough for Connie.

Lieutenant Braxton had also called and said they had arrested some of the "usual suspects" that were involved with violent gang incidents in Chicago, but he was pretty sure that they had not yet found the guilty ones who had shot Connie.

Tommy had called an Uber that picked him up at O'Hare Airport and drove him home about 10:00 p.m. He and Nora visited for a while, but they were both so tired they gave each other a desultory kiss and just went to sleep.

Sunday, June 16

After a night of refreshing sleep, Nora and Tommy were thrilled to see each other and were back to their energetic selves. Today was Father's Day, and no one had made any definite plans, so they made some quick calls and the Duffy and Barry families agreed that it would be a great idea to meet downtown at Old Saint Patrick's Church for Mass.

Old St. Pat's was one of only a few buildings that had been spared by the 1871 Chicago Fire. Periodically it was rehabbed, and the last efforts had been beautifully done. They admired the Irish scrollwork on the walls, the gorgeous stained-glass windows, and the statues of many saints that lined the top of the interior.

They thought that Old St. Pat's choir was one of the best in the city, and the homilies given by the dedicated priests were always well done and effective. Old St. Pat's at one time was near to closing because it had so few regular parishioners, but an emphasis on serving young adults and then their young families had resulted in a vibrant community dedicated to the worship of God, excellence in education and music, and service to others. The Duffy and Barry families prayed for all the fathers in their families who had gone before them.

Tommy had called ahead and made reservations at Fado Irish Pub, and they descended on this attractive restaurant, whose furnishings had been imported from Irish pubs. Its interesting interior held an authentic curragh, a leather-bound boat that hung from ceiling hooks. The menu offerings mimicked what you might expect to see if you were in various Irish cities. A less well-known story was that the vintage building was occasionally haunted by several ghosts.

Nora and Tommy had some familiarity with ghosts since the mysterious events at Duffy Hall Castle in Sneem last year. They couldn't prove this, but they believed they had been helped by the efforts of Bridie the good ghost, the daughter of a long-dead previous owner of the castle, whose picture hung on Aunt Vinnie's wall. They believed that the ghost's whispered warnings and the clouds of honeysuckle perfume she emitted had been effective in saving them all. Nora never disparaged the mention of ghosts, although she certainly preferred Bridie's type of helping the living rather than the kind that scared them to death.

They enjoyed the delicious menu offerings and toasted the fathers in their midst. Gifts were given out to the dads, and many stories were exchanged. Their waitress Erin reminded Nora of Enda at the castle, and they enjoyed hearing the animated girl's southwest of Ireland brogue and tales of her hometown in Killorglin. Erin knew about Duffy Hall Castle and was thrilled to be meeting its owners. Everyone agreed that the day had been a perfect way to celebrate their fathers.

They started toward home after a few hours, but Nora's phone continued to ring, and she saw that Lt. Matt Braxton was calling her. Nora had a feeling that this was not going to be anything good since she thought that Matt and Laura were supposed to have gone to Milwaukee today to visit Laura's grandfather.

Matt usually spent a few minutes of chitchat when he called, but he got right to the point today. A beautiful and nude young woman's body had been found last night by two startled joggers at Maple Lake in the forest preserves. The woman had a drawing of two golden horseshoes with a red slash through it above her breasts. They had no clue as to who she was, and no one answering to her general description had been reported missing.

Nora had been enjoying her day so much, but she could hardly believe this horrible news. How could it be that this nightmare had followed her from Ireland to her own city thousands of miles away? She felt tears pricking at her eyes, and she sent mental condolences to this latest victim. She briefly buried her head in Tommy's shoulder but then asked Matt to elaborate on the details of this latest murder.

Matt asked Nora if she would be willing to come to the Cook County Morgue to see if she could identify the markings on the girl to see if they were similar to those found on the young women in Ireland. Nora said yes, but in her heart, she just wanted to go home and hide under the covers.

When they got to the old morgue building near Harrison and Western, Tommy held her up as Nora steeled herself to see this latest victim. These shabby buildings made an attempt to disguise their purpose, but there were too many comings and goings of ambulances dropping off their sad burdens.

The polite attendant at the desk took their information and said she would guide them to the appropriate place shortly. Nora wondered how difficult it would be to be a worker at this sad place. They saw a few other people in the waiting room who looked as

THE GOLDEN HORSESHOES MURDERS

traumatized as Nora felt, and she pitied them for the ordeal they were about to face.

They were called soon and ushered into a viewing room, where they were shown the body of the young woman. She was blond and thin and had the drawing of the golden horseshoes above her breasts, but Nora was glad to see that the drawing was misshapen and had been done by someone who did not know how to draw very well. Mercifully, there were no green shamrocks included, so this was surely a copycat killing by someone who had heard about the Irish murders but was not aware of the exact details. It would now be up to Matt and his CPD teammates to figure out who this poor woman was and who had killed her.

Laura had waited out in the car for them to view the young woman, and Nora and Tommy visited with her for a few minutes. Matt thanked them for their help, and then they headed back home.

In what was left of the afternoon, they both made attempts to just read and relax. Nora had never finished the charming story she'd started reading on the plane last year about the young couple who'd met on the beach on Cape Cod, and she pulled out the book and enjoyed the peace and the fun that seemed to inhabit its many pages. The dogs didn't get to enjoy having their masters to themselves very often, and Clancy sat next to Nora in her recliner while Satin jumped up on Tommy's lap as he worked on his computer.

Sometime near dinner, Nora's twin sisters appeared at their door and came running in to talk to them. They were both so energetic and were at the height of their good childhood times. Nora hoped that the memories of these days would keep them happy as they entered the more difficult teenage years.

Nora heard a text beep, and it was from Connie, saying that she thought she might get to come home on Wednesday. She hoped that Nora might be around that day to talk to her. Nora responded that she was so happy for her, and she would look forward to the visit. This was much more positive news than Nora thought they would be receiving, and she was so grateful.

Nora often thought how fortunate we are to live in the age of almost instant communication via our phones, and Connie's call illustrated that so well. She thought about the sadness of the families left behind in other countries whose children had emigrated to America. Letters would take weeks or months to arrive, and they sometimes never arrived at all. She silently thanked all the many inventors responsible for making our lives so much easier and happier today.

How many older movies were there where the people were in terrible danger, but if only they had had a cell phone, they might have been rescued. Of course, they would have to make sure they were close enough to a cell tower and that their phones were sufficiently charged, and Nora was hopeful that someday soon the communication companies would solve those problems too.

That night, they felt like they needed a good laugh, so they called up the recording of *Planes, Trains and Automobiles* on their television. It was obvious that the scenes had been staged to elicit the maximum humorous effects, but the interplay between John Candy, Steve Martin, and the other excellent character actors was hilarious. She reflected that it was such a loss to everyone that the talented John Candy had died at such an early age, but his legacy would be long-lasting.

The lighthearted laughter helped them to relax, and they fell asleep early feeling as though they could face the next day's challenges.

Monday, June 17

Nora drove her early teen twin sisters in the morning to their high schools for their summer drama programs and caught up on their news. She was always amazed at how they were "growing in beauty and grace." So far, she had not heard either of them talk about boys except as good buddies. They still looked so much alike, and it always took new people who met them a while before they could tell them apart. They were continuing with their Irish dancing, but now that they were in high school, there were only so many hours in a day for their homework and various other clubs and activities. They would soon be sophomores and felt quite grown up.

Nora recalled that when they first decided to go to different high schools, they were excited but also somewhat scared since they had always done everything together for the first thirteen years of their lives. They were pleased with their choices so far. Tomorrow, they would be participating in the summer science fair projects at both their schools.

Molly was thrilled to be playing her French horn as part of the orchestra at Mother McAuley and was also going to try out for a singing and dancing role when they put on their version of *The Music Man*. She was doing well with her other subjects too, but she was loving the drama and music classes more so far. McAuley was known for its many championship volleyball teams, but Molly was too short and thin to do that. She was enjoying being a part of the swim team and was scheduled for a competition the first week of school.

Caitlan thought that she wanted to go into the field of medical research, and she was enjoying her science and math classes at St. Ignatius. She too had discovered the allure of being part of a theatrical production and was hoping to get a singing and dancing part in their production of *Joseph and the Amazing Technicolor Dreamcoat*. She'd loved playing baseball ever since she was on a T-ball team as a little kid, and she'd now been chosen to be a shortstop for the St. Ignatius team.

Nora was the oldest of the Duffy siblings, and her young sisters thought of her almost like another mother. They thanked her for her advice and always listening to them when they needed help. Nora thought of these two dear sisters almost like her children, and she was sorry to see them growing up so fast.

After Nora dropped off Caity at St. Ignatius on Roosevelt Road, she continued driving downtown. She had been wanting to visit with one of her Irish dancing friends for a long time, and Kristin Harris was excited to be meeting Nora for brunch at the Drake Hotel. The restaurant's menu items were always a treat for the eyes as well as the taste buds.

Nora smiled when she saw her old friend with the laughing eyes. Kristin could be described now as tending to be chubby and was one of those women who seemed unable to lose weight no matter how

BABS L. MURPHY

hard she tried. She threw up her hands in resignation and said she surely would not be able to keep up now with the ceili dances they used to do. She had married Barry Harris and was so thrilled to show Nora pictures of their two adorable children, Rose and David. They caught up on each other's news and talked about the other members of their old team. Kristin said she had heard a little about the murdered girls in Ireland, and she hoped that Nora would stay safe and well. They parted from each other with a promise to keep in touch more often.

As Nora was leaving the beautiful old hotel, she caught sight out of the corner of her eye of a tall and strange-looking woman with long stringy black hair wearing a long black coat and a large pink pom-pom hat. The hat looked very warm, and it seemed strange she would be wearing it since it was a fairly warm day. The Drake often had guests from around the world, and she had not seen the woman's face. Perhaps she was from another country.

Nora forgot about the woman and tried to think about the conversation she had had earlier this morning with the man who wanted to sell her a new car. Little did he know what a timely call this was.

Nora had been contacted by John Keannealy from St. Mary's parish, who owned a Cadillac dealership. He told her that he had seen her driving around in her vintage (a kind adjective, Nora thought) Chevrolet and told her that he would give her an excellent deal on a new car, and he'd also donate a car to their pastor Father Ahearn if she bought a car from him. Nora had some time today, so she gave him a call to set up an appointment, and he asked her to come right over. On the way back from driving her sisters to school, Nora thought about one of her favorite idioms, "A stitch in time saves nine." Her old "red robin" had served her well, but by the time she got to Mr. Keannealy's, the tired old car was close to breathing its last.

As the history buff she was, Nora knew a lot about the founding of the Cadillac company in 1902. From the beginning, they had always been committed to excellence. Some people still used the expression "it's the Cadillac of whatever" when they wanted to point out that something was the best it could be. Nora admired Mr. Keannealy for saying that he would donate a car to Father Ahearn, who surely needed a new one since his car was frequently "in the shop."

The showroom for the Cadillac dealership was shiny and bright with many ceiling LED lights and was a perfect backdrop for eight beautiful cars or SUVs. She had often heard her grandparents say that they missed the huge old Caddies with the big tail fins, and Grandpa Burke still had a silver 1959 Eldorado Biarritz under several tarpaulins in his garage, which he was "saving for the grandchildren."

Mr. Keannealy was excited to have Nora at his establishment and showed her a few of the features in today's cars. He too remembered the big old Caddies and agreed with her grandparents but said we have to live in the present world, and the newer cars were a lot safer. He said if she did not see anything she liked here, she could special order any combination of exterior paint color and interior leather. She jokingly asked if he would like her eleven-year-old Chevrolet, her old "red robin." He said he would have one of his mechanics look at it, but it seemed as though it was no longer safe to drive.

After a few hours, Nora settled on a black CTX-V Cadillac with extra chrome trim with black and cream leather interior for Father Ahearn. She special ordered an Escalade ESV carmen-red exterior paint with white leather seats with red piping on the sides for herself. The main thing she was interested in was that the seats would raise to the right height to accommodate her short legs and foot reach. She thought she would get the bigger car for days when her large family might need a ride.

Mr. Keannealy suggested that she get the best antitheft devices and alarms, and she agreed. She told Mr. Keannealy that she wasn't sure about Tommy's preferences, so they would have to come back at another time so he could pick out a car for himself. The dealer told her that she probably would be able to get delivery of her SUV in about two weeks, so that should work out fine. Father Ahearn's SUV might be available in about a week. Mr. Keannealy strongly suggested that she accept his offer of a loaner car and leave the "red robin" with him to be sent to the junkyard. His mechanics told him its engine was about ready to fall apart, and the brakes were bad too.

Nora knew that he right, and she said a fond goodbye to the red car that had taken her to so many places over the last eleven years. She was thrilled to see the beautiful black Cadillac loaner car and made sure that the foot reach was properly adjusted for her. She thanked Mr. Keannealy profusely and then was on her way.

She still had a few hours before she needed to get home, so she called her grandparents in Long Beach, Indiana, and asked them if they had time for a visit. She told them about her temporary new car, and they said they would be delighted for her to try it out, and she should come and see them right away.

What a wonderful difference a new car makes, was her thought as she maneuvered her way onto I-94 and headed toward her Indiana destination not far from the Indiana Dunes. It made the drive so much more enjoyable when she did not have to worry about the brakes holding or the engine stopping.

She arrived soon at Grandpa John and Grandma Marie Burke's neat little home, and they were anxiously waiting for her at the front door. Grandma Marie had whipped up her favorite cream of chicken soup, and Grandpa John had gone to their local bakery and procured some of their crunchy olive bread.

Her grandparents told her about their latest news and said they were both feeling pretty good, and their friends who lived near them were about the same, except for one of Marie's best friends Sally Curran, who had just been diagnosed with stomach cancer. They then asked her to tell them what in the world was going on with people getting murdered near her castle in Ireland.

They talked for several hours, and then Nora said she should be getting home before rush hour on the expressway. Grandpa John admired her car and said he would be waiting to see the real thing as soon as she had delivery of it. They hugged one another for a long time, and then Nora bid them a fond farewell and started back to Chicago. Sometimes, this drive was agonizingly slow, but the traffic seemed to be flowing smoothly today.

CHAPTER

18

Monday, June 17
Chicago, Illinois; 4:00 p.m., CDT

Nora did not know if it was the traffic or the new car that made the difference, but she arrived back in Chicago quicker than she thought. She called her sister Mary Ann and asked if she had time for a visit. Her little guy Dylan was just about a year old now, and she was always anxious to show off his latest feats.

The two sisters embraced, and then Nora laughed at little Dylan as he ran up to her and hit his head into her leg. He had the family red hair, but it was straight, and he was not only walking but running. Like many of the family, he was going to be an early talker too, and he put up his arms to be picked up by "Bwitsy." Mary Ann's good friend Tracy was also there and she offered to stay outside with Dylan for a while so the two sisters could have a talk.

Mary Ann led her into her bright kitchen and served Nora some of her strawberry lemonade. They shared stories about their lives, and Mary Ann said she was due to start teaching again next month at Rivers High School, and Tracy was going to stay with Dylan during the day. They had a grand conversation for over an hour, and then Nora said she had to go since she wanted to get to the hospital to visit with Connie Carroll.

Connie appeared to be in good spirits and said that tomorrow physical therapy had plans to get her up and walking a few steps. If all went well, they had told her she might be able to go home on Wednesday. Her back was still sore, but she was so happy to hear that she would likely make a full recovery she was paying little attention to the pain.

When she arrived home, Tommy was thrilled to see the new car, and he said he too would like to pay Mr. Keannealy a visit to think about getting one for himself. He had not had a chance to talk to Nora about the visit to Boston, so he told her about the wonderful time he had visiting with his family.

They had all taken the hop-on, hop-off bus tour of Boston, and it was fascinating to see so many places they had always heard about in history books. They also visited with his cousin Christine, who was a sophomore at Harvard. She had taken them all for a tour of the famous university and the nearby buildings. She explained that Harvard University began life named after John Harvard from England, and it was a farm at the time. The first graduating class consisted of ten men who were trained to become ministers.

John Harvard would have been surprised today to know that the most recent Harvard graduates numbered almost seven thousand and included women. He would also be pleased to see that the divinity school was still turning out religious leaders and that Harvard has the largest endowment money of any university in the country, perhaps in the world.

Tommy's family had then attended Maeve's first dance recital with the Boston Ballet. She had told them not to be disappointed in the ballet since she wasn't going to be wearing a beautiful white outfit like she would if it were *Swan Lake*. This ballet was part of the modern suite, and she was going to be clad in a body leotard in a rather ugly shade of puce. She was just part of the corps de ballet for now, but she was hoping to make enough of an impression so the directors would give her more significant roles. The family was not too impressed by the ballet itself, but they could tell that Maeve was excellent in her small role. It was exciting to join the audience in a raucous round of applause. Maeve's brothers were tempted to give her Chicago-style whistles, but their mother urged them to resist.

They were also disappointed to hear that Maeve would not be going to the hotel with them for dinner since she was going to be accompanying the company to their own dinner. Earlier in the day,

Tommy had seen a beautiful restaurant they thought would be good for their celebration, and he had made reservations. They headed there and enjoyed the fresh east coast seafood immensely. They then went back to the hotel, continued the party, and finally turned in for a good night's sleep.

Nora said she was so glad that everything had turned out well for Maeve and Tommy's family. She updated him on Connie's progress, and he was so happy to hear it.

Nora had a call from Chief Brennan in Ireland, who said the garda was still in the process of interviewing anyone they thought might know more about the two murdered girls. They had heard a lot of theories and gossip, but he did not feel they were making any breakthroughs in finding the murderers.

Nora also had a call from Tim Taylor, the stable director on the Duffy Estate in Sneem. He wanted to let her know of several developments in the aftermath of his gambling problem. He had talked to Betsy and given her the full and frank details about his gambling addiction. Betsy loved Tim, but she was no fool either. She said she had no idea why in the world he thought she would want or need a new house and a large engagement ring, and she was horrified to hear of the trouble he was in. She said she would come with him to the Gamblers Anonymous meetings, and then she would give him her answer. If she saw that he was giving in to his addiction, she would have to turn him down, but Tim thought that he had been scared to death and would not be doing that again.

Tim gave her a report on the animals on the castle's estate and said that Jack Boyle's old collie was now staying with Betsy and seemed to be healing up nicely. All the other pets seemed fine, although the red deer seemed to have contracted some kind of skin allergy, which he was treating with a special diet and carbolic salve for those that were badly infected. Nora hoped that everything would be fine about the gambling since Tim was a marvelous veterinarian.

Sean Duffy called Nora to give her a report on the funeral for Jack Boyle that had been held yesterday. It had been so well attended that a number of people were not able to get into the church. Father Lanigan gave a memorable sermon and Sean had recorded it for

Nora. The luncheon at the Sneem Hotel was delicious, and all Jack's old buddies from the Two Squares Pub were there.

The fund to provide a memorial stone for Jack at the Coral Beach had swelled to the point where there would not only be an attractive memorial, but a scholarship in Jack's name would help children who wanted to attend St. Mary's School. Now, if only they could find out who had killed Jack, there could be some kind of closure there.

Nora sent a proposal to the committee, who was gathering donations for the memorial stone, asking if they would be interested in erecting a small lighthouse in Jack's memory. She proposed that the lighthouse could be painted in the tricolors of Ireland with alternating stripes of green, white, and orange with shamrock decorations. She suggested that an artist could paint a life-size picture of Jack with his dog Flossie near the bottom. The committee could decide what an accompanying plaque should say. She received a quick confirmation that Jack's friends thought it would be very fitting indeed for a building that could provide safety for the ships that passed the Coral Beach.

Nora immediately talked to Mr. McGovern about getting the lighthouse built soon, and she asked Enda's Bill Callahan to paint Jack's and Flossie's pictures. They thought the lighthouse could be constructed well before the start of winter.

Nora also talked to Duncan Lloyd about Duffy Medical affairs, and he told her that the board had voted to approve at least looking into reinstating the two officers they had fired last year, Ben Jordan and Fred Carroll. They felt they needed their expertise for several sensitive deals that were coming up, especially the proposal that Duffy Medical become publicly traded on the New York Stock Exchange, and they were hopeful that this would work out.

CHAPTER

19

Wednesday, June 19

B ridie, the former good ghost at Duffy Hall Castle, told Ralph and Hitch, the ghosts who were always getting into such messes, to keep an eye on Nora while she was at home in Chicago to make sure that she was protected. They had agreed, but in their usual fashion, things were not going well.

The ghosts kept flying into each other as they tried to figure out how to get from Sneem, Ireland, to Chicago in the US. This was a much longer trip than they had ever been on before, and they found it frightening to be flying over the large expanse of the Atlantic Ocean.

"Ralph, I'm getting awfully tired of flying," said Hitch. "Can't we take a rest somewhere?"

"Where would you suggest that could happen, my dear Hitch," answered Ralph. "There's nothing but water underneath us, but I understand once we get past the Atlantic, we just look for the big Lake Michigan that points like an arrow to Chicago. Then we find Nora and Tommy and just follow them wherever they go."

"You make it sound so easy," said Hitch. "I'm really getting thirsty, and I need a Guinness about now."

"Patience, please," said Ralph. "We made the turn for Lake Michigan some time ago, and I see Tommy's family's pub is coming right up. They ought to have plenty of Guinness there and Jameson too."

The two ghosts swooped down into the Barry's basement but realized soon enough that Mr. Barry's lids for their barrels of Guinness were even harder to open than Mr. Foote's were in Sneem. Hitch set-

121

tled for slurping up some of the excellent beer from the many glasses that had not been washed yet, but he was not happy. That was never a good sign since that usually meant he would be causing problems.

PJ Barry and his wife, Kathleen, Tommy's parents, were the owners of Barry's Pub on Irving Park Road. On Wednesday nights, they usually had a concert and ceili dance at the pub and featured many members of their families playing, singing, and dancing. They often featured guest musicians too, and tonight, they had imported several musicians from the Two Squares Pub in Sneem, Ireland. Maureen McDermott and Adam Tinsdale had danced with the *Riverdance* company, and a larger-than-usual crowd was looking forward to seeing them.

Nora talked to Maureen and Adam about their *Riverdance* participation and told them that the founder of *Riverdance* and so many other extravaganzas, Michael Flatley, grew up in Chicago just a few miles from her home in Beverly. The two young dancers said they had enjoyed their days with the company very much, but they had decided they could no longer keep up with the pace required needed to do this demanding dancing, as well as the traveling. Now, they enjoyed going to places like Barry's Pub, where the audience thought they were marvelous, but they were no longer subject to the scrutiny of demanding music directors.

The musicians began to play, and the colors of the US and Ireland were hoisted up by the youngest members of the Barry family. Neil Barry played his bagpipes accompanied on the drums by his siblings. The US flag was placed in its holder on the stage, followed by the tricolor green, white, and orange of Ireland. The crowd lustily sang the "Star-Spangled Banner" and then "A Nation Once Again" for Ireland.

The musicians began to play the background music for the young *Riverdance* stars to begin their dancing, and they were partnered by a group of younger dancers, as well as four adorable five-year-olds. The dancers were as good as the crowd expected and were awarded by joyous applause. Then the musicians began to play the crowd's favorites, and everyone resumed eating and drinking.

Soon, couples began to take to the dance floor for a ceili dance, and the clapping and dancing by hundreds of feet made a happy sound. Nora fiddled her way through the evening, and Tommy's baritone voice joined the others in a variety of tunes. The stars from Ireland complimented everyone on their skills.

About 10:00 p.m., PJ Barry announced that it would be time for last call in half an hour, so the guests should get their final orders in now. Many people told the Barry's that this was one of the best gatherings they had had in a long time, and they promised to be back.

Just about then, Ralph and Hitch, the hapless ghosts, swooped up to the ceiling of Barry's Pub and tapped their toes to the ceili dances. Ralph wished that his old sweetheart Rita was here now, and Hitch felt himself getting very sad indeed. He couldn't help himself. The lights in the ceiling were too bright, so he broke many of them with a satisfying sound of glass breaking. The patrons were shrieking in surprise and fear, and that sound always energized Hitch to try for more. He opened the taps behind the bar, and a river of beer was soon flooding the dance floor. Ralph could only imagine what Angel Christopher would have to say about all this!

PJ and Kathleen couldn't imagine what had caused these sudden accidents, and they apologized to their guests and began the long process of cleaning up the mess. No one had been hurt, but it was still very disturbing. Nora and Tommy helped to tidy everything up and briefly visited with his parents and the rest of the family, and then they packed up and headed back south to their home.

When they called Tommy's parents in the morning to see how they were after the events of last night, PJ and Kathleen told them they were fine, except that they had woken up this morning to the terrible smell of sewer gas coming from their basement. They had never had problems like this before, and they wondered what might have caused them.

Oh no, Nora thought. This sounded too much like the shenanigans that had been happening in Sneem, and she hoped that bad luck hadn't followed them back to Chicago.

CHAPTER

20

Sunday, June 30
Chicago, Illinois; 10:00 a.m., CDT

Eileen Duffy made it a practice to get out to the family cemeteries at least twice a year, and she had selected the last Sunday in June for that. It was a good day for the visits since there was no rain, and the sunshine was expected to last all day. The Duffy children knew that any of them who didn't have to be at work or at a school function were expected to be there. After Mass and a quick breakfast, they all piled into various cars for the trips to Holy Sepulchre and St. Mary's. Doctor Duffy had two of the boys help him retrieve the artificial flowers from the garage and put them in the trunk. They also brought along diggers in case the grass needed trimming around the gravestones.

They first drove out west to Holy Sepulchre and the Duffy graves for his grandparents, some aunts and uncles, and one of Doctor Duffy's brothers Robert, who died when he was only four years old when he was hit by a car. During the drive, a few of the children asked questions about the history of the family, and Doctor Duffy, who was an excellent raconteur, obliged with what he knew about the family tree.

They found the gravestones that were not far from the St. Patrick's shrine, and the diggers were needed for the grass that grew so quickly at this time of year. The cemetery kept the grass trimmed pretty well, but green shoots were visible all around the base of the Celtic cross. They then found the grave markers in the military section for Papa Pete Duffy, Grandpa Conor's father, and a cousin Leonard Brown, who had been killed in World War II. They put the artificial flowers in place, said some prayers, and then moved on to the next stop, which the children knew was difficult for their parents.

The twins Molly and Caitlan were the youngest children at fourteen, but two years after they were born, Mrs. Duffy had had a miscarriage of a baby boy. They had named him Conor Daniel, after Doctor Duffy's father and his best childhood friend, and they had purchased graves for all of the family at that time. They headed over to that section and found the statue of the Holy Family with the Duffy name on it. Mrs. Duffy placed a rose on the place that marked her youngest child's resting place, and all of them murmured the prayer she loved the best. They knew that she was thinking what Conor would look like and what he would be doing were he alive. They said a prayer for everyone in the cemetery and then headed over to St. Mary's.

The Burke family graves were a combination of a gray marble monument and flat grave markers. By now, the children knew how to find the graves: look for the grotto with the candles and then follow the first road to the left, then look for the tall gray Ashford tombstone. Doctor Duffy held Mrs. Duffy's hand as the children dug away the grass shoots and then placed the colorful artificial flowers on the graves and concluded with a prayer.

The entire trip had only taken about two hours, but the Duffy's thought it important that all the children should remember their relatives, who not so long ago were just as alive as they were and shared their DNA. They hoped that instilling this habit in the children early would result in them remembering to keep up the practice after they were gone. Mrs. Duffy had two cousins who were buried with their husbands at St. Joseph's cemetery on the north side, but that was a long trip for another day.

Part of the allure that kept the children interested in the trips to the cemeteries was that they then got to stop for lunch at one of their favorite places, the Old Farmstead. Not only did the restaurant have delicious food, but they could visit various farm animals afterward and then have a ride on some of their amusement park attractions.

Everyone agreed on the way home that the first part of their family togetherness week had gone well. Kevin and Brian, with their usual boisterousness, had behaved themselves pretty well, except for accidentally spilling a Coke on Siobhan's new blouse, which resulted in a lot of yelling.

Tomorrow, the family was scheduled to head to the big vacation house that Nora had purchased for all of them last Christmas. Tommy and two of his brothers were heading out to the house in New Buffalo, Michigan, this afternoon to make sure that everything was ready for the onslaught of his and Nora's big families. Nora had prepared a list for him of groceries and cleaning supplies to buy, and a vacation-like atmosphere surrounded all of them. Nora, unfortunately, had to be on duty at the hospital tonight, but she hoped to leave early the next morning to join them.

It was nice that they had enjoyed Sunday so much because rain and a creeping crabbiness invaded the family overnight.

CHAPTER

21

Monday, July 1
Chicago, Illinois; 8:00 a.m., CDT

D octor Duffy started off the day by saying that his lower back
tooth, which he thought had been taken care of a few weeks ago,
had suddenly flared up like a volcano. He certainly could not be gone
for several days with this pain. Then he realized that his favorite bathing trunks were missing from his dresser. Eileen heard him yelling
from the bedroom and came to see what was going on.

"Ei-leen," he bellowed, "where are my trusty old blue trunks? I
can't find them anywhere."

She knew when he said her name with the emphasis on the first
syllable that something was really bothering him. "Michael, those
poor old trunks are at least ten years old, and they have a bleach stain
on them. When I was preparing for this trip, I put them in the rag
bag, and I bought you an attractive pair that should fit you better.
They're already in your suitcase."

"I don't want new ones," her usual even-tempered husband
hotly retorted. "I want the ones that I know are comfortable. And are
you saying that my waistline would no longer fit into the old trunks?
They can't be ten years old. They have years of wear left in them."

"At least try on the new ones. If you don't like them, I haven't
yet given the old ones away, and I can always retrieve them from the
rag bag. I've already called Doctor Annette about your tooth, and she
can see you this afternoon at 1:00 p.m." Eileen resisted the impulse

to tell him that she had warned him not to eat peanut brittle, but she didn't want to exacerbate his bad mood.

Tommy called Nora and said that he had just discovered that his sister Bunny said there was no way that her allergies could stand to have four big old dogs around for days at a time.

"Oh great," Nora replied. "Just now you're telling me this? What are we supposed to do with the dogs at the last minute? This was supposed to be their vacation too. Maybe it's Bunny who should stay home."

Nora could hear Tommy bristling on the phone, and she said she'd see what she could do, but this was certainly a fly in the ointment. She could ask Jesse to stay home with the dogs, but this was her vacation as well.

Jim and Jack also called and said their girlfriends, Trish and Sally, both found out they had to work later in the week so they could come today and tomorrow, but then they'd have to leave. Maureen kept up the bad news by telling them that she too had to work at the hospital tomorrow. And the twins Molly and Caitlan, who were usually so in sync, picked today to have a fight over who was going to get the new pink suitcase, and who would have to use the old black one with the crack.

Of course, they next heard from Mary Ann that toddler Dylan had fallen down a few steps and was bleeding on both knees. Eileen could hear his pitiful cries over the phone. Mary Ann wasn't sure what time they'd be able to get out to the cottage until they knew how he was going to be.

The rain didn't show any signs of stopping either, and worst of all, Nora realized that the new elevator she'd paid to have installed at the vacation house wasn't working. She didn't want the grandparents and Monsignor Callahan to have to try to struggle up the steps. Nora was thinking that the best solution about the dogs would be for her to stay home with them, but then her mother, as usual, came to everyone's rescue.

"The rain will do what it's going to do, but we can come up with some solutions here," said Eileen. "Aunt Honey and Uncle Joe are scheduled to come up later today with Beth and Maeve for a few days. Aunt Ellen and Uncle Bill can stay with the dogs for now and then switch with Honey and Joe for the rest of the week. I think that will all work out.

"I'm hoping that Dad will feel good enough to drive up later tonight, but he can always come tomorrow." Eileen found creative solutions for the rest of the family's concerns, and the rain had suddenly slowed down too.

I don't know how she does it, mused Nora. *I can only hope that I'll be half as good at being a wife and mother as she is.*

Nora had asked Eileen once if she didn't feel like complaining about things herself. Eileen had responded that early on, she realized she had to make a choice as to what was most important to her.

"I feel better when my family is safe, healthy, and in harmony, at least as much as there can be with so many different personalities involved. Complaining never gets me anywhere anyway, so I developed a knack for figuring out how to keep everyone relatively happy. I don't know if you realize it or not, but in the process, I've found ways to get all you people to come around to what I wanted to do in the first place."

Once again, Nora realized how fortunate she was to be a member of this creative family. She wondered if her father realized that sometimes Eileen was manipulating him to do what she wanted, and she decided that he was aware of it and felt grateful that his wife was smart enough to keep them all on the right path. Nora wasn't so sure that Tommy would be as pliable as her dad, but she kept this tip in mind.

Doctor Annette was able to finish off the root canal she had started on Doctor Duffy's tooth last week, and it felt considerably better when she was finished. She suggested a good pain medication in case he needed it, and he felt as though he would be able to get through the week. Chances were that he would not be able to get through a whole week anyway without being called back to the hospital, but his mood had improved considerably by the time he got home. He called Eileen and said that he had tried on the new bathing trunks, and he had to admit that they felt fine, and the old ones did look pretty battered. He said he would drive up in a few hours, and prospects for a good week seemed much brighter.

Tommy called Nora again and said that his sister Bunny had received a prescription allergy medicine from her doctor, and she was now confident that they could bring the dogs along, so crisis averted there. His parents, PJ and Kathleen, would be unable to come since this week was one of their busiest at Barry's Pub, but his brothers Paul, Neil, and Pete would be there, as well as his other sisters Lucy, Kat, and Maeve.

Eileen decided that they would bring their cat Cheshire with them, and Nora would drive out with the dogs. Traffic on the expressway was running surprisingly smoothly once they started driving north, and they made it to the cottage in just a little over an hour. Nora found it humorous that a house with four bedrooms on the first floor, six on the second, and room for about twenty more in the basement should be designated as a "cottage," but that's what everyone had been calling it.

The passengers removed all the suitcases, boxes, and bags from the SUVs, and there they were at their home away from home that faced beautiful Lake Michigan. They started toward the house, and Eileen helped Jesse carry in her suitcases, and they looked forward to happy days.

Nora drove her new Cadillac with Kevin and Brian, and they put all four dogs in the back seats—Reilly, the wolfhound; Billy, the toto mix; Satin, the cocker spaniel; and Clancy, the Irish setter. Mr. Keannealy had given Nora protective rubber mats that fit the seats perfectly so that the dogs' nails wouldn't mark them up. Fortunately, the dogs were together frequently so were good friends. The canine buddies didn't know what was happening, but it must be something different and exciting, and they were "good as gold" on the trip, as Jesse would say.

Eileen and Jesse prepared lunch with the food they had brought along, and everyone took their salads and sandwiches out to the back deck and enjoyed the view of both the lake that was almost like an ocean and the attractive town. Afterward, they spread out to do what they preferred.

When Doctor Duffy arrived, he had had a stressful week at the hospital, and it took him little time before he was snoozing on the hammock. Eileen joined him on the deck and was happy to have some free time to read more of her book club's latest selection *The Gentleman in Moscow*.

Jesse was happy to see that the yard was surrounded by a high fence, and she took the dogs out there so they could run around while she opened her Kindle and read more of her recent books. The family would be surprised to know that she enjoyed reading books by authors like Stephen King, and she was about halfway through *Pet Sematary*. When she tired of that, she took up her knitting and tried to finish the large blanket she had been working on for Dylan.

Most of the younger people got into their bathing suits and either went to the pool or to the beach. Nora had hired a lifeguard for the pool so none of them would have to worry about water safety. When the children were younger, they used to bring along a variety of inflatables, but they now settled for just a few. The girls would not be spending too much time in the pool anyway but would try to get tanned as they lay on the pool chairs.

Later, they would enjoy walking through the town and stopping at Oink's for ice cream. The twins' favorite flavor was bubblegum, a thought that Doctor Duffy found most unappealing. He looked forward to a mix of butter pecan and chocolate. Kevin and Brian said they were holding out for the four-scoop banana split. Most of the girls settled for some flavor of sherbet.

Nora had hired a professional cook for the week so that none of them would have to be stuck in the kitchen. Gina's menu for tonight included steak and lobster for whoever wanted it and chicken shish kabobs for those who preferred something less filling.

Father Ahearn and Monsignor Callahan were expected shortly before dinner, and Jim's friend Moose Darcy, a Chicago fireman and paramedic, said they should have no worries about the elevator since he would just lift the monsignor out of his wheelchair and carry him up the steps.

Screams of laughter were heard from the pool area, and Nora was happy that her gift to the family seemed to be working out great, so far. It seemed like a place that would bring them much happiness for many years to come. The town of New Buffalo went all out during the week with plans for water sports, parades, and fireworks, and everyone looked forward to participating in some way.

The dinner prepared by Gina and her staff was a huge success, and that was followed once it got dark by the telling of ghost stories and toasting marshmallows on a bonfire. Plenty of fresh air and good food led to a general air of sleepiness, and most of the family had dozed off by 11:00 p.m.

Tuesday, July 2

Father Ahearn and Monsignor Callahan began the day by celebrating Mass for them on the deck. Eileen had told a few neighbors that their priest friends would be doing this, and the crowd swelled exponentially. Gina and her crew had planned for this and soon everyone was enjoying breakfast sandwiches and hotcakes.

Most of the men accompanied Doctor Duffy to the local golf course while Eileen and Nora stayed with the younger folks as they attended a parade downtown. They then went to the farmers' market, where they picked up delicious-looking fruits and vegetables for the rest of the week. Later in the afternoon, some of the family drove to the nearby town of St. Joe's and enjoyed their huge beach and shopping opportunities. They really didn't need new T-shirts, but it was always fun to refurbish their wardrobes.

The four dogs got to run in the waves at the beach behind the house and were delighted with the wind and the waves. The cat Cheshire wanted nothing to do with these plebeian activities and enjoyed sunning herself on the back deck while waiting for Jesse to bring her special dinner treats. Most of the humans were ignoring her today, but the little boy liked to pet her, and she waited for him to return.

Later that afternoon, it rained enough so that it was uncomfortable to be outside, and many of the adults went to the Four Winds Casino. Jesse's sister Margaret arrived at the cottage, and the two older women thoroughly enjoyed themselves as they attempted to win a fortune but gradually lost their limit of fifty dollars. Nora found the whole atmosphere rather depressing as she saw so many people shoveling money into the various shiny machines, but it must satisfy some human need to try to beat a challenge since it was immensely popular.

Tonight, they had made reservations at the Copper Rock Restaurant for dinner, so Gina and her crew had the evening off. Salads were a specialty of the house, and Nora looked forward to this meal all year. Everyone ordered their favorite meals, and the manager gave them free desserts since the teenage boys had managed to each eat a huge steak.

Father Ahearn thanked the Duffy's for their hospitality but said that he had to get Monsignor Callahan back to the rectory for his medicine. Nora knew the story that had caused Monsignor John's disability when he saved a young boy from a house fire but had been blown down a flight of stairs, which had permanently damaged his spinal cord. She admired him so much since he seemed to have a huge smile on his face most of the time. He said he had a wonderful time, and if God saw fit to spare him until next year, he would love to come back again. Moose carried the monsignor to his car, and they all said goodbye to the two priests and thanked them for all they did.

They went back to the house and made wishes on the huge moon that appeared to be right over their house. The teenagers made sure they had the right outfits ready to wear tomorrow to the fireworks while the adults checked their phones and laptops for messages and sent responses.

The musicians in the family went out on the deck and began to play their various instruments, and all the girls who were not playing an instrument put on their hard shoes and danced to the music they would be using for their fall Irish dancing competition. Soon the music and the dancing attracted a huge crowd of people that had been at the beach. Molly and Caitlan spotted their friends Kate and Annie, and they asked them to get their shoes and join them. Siobhan and her boyfriend Mick sang a haunting melody while Nora accompanied them on her violin, and then all the other instruments joined in. Jesse and Eileen brought out refreshments for the crowd, and the merriment went on for many hours.

A bonfire was lit on the beach, and everyone joined in toasting marshmallows and s'mores. That was fun until one of the neighbors burned his fingers on the fire, and Eileen had to tend to him with her first aid kit. Finally, Doctor Duffy told the family it was time to return to the house so they could prepare for tomorrow's main event, the fireworks.

Wednesday July 3

Nora and Tommy awoke early and went for a run and were joined by Kevin and Brian, who were supposed to be in training for their track teams. They didn't see too many people yet, but they knew that in several hours the town would be a beehive of activity as it prepared for its annual fireworks display. Today, Gina put out a smorgasbord of breakfast foods and juices that looked delicious.

They always saw other families they knew at New Buffalo, and Kevin and Brian told Eileen that they would like to go to the movies with their friends the McMillans. The twin girls wanted to go with Aunt Honey to spend time with their young cousins. Eileen reminded everyone to be back in time for the fireworks tonight.

Michael and Eileen went down to the beach, and Doctor Duffy got to use his new bathing trunks as he swam laps in Lake Michigan, which today was close to seventy degrees. They were joined by her sister Ellen and her husband, Bill, and Michael's sister Honey and her husband, Joe. They could see some of their children far down the beach, who were pretending they were all alone. Eileen was not a fan of beach sand and was doing her best to remain away from it in her beach chair with the attached umbrella. It was a relief to see blue skies, which augured well for tonight's festivities.

The children had been told to come back to the house early for dinner since they remembered the Fighting 38 on holidays like this. Papa Pete, as Grandpa Conor's father had been known, was a marine in World War II. He fought in many European battles, and he led his thirty-seven comrades in their landing craft to Omaha Beach on D-Day, June 6, 1944. Many of them were mowed down by German fire before they ever got to the beach, and more were killed once they set foot on land. Only eight of them survived the war to come home.

Papa Pete kept the pictures of those friends in a shrine at his home, and Grandma Viv washed and polished those pictures every week. Pete saluted those men every day for the rest of his life until he died at ninety-two. Grandma Viv kept the pictures shiny until she also died just a few years ago.

On days like this, the youngest grandchildren, Molly and Caitlan, took turns reading their names: Peter Duffy, Jocko McMahon, Sandy Gibbons, Bruno Marshall, Frank Pinelli, and on and on until all thirty-eight names had been read. The family then toasted their memories and promised that they would never forget them. Those pictures of the Fighting 38 now hung in the hallway of the Duffy's home, and Grandpa Conor saluted them every night after dinner.

Just as they were going to sit down to Gina's fabulous holiday treats, Doctor Duffy received a call from Holy Savior, asking him to get back to the hospital urgently for one of his longtime patients Ed Sloan.

"We could handle him, Michael," said his partner Doctor Patma Patel, "but Ed has had a major heart attack, and he's asking for you."

Doctor Duffy assured Patma that he would be there as soon as he could. He told Eileen about it and asked her to come with him. "I've been worried about Ed for some time now, and he's almost surely going to need surgery."

Eileen agreed and asked Nora to handle things at the cottage. Everyone gave their parents a hug and wished them good luck. In a family of doctors, everyone knew that revelry is only temporary while the business of life and death goes on as usual.

As it neared 9:15 p.m., the family could see the first tentative lights from the fireworks begin, and then the night sky was aglow with lights of every color and the noises from many explosions. They enjoyed it all, but their thoughts turned to their parents as they battled once again the ills that could invade the human body. Nora silently sent them her love and prayed that Mr. Sloan would be able to survive. His daughter Melanie was about her age, and she knew that she was devoted to her dad.

After they got everyone back to the house and settled, Nora sent a text to her mother and asked how things were going. She also sent one to Therese Cummings at the Children's Cancer Clinic at Holy Savior Hospital. It would be dawn in Ireland, and she sent a text to Sean Duffy at the castle and to Chief Brennan to see if he had any news about the murders. Nora slept fitfully as she waited to see if she would receive any responses.

The family decided that they would close up the house on Thursday and head home to see how their parents were doing. They had had a great time for a few days, but it was now time to get back to real life. The girls were anxious to go shopping for their trip to California next week and for school clothes. Life is a series of next steps, and they were beckoning to them now.

CHAPTER

22

Friday, July 5
Chicago, Illinois; 8:00 a.m., CDT

The women in the Duffy family got up early on Friday and went to their favorite breakfast place Beverly Bakery for omelets and scones. They were anxious to get to the stores to see if they could find summer clothes bargains and fall school clothes and supplies.

Doctor Duffy and Eileen were at the hospital caring for Ed Sloan, who had survived the initial operation but had a long way to go. Nora had to go in for a shift at the cancer clinic.

Mary Ann said she would drive her sisters to the stores, but they had a difference of opinion as to where they should go. The older girls wanted to go out to Oak Brook, but the younger ones wanted to stay closer to home since their friends had called and said they might be able to get tickets for a concert tonight at the amphitheatre in Tinley Park.

The older girls remembered what it was like to be looking forward to a rock concert, so they deferred to the younger ones and settled for Orland Park shopping mall. They were able to pick up a number of bargains at Macy's, and in the process, the twins spotted dresses they thought they might like to wear for the upcoming high school dances. Molly and Caitlan looked for school shoes, but they did not see anything that appealed to them yet. They were going to have to make a decision soon since school would be starting in less than a month.

They decided to have lunch at The Cheesecake Factory, and each girl looked forward to their favorites. Maureen and Siobhan were old enough now to worry about putting on a few pounds, but the others said they would give them a bite of theirs. Molly's favorite was the white raspberry chocolate, and Caity preferred the carrot cake. Each piece was too big to eat at one sitting, so they boxed up the remains to bring home. The entrees had been good, but the desserts were the stars of the show.

Mary Ann paid the bill, and they were about ready to leave when they noticed a strange-looking woman wearing a black raincoat with black stringy hair and a pink pom-pom hat. She seemed to be waiting for someone and was just sitting on one of the front benches, but Mary Ann thought she remembered Nora saying that she had seen a similar person. Mary Ann was responsible for her younger sisters' safety, so she called Nora and asked her how concerned she should be about the woman. Nora told her she had no idea who the woman was, and so far, she had done nothing threatening, but she thought they should get out of there as fast as possible. Mary Ann gathered everyone together and shepherded them to the entrance, but by the time she turned around, the woman in the pink hat was gone.

The males in the family had gone to Ridge Country Club and played a round of golf, but the younger guys' friends also called, and said they were able to secure tickets for the concert at the Tinley Park Amphitheater. It was going to be a fun Friday night, especially since they could meet up with the girls.

Tommy and Nora had plans to meet their friends Alan Pepper and his wife, Pam, for the Grant Park Friday night concert. The Chicago Symphony was playing a repeat of the third of July concert, which was always spectacular. Nora wondered how many people in the audience realized that the magnificent *1812 Overture*—climaxed by cannon fire, ringing chimes, and brass fanfare—had been written by a Russian, Pyotr Ilyich Tchaikovsky, to celebrate the Russian victory over Napoleon and had nothing to do with the US, except that Tchaikovsky had conducted the concert himself at the dedication of Carnegie Hall in New York City on May 5, 1891.

Alan Pepper was a colleague of Tommy's at his law firm, and he and Pam were professional musicians, so they knew a lot about music and were enlightening without being pretentious. Neither of them seemed to care a whit about Nora's money, probably because both of them came from old money families. Alan had grown up in New York City and had met Pam at the University of Chicago. After they got married, they decided to settle down in Chicago and they had a spacious apartment on Lake Shore Drive across from the Drake Hotel.

The two couples then headed to the Signature Room at the 95th restaurant for a holiday-themed dinner. Their friends took the occasion to tell them how excited they were to find out that Pam was expecting their first child early next year. They had been married for five years now and were just about at the stage where they thought Pam couldn't get pregnant, so they were thrilled. Pam said the only drawback was that she could see the 95th's excellent wines in front of her, but she would not be able to sample them since she was pregnant.

Nora reminded them that she and family were going to be traveling out to Sonoma next week for the wedding of her cousin, and Alan asked her if she could find some Ramazzotti wine for them since it was their favorite. She said she would find it for them, as well as wine from her aunt and uncle's La Bella Maria vineyard. Pam could save the wine to toast the new baby when it arrived.

They were all starting to get sleepy about 11:00 p.m., so they said goodnight and agreed that it had been a magical evening for all of them. Nora had already thought about when she might host a baby shower for Pam.

Saturday, July 6

In the morning after Mass and visiting with friends, Nora went home while Tommy drove out to his parents' pub to help them paint their living room. Nora took a look at the room that they had designated as a file room for both of them at their new home. They had started off right by having Mr. Kamin procure a row of pink file cabinets for Nora, blue ones for Tommy, and tan cabinets for the house files. A row of bookshelves stood all across the back wall that were designed to hold photo albums, trophies, and awards. Unfortunately, their original good intentions had not yet panned out, and most of the paperwork sat on tables and even on the floor, and nephew Dylan's baby paraphernalia filled up all the corners.

Nora decided that this was the day she was going to whip this room into shape. The trouble with good intentions like that is she had to read much of the paperwork to decide where it should go. By 2:00 p.m., she had made considerable progress in filing things that needed to be done, bills, receipts, and school and work documents. She turned on the overhead lights, went to the kitchen for a sandwich, and kept going for another hour. The room looked much better now, and one happy result was that she found a wedding card from one of their friends that she had not seen before. She also realized that she had not yet renewed their subscriptions to the Chicago Symphony and Lyric Opera seasons.

She came across pictures of her old Irish dancing team and decided that she should arrange for a reunion for them. Their sweet faces smiled back at her in the large photo, and she recalled the exhilarating feeling they had all experienced when they had come in First Place at the World's Championships. Nora vowed to file things away as soon as she received them in the future. If there was a patron saint for filing, she asked for his or her help.

Nora had heard her phone ring a few times while she was busy but decided not to answer it. When she looked at her phone, she realized one of the calls was from Chief Brennan. She called him back, but he was also not reachable at the moment.

She also had a call from Mr. Kornan's secretary Norma, telling her that that Mr. Kornan wanted it to be a surprise, but Tommy was going to be made a partner at the law firm, so they wanted to be sure that they saved the date of two weeks from next Saturday for the celebration. Nora was thrilled to hear about this, but there were so many other things coming up in their schedules too. She immediately wondered what kind of gift she could get for Tommy for this important milestone. She thought she would like to get him a painting for his new office, but she had no definite ideas as to what that would be. Perhaps she would find something in California.

Nora kept an eye on the clock since she and Tommy were taking their parents, grandparents, and Sister Mary Cecilia and her friend Sister Mary Lydia from Holy Savior out to Ravinia, the oldest outdoor music festival in the US tonight. Everyone was supposed to gather at their house, and the limousines were due there by 4:00 p.m. Nora was excited because they were going to see Ringo Starr from the Beatles and the Beach Boys. She knew that both groups were excellent musicians as well as being so popular.

When she and Tommy went to Ravinia by themselves, they preferred to take the two trains, the Rock Island and then the Northwestern, which let them off right outside the park. That required quite a bit of walking, so they had ordered the limos to make it more comfortable for their older guests.

Nora rather envied the many people they saw who were going to have lawn seats, bringing along beach chairs and picnic lunches. Some of them brought along lamps and ribbons and bows and their displays were lovely.

Tonight, Nora and Tommy and their guests would have dinner at the Ravinia Restaurant on the grounds, and then they would sit under the covered pavilion.

Nora quickly took a shower and dressed in her '60s flowered dress and sandals. Tommy arrived with his parents and grandparents, and Doctor Duffy came in with the two nuns from the hospital. The Burke and the Duffy grandparents arrived, and everyone greeted each other and said they had been practicing their singing for tonight's entertainment. Jesse had prepared hors d'oeuvres and drinks for them, and "Good Vibrations" was playing in the background.

The limos arrived on time, and everyone entered their waiting chariots and prepared for their fun evening. Nora was happy to be heading to one of her favorite destinations. Last year had been so busy that they had been unable to attend any of Ravinia's appealing offerings. The limos made it to the entrance to the parking lot, dropped them off, and gave Tommy directions for how to find them afterward. It was exciting to see the crowd of music lovers dressed in their summer finery.

The dinner was delicious, as usual, and then the group headed over to the pavilion to be seated. Nora noticed that Sister Mary Lydia was limping, and she told her that she had injured her foot when she was playing touch football with her nephews. She was so happy to be here tonight since she was a big fan of both music groups.

When the music started, Ringo and his large band and the Beach Boys were greeted with deafening applause. The concert was just as entertaining as they hoped, and most of the audience hummed or sang along with their famous music.

Tommy noticed that the grandparents were starting to wilt a bit after 10:00 p.m., so they left promptly at the concert's end. Everyone agreed that it had been a marvelous evening, but the traffic leaving the park was heavy, and they didn't make it back home until after midnight. The Burkes were staying at the elder Duffy's home overnight.

Nora and Tommy were still in the thrall of the music they had just heard. They had bought a tape of the concert before they left the park, and they danced around their living room to "Yellow Submarine" and "California Girls" and felt as though they could have danced all night.

When they finally settled down for the night, Nora began to think about their trip to California on Wednesday for her cousin Sheila's wedding. She had a lot of clothes already, but she could use a new dress for the rehearsal dinner, which she was sure would be very glitzy. Visions of ball gowns flitted through her head, and she gradually fell asleep humming some of the music she had heard earlier tonight.

The next day, Eileen Duffy and all of her daughters, plus the brothers' girlfriends, Trish and Sally, traveled to their favorite boutique Monique's and looked for dresses. Nora usually had trouble finding something with her small size, but Monique helped her to find a pink and white "goddess" design that fit her small frame well. The helpful store owner said she would hem it up by Monday so the length would be better for her. The rest of the ladies in their party found dresses they loved, so it had been a successful trip.

Nora wondered what new adventures they would encounter during their trip to California and hoped for good weather and happy days. Tomorrow was their block party, their first in their new house, and she mentally reviewed the plans for that fun day.

Sunday, July 7

Nora had been so busy recently, she had not been able to help out much for the plans for their block party, but she was sure that the talented people on her block had everything well in hand. The weather looked iffy at the moment, but the festivities would go on, good weather or not.

The men had sent around warnings to the residents a few days ago to make sure to move their cars since they were going to block off the ends of their street by 8:00 a.m. Sounds of the younger children riding back and forth on their bicycles and big wheels began about 8:05. It was exciting to see the homes decorated and the tables covered with red and white paper cloths set out in the street awaiting delicious foods and drinks. A few neighbors could be seen setting out their lawn chairs and visiting with each other. Loudspeakers had been set up and some Disney tunes were blaring loudly.

Jesse had helped Nora prepare morning treats for everyone, and those were brought out about 9:30 a.m. and quickly disappeared. Other tables contained a plentiful supply of sweet and salty treats and various drinks.

Nora and Tommy visited with a few of the elderly people and made sure that they had chairs in front of their homes that were set up in a safe spot so they would not get hit by flying Frisbees or balls. They helped a few people to get down their steps and brought them plates of snacks.

They knew that Mrs. Erkland had recently lost her husband and didn't emerge from her house much these days, so they went to see how she was. She told them she was not feeling very well and would not be able to participate this year. Tommy said that they could help her get to their house, where she could sit outside with Nora's grandparents, and she finally acquiesced and said she would give it a try.

Baseball, touch football, and a variety of games for the young children were started, and that took care of the younger and older people's needs. As usual, most of the teenagers thought they were too cool for these activities, but when the lunch arrived from their local deli, they managed to make an appearance. As Nora had thought, the women on the block had everything organized well, and various people were responsible for setup and cleanup.

The afternoon was taken up with the kids having fun in the bounce house and bingo games for those who were so inclined. When Nora was little, a fire engine would give rides to the kids on its roof, but that had been deemed not safe enough now since it was not equipped with seat belts for everyone. Nora and Tommy's contribution to the day was to provide pony rides for the little ones with a guard for each individual pony as well as helmets for the riders. That was a popular addition to the day, and all seemed to be going well.

The adults drifted in and out to do various chores at home, but about 5:00 p.m., the smells of charcoal fires filled the air, and many delicious looking foods and salads were brought out for the shared supper. Nora knew that Gloryann Graber, her administrator for Duffy Medical Foundation—US, would also be supplying vegetarian and gluten-free dishes.

Unfortunately, just as dinner was about ready, the threatened rain arrived, but the organizers had made plans for that as well. Six garages had been cleaned out and outfitted with tables and chairs, the food was distributed among them, and people finished up eating in there. Ice cream treats and delicious-looking cakes appeared, and some games continued for a while.

At 7:30 p.m., the drawing for the grand raffle occurred in the Murray's garage. Those who had participated had taken chances for five dollars each, and there were three prizes. Tommy and Nora had supplemented the fund with a generous amount, so the prizes were substantial. Mrs. Erkland won one hundred dollars, the Browns won five hundred dollars, and the McIldowneys won one thousand dollars.

Those who had not won the big prizes all received twenty-five-dollar gift cards, so even though it was still raining, the organizers felt like all their efforts had gone well.

When it became apparent that the rain was going to continue, they decided to end the day's activities. It had been nice to visit with neighbors that they rarely saw, and everyone seemed to agree that it had been a happy time. It was unfortunate that the trivia game that was supposed to be played after dinner had to be postponed, but they would try to do that at the Labor Day party. Nora's parents and siblings returned to their house and said they would look forward to having Nora and Tommy attend their block party in a few weeks.

Tommy was about to go into the house when Don Wright from next door came running over to him. He said he knew that the block party organizers tasked with safety measures for the day had nixed the idea of fireworks, but he had obtained some from his friend in Indiana and hoped to set them off as a surprise for the kids. When the rain came, that was the end of that, but he had just opened his garage door to put away tables and chairs and noticed immediately that there was a powerful smell of gasoline. He looked for its source and realized that someone had poured gas over the boxes of unopened fireworks. All it would have taken was a spark to set them off and the whole pile would have gone off at once. It could have resulted in a fire that would have burned down the garage and possibly injured many people. Don shakily asked Tommy for his advice.

Tommy immediately phoned Nora and told her to meet him in the backyard. Then he called his fire captain friend and the District 22 Chicago Police Department. He told Don to get his family out of their house and to tell the neighbors on each side of them to leave their homes until the fire department had a chance to remove all the saturated fireworks. About an hour later, they had been doused with foam and removed, but the police and firemen had many questions.

Don apologized to everyone and had to admit that he had been told not to have the fireworks. He received a lecture from the fire captain on the dangers of having these around children, and his wife, Terri, looked at him as though he were crazy. He was given a citation and was told to leave open the doors to the garage until the fumes had disappeared and to scrub down the floor. The police had questions about who could have done this and why. No one had answers to that.

Nora realized that she had not noticed before how much the Wright's garage looked like theirs. She wondered if the perpetrator thought he was trying to harm them rather than the Wright's. She did not mention that disturbing possibility, but she called her friend Lt. Matt Braxton and made sure that he was aware of this latest threat that might have been directed at them.

Tommy and Nora said goodnight to all their friends on the block and thanked them for making the day so successful.

CHAPTER

23

Wednesday, July 10
In Flight to California; 11:00 a.m., PDT

"Why are dreams so ephemeral?" Nora wondered for the thousandth time as she woke with a start. Just a few seconds ago, she had been talking to a man who looked a lot like her cousin Sandy Moynihan, who had just shot the person across from him, and she had pleaded with him to stop, and he looked at her with hatred, and then she woke up. She thought she might always remember the man's florid face and straight reddish-colored hair, but she couldn't recall any of the other details. They were all just gone, like iridescent soap bubbles that vanish with a sudden splat.

She usually didn't have violent dreams, and she wondered if this one reflected her recent exposure to violence. If only the brain had a way to capture the people and images we experience when we dream on a computer, Nora felt sure we would learn something valuable. What happens to the dream people that seem so real to us for a few hours? Nora had seen a number of patients transition between life and death, and some of them mumbled words during their last sleep that seemed to indicate they were children again. Sometimes, she wondered which was reality, the hours we spend dreaming or the rest of the time we deem as being "awake."

Having engaged in her attempt at metaphysical musings for the day, Nora looked at the clock on her end table, said a quick prayer of thanks for another day, and jumped out of bed. She had been at the Children's Cancer Clinic later than she had expected last night, so she had slept twenty minutes longer than she had planned. Today was one day when she wanted to savor every moment. In a few hours, most of the members of her family would be traveling to California for her cousin Sheila's wedding.

Nora showered and finished her preparations for the trip and brought her dogs over to her parents' home, where pandemonium reigned as everyone finished getting ready. They talked to Jesse about their plans, and she said that she and her nephew would take good care of the four dogs. She fed them a quick breakfast, the suitcases were put on the front porch, and they were ready.

Three limos arrived at the Duffy's to pick them up for their trip to O'Hare Airport. Eileen Duffy made sure her large brood was all accounted for. There would be no one left "home alone" while she was in charge. Doctor Duffy and Tommy would be joining them a few days later, as would Mary Ann, Al, and baby Dylan.

The trip to I-294 went smoothly, although there was a glitch as they were about to enter the tollway. Once they got past that, they made the trip in record time, and everyone alighted at the United Airlines terminal. They were bound for OAK, Oakland, California, from ORD, Chicago, Illinois, and they checked in their luggage, got their boarding passes, and gathered for a snack at the deli.

They proceeded to their gate, and most everyone was able to get a seat in the waiting area. As they were sitting there, Nora again noticed the tall and strange-looking woman with the black coat and long stringy black hair wearing a large pink pom-pom hat. Who was this person with the distinctive hat who seemed to be appearing wherever she went? So far, this woman had not done anything threatening, but it could not have been an accident that she kept spotting the hat wherever she happened to be. It was unnerving. She thought the woman was waiting to get on her flight, but when she looked up, the woman had disappeared.

Then there was a mad dash to get seated on the plane, and the Duffy family took up most of the seats in first class. They got settled and took off. Then they were served a small lunch, and Nora drifted off to sleep.

Sometime later, Nora Duffy's young sisters elbowed her in her ribs, telling her that she was moaning and to wake up. Nora sat next to the window, and the twins took up the middle and aisle seats. Their mother, Eileen, and grandmother, Marie, were sitting behind them. "You promised you'd tell us what we're flying over," said Molly and Caitlan, the fourteen-year-old identical twins. "What are those black hills below us?"

Nora grabbed both her little sisters' hands and said she was sorry she had dozed off. She had a late shift at the cancer clinic last night, and she was still sleepy. She explained to them that the green and brown geometric shapes they had passed over were farmlands and reservoirs, and they would soon be flying over the Sierra Nevada Mountains. They might look like hills from up here, but they are about fifteen thousand feet high.

"What's California like?" asked the girls.

"That's a good question," answered Nora. "Remember those books you were reading last year called *The Land of Stories*? I think that's a good description of California. Everything there seems to be an extreme story, from the people, to the land, to the ocean, to the earthquakes, mudslides, and fires. So many places are incredibly beautiful, but those tan hills they feature in pictures that look like they are covered in rolling wheat are really vegetation that has been burnt to a crisp by the sun. In the spring, those same hills are covered in bright green plants and golden mustard flowers, but once the sun parches everything, that doesn't last long.

"Many of the cities we'll see are named after the famous missions that the Franciscans established up and down California many years ago. San Francisco was named after Saint Francis and Los Angeles is the City of Angels.

"California is the richest place, but there's also a lot of poverty. The tourist towns are filled with beautiful shops and restaurants, but many workers cannot afford to go there. Buying a house is often beyond their abilities since even a small home can cost over a million dollars. Most people appear to be very liberal in their political views, but many others are just as conservative. As Winston Churchill said about a different subject, 'it's a riddle, wrapped in a mystery, inside an enigma.'"

Nora continued, "California is so big that it could be its own separate country. It has the fifth largest economy in the whole world, and it is just one of our states. Even though they are in the same state, Cousin Karen lives near Hollywood, where it is usually warm, but she is five hundred miles away from Aunt Janet's near San Francisco, where it's relatively cool much of the time. The vineyards are pictur-esque, but they take so much work to plant and protect the vines and to harvest the grapes and then make wine out of them. You just will not believe how many vineyards there are!

"The middle of the state grows most of the flowers, fruits, veg-etables, and nuts produced in the US. Although we think about Wisconsin for dairy products, California has almost as many so there are lots of dairy cattle. Some of the most beautiful horses in the world can be found on their ranches. I hope we have time to visit the big redwood trees that are close to Aunt Janet. They are so big and tall they look unreal, and the smell is so unique. San Diego in the south has one of the most stable climates in the country, where it's usually seventy-five one day, seventy-six the next, all year long.

"You're likely not going to see any of the problems, and I know you're going to just love it. After the wedding, we are planning to drive down Highway 1 all the way to Los Angeles, and then you'll really get to see spectacular views of the ocean.

"The last really big earthquake occurred in San Francisco and the surrounding areas in 1906, with a magnitude of 7.9, one of the biggest quakes recorded. Much of the city was destroyed, and thou-sands of people were killed or injured. California has smaller earth-quakes every day, and a big quake in Los Angeles in 1989 was also serious. You remember when you were studying about tectonic plates slipping along fault lines? There are several large faults in California, and one of the biggest is the San Andreas. The likelihood of a major earthquake looms as time goes by, but hopefully, we won't see any-thing like that."

A stewardess appeared at their side and asked if they needed anything. She queried, "You're Nora Duffy, aren't you? My friend thought I was wrong, but I told her there was no mistaking your small stature and big red curly hair. We're all happy to have you and your family on our flight today."

Nora responded that they were doing well, and yes, she was Nora Duffy. The downside of all the publicity about her and her family over the last six months was the loss of anonymity. Most people had seen those newspapers that termed her the "Mighty Rich Midget." Nora explained to the stewardess that they were on their way to a town in Sonoma County to attend the wedding of her cousin, and they chatted about that for a few minutes.

Eileen Duffy reached through the seats and patted her daughter on the back and said they should be arriving in Oakland in about an hour. Eileen had always been attuned to her eldest daughter's moods, and that connection had become even stronger after they had faced down an irrational murderer last year. The recent murders Nora had encountered in Ireland had not helped either. She was hoping that this trip to visit her sister Janet, and her family in California would take Nora out of her routine and help to restore her usual positive attitude.

Nora thought about her cousin Sheila Kelly and her upcoming wedding to Tony Capodice next Saturday. Sheila was a speech coach, and she spent her days helping executives to hone their speechmaking skills. It was a perfect profession for her since she rarely stopped talking. Tony, a sweet and happy guy of Italian descent, could outtalk even Sheila, so their children should be very articulate.

Of all the many cousins, Sheila looked the most like Nora since she had inherited the thick red curly hair, although she was a foot taller than Nora, who was only four feet five inches tall. Nora expected the wedding to be a lot of fun, and she was to be one of the many bridesmaids. She would not get to try on her bridesmaid dress until tomorrow, but she had seen pictures of the coral pink dresses, and she thought that Sheila had chosen well.

She was looking forward to spending time with her godmother Aunt Janet; Uncle Joe Kelly; Sheila and Tony; and the other Kelly cousins Carolyn, Suzy, and Andy. She loved their beautiful Italian villa home at the top of a hill overlooking their large vineyard in Sonoma.

As they were about to arrive in Oakland, they could see that, contrary to the popular song, it did sometimes rain in sunny California. Nora hoped the rain would not last long so that nothing would mar Sheila's beautiful day. It was exciting to see their first views of the Pacific Ocean, and suddenly, after their long flight, their talented pilot and crew ensured that they had a smooth landing.

Their large group picked up their luggage, they found their limousines, and they were on their way to Sonoma. As they passed the huge cranes that serviced the many large ships in the Oakland Harbor, everyone agreed that they looked a lot like the walkers in the *Star Wars* movies. It was a longer ride than they thought to arrive at Aunt Janet's, but they were happy to see that the rain seemed to be coming to an end.

Once they started seeing vineyards, their limo driver explained to them that they would reach La Bella Maria in about half an hour. The people from the vineyard were always happy when they saw rain since it was needed so much. The twins were thrilled to see the mountains that seemed to soar so close to them. Soon, they could see that unending vistas of vineyards that Nora had said they would, and they found it amazing that the plants seemed to cover every plot of empty earth as far as the eye could see, even up on the hillsides. Nora pointed out to them that some of the wines they could find in Chicago stores were manufactured right here like Gallo and Kendall Jackson.

The limos slowed down as they came around a corner, and there was the beautiful hand-painted archway sign for La Bella Maria Vineyards. Sheila and her brother and sisters were waiting for them at the gatehouse and greeted them with bouquets of flowers. They told them to drive right up to the house and they would join them in a few minutes.

Aunt Janet and Uncle Joe waved to them from the spacious front porch and welcomed them to their home. Workers came and picked up their luggage, and those who wanted to wash up were directed to their rooms upstairs while those who wanted to relax were invited to join them for a drink on the porch. After greeting her sister and brother-in-law, Eileen took some of the younger children in the house to get them settled. Gorgeous flowers decorated the inside and outside of the home, and recordings of popular singers provided a festive atmosphere. Nora could hear Elvis Presley crooning the "Hawaiian Wedding Song."

Nora remembered meeting the Kelly's happy cook and housekeeper a few years ago, and after they'd had a chance to relax for a while, Auntie Anna asked them all to enjoin to the yard for a barbecue meal. The delicious smells coming from the backyard encouraged them to hasten their steps, and they sat down at a pink and green covered table with grapevine china and glassware. Workers gave them generous helpings of salads, fruits, and meats, and, of course, wines and juices of various types. Many toasts for good health, happiness, and wealth were given to the young couple. Then Nora was asked to play her violin and join in a serenade to Sheila and Tony. She knew that one of their favorites was "True Love," and she played that beautiful song while everyone sang to them.

A big moon got bigger by the minute, and the ambience of the celebration reached its climax as Eileen realized that her youngest daughters were starting to fall asleep. They had started off the day early in the morning, and the excitement had tired them out. Eileen took some of the children into the house and helped them get ready for bed, with the promise that they could get up early tomorrow to prepare for more adventures.

CHAPTER

24

Thursday, July 11
Sonoma, California; 7:00 a.m., PDT

Nora had gotten up early and used the binoculars in Uncle Joe's study to gaze out over the peaceful vineyard. She was always amazed at the mathematical precision of the rows of grape vines, and she asked how that came to be. Uncle Joe had explained to her that in the old days, planters relied on many spotters and strings, but he had taken advantage of the newest technology and used a truck equipped with a laser beam. That had advantages at both planting and harvest time.

As she scanned back and forth across the field with the binoculars, she came back to a spot she'd been looking at a minute ago. She wasn't imagining it; a person in a bright blue outfit was lying supine on the ground. Either he was taking a nap in a strange place, or he was dead. Nora thought she might have been imagining things since she had seen so much violence lately, but she didn't want to take a chance. She ran and found Uncle Joe and asked him to look through the binoculars at about, in military terms, three o'clock. Uncle Joe agreed with Nora that it was suspicious that the person was lying there so still, and he called his foreman George Pickerell and told him to get out there to investigate right away.

George fired up his two-by-four vehicle and raced to the spot. It turned out that the man was a worker who had fainted, but if Nora hadn't spotted him, he could have died in the heat. Uncle Joe, George, and the rescued man, Matthis, thanked her profusely for her sharp eyes. Matthis was taken to the hospital for observation since this had never happened to him before.

Most of the young people joined for an afternoon of singing and dancing with a DJ. Eileen and Nora Duffy joined Aunt Janet and Uncle Joe for a chance to have a trip down memory lane talking about how the Kelly's happened to meet and how they had started their vineyard. Uncle Joe reminded Nora that this property had originally been owned by his grandfather, but it wasn't very big at first. Joe's father, Andrew Kelly III, liked to live the simple life and had no wish to engage in the physical labor it took to keep a vineyard being successful.

Joe said that his father had been a happy-go-lucky hippy, who sometimes hung out with the original Beach Boys, used pot, and had affairs with winery workers' wives. His mother, Carolyn, probably should have left him, but she was smart and faced the situation squarely. She loved him, but she saw a good lawyer and made sure that the control of the money was in her hands. Eventually, her good sense and influence made Andrew come around, and they'd now been married for sixty years. "They live in the big cottage you can see when you pull into the grounds, and they'll be here shortly," said Joe.

Nora had heard that it was Uncle Joe who had the expertise to turn La Bella Maria into a thriving winery, and he and the whole family had spent years building it up into what she saw today.

Sheila came and joined the group and asked Nora if they could walk around a bit. Sheila asked Nora if her wedding gift to her would involve money, and Nora said that it could. Sheila explained that her father wouldn't want anyone else to know about this, but he'd been diagnosed with a seriously blocked heart artery. She was hoping to hire a manager for the vineyard and have her father stay involved but just in the wine tasting room or in the office. She'd already talked to the current manager George Pickerell, and he had recommended a good man to her, but he wouldn't come cheap. Any money that Sheila and Tony received for a wedding present would go for that.

Nora agreed that she would do that, and she said she hoped that Joe would agree to have a second opinion from her father when he arrived tomorrow. She also wondered what Joe would say when he

155

realized that his family was making other plans for him behind his back. It was plain that he thought of La Bella Maria as his kingdom.

It was time to prepare for the wedding rehearsal, and everyone was asked to get dressed for it. Nora went to her bedroom and put on her pink and white gown. Everyone in the wedding party was asked to assemble on the back deck, and Nora was introduced to all the bridesmaids and groomsmen. Sheila was especially glad to introduce her to Lisa Montgomery, her best friend since kindergarten. Lisa was tall and blond and good-natured. Later, they found her husband, Ken, at the bar, and he was already quite drunk.

Ken was introduced to Nora and said, "Wow! Lisa told me you'd be here, but you really are a midget and a funny looking one at that." He lurched toward Nora. "Are we supposed to be impressed that you're here with all your money? I think you're just using Sheila as another opportunity to get your face in the news. I would offer you a drink, but I understand you're the sweet little angel who doesn't like alcohol. You should try it and maybe you'd be less of a witch."

Nora was surprised by this outburst and wasn't sure how to respond at first, but she had discovered that silence was usually the best policy in cases like this. She didn't feel the least pressured to explain to him why she didn't drink, which was her personal preference. She never tried to influence others not to drink, but she expected the same courtesy from them.

Lisa and Sheila were horrified at Ken's outrageous behavior and tried to get him to stop talking, but he was on a roll. "My family had money when yours was still digging for potatoes. Why don't you go back to the bogs, where you belong," Ken slobbered out as he tripped over a pillow and hit his head. Nora took a look at the sore spot on Ken's head, but the fall appeared to have caused just a scratch. Several of the men grabbed Ken by the arms and began to drag him away from the bar, but Nora intervened.

"Mr. Montgomery, I'm sorry if you're disturbed by my being here, but I'm Sheila's cousin, and I'm to be a bridesmaid, like your wife. Neither of us can help having money, and I notice by your clothes and your jewelry that you use it quite liberally. You are embarrassing your wife and the bride-to-be, and your outrage would be more believable if you didn't need alcohol to give you false courage. I'll go back to the other room and get out of your way." Nora quickly trotted away in her pink Louboutin stilettos.

Lisa tried to apologize to Nora through her tears, but Nora went to find her mother, and Ken's friends convinced him to go back to the house. Lisa looked as miserable as could be.

Nora looked back and saw Sheila wrapping Lisa in her arms and trying to comfort her, but she knew that this poor young woman was in for many heartaches. How many times had she seen people at the hospital, whose families had been torn apart by alcoholism say, "He's really a nice guy when he's not drinking." When it got to the point where there was almost never a time when the person was not drinking, there was little hope for them to return to "nice guy" status.

Eileen Duffy was visiting with Aunt Janet and Uncle Joe in the living room, and there were several guests they wanted Nora to meet. Austin Tennill was a famous artist who specialized in painting large landscapes of the many different areas of California. One of his canvases filled the space above the Kelly's huge fireplace and featured the magnificent Malibu coastline, Uncle Joe's old home. Another smaller picture of the brilliant fields of flowers in the Central Valley hung above the Louis XIV desk. Nora complimented this talented artist and held out her hand to him.

Mr. Tennill greeted her warmly and said he'd heard she was going to be there and was delighted to make her acquaintance. After her frosty and uncomfortable reception of a few moments ago, this was a much more pleasant greeting. Austin was accompanied by an attractive woman wearing a gorgeous gold-textured Indian sari. A few minutes of conversation revealed that Mari Tennill had been born in Los Angeles and had gone to Berkeley, but she loved the traditional garments of the Indian women and often wore them. Mari was an artist and sculptor and one of her graceful bird sculptures could be seen outside the picture window. Mari had the voice of a soprano when she spoke, and it was easy to see why she was so popular.

Nora talked to Austin Tennill and asked him if he would have a suitable painting that she could use as a gift for Tommy now that he was going to be made a partner at his law firm. Austin said some of his paintings were displayed in a gallery in the nearby town of Windsor. He asked if she could meet him there on Sunday night to make a selection. Nora agreed that she would, but she told Austin that this was all to be a surprise for Tommy. She would have to make sure that Tommy was suitably occupied then so he wouldn't want to come with her.

A man dressed in black with a long, narrow face and a marine-type haircut sat quietly in the corner and seemed to be observing all of them as if they were scientific experiments. Nora walked over to him and introduced herself. The man didn't respond right away, so Aunt Janet came over and told her that Robert Durkin was a movie producer from Hollywood. He and Tony, the bridegroom, had gone to school together, and Tony had asked Robert to produce a movie about the California vineyards. Robert had decided to include Sheila's wedding in the movie and was here to meet the family.

Robert asked Nora to sit down next to him, and from just those few words, she thought she detected an Irish brogue amidst his attempted British accent. She told him that she was glad to make his acquaintance since she had been trying to get a movie made about her castle in Ireland, and it had not been going as well as she'd planned. She said she would appreciate his advice, and Robert said he would be glad to talk to her after the wedding about it.

Nora had the strongest feeling that she might have met Robert Durkin before. Something about his face was nagging at her memory. She had absolutely nothing tangible to base this feeling on, but one of her fairy fey moments seemed to be telling her to tread slowly and be wary in dealing with Robert. When these moments occurred, she filed the warning away in the back of her mind and waited until future events could discount it—or not.

Fr. Joseph Flynn, a Maryknoll priest and friend of the Kelly family for many years, was to be the celebrant for the wedding Mass. He had been a missionary in Tanzania for most of his priesthood but had recently developed amoebic dysentery and then liver cancer, so he had been sent home to California. The Kelly family had been his mentors for many years. He usually traveled little these days, but when his old friends asked him to preside at Sheila's wedding, he said yes. It would be a continuum of being involved with Sheila's life since he had baptized her twenty-five years ago.

Father Flynn had probably been a handsome man in his youth, but hardships and illness had caused him to become extremely gaunt and wrinkled. Nora found his description of his work in Africa fascinating, and his voice was still strong and vibrant. Nora looked forward to what he would have to say to the young couple during the wedding Mass.

Aunt Janet announced that it was time for the wedding rehearsal to begin, and Sheila's friend Camilla Harris soon got everyone organized. There were to be ten bridesmaids with matching groomsmen, and Nora would walk down the aisle with Tommy first since she was the shortest. Camilla reminded Nora of her friend Connie, who had been such an excellent planner, and the rehearsal went without a hitch and was quickly brought to a close.

It seemed as though the group was going to work together very smoothly, with the possible exception of Ken, and Nora swore that she would try hard to avoid talking to him since he seemed to be so annoyed by her presence. She had pretty much gotten used to the fact that she was wealthy now, but this was another case where she wished that she did not have to worry about the effect it had on some people.

Nora went to visit with Auntie Anna and her crew in the kitchen and had more fun with them than she had with some of Sheila's wealthy friends. She asked Auntie Anna to tell her about her background, and she said that she had been born outside of Los Angeles to very poor parents, and she had twelve brothers and sisters. Their parents insisted that they all get as much education as they could, and they had all become fairly successful. One of her brothers was the mayor of a small town. Anna had run the Kelly's household for twenty years now, and she loved the children as though they were her own.

Nora told her stories about her nine siblings and her parents and grandparents, and she knew it was true that you just share chemistry with some people, regardless of their station in life. Nora invited Anna to come and visit them in Chicago, or even in Ireland, if she ever got the chance for some free time and told her she would be glad to pay for her fare. By the time the visit was over, they knew they would be fast friends.

Eileen came looking for Nora and said she was tired after their busy day, so she was going upstairs to bed. Nora said that she would be coming up shortly, but she went to find Sheila and Tony to wish them a happy good night.

CHAPTER

25

Friday, July 12
Sonoma, California; 8:00 a.m., PDT

The wedding party and most of the guests were going to see the giant redwoods at Muir Woods near San Francisco today. Eileen stayed behind at the house with Aunt Janet and Uncle Joe since she had visited the awesome trees a number of times in the past.

Everyone had an early breakfast and began their preparations. Sheila warned everyone going to the woods to wear comfortable but warm clothing since the sun did not penetrate too much into the woods. She told them it was essential that they wear comfortable shoes suitable for climbing since they would be doing a lot of walking.

They were picked up by a bevy of limousines, whose drivers were part-time tour guides and comedians, and they were soon laughing as they enjoyed the scenery on their way to the big woods. The drivers got serious for a while as they relayed the history of how Muir Woods came to be protected, and the part that John Muir had played in saving these majestic trees. They told their passengers to watch the Ken Burns's documentary about the national parks for a lengthier explanation about John Muir and his compatriots, but he was indeed a hero. If it were not for him, the loggers of the nineteenth century might well have cut down every tree. As it was, about ninety-five percent of all the "old growth" trees had been removed from the face of the earth to make everything from jewelry boxes to houses and then firewood.

To get to the woods required driving up impossibly steep, twisting, and bumpy roads, and the wedding guests were told to hang on tightly until they were able to pull into the parking lot. Jim and Jack Duffy were huge fans of J. R. R. Tolkien and his books and said this trip reminded them of the road to the dreaded Mirkwood forest in *The Hobbit*. They could see that the trees on each side of the cars were gradually increasing in girth.

Finally, they saw the sign for the entrance to Muir Woods and were able to pull into the parking lot, which seemed incredibly crowded, even at this early hour. The drivers showed their passes to the guides at the entrance; they were finally able to park, and when everyone was out of the cars, their tour guides told them to read the directions at the front entrance. They especially stressed that it was most important that they stay together, and under no circumstances should they leave the well-marked paths. They made sure they understood that there was no cell phone or Internet access here.

Once they read the interesting signs that had been posted at the entrance and got past them, first timers experienced the "cathedral effect" as they realized that the outside world seemed to have disappeared. Their bottoms were still stinging from the bumpy ride on the bus, so they knew the world was still out there, but it was so very quiet here that it was a little scary. They felt like they were the aliens among these huge survivors. The smells coming from the trees were overpowering and pleasant but like nothing else they had ever experienced.

At first glance, they did not see any animals, although they did hear some bird calls. Their guides told them to look for Steller's jays, beautiful birds with dark blue feathers that occasionally flitted from one tree to the next. They assured them that a variety of wildlife was here, although they might not see any of them. One interesting fact was that there were almost no bugs here since the tannin from the trees was not hospitable to insects.

The breadth and height of the trees was hard to believe, and every so often, they came across a tree that had what appeared to be a giant mushroom effect at its base. These helped to protect the trees from the fires that could occur from lightning strikes. There were plenty of places for photo ops, and one of Nora's favorites was of the four youngest cousins who fit into a "hole" in one of the giant trees. Every so often, they came to a tree marked by a sign that explained that this tree was of particular interest.

The younger hikers wanted to go hiking on the more difficult trails, and Nora carefully counted who was going to do that. They were warned that they had to be very fit to take these trails since they would be going "uphill and down dale," and fifteen of their number prepared to go off on their adventure. They had a map to follow, and Jim said he would keep an eye on them, and they would meet up with the rest of the party back at the entrance gate. The older folks stayed on the easier main trail and enjoyed reading all the historical information about the incredible age of the trees, how they came to grow there, and why they needed the moisture that came from the nearby ocean and the frequent fogs that nourished them.

They didn't get too far on their hike when Nora once again spotted the strange-looking woman wearing the long black coat with stringy black hair covered by a pink pom pom hat, peeking out from behind one of the huge trees. *This is no longer a coincidence,* Nora worried. *I saw her a few times in Chicago, and now here she is in California in this specific place. She must be following me.* She tried to pay more attention to what the woman was wearing and what her face looked like, but the pink pom-poms disappeared around the bend in the redwood grove, and Nora lost track of her.

Jim and Jack, the oldest boys of the Duffy clan, were happy to be hiking together again. They used to do this kind of thing often, but they were so busy with their demanding jobs that they hadn't gone hiking for a long time. They lived together in a downtown Chicago apartment, but between their jobs and their girlfriends, they didn't spend much time talking to each other about anything substantive, so they welcomed this opportunity.

These trails were demanding in spots, and the gnarly roots of the huge trees could be tripping hazards, so they frequently warned the intrepid group behind them of potential trouble spots. They had been told by Nora, who had stayed behind with the older people, to especially keep an eye on the young teenage twins Molly and Caitlan, and they looked for their yellow sweaters to make sure they were still keeping up with them.

At some point, the twin girls lagged behind a bit when they heard some soft mewing sounds off to their left. They told their older sister Siobhan that they would catch up with them in a minute since Molly wanted to tie her shoes, but they went looking to see if there were animals making these soft noises. At the base of a tree that had particularly large roots, they found a group of baby somethings that Molly thought might be wildcats, but Caity told her she was sure they were foxes. Mama fox didn't seem to be around at the moment, so they got a little closer to watch the cute little cubs as they tripped over each other and cried pitifully. They were so adorable that Caity wanted to pick one up, but then she remembered hearing in one of their science classes to never pick up a wild animal.

The girls were so entranced by the babies that they didn't notice that two young men dressed in black plaid shirts had come up behind them. The men grabbed the girls' arms without warning and tried to drag them away. Molly and Caitlan had both taken self-defense classes, and they initially fought the men off for a few minutes, but they were so much bigger than they were. The men threatened to kill them if they didn't quiet down, but the girls had no such intentions and began to yell and scream. They realized that the big trees acted like a wet blanket that muffled noises, and they were just about getting really scared when the woman they had seen once before at the cheesecake restaurant in Chicago appeared.

She was dressed in the long black coat with the scraggly black hair and the pink pom-pom hat, and she was holding a drawn gun. She warned the men to back off from the girls immediately and assured them that the gun was loaded, and she was a good shot. Her no-nonsense voice and her stance as an experienced gun handler convinced them to step away from the girls quickly. She told them to take off without stopping, and they soon saw the backs of their plaid shirts running away down the nearest path.

The girls thanked the strange-looking woman for her help and said they thought they were fine, but they couldn't wait to get out of here and back to Nora. They soon heard their names being frantically called, and Jim and Jack and the rest of the party found them and hugged the girls and wiped away their tears. The twins started to explain about the baby foxes and the two guys who had tried to kidnap them and how they had been saved by the woman in the pink pom-pom hat, but when they went to look for her, the woman had disappeared.

Jim and Jack kept the twins right beside them, and they looked at the map for the quickest way to get back to the entrance gate. Maureen and Siobhan would have given the girls a lecture about paying attention to directions, but they saw that they had been properly scared, so they just held their hands. All of them wondered what the men's intentions had been, and they knew that Nora was going to be furious when she heard that the girls had been left alone.

Jim and Jack and their party made it back to the entrance before Nora and the older folks did, and they looked for a park ranger so they could report the twins' incident. The ranger reported their story to the local police, who came quickly. Just then Nora and her group met up with them. Her siblings were right that Nora was so upset with them when she had told them over and over again that the girls could be kidnapping targets, but right now, she wanted to get them out of here as soon as possible.

The police told them they were sorry that they had such a frightening experience, but they recognized Nora Duffy from her pictures. They were particularly curious about the woman in the pink pom-pom hat with a gun, but no one had more information about her. Nora silently thanked her, whoever she was, for protecting her sisters. Molly and Caitlan knew they were in for "a talk" later, but they were just so glad to be standing here with their arms around Nora. They wouldn't need any more warnings in the future about wandering away from the group.

Tony and Sheila had hired a professional photographer to take pictures at the park, and the Duffys recovered enough to pose for them. Then the party headed back to the parking lot. Nora looked for the woman in the pink pom-pom hat, but she saw no signs of her.

The limousine drivers then took them to the town of Sausalito for lunch and an opportunity to do more shopping. They had made reservations at Scoma's Restaurant, which was right on the water with a fantastic view. Everyone was hungry after being out in the open air and enjoyed the cocktails and delicious food. They were given an hour for more shopping at the many nearby stores and boutiques, and then the group gathered again for the return trip to La Bella Maria.

On the way back, Uncle Joe and Aunt Janet had made provisions for them to stop at Korbel Champagne Cellars for a visit to their tasting room and a tour of their beautiful grounds. La Bella Maria was a medium-sized vineyard, but they also wanted them to see the operations of one of the giants among the industry. The professional photographers had many opportunities for posed pictures of the group.

Since Nora was not a drinker, she took her younger siblings and cousins for a walk through the huge grounds that provided their bubbly specialties to virtually every city in the US and around the world. They were able to sample nonalcoholic beverages that were so tasty too. The flowers that covered almost every square foot of ground not planted with grape vines were gorgeous, and they spotted many varieties of birds who were singing their hearts out.

It was finally time to return to the Kelly homestead, where they had an opportunity to rest up. The twins found their mother, Eileen, and relayed the story about them almost being kidnapped and being saved by the woman in the pink pom-pom hat, and she was horrified. Nora had suggested to her mother and father before that it might be a good idea to hire someone to act as bodyguards for the girls, but they had resisted that suggestion so far. It might be time to revisit that decision again.

The guests were going to be treated tonight to a formal dinner under the many tents that had been erected in case of rain tomorrow. Auntie Anna and her crew were busy preparing an Italian meal for them with all the trimmings, and the delicious smells whetted their appetites. They had said in Sausalito that they were so full they couldn't possibly eat again, but there was always room for more Italian food.

Nora had a call from Tommy who said that he, her dad, Mary Ann, Al, and Dylan had landed at Oakland, and they should be there within the hour or so. That made her feel so much better and safer, and she anxiously waited for his arrival.

When the latecomers arrived at the vineyard, Tommy remarked that Nora looked even more beautiful than usual. She told him she put her enhanced coloring down to being outdoors and hiking among the huge trees, but the compliment was nice to hear. Doctor Duffy said that Ed Sloan appeared to be doing much better about his bypass, and everyone greeted Mary Ann her family with many hugs and kisses.

Auntie Anna invited everyone to come and be seated at the banquet tables, and at each place, they found good-sized towel bibs that had pictures of the bride and groom on them to wear over their dressy clothes. Over the next two hours, they were served a nine-course meal of Italian favorites. Although that sounded like a lot of food, Auntie Anna knew the old ways that made each course consist of a small but exquisite portion of food, and there were several changes of wines. Much toasting was done to the happy couple in between courses. Authentic Italian musicians provided just the right atmosphere, and by the time the meal was over, everyone was happily singing. Aunt Janet looked pleased that her planning had resulted in an unforgettable evening, and nature did its part by providing a full moon.

When things quieted down, Nora told her father about Uncle Joe's heart condition, and she asked him if he would be willing to give Uncle Joe a second opinion about what should be done. Michael Duffy agreed that he would be happy to do that whenever Uncle Joe requested it. He said he was sure that surgeons in the State of California had plenty of diagnostic tools at the ready, but he could listen to his heart and see if there was any advice he could add.

Joe greeted Michael Duffy cordially, and Doctor Duffy shook his hand while taking in his general appearance. It was not always possible to diagnose someone just by looking at them, but in Joe's case, his air of general tiredness, pale complexion, and labored breathing did seem like ample cause for concern. Doctor Duffy asked Joe if what he had heard was true and if he would like him to do a brief examination. Joe would normally have told him to get lost, but it was clear that he was worried, and he said he would be glad to have him do that.

Doctor Duffy got his bag from his bedroom, and Joe led him to the workout room, where there was a flat table that would work as an exam table. Doctor Duffy listened to his heart for a long time, gave him a general exam as well, noticed that Joe's feet were swollen (a bad sign), and then listened to his heart again. Doctor Duffy said without more sophisticated tests, he couldn't give him a definitive answer, but there was definitely something amiss with his heart rhythms, and he probably had edema. He suggested that his good friend stay away from alcohol for the next few days, remain as quiet as he could during the upcoming festivities, and let Doctor Duffy know if he experienced any sudden changes.

Michael also told Joe to talk to his cardiologist and get to the hospital as soon as the wedding was over. If he had congestive heart failure, that would affect his kidneys as well as his lungs. Michael told him there was every chance that his surgeon would come up with a good solution, but he shouldn't let things go on too long. Michael said if Joe were his patient, he would tell him to get to the hospital right now. Joe was sure Michael was right, but he just could not miss his daughter's wedding. He thanked Michael for his help and said he would listen to his advice.

Aunt Janet knew of the exam and thanked Michael as well and said she would be keeping an eye on her usually rambunctious husband. The couple was worried about the future, but at least they had some warning, and they were fortunate that Michael would be there for a few days. They all conspired to keep Joe's condition quiet from the children and said they would do more about it right after the wedding.

CHAPTER

26

Saturday, July 13
Sonoma, California; 8:00 a.m., PDT

The morning of the wedding day dawned clear and cool, and Tommy and Nora joined the young people for a horse ride. Tommy was given Shooter, a chestnut horse with a white patch around both eyes. Gizmo was the horse assigned to Nora, and she was an old and short white horse, who could barely do more than trot. They didn't want to take any chances of Nora being hurt, but she thought that Gizmo was a sweet girl, who was happy to see her and nuzzled her cheek. They rode around the wine making vats and went up to the top of a hill, where they had an expansive view of the beautiful valley.

After their ride, they were hungry, and Auntie Anna had prepared a generous but healthy brunch for all of them. Nora and Tommy had stayed at the stables for a while to make sure the horses had a good rub down and feed, and they talked to the stables director Gary Pinkett. Gary told them that horses were essential to their operations since the animals could travel through the vineyard easily without trampling down any of the precious vines. The animals were all very carefully tended since they were essential to the business.

Nora asked Gary why there were rose bushes in front of the rows of vines, and he responded that the health—or not—of the rose bushes told the vineyard managers the location of possible diseased vines. The couple realized that a successful vineyard required the hands-on approach of everyone who lived there.

Nora and Tommy jogged back to the house and took showers and prepared for the brunch, where they enjoyed visiting with family and guests. Nora had told Tommy about her experience with Ken Montgomery and asked him to keep an eye on this potentially dangerous man.

The wedding was scheduled for 5:00 p.m., and the beauticians arrived about noon to do hair and nails. Camilla, the wedding planner, checked to make sure that the flowers were all in place. The cooks had gathered all their equipment and were checking out the food. Magnificent hors d'oeuvres were made and stored in huge refrigerators. The orchestra began to arrive about 3:00 p.m. and began to play. Camilla directed the bride and bridesmaids to the bedrooms, where their gowns awaited. Nora put on her beautiful bridesmaid dress that was a little long, but once she put on her high heels, it would be okay. The panorama of the girls in various shades of coral pink would make a beautiful tableau.

Cars began arriving to park about 4:00 p.m., and a bevy of parkers took their cars and directed the guests to the appropriate places. Comfortable chairs enhanced with white ruffles awaited the many guests. The orchestra had begun to play "San Francisco," and the words to the various songs appeared on big screens so the guests could sing along. Nora thought that no one could sing that song better than Jeanette MacDonald in the movie *San Francisco,* but she added her voice to the others who were starting to have such a good time. Waiters handed out hors d'oeuvres and flavored waters.

The groomsmen gathered with their formal black tuxedoes, and they looked quite distinguished. Tommy noticed that the man Nora had pointed out to her, Ken Montgomery, appeared to be drunk already, and he hoped that no disturbance would be happening during the wedding or reception.

Sheila finally emerged from her isolation room. She was tall and thin enough to wear a white silk formfitting dress that emphasized her many curves. She did not wear a veil, but her head was covered with copious white blossoms. Her only jewelry was a diamond pendant that caught the flickering of the sun.

Two altar girls lit the many candles around the altar that had been erected on the Kelly's large deck. A young priest, Fr. Tom Prince, from Father Flynn's residence, would assist the elderly man and keep an eye on his health. The parents and grandparents were escorted to their places and the orchestra intoned the opening notes of Vivaldi's *Four Seasons* music that formed the perfect backdrop for the wedding party to step off.

Many brides today thought it looked more elegant to carry only a small bouquet, but since La Bella Maria grew so many flowers, Nora's very full bouquet of twelve different species was gorgeous and fragrant but heavy, so she was glad she didn't have to walk very far. The other bridesmaids met their guys who had been standing at the front of the deck, and then it was time for Sheila to walk down the aisle.

All eyes were on her, and she looked fabulous as the orchestra switched to the "Wedding March" from Lohengrin. She met up with Tony, and they looked so happy as they anticipated the wedding Mass and ceremony.

Father Flynn looked so fragile, but he moved with surprising grace and strength. When it was time for the homily, he said he had only five pieces of advice for the young couple, and they all began with love. He reflected that when he was a young man, he thought he had all the answers about what it meant to love God and his people, but he had soon realized that it took so much hard work that he had been tempted to quit many times. He thought that must surely apply to two people who had to learn to live together harmoniously while still maintaining their individuality.

The old priest said that he had found strength from the apparently poor people of Tanzania. They had learned to survive and prosper by realizing that they could not do things on their own. They needed the love of God and of each other, and when things seemed too hard, they had found creative ways to deal with them within their community. Tony and Sheila had more material blessings in one day than some of his people had in their whole lives, but he hoped they realized that they needed God, each other, and their families.

He had one piece of practical advice for them too. In a few minutes, they would pledge themselves to each other, and that would be easy on this happy day, but he asked them to have a monthly anniversary ceremony and write a new pledge of their love to each other and keep those papers in a special place so they could refer to them in the years to come. There might come a day when that promise would not be so easy to make, but looking at past pledges of love should help them in the future.

Nora and Tommy were impressed by the kind priest's simple words and thought that Tony and Sheila would be too. The wedding had been beautiful and fun, and they thought the young couple should feel satisfied that all their plans had turned out so well.

Nora stood on the top of the stone bridge that overlooked the Kelly estate, and it seemed to her that the tableau below her of all those people dressed in their finery was impressive. She also thought that in Tony and Sheila's world, it was money that mattered.

Lots of time, effort, and money had gone into turning the flat area behind the house into a bower of flowers and beautifully dressed tables with Vera Wang china, crystal, and silverware. The menu had been designed to mimic what they would find at an Italian villa, and the guest chefs came from all over the country to serve the 1,500 guests with the finest wines and food. For those ladies who were concerned about their waistlines, more experts had been imported to provide low-cal and gluten-free foods.

Flowers adorned as many surfaces as possible, and the orchestra kept the guests entertained with a variety of music genres. The music and dancing went on for hours, and all seemed well, except that Ken Montgomery had been drinking during all those hours and was in fighting mode.

When Ken discovered that the tall groomsman standing next to him was Nora Duffy's husband, he began to assail him with insults and then tried to hit him in the jaw. Tommy was in much better physical shape than Ken and easily sidestepped his clumsy punch. He had been warned about Ken and had been trying to ignore him, but when he saw Ken punch his wife in the stomach, Tommy stepped in quickly and threw him to the ground. He asked some of the other men to help him get Ken back to the house, and the women took Lisa back to her room and tended to her.

THE GOLDEN HORSESHOES MURDERS

Lisa alternated between apologizing for her husband and crying about her injuries. She sobbed out to Nora that she thought she might be pregnant. Nora told Sheila to call an ambulance immediately and have Lisa taken to the hospital to be checked out after she had suffered such a vicious punch in the abdomen. They waited until the ambulance arrived, and Lisa's friend Beth said she would go with her and her parents to the hospital.

They were not sure how to handle the issue of Ken. They did not want to spoil the happy day by calling the police, but some of Tony's friends said they would take Ken back to his house and stay with him until he sobered up. It was clear that something more would have to be done about this situation and soon. Ken had gotten to the point where his alcoholism had made him so violent that he thought nothing about hurting his wife and potential child. Lisa had been putting up with him for a long time, but tonight's events would probably be the end of that.

Early the next morning, Tony and Sheila left to begin their honeymoon in Italy. They were scheduled for five days in Venice, and five in Florence, where they would be spending some time at a winery in the Tuscan Hills, and then five days in Rome. They were then going to visit Duffy Hall Castle in Ireland for a few days. They had made arrangements in Italy and Ireland for more genealogical information about both their families, and they looked forward to the next few weeks with joy.

Sunday, July 14

Joe and Janet Kelly were glad that the couple had gotten off on their trip, and then Doctor Duffy waited until Uncle Joe had called his cardiologist and arranged to meet him at the hospital. Doctor Duffy was concerned about Joe, but the last two days did seem to have perked him up, and he seemed to be breathing better. One never knew about congestive heart failure, and some people lived with it for years.

Michael urged Joe to take advantage of the offer by his children to hand over the day-to-day operations of the vineyard to a younger man and said he should enjoy the coming years and all the success he was responsible for. Michael went with Joe to see the cardiologist, who recommended that Joe get checked into the hospital.

On Sunday afternoon, Nora made sure that after lunch, Tommy went with the men for a round of golf. She then used the rental car and drove to the town of Windsor to visit the art gallery, where Austin Tennill's paintings were displayed. He greeted her warmly, and she was so impressed by the charming town, the gallery, and Austin. One talent Nora never had was the gift of drawing, and she admired those who had it. Austin shepherded Nora through the two-story art gallery, and she admired his many seascapes, photos of vineyards, flowers of all varieties, posters, and portraits. She was about to give up on finding the right thing when she spotted a smaller picture in a dark corner.

Austin said he had painted this when he was a young man and entitled it *Impartiality*, but people in California seemed more drawn to his larger paintings of California scenery. Nora recognized the site of the painting as the Old Bailey in London, one of the centers of the British Empire's legal profession. This area had been made famous by Charles Dickens and a number of other authors and in television shows like *Rumpole of the Bailey*.

The painting portrayed an impressive judge with his white curly wig seated at a big old desk in an old-fashioned courtroom, gesturing to several barristers, a morose-looking defendant standing in the dock, and many other people with emotion-filled faces. Nora believed that when you find something that is "just right," you knew it, and she thought that this would be the perfect painting to hang over the fireplace in Tommy's new office. They settled on a price, and Austin had the painting carefully packaged up for her.

Nora had made arrangements with Tommy's secretary Mary Lou Walsh that the painting would be express shipped to her and should be hidden so that Tommy would not see it until the night of his big party. Nora thanked Austin and said she looked forward to seeing him in Ireland when they were to begin the construction dig for the Duffy Medical Research Building in a few weeks. He thanked her for inviting him, and he hoped to be there. He was sure that he would find many places worth painting in Ireland.

On Monday morning, the Duffy's bid everyone at La Bella Maria a fond goodbye. They found Highway 1, the magnificent coastal drive that stretches the length of California. They stopped for lunch in Santa Barbara and enjoyed watching the big brown pelicans on the pier and took their pictures. The children had a surprise when the pelicans turned around and started chasing them down the pier. They continued on to Hearst Castle, San Simeon, the incredible home of the former king of newspapers William Randolph Hearst. He had acquired 250,000 acres of land and built his fabulous mansion on the top of a hill called the La Cuesta Encantada or The Enchanted Hill.

The property is so large, it was possible to go on multiple tours of the inside and outside of the building, but they had made prior reservations for the tour of the main house and swimming pool. It was a gorgeous building that exemplified that whatever the mind of man can imagine, money and talent can usually achieve.

They continued driving on Highway 1 and came to the enchanted town of Carmel-by-the-Sea, where they were to stay overnight. They visited the beautiful Carmel Mission, formally known as San Carlos Borroméo del río Carmelo. The grounds and the church were beautiful and historic, and they took advantage of the tour guide, who explained it all to them. Tommy found many places that challenged his photographic skills, and he thought that they would now have even more pictures to hang on the walls of their new home.

They took the seventeen-mile drive that led to the Pebble Beach Golf Course and admired the cypress trees and the magnificent scenery. Doctor Duffy and many of the boys decided they had to play a round of golf on this world-famous course, but they lost a number of balls. The water holes here consisted of the ocean itself, and it was windier than they thought. Their pitiful scores emphasized the fact that they would not be challenging the top golfers any time soon, but they had fun.

Eileen Duffy and the girls went to the town of Carmel and took advantage of the shopping at so many beautiful stores. They went down to the beach after they had dinner at the Carmel Steakhouse and then went to bed early.

It seemed a shame that they would be so close to Disneyland and not stop in, but Doctor Duffy assured them that they would take a trip to Disney World in the spring. There were only so many hours for this trip, and they just would not have time to take in all of California's many attractions.

On Tuesday morning, they drove through magnificent ocean vistas in Malibu and then finally arrived in Los Angeles. It was exciting to see the huge letters that spelled out HOLLYWOOD up in the hills. They called Cousin Karen, who lived nearby, and she joined them for lunch at the Hooray for Hollywood restaurant. Karen Duffy had been working in Hollywood as a screenwriter for five years now, so she was able to act as their tour guide as they hit the shops on Rodeo Drive.

Maureen said she was sure that she had seen Paris Hilton exiting from one of the stores, but there were so many beautiful people here, it might have been someone who looked like her. They took the tour buses for a guided tour of the city and returned to the hotel to get a second wind for their last night in La La Land.

They had a little excitement as they were preparing for bed when their room seemed to shake for a minute and the mermaid statue that Siobhan had bought at the farmers' market fell off the shelf and broke. The hotel desk called and told them not to worry since it was just one of the many small earthquakes that they experience frequently.

They called Janet and Joe at the vineyard to see how things were for them. The good news was that after a checkup, Joe was told he could go home if he remained relatively quiet. Janet said that after some push back about giving up control of the day-to-day activities at the vineyard, he had come around to thinking that he might enjoy being the lord of the manor. He had met the younger man that Sheila had recommended, and he seemed to think he could do a good job of taking over the busier jobs. Janet was grateful and said she hoped they would have happy years to come.

However, Auntie Anna had exerted herself so much over these past several weeks, she had been taken to the hospital with heart palpitations. The doctors told her it was time for her to get some rest too, but she was not being as pliable as her employer so far. Nora could imagine how Anna would react if she were told to relax, but she hoped she would.

Lisa Montgomery had survived her husband's brutal blows, and the doctor thought the baby should be fine, but they had scheduled more frequent doctor appointments for her. Ken Montgomery had apologized and said he realized that he needed to go to a rehabilitation facility, and he had promised to do that next month. They were all hopeful that this would actually be the case, but Lisa had heard these promises from him before, and she had moved out of her home for now and had gone to stay with her parents. She doubted that there was much hope for Ken, but she was now making their baby the focus of her concerns.

Everyone agreed that the trip had been wonderful, and the girls told Nora she had been right that they hadn't seen too many problems, other than almost being kidnapped. However, they noticed that the workers on the vineyard looked like they worked much too hard in the sun, and the only shelter they seemed to have was a small roof tent. The girls said they had also noticed that behind the mansions, there were small houses with old-looking screen doors that were open, so they must not have had air conditioning, and the kids playing outside these rickety-looking places looked poor.

Eileen Duffy was glad her children had noticed these people and hoped that they would not forget them. Most tourists just see the mansions.

Wednesday, July 17

On the way home, everyone agreed that each of the places they had visited in California deserved a month's visit rather than a few hours, and they hoped to get back to see more in the future. What a summer they had been having! They had brought home quite a collection of classic movies from places they had visited like *Vertigo*,

The Birds, Citizen Kane, Cannery Row, Play Misty for Me, and *Sunset Boulevard.*

Nora talked to the castle in Sneem, and nothing new seemed to be happening, except that Enda sounded excited that her Bill sounded as though he was getting close to proposing to her. Chief Brennan said they had been trying to make progress on the murders of the young girls and Jack Boyle, but he did not feel they were much closer to identifying the murderers. Nora talked to Matt Braxton in Chicago, and he reported a similar story about the murdered Chicago girl.

CHAPTER

27

Thursday, July 18
Chicago, Illinois; 9:00 a.m., CDT

Nora had had a perfectly ordinary day so far. Tommy was at work downtown, and they and the dogs had slept well. She had had no calls from the hospital, and she did not have to leave for her shift until this afternoon. A call to her parents and siblings, who lived nearby, revealed nothing unusual. She checked her texts and e-mail messages and saw nothing strange there. She turned on the news and did not hear anything that had not been said last night. So why was she experiencing another *fairy fey* moment, feeling that something was really amiss?

She brewed some Earl Grey tea and toasted two slices of brown bread that had been delivered yesterday from Duffy Hall Castle. The familiar smells were calming, and she felt a little better. "I suppose I should call Kitty at the castle and check with them that everything is fine there," Nora decided.

She dialed the Irish telephone code for Kerry and the number for the castle, and Enda answered on the second ring. "Enda, it's me," Nora identified herself to spare the always-happy receptionist from having to repeat the usual long greeting. "How are you today, Enda?"

"Oh, Nora dear, I'm fine, and it's a grand day here, even though we've had rain for two days straight. How are things in Chicago for you and Mr. Tommy?" Enda asked.

"We're doing fine here, and our weather has been about the same. How is your Bill doing?"

179

"He's grand, as far as I know, but he's visiting his sister for a while who lives in London. I can't wait until he gets back next Saturday."

Nora asked to speak with Fiona Finnegan, the solicitor, and Enda transferred her quickly. Nora chatted with her for a while and confirmed that everything seemed to be going well there too. Fiona reminded her that the next meeting of the Board of Directors would be in three weeks, and Nora assured her that she had it on her calendar. Fiona reminded her that they would need to make plans for the Duffy Medical Christmas meeting and ball soon, and Nora asked her to send her more details via e-mail.

Well, my Spider-Senses must be mixed up today, Nora thought to herself and decided to get dressed and take the dogs for a walk to see their friends at her parents' house. A visit with Jesse, the indefatigable housekeeper, and whoever else was home at the house should perk her up and help lessen her concerns.

On the way to her old home, Nora Duffy wondered how long the scars from psychological trauma take to heal. She would think that she had recovered from the murderous assaults that had plagued her and her family last year, but every so often, especially when she was stressed, she'd have an episode where she once again saw those bloody footprints on the flagstone floor of her castle in Ireland, and her heart would race uncontrollably.

The perpetrator was now long dead, but the evil that had been unleashed lingered on like a piece of ugly paper stuck to Nora's inner being that she could not shake loose. And now these latest murders in Ireland and in Chicago had renewed her unease.

Nora put leashes on Satin, the black cocker spaniel, and Clancy, the Irish setter, and they started out on their run to the Duffy home. Nora had to keep an eye on them since she had trouble keeping their boisterous natures in check with her small stature. She waved to the Murray's and Mrs. Brown on her way and was soon at the Duffy's door. Her old pals Reilly, the tall gray wolfhound, and Billy, the small black-and-white "Toto" mix, heard them coming and greeted them with friendly barks and briskly wagging tails and could not restrain their excitement when they saw Nora.

THE GOLDEN HORSESHOES MURDERS

Jesse heard them coming too and opened the door with a huge smile. "Bitsy, dear," Jesse greeted her with a kiss, "I didn't expect to see you this morning. Come in from the rain. Your mom and dad are already at the hospital and the others are at school. Don't you have to be at the hospital? Please tie up those dogs and put them on the sun porch. I just finished washing the kitchen floor." Jesse gave the visiting dogs a quick petting but then led Nora into the living room.

Nora assured her that her shift at Holy Savior would not start until 2:00 p.m., so she thought she would spend some time with Jesse this morning. "That's grand," Jesse responded. "I've just put a raisin coffee cake in the oven, and it will be ready soon. Sit down and tell me what your latest news is."

Nora's old cat Cheshire jumped up on her lap and waited to be petted. Nora began, "I woke up this morning feeling as though something bad was going to happen, but I've checked, and everyone seems to be all right. Is everything fine with you?"

Jesse ran both her hands through her salt and pepper curls, and Nora could see the start of tears in her eyes. "You know, I always did think that you had some fairy child in you, Bitsy dear," Jesse said, addressing Nora by her nickname. "You always seem to know when I am having a spot of trouble.

"I went for my regular mammogram yesterday," Jesse related, "and I could tell right away that they must think they saw something amiss. They took a lot more time than usual, and they did something called a needle biopsy. I'm sure they must have identified an abnormality."

Nora felt a hole open up in the pit of her stomach since judging by what Jesse told her, it did seem likely that the technicians had encountered a suspicious lump in her "other mother." Nora tried to reassure her, but she knew that uncertainty and worry plague those who are anxiously waiting for their diagnosis. Jesse had been taking care of the Duffy children since Nora was a baby and was more like a beloved family member than a housekeeper.

Nora's mind fast-forwarded to how things would have to change around the Duffy home if it were discovered that she had cancer. Nora had no doubt that Jesse would face things with her usual deter-

181

mination, but strong chemo tires out the strongest person. They would have to move her into the first-floor bedroom, and family members could take turns driving her to the hospital for tests. Well, no sense in worrying too much now. Nora asked Jesse for a piece of the warm and fragrant coffee cake and tried to continue on with their usual easy conversation.

After they had finished their snack, Jesse insisted that she would like to know what she faced if the tests were positive. "I hadn't noticed anything lumpy or hurting. You know that being prepared for the worst is better for me," Jesse said. "I've never been one to think that putting my head in the sand is a good idea. You work with children's cancers all the time, but I'm sure you can give me the best advice too."

Nora held Jesse's hand and explained, "The cells they extracted from you during your biopsy test are being analyzed now at the lab. We'll say a prayer that the results are negative and that they are only doing this as an extra precaution. Many women have dense breast tissue, so the technicians want to be sure they are not missing something. It is a good sign that you haven't noticed any lumps. You will receive a call in a few days telling you the results of the tests.

"If the tests are positive for cancer, there are a number of optimistic things to focus on. I know that you have been going for regular mammos, so anything they find should be in the early stages. The doctors at Holy Savior's breast cancer center have treated thousands of cancer cases, and they have a high success rate.

"There are different types of breast cancer, so the first thing they would do is find out which kind it is. That helps the doctors determine the best treatments to use. They would call you to schedule an education session about your proposed treatments and would give you materials to read. I could help you to understand them. They would then assign you a specialized nurse that you can call with questions and concerns. I know you have an excellent insurance policy, and that is a great thing, because cancer treatments are frequent, and each one is expensive.

"Then you and people you designate will meet with an oncologist or cancer doctor and probably also the surgeon and radiologist, who will explain the course of treatment and answer any questions.

You know that Mom, Dad, and I would be there for all of this," Nora assured her, "so you would have three additional medical professionals looking out for you. They often use chemotherapy first, which is given intravenously, probably once a week. Those treatments often kill off all or almost all of the cancerous cells by the time all the chemo treatments are finished.

"I hear various comments from women as to how they react to chemo treatments, and at least some of that involves their general predisposition to challenges in life, as well as the intense fear that people have when told they have cancer. Some women are terrified, which is understandable, especially if they are young and have children. Others, like you would be, use a 'let's get on with it' approach. It is both interesting and sad that our chemo treatment room has thirty comfortable chairs, and they are usually filled with patients all the time.

"They would likely insert a portal or tube into your shoulder area, so the chemo drugs would be put in there. The treatments themselves don't hurt at all, except a little bit for the initial needle stick, and the experienced nurses who administer the treatments know just what to do. It does tend to be cold in the room, and the treatments usually last several hours, so people bring a comfy blanket. Some watch television, many read a book or talk to the person next to them, while others even take a nap.

"After each treatment, they will do a blood test to determine if your white blood cell count has dropped, and you may need to occasionally come back for injections. I am sure you've seen those ads on TV for the patch that attaches to the back of your arm, and they will likely use that. The most common side effect from strong chemo is extreme tiredness, and some women experience this more than others. That tiredness doesn't happen for several days after the treatments. Some women experience quite a bit of nausea.

"We wouldn't want you to get out of practice though, so we'd still expect to enjoy your delicious dinners and baked goodies, at least occasionally. You could probably just stay at your house, but you could certainly stay in our first-floor bedroom. You would also lose your hair, but the hospital receives donations of wigs, and a trained person will help you decide which one looks the best on you. This is often traumatic for younger women, but I suspect you would appreciate not having to worry about curling your hair for a few months, and the wigs are cute. Many women receive more compliments on how attractive the wig is rather than when they had their own hair.

"After the chemo treatments are completed, they will do more tests and the oncologist will decide if you need surgery. Often the surgeon will just do a lumpectomy, which means they just cut out a small spot of cells, which might leave only a small scar. If needed, they might have to remove one breast or both of them, but again, there will be experts to assist you all through the process, and of course, you would have us to rely on at any time.

"After you heal up from that, they would almost certainly recommend radiation therapy. You would lie on a table next to a huge machine, and there would be lots of whirring and beeping, but those treatments don't hurt at all. I think you would find it interesting that they prepare a specific template for each person. The good news about those treatments is that the time they take is much shorter, although there are usually quite a few of them for a month or more. Some women get through them with nothing more than tiredness.

"So that's a general summary, but the treatments could take place at different times than I've mentioned. Afterward, you would have to have more frequent mammograms, but when your hair grows back, it will be cuter than ever. We'll just hope that none of this is needed, and you should be hearing from the hospital soon. By the way, be sure to tell my mom and dad about this, but please don't mention it to my brothers and sisters until we know more."

"Well, thanks, Bitsy dear, for the explanations. I think I could make it through the treatments, but I was afraid I would have to stop working for the family all together. You've made me feel much better," Jesse said with a smile. "Where does this cancer come from?"

"Well, if you can find the answer to that, you'd be a gazillionaire," replied Nora. "Doctors ask themselves that question all the time. There are so many theories about it coming from stress, the foods and drinks we ingest, smoking, the environment we live and work in, or the air we breathe, and it seems likely that it's a combination of

THE GOLDEN HORSESHOES MURDERS

all these things. Most studies show that there is a genetic connection, but even then, that's not always the case. Thousands of researchers around the world are working to find a solution, and an occasional breakthrough happens, but a cure can't come soon enough."

Nora and Jesse continued their conversation about the family and the neighborhood for a while, but Nora then gathered up the dogs, gave Jesse a kiss, and headed out the door to continue her run. She worked with cancer patients every day but had never experienced it in a family member before and did not like the prospect of it at all. She had not mentioned to Jesse that sometimes even after the treatments were done and women had survived for years, a future exam might reveal that the cancer had returned and sometimes in a different place. Cancer is an implacable foe that requires our utmost attention.

Two days later, Jesse received a call from the Holy Savior Cancer Center, telling her that the lab tests confirmed that she did not have breast cancer. However, she had dense breast tissue, so they wanted her to talk to her oncologist about having more frequent mammograms. Jesse hardly heard what they were telling her after she heard them say the tests showed no cancer!

She first called her sister Margaret to tell her the good news and then her dear friend from the parish Carolyn Swift. When Doctor and Mrs. Duffy and Nora and Tommy returned home that night, she told them about it and was so grateful for the diagnosis. She told Nora that she would be doubling up prayers for all the women who receive a positive diagnosis now that she knew the terror that they must be feeling.

Eventually, the other Duffy children found out about Jesse, and they were all thrilled and said they would do their best to make Jesse's job easier after the stress she had undergone during these past two weeks.

Saturday, July 27

The plan agreed to by Nora and Tommy's secretary Mary Lou Walsh for keeping Tommy in the dark about him being made a partner had been working so far, and they thought he did believe that tonight's party was a surprise for his boss Mr. Kornan and not for him. Mary Lou had clued Mr. Kornan in too, so he knew what to expect. Nora told Tommy that they had to be at the office by 6:00 p.m., so she could help out with the dinner, and he seemed to have bought that story well.

When it was time to get dressed, Nora told her husband that she had seen a black suit for Tommy when she was in California, and she'd ordered it for him in Chicago. She asked him to try it on, and it fit him perfectly. She knew that blue was usually his favorite color tie, but she suggested that he wear the gold and maroon stripes from his alma mater, Loyola Law School.

Nora had bought a new dress in Carmel, and she tried it on again. She usually stayed away from red since she thought it too much of a contrast with her red hair, but this dress was a darker, red and Nora thought the semiformal design flattered her short figure. It also complemented Tommy's tie. She had found a pair of red Jimmy Choo heels that she had been walking around in for a few days so that they would be comfortable for tonight.

When they opened the door of the firm, they were greeted by shouts and applause, and Tommy realized that the clapping was not about his boss but for him. He had spent several years as a hardworking associate and had become valuable as he learned more about the international law community. He was happy that Mr. Kornan and the other owners of the firm thought enough of him to give him this honor, and he was thrilled at the thought of being a partner.

He stared at Nora with a huge smile and realized that she had known all about this. No wonder she was wearing her new red dress and new shoes. Everyone was seated around the large boardroom table, and several of his friends made introductory speeches, followed by Mr. Kornan, who was always so eloquent. Tommy wished that he'd had more time to prepare remarks, but then he'd been preparing for this moment for a long time, so he was able to tell them all how happy he was about this day and what it meant to him and to Nora. He thanked them for their faith in him, much clapping ensued, and then dinner was served.

Tommy and Nora sat next to their friends Alan and Pam Pepper, and Nora told them the Ramazotti and La Bella Maria wines were in their car, and they could pick them up after the party. Pam said that her pregnancy was going well, but she had some morning sickness that was a problem. The Peppers were so happy for Tommy and said his promotion was well deserved.

Many cards and gifts were given to Tommy, and then Nora led Tommy to his new office, where the Austin Tennill painting of the Old Bailey held pride of place over his fireplace mantle. Everyone again clapped and said what a perfect gift this was for an international lawyer. One jokester said he thought that the boy in the background holding the chamber pots looked a lot like Tommy.

Tommy gave Nora a kiss and said that he loved the painting and that it was a perfect gift from a perfect woman. Nora gave him an "aw shucks" look, but she was pleased that he always knew the right thing to say. He was going to make such an articulate partner!

Nora was happy that the party had gone so well and was so timely since they were scheduled to leave to go back to Ireland, where construction of the medical research center behind Duffy Hall Castle was about to start.

CHAPTER

28

Sunday, July 28
Chicago, Illinois; 12:00 p.m., CDT

Nora had packed their suitcases during the week, so after the usual Sunday morning activities, they tried to relax for a while. This would be a quick trip to Ireland since they had been taking too many days off this summer, but Nora and Tommy were excited that the planning that had been going on for months for the start of the research center was finally going to come to fruition.

Their parents had too many things coming up in the next few days, so they would not be able to come, but many of their siblings and friends were happy that they had been invited and looked forward to the trip. Michael and Eileen gave Nora a kiss and told her they were proud of her, and they knew Uncle Cy would be too. They asked Nora to extend their greetings to the castle's staff.

Limos picked up the hearty band of travelers, and they made the trip to O'Hare once more and went through all the steps to board their Aer Lingus flight to Dublin. Nora fervently hoped they would not encounter any more violence once they arrived. The trip from Dublin to Sneem went smoothly, and they soon caught sight of the ramparts of the castle.

The staff at the castle were lined up to greet them on either side of the entranceway, such as one would see in a movie like *Downton Abbey*. They clapped for Nora and Tommy and the many guests. Tim Taylor, the veterinarian, had been holding tightly to the dogs' leashes, but they could not be controlled when they realized that their beloved mistress was back. Liam, the white wolfhound, and Bran, the Irish setter, almost knocked Nora over with their enthusiastic welcomes, and she spent a few minutes with them giving them hugs and kisses until they finally calmed down.

Mr. Sean O'Keefe, the butler, and Mrs. Sheila Doyle, the housekeeper, helped everyone to get settled in their rooms once the first-timers tired of craning their necks to look at the castle's impressive architecture and furnishings. Mrs. O'Hara was delighted to see Nora and Tommy "back where they belonged" and outdid herself with a meal of celebration. She said she was so proud of them that they were ready to add to the cachet of the castle yet again.

Nora was happy to see that Gemma Doherty had completed the huge painting of Duffy Hall Castle, and it now hung over the main fireplace in the great hall. Gemma had done a masterful job and the oil painting that reflected the ceiling lights added the finishing touch to this room that they had not realize it needed.

Siobhan sat down at the piano in the great hall, and Nora accompanied her with her violin, and the guests enjoyed being serenaded with a medley of Irish tunes. The twins could never resist the lure of Irish music, and they found their hard shoes and began to entertain the crowd with the dance they had done to win first place at their recent competition.

Finally, everyone knew it was time to get to bed since they would be expected to get up early for tomorrow's festivities. They thanked the staff for the wonderful welcome and then drifted upstairs to their rooms. Nora said a prayer to Saint Patrick that tomorrow would be as successful as all the planning promised it would be.

CHAPTER

29

Monday, July 29
Sneem, Ireland; 6:00 a.m., IST

The long-awaited day to begin construction of the medical research center behind Duffy Hall Castle on the Kerry coast dawned awash in sunshine and high hopes. Nora had woken up many times during the night, thinking of the many people and events that had led to this exciting day, but a glance at her phone now told her that it was already 6:00 a.m. She realized she was humming "Oh, What a Beautiful Mornin'" from *Oklahoma* and thought that it seemed like everything would be going her way today.

She yelled to Tommy, who was in the shower, that she was going to take a quick run, and she dressed in her new pink Skechers and blue sweats with the "If you want a helping hand, look at the end of your wrist" logo. She clipped leashes on her beautiful dogs so they could accompany her, and they were so happy to have Nora home they were behaving quite well.

She skipped down the filigree and marble staircase and was thrilled to see that just a few gray clouds appeared in the sky far out over the Atlantic Ocean. So many prayers had been said for good weather for today, and it looked as though that was going to be the case. The castle grounds looked gorgeous with summer flowers blooming abundantly in their well-manicured beds. Mr. Gilbert had done an outstanding job on the hill leading up to the castle with the huge letters that spelled out DUFFY in brilliant gold, red, and purple chrysanthemums.

She began her usual run past the red deer enclosure, waved at Bambi and his family, and was glad to see that Tim Taylor must have found the proper medication to treat the rash that had been plaguing the deer. She then jogged over to the lake to watch the ducks, geese, and swans. The bird babies that had recently been born were gaining in size every day, and she rejoiced in the circle of life that was so evident here. The dogs could sense her excitement, and Nora had trouble keeping up with them. This was one of those times when she wished she were taller than only four feet five inches so she could see better and run faster.

People had started to arrive in the parking lot already, so she changed course and ran past the tombstones of Uncle Cyrus and Aunt Emily. She sent them all her love and asked for their help today. She thought they would be so pleased that their long-ago dreams to cure people of illness and disease would be taking a big leap forward after the new research building was completed.

Nora's pink Fitbit watch confirmed that she had made the return run in record time. She arrived at the front entrance of the castle and bounded up the twenty-eight steps to the big bronze doors with the Celtic carvings. Enda the receptionist had been attempting to expand Nora's knowledge and pronunciation of Irish phrases, so Nora greeted her with *Bail ó Dhia ort* (*Bal oh Yee-ah urt*), or "the blessing of God on you."

Irish was the official language of the Republic of Ireland, and since Nora was now the owner of Duffy Hall Castle and chairman of the board for Duffy Medical, she had been practicing the basic Irish phrases, but it was hard going. Nora had been trying to devote fifteen minutes morning and evening to this pursuit, and she could now write a few respectable sentences in Irish. However, learning the English pronunciations without her guidebook was going to take more time.

Nora stopped to send a text on her phone to Hal Carmody, the construction supervisor, and asked him to meet with her in the kitchen in half an hour. She ran up the steps to her bedroom and found her handsome Tommy starting to get dressed in his charcoal gray Armani suit that made him look like a younger version of

Cary Grant in *North by Northwest*. They had been married for a few months now, but she still felt her legs go weak when he flashed his electric smile at her. They embraced and gave each other a hug, but Nora had to hurry since she'd uncharacteristically overslept.

She had ordered a new outfit for today from her favorite Irish designers. She'd turned to Louise Kennedy for a green and blue classic looking dress, a gorgeous blue velvet hat by Margaret O'Connor, and lovely and comfortable green leather boots from Kate Appleby. She was especially grateful that the boots fit well since they had to be especially made for her size three feet.

She asked Tommy to tidy up and take the dogs downstairs while she took a quick shower with the soaps that were made from the lavender clumps that grew on the castle grounds. She spent a little extra time today on her mop of long curly red hair and started to don her new clothes. As she looked in the mirror, Nora said a silent thank you to those talented women who made her look just how she had hoped she would.

Nora asked for God's help as she and Tommy ran down the stairs to face the day. She thought of the inspiring words of the psalm: "This is the day which the LORD has made; let us rejoice and be glad in it."

She was always aware of Uncle Cyrus's lingering presence when she was at the castle, and she hoped he would approve of what she had been able to accomplish so far with the huge inheritance he had left her. She chuckled as she thought of some of the jokes that he had told her over the years, and she loved the idea that he'd thought of her as his daughter. Nora also felt Aunt Vinnie's presence, but she tried to remember only the good things they had shared about flowers, perfumes, Harry the spider, and poetry.

She found Hal Carmody and a number of other Duffy Medical personnel, as well as family and friends, waiting for them in the kitchen and great room. Nora hugged all the members of hers and Tommy's extended families and friends, who were able to attend on this historic day.

Mrs. O'Hara served them all her special Irish bacon and Kerry cheese quiche with brown bread, a delicious meal that could be eaten quickly. Nora and Tommy thanked Mrs. O'Hara for all her work and greeted John O'Malley, the CEO; Duncan Lloyd, the solicitor; Fiona Finnegan, her personal solicitor; and Chief Michael Herlihy, security officer of Duffy Medical; as well as the other board members and castle staff.

She asked Mr. Carmody if he had any last-minute advice for them about what they might expect, but he said he thought everything they had talked about yesterday appeared to be right on schedule. The soil samples they'd sent to Cork had come back, and there didn't appear to be any problems that would affect the foundation of the one hundred thousand square feet building that would house laboratories, offices, a digital and book library, an auditorium, and sleeping rooms for doctors and scientists who might spend the night.

A huge throng of people had gathered at the back of the castle to watch the festivities and enjoy the castle's signature coffees, teas, and scones, as well as Tommy's straight up Coca Cola and Tayto chips. Invitations to the event had appeared in newspapers and television screens all over Ireland, and people always enjoyed the Duffy hospitality.

A large contingent of print and television media representatives from Ireland, the UK, Canada, India, Africa, and other countries where Duffy Medical had customers were in attendance, as well as many from Chicago, New York, and other US cities. Nora and Tommy said hello to many of them and promised them an interview when the morning's festivities were done.

At the stroke of 10:00 a.m., Nora intoned the music on her violin, and a group of young people on the dais from St. Brigid's Orphanage joined her and began to proudly sing the anthem that was acceptable to both the North and the South of Ireland. After the talented boys and girls were finished, the crowd was invited to join in singing the stirring lyrics of "Ireland's Call":

Come the day and come the hour
Come the power and the glory
We have come to answer Our Country's call
From the four proud provinces of Ireland.

Ireland, Ireland
Together standing tall
Shoulder to shoulder
We'll answer Ireland's call.

A group of bagpipers, drummers, and fiddlers continued playing the stirring melody as they walked around the spray-painted orange marks that outlined the perimeter of the large new building. A large throng of young children followed in their wake holding huge green, white, and orange helium balloons. The Duffy Hall white pigeons flew back and forth and added to the festive mood.

Nora and Tommy grabbed the microphone and addressed the crowd and said this was a proud day for Duffy Medical, Ireland, and the world. They thanked everyone who had helped in the planning and reminded them that it had all started fifty years ago when her uncle Cyrus and his wife, Emily, had begun Duffy Medical with just scalpels as their first products until today when Duffy Medical had become one of the premier medical supply companies in the world.

Nora asked everyone to look at the brochures that had been handed out that illustrated the limestone foundation of the new building topped by two stories of glass and steel. She assured them that everything in the building would be as ecologically friendly as possible. The building would be not only beautiful but would be a place where worldwide scientists and doctors could do research that someday might lead to a cure for baffling rare diseases.

Tommy explained that one likely disease they would be focusing on would be Tay-Sachs. This disease cripples and slowly kills the young children of some Jewish people but also affects a number of people of Irish descent. Those children suffer for years as their bodies gradually lose muscular control and they usually die before they are ten years old. The center would also be doing research on a number of other diseases that are so rare that the medical community and the pharmacology companies don't put much money into finding cures for them. Another good side effect would be that the center would be a source of employment for many of the local people. Nora and Tommy were interrupted many times by exuberant clapping and whistling.

Everyone in the crowd received a green hand digger so they could also participate in the digging. Nora, Tommy, and their smiling team grabbed their ceremonial green shovels emblazoned with the Duffy Medical logo of a four-leaf clover surrounding a gold capital D. Everyone pushed their shovels enthusiastically into the rocky Irish Kerry soil, and the loud applause continued. Lights and clicking noises from a thousand cameras recorded the scene.

The roar of Caterpillar tractors was heard as they prepared to take the first chunks of soil and limestone out of the earth. Nora gave the signal, and the tractors lunged forward and lowered their huge shovels. The plan was to have the tractors remove the soil and rocks around the perimeter of the orange marks and a large spot in the middle before the crowd was dispersed today. People gave each other high fives and toasted Duffy Medical with their drinks. Good-sized deep holes soon took shape, and anticipation ran high.

After just a few minutes of such gaiety, Hal Carmody, the construction supervisor, whistled loudly and gave the order to stop the tractors' engines. "What's going on?" the crowd asked in unison.

Mr. Carmody looked up from his binoculars and pointed to the middle of the hole on the left side, and the bystanders could see that some kind of thin brown rods were sticking up out of the ground. He walked down into the hole to take a better look, but Hal was already sure that the brown sticks were bones, and there appeared to be a lot of them. The digging would not be able to proceed until the authorities arrived to determine if the bones had belonged to animals or humans.

When Nora's grandfather Conor got frustrated, he often said, "What a revolting situation this is!" and she thought that about summed up her feelings right now.

CHAPTER

30

Monday, July 29
Sneem, Ireland; 11:00 a.m., IST

Nora reluctantly agreed that Hal Carmody was right. In a small and rocky country like Ireland, construction crews sometimes dug up the bones of ancient inhabitants and their belongings that had not been buried too deeply. If these were human bones, she asked herself a number of questions. *How did the bones get here? Why didn't we know about them? Were they ancient or recent?* If they were recent, she knew that this would be declared a crime scene until they could determine a cause of death and what to do with them. The start of construction could be delayed for a long time.

Nora got out her phone and again called her old friend Chief Jack Brennan of the An Garda Síochána and asked him to come to the castle as soon as possible and explained what had just happened. Chief Brennan responded, "Nora dear, it's disappointed I am so to hear this news. I'll be there as soon as I can, and I'll bring some gardai with me for crowd control and to seal off the entire area."

Chief Brennan was still investigating how the nude girl on the Coral Beach and the other victim at the Ballybunion Golf Club had appeared there, and who had placed a symbol of the golden horseshoes with a red slash through it on them. It was unusual for their area of the country to encounter so much violence.

Nora again called the coroner Lucy Sullivan and explained why they once again needed her help and asked her to come to the cas-

196

tle today. Lucy would be able to at least tell them if the bones were human and their approximate age.

Nora grabbed Tommy's hand and said, "Let's do a little damage control while we're waiting for the garda and the coroner to get here." Nora saw Mrs. O'Hara, their master cook, standing near the side door of the castle. She asked her to get her crew together and bring out refreshments for all the people there and serve them outside. Tommy used the bullhorn to invite the workers, bystanders, and reporters to move toward the outdoor garden, where they would find drinks and snacks. That mollified the people, whose expectations had been changed so quickly, and Nora and Tommy promised to keep them updated as they learned more. Speculation and gossip spread through the crowd like wildfire about these surprise developments and what might happen next.

Those dark gray clouds that had been hovering over the Atlantic moved over the castle grounds with surprising speed, and a cold rain began to fall, which encouraged the bystanders to make a quick exit. Mr. Gilbert and his team found large blue tarpaulins in the storage shed and covered the trench where the bones had been exposed. Nora wanted to keep the bone pit as dry as possible until tomorrow when more explorations could be performed.

Garda Chief Brennan arrived at the castle quickly, and that made Nora feel somewhat better right away. He had brought along three gardai today, and Nora recognized them and smiled her thanks to them. Tommy said he would supply the details to the chief and his team while Nora called home and updated their families on the disappointing news.

Nora first called Tommy's parents, PJ and Kathleen Barry, at Barry's Pub, which was also their home. Mrs. Barry answered the phone on the second ring with her usual greeting, "It's always a grand day at Barry's. How can I help you?" When Kathleen heard Nora's voice, she said she was so glad to hear from her and asked. "How did the festivities go?"

Nora briefly explained the events of the last few hours, asked how everyone there was, and said she had more phone calls to make, but they hoped to be home on Saturday, unless they ran into more problems. Kathleen added that her daughter Lucy and fiancé Kevin had set their wedding date for next April. "I think they may be asking you if they can use the castle as the site for their wedding around Easter, so there's a lot to figure out, but they are over the moon with excitement. Of course, Grandma O'Sullivan will be making all the dresses."

"That should work out fine," responded Nora, "although now the timing for having the new building completed is still to be determined, but Tommy and I would love it. I can't wait to talk to Lucy." *I'm so lucky to have the Barrys and their children as in-laws*, Nora reflected. *They are so talented and so much fun.*

Next, she called her parents' house and was glad that her "other mother" Jesse Meyers answered. "Your parents are at the hospital, Bitsy dear, but we've all been wondering how the opening day went for your new building." Jesse almost always used Nora's nickname of Bitsy, given to her at her birth since she was such a tiny little thing. Jesse again thanked Nora for her help in understanding what the oncologist had said about her not having cancer but reminding her to have more frequent testing. Nora told her she was still thanking St. Brigid for her help and that they would be home in about a week.

Nora explained to Jesse what had happened today and asked how everyone there was doing. Jesse gave a brief rundown on Nora's nine siblings and relayed that all seemed well, except that the dogs unfortunately had discovered a wasp nest in the backyard and suffered quite a few stings. "Your dad took care of them and they seem better today, although Reilly keeps licking his paws. Your dad called an exterminator, who got rid of the large nest in the ground." Jesse said the twins Molly and Caitlan had told her their latest news. "I think they've both been invited to the fall dances at their high schools and they need your advice." Nora and Jesse chatted for a few more minutes and then Nora said she had to go.

Nora called the Children's Cancer Clinic at Holy Savior Hospital and reached her friend Therese Cummings, who relayed that all seemed calm at the moment, but they were all anxious for her to get back. "Doctor Whiteside has been like an old bear since you've been gone. You have a way to get him to smile, which is good for all of us." Nora told Therese about the disappointing news there and said she hoped to see her next Sunday.

Lucy Sullivan, the coroner, wondered what she might face as she thought about the request from Nora Duffy to come to Duffy Hall Castle to examine bones that had been uncovered. She knew the garda were still trying to figure out how the two murdered girls got to their death sites, so all this violence was unusual.

Nora recalled when she had first met Lucy and her sister Gemma at one of the monthly festivals hosted at the castle. Most of these events were recreational, but Duffy Medical occasionally hosted a medical-themed event. Lucy had been particularly interested to attend a seminar on the reemergence of old disease foes like measles. Some parents were more concerned about the effects of inoculations, which had taken decades of work and research to perfect, than they were about protecting their children from the actual diseases. She knew that measles could have side effects, but she had learned a lot about just how dangerous this ancient foe could be. Some people experience swelling of the brain, leading to hearing loss or brain damage, pneumonia, and other complications.

Lucy also enjoyed browsing through the magnificent flowers grown in the surrounding villages at the castle's flower show and visited the tents that sold everything from antique jewelry to furniture. She and Gemma had also enjoyed delicious food and drink offerings under the dining tents that had been set up behind the castle.

Lucy recalled the excitement that had led to Nora Duffy becoming the owner of the castle and the chairman of the board of Duffy Medical. The locals were surprised to hear that Nora's uncle Cyrus Duffy had left most of his estate and fortune to Nora, whom he considered to be his daughter. That had been front page news for months. Lucy had heard that Nora, an American from Chicago, had had difficulty adjusting to the idea of being very wealthy, but it seemed as though she had worked through things well so far. Her husband, Tommy Barry, a solicitor, was certainly a good-looking guy, and they seemed to be very much in love.

Lucy would not have minded if someone had left her billions of dollars. She had grown up on the Ring of Kerry, a beautiful place for scenery and charming people, but she'd be out of there like a shot if she could afford to have houses around the world. She thought that someplace consistently warm and beautiful without much precipitation sounded ideal.

Lucy and Gemma strode through the rain, which was diminishing, and greeted Nora warmly and told her they were sorry to hear about the unexpected developments today. The two sisters said they would promptly examine the bones. Mr. Gilbert, the groundskeeper, and his crew led them to the pit and said they were standing by to help. Lucy said she was glad they had not disturbed the bones that would be better examined in situ. The sisters put on their waterproof outfits and boots and jumped down into the pit. After a brief look at the bones, Lucy declared that they seemed to come from various animals like horses, deer, sheep, and dogs. This must have been the burial site for favorite animals of the castle's owners. Nora started to breathe a sigh of relief, but Lucy said they had more disturbing news for her.

Gemma pointed out to Nora that a few of the bones were almost certainly human. She showed her some that had remnants of dark blue material attached to them, possibly fabric from a garment like a jean jacket with silver buttons. The shape of the pelvis indicated that it was likely that these particular bones belonged to an adolescent female person, although there was no skull attached to the spine, which would give them more confirmation. They would have to do more looking amidst the bones tomorrow, but Lucy wanted more help from an expert forensic pathologist before proceeding.

CHAPTER

31

Monday, July 29
Sneem, Ireland; 12:00 p.m., IST

Lucy Sullivan knew that there was a time constraint about this investigation, so she promptly called her more experienced coroner colleague Aloysius Stec, the "Polish prince," and asked for his assistance. Nora said she had heard about this famous pathologist with the Polish name and the very pronounced Irish brogue. She hoped that Aloysius would be available on such short notice.

The story Nora had heard was that Aloysius's great-grandparents had seen the handwriting on the wall about the coming of war in 1935 and moved from Krakow to Cork. Edward Stec spoke some English at that time, but there were no job openings in Ireland for Polish professors with a royal past. He was happy to be alive and free and was willing to work hard. Through a friend, he became a farmer, and he and his wife, Ewelina, spent the war years raising wheat and children while grieving for their relatives and friends who were caught up in the Nazi blitzkrieg.

One of Edward's best friends in Poland was Anton Erlich, a Jew who refused to listen to the warnings about the Nazis' ambitions and thought they were exaggerated. In 1940, Edward heard the terrible news that the Erlich family was one of the first to be sent to Auschwitz, and they were never heard from again.

The Stecs grew to love Ireland and their neighbors and vowed to give their children as good an education as possible in their new land. After three generations, the family spoke English with as fine an Irish brogue as could be wished. Aloysius's cousin, like many other emigres, had changed his name to Stark to better fit in with the Irish population, but Aloysius was proud of his heritage and refused to anglicize his name. He did not currently practice any religion, but he did give pride of place in his home to the Polish Madonna that his great-grandparents had brought with them. He also did not like nicknames, especially his own. If someone called him Al, he reminded them that he preferred to be called by his full name Aloysius. "And no," he would say, "it's not Aloy-sius. It's Alo-i-sius."

Aloysius had blond wavy hair, bright hazel eyes, and wore tailored suits that enhanced his athletic body. He was often seen squiring different women to dining or recreational events, but the rumor was that he was the epitome of the confirmed bachelor. He lived in a newer home with all the mod cons that faced Cork Harbour. He rather enjoyed hearing people call him the Polish prince and purported himself accordingly. He felt most comfortable when everything around him was clean and organized, and he kept himself, his home, and his laboratory in the same fashion. "Everything in its place" was his religion. He had developed a reputation as being as thorough and knowledgeable as could be, and the garda often called him in to examine unusual cases.

Many coroners developed a habit of cloaking the more distasteful aspects of their difficult profession by making jokes about death. Aloysius had a fine sense of humor, but he would never do that, and he discouraged it among his team. His grandparents' reverence for life and fear of anything that would lessen it were always fresh in his mind. Whether he was prodding the remains of a body filled with maggots or holding a puzzling bone in his hands, he treated every part of the human body with reverence and remembered that, not so long ago, this person was as alive as he was. He felt he owed it to the owner of those bones to find out why this person had ceased to be among the living.

Aloysius and his assistant Paul McShane arrived at the castle to meet Lucy, Gemma, and Nora and were cordially welcomed with tea and scones. Lucy found Aloysius to be very good looking, but Aloysius was all business. She filled him in on why she needed his assistance and the reason for the hurry in this case. Nora said she would make arrangements for a waterproof tent to be erected over the animal pit tomorrow. For now, they could use the gardening room at the back of the castle as their office. Aloysius and Paul removed their suits, changed into their lab gear, and were directed to the bone pit.

Lucy and Gemma had already separated some of the bones into piles of animal and human bones, but she asked him to take another look just to be sure. Aloysius was disappointed that they had moved any of the bones, and he asked them not to do any more with them until he had had a chance to do measurements and sketching of what the digging had revealed. His trained eye agreed with her conclusions about the animal bones, and then he turned his attention to those she thought could be human. Lucy reminded him that the construction crew had stopped digging early on, so there were probably many more bones to be found.

After some preliminary assessments and an initial examination, Aloysius and Paul began to construct a skeleton. The careful pathologists counted and catalogued the bones as they went along. The skull was missing, as were many of the 206 bones that belong to an adult human. Bones from the middle of the excavation site likely belonged to an adolescent female person judging by the heart-shaped pelvic area bones. It was clear that they were recent, probably less than ten years old. The pieces of clothing stuck to the rib cage were tattered but still recognizable.

When Aloysius found more than two femurs, it was apparent that there was likely a second body too, most likely a male. They began to move away from the central area and kept looking for a skull or two. Chief Brennan had asked them to look for telltale signs of violence, but that was hard to assess when the bones had been all jumbled up in the very moist earth. They recorded anything that might indicate a violent attack, and some of them did have nicks and scratches, but that could have been from natural causes.

The persistent rain kept falling, and the pathologists decided it was more important to keep the bone pit as dry as possible, so they planned to return tomorrow. They had constructed the skeleton pieces on adhesive cloth, and they very carefully moved this exhibit into the room at the back of the castle. They gratefully accepted the offer to clean up and then have lunch.

Lucy explained to Nora that some of the bones were human and likely belonged to an adolescent female as well as a possible male, so the site would have to be shut down for the foreseeable future. They would be coming back out there tomorrow morning to see if they could find more pieces of possibly two skeletons. She asked Nora to make sure that the garda had surrounded the crater with crime scene tape until they had a chance to determine if this was a case of homicide. Nora had called an exhibition company in Killarney, and they arrived and constructed a temporary tent over the entire area of the bone pit.

Nora recoiled from the impact of the word homicide since she recalled only too well the murder that had taken place at Duffy Hall Castle just a few months ago. She relayed Lucy's information to Garda Chief Brennan and asked him to look through the police records to see if there were missing young persons in the area from ten years ago or less.

Nora was disappointed with the construction delay, but she was most concerned with how a young woman, and possibly a young man as well, had ended up in a pit that must have been tradition-ally used to bury animals from the estate. Nora had many ques-tions for Hal Carmody, the construction head, and Mr. Gilbert, the groundskeeper. *Did they use modern planning and excavation methods to determine what was underneath the ground? Why didn't anyone know about the animal pit?*

Uncle Cyrus and Aunt Lavinia, former owners of the castle, were both dead now, and Mr. Gilbert had not been in his position too long, but it seemed as though someone should have been aware of the buried animals. Nora had talked to one of their neighbors a few times, an old woman named Kathleen McGrew, and she wondered if she might know more than they did about the castle grounds. Nora would try to visit her later today.

Nora could feel herself getting angry that after all the detailed planning that had been done, not one person had mentioned any-thing about an animal pit on the grounds. She had only been the owner of the castle for a few months, and her uncle Cy had never mentioned anything about it. Not only was this embarrassing to have happened in full view of the reporters and television cameras, but a protracted delay could lead to additional problems from the Kerry weather that was always unpredictable as it got closer to the start of winter.

Nora jogged over to Mrs. McGrew's home and asked her if she knew about the animal pit, but she said the castle had been abandoned for decades before her uncle Cy purchased it, so the animal bones must be really old indeed. It looked as though the mystery surrounding these bones was not going to be solved any time soon. There would likely be a long delay before they could start the digging again.

CHAPTER

32

The dogs were always sensitive to Nora's moods and nuzzled her hands to see if that would help. Nora was grateful for their companionship but noticed that Bran needed some grooming attention. Irish setters needed frequent washing and trimming to keep that flowing red coat glossy and tangle free. The more rugged wolfhounds didn't need as much careful attention, but she was sure Liam wouldn't mind having a wash too. She added that to the reminders on her phone's to-do list.

Nora had previously arranged for their guests to go on a tour of the Ring of Kerry towns with her favorite guide, John O'Shea, and he arrived at the castle with his tour bus. It was only 1:00 p.m., so they should have time to proceed with the 111-mile tour. The guests were thrilled with the scenery, the history, and the shopping opportunities.

They returned to the castle in time for a rest and a wash and change of clothes and then headed into Sneem for dinner at the Sneem Hotel. Tommy had told them about the fairy houses and Pyramids near the hotel and said that if they had time, they could take the walking trail among them. They enjoyed the delicious dinner and the interesting conversation, and they said they would like to take a walk. It was a beautiful night, and they all acknowledged Nora's generosity.

They headed back to the castle and spent the evening sipping wine and sharing stories while the soothing music of Enya played in the background. They talked about what the discovery of human bones might mean for the research center and wondered how long such a delay would last. Gradually, they ran out of steam and drifted off to their bedrooms.

Nora called her parents in Chicago who had been unable to come to Ireland at this time since they had busy schedules at the hospital. Eileen Duffy shared stories about the local news, and Doctor Duffy told Nora about Holy Savior's gossip mill.

Chief Brennan arrived at the castle and revealed that they had found records of ninety missing young Irish people from ten years ago or less. There were notations on the records that most of the cases had already been solved, in one way or another, but they had begun the process of checking up on those that remained. Several of the missing came from the Travellers people, also known as Tinkers or Gypsies, who could be found at various places on the Ring of Kerry. Since they moved so frequently, it was difficult to know if they were really missing. He told her that he was hopeful their work would pay off soon. Nora offered him a piece of lemon meringue pie that she had brought home from the hotel, and the chief looked more relaxed than she had seen him in some time.

CHAPTER

33

Nora had plans for the day, so she asked Kitty and Sean Duffy to act as hosts and tour guides for their guests who were still at the castle. Since the external construction of the Duffy Medical Research Center would be delayed for possibly a long time, Nora called Mr. Jack Gainer, director of the Restoration Company, and asked if they could speed up their plans to excavate the old ruined section of Duffy Hall Castle. Mr. Gainer told her that they first had to ensure that the roof and loose stones that had fallen in were removed and catalogued so they could be reconstructed later. They especially had to make sure that the remaining walls were stable enough to stand alone.

Mr. Gainer and a conservator archeologist Doctor Alice McGillicuddy came out the next day and said they would begin by making measurements on the inside of the castle's rooms that faced the backyard and the caved-in part of the old castle. After a few hours' work, they told Nora that it was just possible that there could be a hidden room, which appeared to be adjacent to the library. It was the only thing they thought could account for the difference in measurements. Such rooms were fairly common in the homes and castles from the 1600s.

Nora led them to the library, her favorite room in the castle. She had nicknamed it "Emily's domain" since it was Uncle Cy's wife who had first decorated this room so beautifully with an eye for traditional decor while ensuring that the books and their organization were the main focus.

After more measurements, knocking on walls, and crawling on the floor, Doctor McGillicuddy said she wondered if there could be a small opening into the hidden room under the library's lower shelf in the north corner. She asked permission to remove the many priceless books that sat on the lower shelf, and she and her team carefully piled them up on a nearby table.

The archeologist preferred to be called Doctor M., and as she had hoped, there appeared to be a small sliding door underneath that bottom shelf. Nora had certainly not been aware of it before, and no one had mentioned anything about it.

Nora remembered the stories about the opening of King Tut's tomb in Egypt when so many of the "first openers" died soon afterward. Initially, it was reported that Lord Carnarvon and his teammates had died because of "the mummy's curse," but scientists thought it likely that at least one contributing factor to these deaths was the ancient bacteria and mold-laden dust they had inhaled that had destroyed their lungs.

The Duffy Hall hidden room would be much more recent, but no sense in taking chances. After more knocking and listening, the Restoration Company and Doctor M. drew up detailed plans for how they would approach opening up the small door and the safety procedures they would need to follow when they did so. They told Nora it would take them a few days to formalize the plans and order the necessary safety equipment.

Two days later, Nora and Tom met with Sean and Kitty Lloyd, the caretakers of the castle; Mr. Gilbert, the groundskeeper; Mr. Gainer from the Restoration Company; and Doctor M. They discussed what they might be likely to find in a hidden room in an old castle and what the plan would be if they found anything of value.

Each person who was going to enter the hidden room was outfitted with a "moon suit" and boots, safety helmet, laser lamp, protective glasses, knee pads, gloves, and a good quality breathing mask as they prepared for the unknown. They also had small containers with them in which to place samples. They were concerned that the collapse of the old part of the castle might have also damaged the stability of the room itself, and they discussed what they would do if that proved to be true. They had cell phones to communicate with each other and to take pictures, but they also brought along several cameras.

Nora made sure that her breathing mask and laser lamp were working, and she turned on the recorder that hung from her neck. Since she was the smallest of the group, she went first. She lay on her stomach and tried to push open the sliding door. It was easier than she thought, and as she crawled crablike into the opening, Mr. Gilbert asked her if she could see anything.

"To paraphrase Howard Carter when he first saw the interior of King Tut's tomb," Nora responded, "yes, wonderful things." She said that from what she could see so far, this must have been a "priest's hole" or chapel where a priest would have come to celebrate Mass with his small congregation when it was against the law to do so in Ireland. King Henry VIII's laws like this lasted for hundreds of years and were only set aside in 1829.

There were plentiful spiderwebs, which she swallowed hard and brushed aside. She knew these small and fascinating arachnids provided a useful role in creation, but only a real gardener like Aunt Vinnie could appreciate spiders. Vinnie had told her that Ireland did not have too many venomous spiders, but Nora hoped not to encounter any of them. She placed some of the web material in a sample jar and moved on.

Once she could stand up and focus the laser lamp, she was astonished to see a beautifully carved white altar with a large crucifix above it, several statues of saints, and ten long benches. She could see several cabinets with closed doors, as well as fourteen carved stations of the cross depictions and woven tapestries on the walls. She kept a running commentary going so that the others could hear what she was seeing.

There were also five large wooden trunks along the walls, and she was anxious to see what they contained. Nora was tempted to sit down on one of the benches to get a more relaxed view of things, but she did not want to disturb the dust or any critters that might be around. She yelled out that she would start taking pictures, and she encouraged Tommy and Alice to suck in their stomachs so they could squeeze through the narrow opening and join her.

Nora asked Tommy to take the measurements of the room with the surveying equipment he had brought along. He also kept taking pictures of the altar and walls. Nora asked Doctor M. to join her in opening the chests. The doctor asked Nora to please call her Alice. They planned to catalogue everything they found on their phones, but they also brought along a computer as well as pens and paper, just in case modern technology was not working, to make sure they didn't miss anything. Their gloves should prevent them from putting their fingerprints on anything they found, but they made sure they fitted tightly and brought extras along.

Nora and Alice turned their attention to the first wooden chest that was about four feet wide and three feet tall. It would have been built according to metric measurements, so the inches and feet were approximate. The chest had been painted a dark green, and the cover was decorated with carved Gaelic runes. Tommy's carpenter eyes noticed that the chest had been masterfully built. They were afraid the chest would be locked, but it opened fairly easily after a few squeaks. The contents were covered by an animal skin, probably cow leather. After taking several pictures of everything, they began to lift the covering carefully and set it aside on the plastic mats Alice had brought along.

The animal skin had been covering a number of pieces of cloth-ing and cloth—altar cloths trimmed with intricate Irish lace, albs and belts for the priest to don, small linen cloths, and still-brilliant chasubles or cloaks in several colors. The garments appeared to be fragile but were in surprisingly good shape after two hundred years. Alice asked them not to unfold anything just now, but each piece was photographed and catalogued and then returned to the chest. They were excited and held onto each other's hands as they realized they were the first people to see these linens in more than two centuries.

They moved on to the second chest, which seemed much heavier, whose contents were similarly protected by a leather cover-ing. Within, they found metal objects that appeared to be made of gold, such as chalices, patens, censers for incense, and a magnificent monstrance that would have held a consecrated host during benediction. Nora could see that underneath her protective glasses, Alice was looking a little pale as the import of these discoveries was revealed.

The third chest's contents did not appear to be connected with a religious service but brought gasps of astounded recognition from Nora and Alice. There were twelve paintings by famous artists such as Michelangelo, Leonardo da Vinci, Rembrandt, Rubens, Pisanello, Plutarch, and more. They pulled them out of the chest just enough to see the signatures and then slid them back again. Some of these paintings were likely much older than the objects in the chests they had already examined. The paintings would all have to be examined by experts, but if they were authentic, this chest held a fortune in lost art. Why were they here? Who had they belonged to? What a miracle that they had survived so well and how lucky were they to be their discoverers!

It took them some time to catalogue the contents of chest three, and then they turned their excited attention to chest four. By this time, they thought that nothing would surprise them, but they were wrong!

Under another leather covering, they found a cache of books. At the top were prayer books and song books in Latin and Irish and several Douay-Rheims Bibles. Alice removed the Bibles and then gave a startled cry. At the bottom were volumes by Aeschylus, Cicero, Chaucer, Jonson, Bacon, Dante, and others. Alice was so excited she could barely suppress yelling as each book was revealed.

Way at the bottom, wrapped in a separate protective covering, was a little volume that Alice recognized immediately but thought it must surely be a fake. She put on fresh gloves, touched the book gingerly, opened the cover ever so slowly, and realized that it might be real after all! It appeared to be a lost First Folio of Shakespeare's first thirty-six plays published in 1623, including eighteen plays that had not previously been published. About 750 First Folios had originally been printed, and there were supposedly 235 known to exist today, some of which were incomplete. These books are among the most valuable in the world, worth many millions of dollars or pounds.

Perhaps their little volume was a complete copy and the 236th? What a dramatic discovery that would be!

The cover proclaimed it contained *Mr. William Shakespeare's Comedies, Histories, & Tragedies*. On the title page was the telltale "Droeshout portrait," the only known portrait of Shakespeare that was considered authentic. On the page preceding the portrait was the introduction by Ben Jonson, Shakespeare's nearest literary rival:

> This Figure, that thou here feest put,
> It was for gentle Shakespeare cut:
> Wherein the Grauer had a strife
> with Naure, to out-doo the life:
> O, could he but haue dravvne his vvit
> As vvell in frasse, as he hath hit
> Hisface; the Print vvould then surpasse
> All, that vvas euer in frasse.
> But, since he cannot, Reader, looke
> Not on his picture, but his Booke.

Tucked into the back of the book were folded sheets of fragile paper. Alice gingerly unfolded the pages just slightly, and it appeared to be a play titled *The King of Ireland* that had been signed by William Shakespeare. Could this possibly be real?

Alice quickly scrolled through the list of the famous author's plays in her mind and recognized that this work was likely a "foul paper," or working draft of a completely unknown work by Shakespeare. Alice held her breath as she calculated how much such a document by the Bard would be worth and the excitement around the world this would cause! She resisted the temptation to open the pages to read more. She would wait until she could get it back to her laboratory to open it in safe and appropriate conditions.

The small cabinet under the altar held glassware, candles, unconsecrated hosts that still seemed to be usable, teas and teapots, cups and saucers, and cleaning supplies—all of them also antiques.

Alice told Nora that they would have to call in more experts to examine everything. Nora breathed a prayer of thanks that the treasures in this long-hidden room seemed to be completely intact. As usually happened with her active mind, she had fast-forwarded already to what a television program these discoveries would make!

How did they get here, and what would they do with them? Should they remain here or be given to museums or libraries in Dublin or London or Chicago or other places around the world? What would this mean for Duffy Medical and the Duffy Family?

As soon as Nora crawled back into the library and removed her breathing mask, she called Fiona Finnegan and Duncan Lloyd, solicitors for Duffy Medical; told them of the treasures they'd found; and asked them to begin to research how to protect these discoveries and to find out what legal questions they thought they would encounter. *Would they belong to Duffy Hall Castle since they had been found here?*

Nora thought that this was a good example of Newton's third law of motion: "For every action, there is an equal and opposite reaction." They would have even more wealth and fame now, but the price to pay was more worldwide scrutiny.

Alice advised Nora and Tommy and the others at the castle to keep quiet about the discoveries for now since violent robberies and murders had been known to be committed over far less. She thought they should not even send texts to their families or make phone calls about them until they could think carefully about how to proceed.

These priceless items had been protected now for hundreds of years from light and dust, and she strongly suggested they leave them where they were. She also told them they should hire extra security for the entire castle until things had been sorted out.

Nora and Tommy thanked Mr. Gainer and Alice profusely for their help so far and invited them to stay for dinner. They talked far into the night about the historical period that these pieces had come from and the laws that would have driven a Catholic community to take refuge in a hidden room. They started to think about the potential value of the items and what should be done with them.

Alice said she had been thinking that since the walls surrounding the hidden room had collapsed so long ago, she wondered if they should get them out of the hidden room sooner rather than later. She would not want their efforts to contribute to the collapse of any more walls. They could order large strong safes for now and insert the treasures in them until they decided how else to proceed. There must be a larger opening somewhere into the hidden room that had enabled the community to get the benches and chests into the room, and they would do more looking to find this. For now, Alice could order protective bags for the treasures, and they could remove them one by one.

Finally, they realized that it was almost 11:00 p.m., and Mr. Gainer and Alice said goodnight and left the castle. Nora found it impossible to sleep as she contemplated who had put all these priceless objects in the hidden room and what would be happening next. She wondered what Uncle Cy would think about these treasures that had been completely unknown to him when he had purchased the castle so long ago. She asked God to give them guidance so that they would make the right decisions, and she tried not to think too much about Alice's words that "murders had been committed over far less." She did not need any more exposure to murderers!

What a difference a day makes! Yesterday, they didn't even realize these treasures were there, but now that they knew about them, protective measures needed to be taken immediately. In the morning, she called in Chief Herlihy and asked him to hire a team of quality armed security people to surround the perimeter of the castle. She did not explain why they were needed, but the chief saw the anxiety in Nora's eyes, and he had a team in place by noon.

Nora also gave a call to Garda Chief Brennan and told him what was happening. She did not tell him why armed guards were needed, but she wanted him to know they were there. The chief was curious but did not press Nora for more details, but she knew she would have to tell him eventually.

A watchful neighbor saw the security vehicles pull into Duffy Hall Castle's parking lot carrying a contingent of armed men. He wasn't born yesterday and figured out that something very valuable must have suddenly been unearthed in the castle in this out of the way town. He intended to scope things out and see if he should be thinking about acquiring whatever it was for himself.

Nora and Tommy finished up their exciting adventures and then returned their attention to their guests' comfort. The guests would be leaving in the morning to return to Chicago, so they celebrated their stay with one of Mrs. O'Hara's delicious dinners and a sing a long in the great hall.

CHAPTER

34

Thursday, July 31
Sneem, Ireland; 5:00 a.m., IST

Nora and Tommy helped the guests who had come to celebrate the aborted dig for the medical center to prepare for their trip home. They all gave each other hugs and kisses, and Nora assured the twins that she would be home in a few days. Old Tim McMahon made sure that all the guests and their luggage were safely stored away, and then they left to get to Dublin Airport.

Nora checked her messages on her phone and saw that she had a text from one of her friends Cathy O'Mara. Nora wondered how things had been going for Cathy and her husband, Adam. She had told her quite a story about their journey trying to adopt a child.

Cathy was one of the volunteers who helped out with the castle tours. She had told Nora that she wished she could get pregnant, but she had had three miscarriages. She and her husband, Adam, had talked it over and decided they'd like to adopt.

Nora had told her about the lovely St. Brigid's orphanage that Uncle Cy had helped so much over the years. Cathy said she would be interested in going there, so Nora arranged the visit to St. Brigid's by the thirty-five-year-old couple. Adam and Cathy O'Mara talked to Sister Mary Ann about what they had in mind and wondered if there would be a child like that at this orphanage.

Cathy relayed some of the details of the orphanage visit to Nora. Sister Mary Ann said one way they had to help couples like the O'Maras to help make their decision was to watch the children at play outside from a large window. Then they did the same inside from a two-way mirror into the dining room. After doing both, the O'Maras said they would like to know more about one of the older girls, the one with the long brown hair in a ponytail. They noticed that she frequently left her place to help the younger children. Sister Mary Ann said she could arrange for them to talk to the girl Peggy O'Reilly, but she warned them that Peggy had been asked for before but always told them that she had decided that she would just stay at the orphanage.

"Why?" queried Adam O'Mara. "Is there something wrong with her?"

Sister Mary Ann said that Peggy was very smart but had special needs of an unusual kind. She would arrange for them to talk to her, and they could make their own decision afterward. The O'Maras followed the smiling nun into a side office that was tastefully decorated in old fashioned decor. She said she would send Peggy in to talk to them, and she would return when they were finished.

Peggy entered the room soon after, and they introduced themselves to each other. Peggy sat down on the settee across from their chairs, and it was not until then that they noticed that she had a large red scar that ran the length of her left cheek. Peggy sat ramrod straight and waited for the couple to make the introductory remarks. She recognized their encouraging but nervous smiles from the last time a couple had asked to adopt her.

"Peggy, we came here today prepared to do whatever is needed to adopt a child," said Adam, a youngish looking man with curly brown hair and a happy smile. "We've watched you for several hours today, and you look like the type of child we think would be happy in our home. We are not wealthy, but we are fairly well off. You would have your own room, and St. Michael's school is just two blocks away. There are many children in our neighborhood, and you could make new friends. Sister Mary Ann told us that you are very smart and love to read. We have many books at our house, and we live near the university library.

"You'll want to know something about us: I'm a successful car dealer, and my wife, Cathy, teaches fifth grade at a nearby school. We like to have fun on the weekends, and we try to do something interesting. We often take trips around Ireland and occasionally to other countries. Our parents are alive, so you'd have grandparents too and some aunts, uncles, and cousins. We've been married for ten years but we haven't been able to have a child."

Cathy O'Mara had a hopeful grin on her freckled face as she explained that they had heard about the orphanage through her friend Nora Duffy, who had invited them to come here. "Would you consider coming home with us for a few weeks to see what we and our home are like?"

Peggy stared at the couple with a crooked smile and then began to speak in a harsh whisper. "Mr. and Mrs. O'Mara, you seem like a wonderful couple, and I'm sure you'll make great parents for some lucky child. I do not believe that child is me. You are offering me what all of us kids here dream about. By the time we are five years old, we realize that although we're well cared for by the nuns, have plenty of food, and receive a good education, we'd rather live with a loving family. Most kids get to leave here before they are my age.

"I've thought about it a few times, but I want to be honest with you and tell you why I don't believe I'm adoptable material. I'm damaged goods in more ways than one. I have no idea who my father was, but my mother was a prostitute until she was knifed to death. Before I came here five years ago, I had been abused in too many different ways. I'm ugly because of this burn scar on my face, and I'm messed up mentally. I made up my mind last year that I would just bide my time here until I'm eighteen years old, and then I'll pursue higher education and get a job that doesn't require too many relationships with other people.

"You want someone that you can love and who will love you back and that you can be proud of. I thank you for even considering me, but there's a little girl downstairs, Patty Butler, who just had her fifth birthday, and she is just dying to be adopted. She is so sweet and pretty, and I think she'd be perfect for you. I hope you understand, and I wish you good luck."

Cathy responded to Peggy by asking her to tell them a little more about herself. Peggy continued in a monotone voice, "I can see that you think I'm exaggerating, but one of my earliest memories was watching my mother and one of her men have sex. They were both making so much noise, I thought he was hurting her, so I picked up a bottle and started hitting him. I was too small to do much damage to him, but he was furious and picked up my mother's hot curling iron and deliberately put it on my face and my back. My mother was too strung out on drugs to help me, and she was mad too because she wanted the money. They locked me in the bathroom, and I remember screaming for a long time.

"Other men did terrible things to me that I can't talk about. I'm smart and strong, and I'm a good worker, but I often have nightmares and panic attacks. My burns require frequent care that is painful and brings back terrible memories. Even though I know my mother did bad things, I miss her. I used to cry a lot, but I think I've forgotten how to do that. I'm pretty much of a mess, and there's no way to fix things.

"The nuns have been good to me and discovered that one way to help me on my bad days is to let me spend time in the chapel. I don't think I believe in God, and I gave up praying a long time ago, but it's comforting to think of Mary as our mother. The quiet dark and the smell of the beeswax candles calm me down. Many people like to clean, but for me, it's therapy. It makes me feel better to scrub the chapel floor tiles over and over, although no amount of soap and brushing can make me clean like a ten-year-old should be.

"Sister Cecilia told me that I'm like Mrs. Macbeth who kept saying, 'Out, damn spot.' I've become useful around here because I like to take care of the flowers, and I've learned to play the piano. I notice when the little kids have some need that I can fix, but I don't think I know what it means to love them. You'd be better off with someone uncomplicated like Patty. She's only here because her parents were killed in an accident."

Peggy stood up and shook hands with the O'Maras and turned to leave, but Adam asked her a question that stopped her in her tracks: "We don't want someone who's sweet and pretty, Peggy. We want you. Won't you give us a chance? We've just moved into a new house, and if nothing else, you could help us clean up all the dust and get the garden started since those are things you like to do. We'd all know after a few weeks whether it was a good idea or not."

Cathy O'Mara, a blond cheerleader type, held out her hands to Peggy, who grabbed them for dear life.

Cathy's text reported the good news to Nora that things were off to a bit of a rocky start, but they were going to be bringing Peggy home with them today. She told Nora that she would tell her more about everything in a few days. Nora responded that she was thrilled for all of them and hoped that everything would turn out very well.

Nora had a call from Chief Brennan, who said he would like to come to see her and explain what he had found out so far in their investigations of the two skeletons found in the bone pit at Duffy Hall Castle. He explained that he and Molly Norris had visited St. Michael's high school and interviewed the principal, Mrs. Mary Meachem. They told her that they were investigating the disappearance of at least one and possibly two students of Travellers' families who used to attend St. Michael's high school. They said their research led them to believe that the pair might be Tia Taylor and Jake Madden who had disappeared about six years ago.

Mrs. Meachem told them that that school was not yet in session with children present, which would not happen for another two weeks. She had only been at the school for four years, so she would have no firsthand knowledge about the students they mentioned, but Dr. Richard Allenby, the history teacher, was there at the time. He seemed to have a personal mission to help the Travellers kids and knew how to get their attention.

Mrs. Meachem told them that Doctor Allenby taught a world history course that was fascinating. "I make all the teachers take it too. He starts with an overview of the earth when all the land mass was unified as Pangaea. Over eons of time, this one piece of land floating on the oceans gradually split up to produce the various continents we are familiar with. He also explains how the various countries developed and concentrates on Ireland and the British Isles but also includes all the other current countries on earth.

"If any student has a spark of curiosity, they usually get interested in the course and write fascinating papers about a particular country and its more important physical and cultural features."

Mrs. Meachem said she would introduce the doctor to them and took them to the teachers' lounge, where Doctor Allenby was having a cup of tea and talking with two other teachers. Mrs. Meachem asked the history teacher to come and speak with their visitors.

The garda are naturally watchful of all the people they interview, but Doctor Allenby seemed to be a strange one. Everyone had mentioned how intelligent he was, but then, why was he teaching at a small high school in a remote part of the country rather than at a university? They asked him that question.

"The short answer is that colleges and universities want their teachers to give more of themselves than I'm willing to do at this stage of my life. They want their professors to take more courses and write books, but that would interfere with the three hobbies I've developed over the years—music, languages, and travel. My position at St. Michael's High School enables me to take advantage of all of them.

"Last summer, I went to Nashville, Tennessee, and visited Elvis Presley's Graceland and the Grand Ole Opry. On my next break, I'm going to Poland to a conference on Chopin and polkas. Next summer, I'm going to Berlin to attend all five of Wagner's Ring Cycle operas. I've been teaching history here for so long it's easy for me to do. My high school students for the most part think that I am smarter than they are, which is nice. Quite a few college students these days would try to prove that it was the other way around. I'm happy with things the way they are," said Doctor Allenby.

Chief Brennan's assistant Molly said she had heard the words that Doctor Allenby said, and they sounded reasonable, but she was still skeptical about his explanation. Molly asked Doctor Allenby why he had developed an interest in the Travellers people, and he responded that it originally started out of curiosity about their Shelta language. Then he had gotten to know a few of the students and found them fascinating. They were strongly tied to their nomadic way of life, and most of them spoke some version of Shelta as their first language. He had wanted to know more about that and took a personal interest in helping these people enter the modern world, if they wanted to.

"As for Tia Taylor, she was a sad and fascinating girl. She was very smart, but she'd learned to keep that side of her suppressed. She was not beautiful in the conventional manner, but her face held your interest. She had her mother's prettiness around her nose and mouth, but her hazel eyes and broad forehead came from her father. She had long curly chestnut hair. She could understand complicated math problems, and she seemed to love history. She was stuck in the middle between wanting to be part of the 'settled' community but still drawn to her family's way of life.

"Her mother was probably very pretty as a young person, but these Tinker ladies have to work much too hard and have too little money, so they don't stay attractive for long. Tia's mother, Giselda, made an attempt to provide an education for Tia by working at our school as a classroom assistant off and on. Many of the Travellers' girl children don't get much formal education since they are married off before they are twenty. After that, they are expected to just be wives and mothers and nothing more.

"I met the father once, a large hulk of a man with piercing dark eyes. Most of their men have difficult lives and work in the metals industry or farming. As their wagons traveled around, these men used to sell and repair metal pots, so they were known as Tinkers, which today is considered a pejorative term. Mr. Taylor had become hard as nails and had no qualms about taking his frustrations out on his wife and daughter. Every few weeks, Tia would show up for class with a red slash on her cheek or a purple eye.

"A few weeks before she disappeared, she wrote me a heart-breaking note. I kept it in case anyone wanted to know more about what she was like, but after the first few weeks of her disappearance, no one asked me about her. I keep yearly files in my file cabinet, and I should still have a note that Tia wrote to me shortly before she disappeared."

Doctor Allenby opened a bottom drawer and removed a large file folder for 2014. He looked through it and showed them a piece of blue paper with carefully drawn lettering.

Dear Doctor Allenby,

I like hearing you talk about things that have happened in the world before us. I think I could learn about these things, and I'd like to be a teacher like you some day. But I would have to leave my family to do that, since our girls are expected to get married young. Timmy Beatty is a nice guy, and we're supposed to announce our engagement next month, but I don't want to get married yet, and not to Tim. If I don't, my father will take it out on my mam, and he might kill me. There's another boy, Jake, that says he likes me, but it's the kind of liking I want no part of.

If I knew what to do, I'd run away to Cork or even Dublin, but I don't have any money, and I know what happens to girls like me in big cities. I liked that story you read to us about *David Copperfield* and how he walked over 70 miles to get to his aunt's house who gave him a proper upbringing, but I don't know anyone like that. I don't have any friends outside of our group. The other girls at school make fun of me. I'm scared and I have no one to give me advice. You told us that we could be anything we want to be, but I don't think that can happen for me. You're so smart. Is there anyone that can help me? Thank you.

Tia Taylor

Doctor Allenby continued, "Most of my students are pretty needy, and I don't have the time to follow up on all of them. I'd been trying to think of what I could do to help her, but one day, Tia didn't show up for school, and then that stretched to a week and then a month, and we never saw her again. I've always wondered what happened to that intelligent but trapped girl, and I am not surprised to hear that she may have been murdered. Some of the young people do leave the Travellers' community, but the odds were stacked against her from the beginning.

"If there's a skeleton of a male, it might be Jake that Tia mentioned in her letter. He was a tough and mean-spirited young man, and he was always buzzing around her. I believe he disappeared about the same time as Tia did. I always hoped that she hadn't run off with him since her future would not have been very bright with a lout like him."

Chief Brennan asked if he might have pictures of Tia and Jake. Doctor Allenby replied that he doubted there were individual pictures, but he thought there would likely be a class portrait out in the hallway. He led the group past many class portraits of smiling girls and boys from years past. He located one from the years that Tia had been at St. Michael's and pointed out Tia Taylor, who was short and stood in the first row. Most of the children made an attempt to smile, but Tia looked at them with a sad expression on her pale and freckled face that was framed by long chestnut curls. She was wearing a dark blue jean jacket that looked too large for her small frame. Jake stood in the back row. His long and narrow face was partially hidden by lanky black hair, and there was no hint of a smile.

Nora heard what the chief had to say and wiped away tears as she wondered if the skeletons they'd found in the bone pit belonged to Tia wearing this same blue jacket, and maybe the other one was Jake. The chief continued his story and said they had said goodbye to the people at St. Michael's and then headed to an interview with Tia's parents.

Giselda, Tia's mother, said that Tia was a mixed-up girl almost from the start. "She'd seen enough of the settled life to know that she wanted to have many of the things they did, but her father was a hard man and wanted none of that for her. She learned to read at an early age, but when I brought home books for her from the library, he would rip them up. We had both learned to be afraid of him. I've missed my girl so much over the years, but it would be a relief to know what really happened to her. If she's dead, I'd like to know it so she can rest in peace."

Tia's father, Christopher, appeared to be the lout that Mr. Allenby described, and then some. When they asked about her, his response was, "She was a slut from the beginning, and good riddance to her. She had every chance to marry a good man from our clan, but no—she had to take up with the good-for-nothing Jake Madden from the village."

Nora found it hard to believe that a father could be that hard hearted about his own daughter. Molly asked Christopher if he wasn't curious as to what happened to Tia. He responded that it made no difference to him since she was never coming back to be a comfort to her parents now. The garda warned Christopher about hitting his wife and said they would be keeping an eye on him.

They then left to interview Jake Madden's parents. They had been told that Jake's father, Simon, had died under mysterious circumstances long ago. They had no proof of anything, but they understood that sometimes Travellers women took only so much, and then they found a way to get rid of the offending husband. They talked to Derval Madden, Jake's mother, who told them that the boy had learned his mean ways from his father. She said, "By the time he disappeared, I was afraid of my own son. I was surprised to think that Tia went with him since she seemed to be so smart. I've never had so much as a note or call in all these long years. I have two younger children to be concerned about, but I ask God to take care of him, wherever he might be."

All in all, the chief told Nora that the afternoon's interviews had left all of them with a sour taste for the Travellers' difficult way of life.

CHAPTER

35

Wednesday, July 31
Sneem, Ireland; 2:00 p.m., IST

Nora returned to the castle and received a call from Lucy Sullivan, the coroner, saying that she and Aloysius Stec had finished their analysis of the human bones that had been recovered from the back-yard of the castle. They belonged to the adolescent female and the young adult male they had talked about, and they had not found any other human bones. They had looked at all the other bones in the pit, and they were from various animals that must have been special pets of the owners. Lucy said that she and Aloysius Stec had signed a document attesting to their conclusions, and she thought that as soon as they reinforced the pit and received clearance from the garda, they should be able to resume the dig for the medical research center

That was a relief, and Nora made several phone calls to see when they could resume their plans for a new construction date. She also asked Lucy to notify the families of Tia and Jake to see if they wanted to have a ceremony and a proper burial for their children's remains.

That night, Nora had *that* awful dream again about the bloody footprints on the flagstones in the hallway that led to the studded basement door of the castle. The killer at Duffy Hall Castle last year had been covered in blood after the murder and had trapped her parents in the basement. Nora had been so sure she would find them dead, and it was the worst time of her life. She tried not to think about those days, but they reappeared in her dreams with some frequency.

Nora knew that it was futile to try to get back to sleep in her comfortable bed. Tommy had an early morning meeting in Cork to try to hire another solicitor for his law firm, so he had spent the night in their favorite B&B place on the River Lee. Nora started to get up, and the two dogs Liam and Bran followed her around.

She tried to take comfort by admiring the view of the Milky Way as she peered out over the Atlantic. Here so close to the ocean, it was literally black as pitch. No wonder the ancient peoples knew so much about the stars. They wiled away their evening hours by finding patterns in the only lights they could see in the night sky and gave them enchanting names like Aquarius, Gemini, Cancer, Orion, and so many more.

Nora padded out to the patio and turned on a few lights. She removed the plastic covering from the daybed and lay down to try to get a few more hours of sleep. It was chilly, but she had put the new Irish wool quilt from Avoca Handweavers out here yesterday. She tried to forget about the violent events that had produced those bloody footprints in the hall and resulted in her dear aunt Vinnie's murder. She had come to love the older woman, who thought of her as her daughter and had learned so much from her. She missed her wise counsel and wondered what she would have to say about these recent events.

Nora pictured her large family in her mind and said some prayers for them. The dogs lay down next to her; all seemed quiet, and she started to doze.

Her studies of the brain had told her that females' brains have more connections going left and right across the two halves of the brain. Scientists think this could be a holdover from the caves when women had to be responsible for concurrent multiple tasks. Men were responsible for the food and procreation, but women protected the babies, made things pretty, liked to visit and talk with each other, and organized things for the betterment of the whole community. Most women were still like that and were used to doing it even during rest, and that was a good thing for Nora.

She realized she was suddenly wide awake, and Liam was vigorously barking and standing over her, and his whole body was quivering. A noxious smell made her gag, and she reached over to turn on the rest of the lights. A shadowy figure in black was climbing over the garden wall, and she only saw his back.

Nora knew that she had to get back in the house but realized that she was having a hard time moving. She got on her hands and knees and crawled back to the door, calling the dogs to her. She was able to close the patio doors behind her and could see some kind of round container sitting next to the wall, which she suspected might be a gas canister. She got out her phone and once more called Garda Chief Brennan on her speed dial.

She asked him to come to the castle immediately and to bring someone from the bomb squad with him and a doctor. She told him she was in the back of the house near the patio, vaguely recalled a lecture in medical school on the possible dangers of nitrous oxide, and then she passed out.

The police doctor that Chief Brennan brought with him made sure that Nora was fully conscious, and then the chief asked her many questions about this latest experience. Obviously, there was a problem with the castle's security that someone could so easily have climbed over the garden wall, and they were looking into that.

There was no denying that someone planned to hurt or kill Nora, but as to who and why, that remained a mystery. Nora had a headache, and they called Doctor McGarry from the castle and asked him to stay with her. Chief Brennan left Garda Molly Norris at the castle, and he headed back to his office.

Nora called Tommy and told him about her latest experiences. It was hard to know if this latest attempt on her life had to do with uncovering the hidden treasures or the murders that were still being investigated.

CHAPTER

36

Nora was about to call Chief Brennan the next day when she saw that he was calling her. He wanted to tell her the amazing news that he had discovered about the murderer of Tia and Jake, the owners of the bones in the bone pit. The chief had been notified that the brilliant history teacher at St. Michael's high school outside of Sneem Doctor Allenby was in the hospital with a major heart attack and was scheduled for an operation. His condition was grave, and the doctors did not give him much hope.

Doctor Allenby was barely conscious when the chief arrived at the hospital, but he told him that he knew he had little chance of surviving the operation, so he wanted to tell them about the dead girl and boy that were found in the bone pit. Doctor Allenby explained that he had had a severe case of mumps as a teenager, and it had left him impotent. He had consoled himself by concentrating on his studies and enjoyed being an expert on the Travellers people. He was well-liked, the students seemed interested in his classes, and he traveled extensively, which contented him for many years.

About six years ago, he had had Celestia Taylor as a pupil, and for the first time in his life, he wanted to have a physical relationship with a female. He knew that he was old enough to be her father, but he hoped that he might have a chance if he planned well. He started off over a number of weeks by talking to her about the things he knew she liked such as nature, pets, music, and the ocean. He told her about enchanting things she had never heard about, and he bought her small gifts he thought would appeal to her.

One night, he tried to take it a step further and asked if she would mind if he kissed her. Tia was no fool and figured out right away what he wanted and tried to pull away from him. He was so stung by her rejection. He had been gardening and moving bricks, and he still had one in his hand. Without even thinking, he struck out at her with the brick, and it hit her much harder than he thought. He saw the blood gush out from her temple with horror. When she fell down at his feet, he panicked and attempted to revive her, but he could not. Chief Brennan could see by the terror-stricken look on Doctor Allenby's face that he felt terrible about it and wished he could reverse events, but it was too late.

Doctor Allenby said he had dithered around for a few hours while he tried to decide what to do, and he finally came up with a plan. He called the lanky and mean Jake Madden and asked him if he would like to make a lot of money. When Jake showed up, Mr. Allenby told him there had been an accident, and he would give him one thousand dollars to put Tia's body in his car and dig a hole in the bone pit at Duffy Hall Castle so he could bury her in there.

Jake had not even been aware that there was a bone pit at the castle, and he hesitated for some time while he tried to assess the weak points in this plan. He needed the money, so he finally agreed. Doctor Allenby helped load Tia's body into Jake's pickup truck, and he had no trouble once it was dark driving over to the bone pit, digging a good-sized hole, and dropping Tia's body into it.

Meanwhile, Doctor Allenby had had second thoughts and realized that letting Jake live to tell the tale and opening himself up to blackmail someday was not a good idea. He had been hiding behind a nearby tree next to the bone pit, and after he saw that Jake had deposited Tia's body into the hole, Doctor Allenby shot Jake with a rifle and added his body to the hole too. He made sure both bodies were covered well, tamped down the earth, and drove Jake's truck out the way he had come and left it in the Coral Beach parking lot. Doctor Allenby then had walked back to his house, and no one had ever realized what he had done.

Doctor Allenby said he was sorry for what had happened, but it seemed like the only alternative at the time. He knew that Jake would not be missed much, and Tia's family was never too sure about her activities since she hankered after so many of the settled people's ways.

Chief Brennan talked to the doctor, who told him that he thought Doctor Allenby probably did not have more than a few days of life left. The chief asked Doctor Allenby if he'd had anything to do with the girl on the beach, Jack Boyle, or the girl at the golf course murders, but he insisted he did not, and they let it go at that.

So, it seemed as though the two long-ago murders at Duffy Hall Castle might have been solved. If that were the case, they should be able to begin again with their plans for the construction of the medical research center, but the search would have to go on for another murderer or more.

The chief thought, not for the first time, that the human heart and mind were the most dangerous things on the planet. Imagine that Doctor Allenby, who seemed so sophisticated, was just another in the long line of thugs that he had encountered in his career. Since he was so near death, they probably would not be able to do more to him now, but he would soon be facing the Ultimate Judge, and that probably would not turn out very well for him.

Nora thanked the chief for the call and said she appreciated the update, but she too found it hard to believe that the charming professor was all a miserable facade, despite all his book learning. She told the chief that she and Tommy would be going back to Chicago on Saturday, but they would return to Ireland as soon as they had clearance for a new construction date for the medical center. She asked him to call her if there was any further news about Doctor Allenby.

CHAPTER

37

Saturday, August 3
Chicago, Illinois; 9:00 a.m., CDT

Nora and Tommy left Ireland to go back to Chicago after the usual planning and goodbyes. The timing was good since her siblings who were still in school would be starting soon, and it was always fun shopping for clothes, shoes, and supplies. They had tickets for the first Notre Dame and Bears football games that would take place in a few weeks, and they loved all the fall activities their families enjoyed. Nora thought it would be fun to host a big Halloween party at their house and she gave some thought to that.

After they got back to Chicago, Nora talked to Kitty Duffy at the castle, who told her that Jack Boyle's wake and funeral would have pleased the kindly old man so much. Just about every soul from the estate and the village had come for it, and they had collected so many stories about him. One thing they had found among his effects was an English-Irish dictionary with pronunciations that he had started, and Nora said she could certainly use that. Sometimes when people die, they are hardly missed, but the villagers realized that Jack's absence would leave a large hole in their tight-knit community.

Kitty said she didn't think that Chief Brennan had made any progress in finding out who had killed him, but every few days, the chief had come back to the castle and given a report to Nora's solicitor Fiona Finnegan. Kitty said she realized they had just left Ireland, but they were looking forward to seeing them for the next construction attempt for the medical center. Nora responded that she thought the major hurdles had been cleared, and she would let her know an exact date soon.

Nora had started sorting through the stacks of mail that had accumulated while they were in Ireland, but she was interrupted by a call from her police friend Lt. Matt Braxton, who said he'd had a call from his colleague at the Cook County Forest Preserves Police. "Bud knows that you're a friend of mine, so he called me and said they had received a call from a guy who says that he killed the girl they found near the lake in the forest preserves. He says he'll turn himself in, but only if you are there. The police often receive calls from crazy people who think they had something to do with violent crimes, but Bud said this guy sounds like he might actually have done it. Will you come with me to the police station to talk to this fellow?"

Nora was upset by the whole conversation, but she agreed to accompany Matt to the Forest Preserves Police headquarters. Matt said he would come and pick her up. Nora explained this latest development to Tommy, who was busy preparing a report for his office, and she said she should be back by dinnertime.

Bud and his team told the supposed killer that Nora Duffy had agreed to talk with him. "Danny" told them to meet him at Maple Lake, and they found a small man there dressed all in black who was waving to them. He showed them where he had parked his car last night and how he had dragged the girl's body down to the lake. He seemed to be quiet and lucid at the moment. They put him in one of the police cars and drove over to the office.

Bud and his partner Gus put "Danny" in one of the interviewing rooms and waited for Matt and Nora to arrive. The man in black kept asking if they were sure that Nora Duffy would be there. He said he needed a Coke and a cigarette badly, so they gave him a can, which he drank down in several gulps. He lit the cigarette and seemed to be getting more agitated, so Bud hoped that Nora would arrive soon.

Matt and Nora arrived shortly, and Bud explained the little he knew about "Danny" to them. He said he was reluctant at first to believe that this little guy could be the killer, but the longer he was alone, the more violent he seemed to be getting. "Danny" had not yet revealed why he wanted to see Nora so badly. When Bud looked at Nora's small size, he asked her if she still wanted to do this, but she said she was willing, and she trusted them to keep her safe.

Bud, Gus, and Matt preceded Nora into the interview room, and the man in black stood up and seemed to bow to Nora. The policemen told him they would be taping the conversation, and then they asked him to tell his story.

"My name is Danny Moody, and I killed the girl you found at Maple Lake." Danny couldn't seem to take his wide-open brown eyes from staring at Nora's face.

"I'm crazy, but I'm just a little crazy, and you can be sure that I'm going to tell you the truth about me and the girl. I'm sorry that I killed her, but it's partly your fault, Miss Nora. I've wanted to see you in person for a long time, and I sent you three letters asking you to meet with me, and I got no response from you at all. I told you that when I had one of my episodes coming on, I wouldn't be able to stop myself.

"My father was a drunk, and he hit me in the head for years. He tried to do it again on my seventeenth birthday, and I turned around and hit him so hard, he never got up again. Nobody knew it was me at the time, but somebody had to stop him. Sometimes, I get such pain in my left ear that the only way to stop it is for me to hit something.

"I saw the news about you in Ireland with the two murdered girls, and I thought I might get your attention if someone was murdered here in the same way. I was washing windows at a store on Clark Street when I saw this pretty girl get off a bus, and it seemed like it would be so easy to kill her. I followed her down the street until she turned the corner, and I just kept hitting her and hitting her, and she froze up and just let me do it. I imagined I was doing it to you, Nora," Danny said with such malice in his voice.

"It would have been a nice touch to put her body on Oak Street Beach, but I'm not very strong, and I couldn't figure out how to do it, so I put her body in my car, and I drove her out to Maple Lake. I wanted it to seem like a copycat killing, so I drew some gold horseshoes with the jagged red X through it on her breasts, and I dragged her over to the lake and dumped her in. All the time I was doing it, I thought I would make you feel bad about not contacting me.

"Yesterday morning, I woke up and my headache was gone, and I realized what I'd done. I wish I could take it all back, but it's too late now. Why didn't you get in touch with me, Nora dear?" whined Danny as he reached for her hand.

When Nora didn't respond to him immediately, he picked up the table and tried to throw it at her. His calm exterior had disappeared, and it took all three policemen to grab him by his arms and forcibly sit him down again.

"I thought you were different, but you're just like the rest of those women who pay no attention to me," Danny screamed out to Nora.

Nora quickly tried to process everything that Danny had said. Sometimes, her secretaries opened her letters and put them in categories for her to answer. Maybe they had put Danny's letters in the "Answer When You Can" pile, but she did not recall seeing them. As to Danny calling her "dear," that was very disturbing. If she had met with him and he got upset, there was every possibility that she would be the one in the morgue. The poor girl who was being autopsied today had become fodder for a half-insane man's fantasies about her.

Nora's physician's eye had noticed that Danny had to stop talking periodically to wince from pain, and there was every possibility that the beatings he'd suffered at the hands of his father had left him with a punctured eardrum, a fractured skull, or more. The mental pain he must have endured over the years was hard to calculate.

The chain of "victims" in cases like this is a long one and probably stretched back many generations in his family. This endless cycle of violence had now claimed yet another victim in the girl Danny had murdered.

Nora thought that Mr. Shakespeare had such good observations about almost everything, and his quote from *The Tempest* seemed so appropriate in this situation: "Hell is empty and all the devils are here."

There was little hope for Danny in this world now, but she silently sang the "Agnus Dei" prayer for him:

THE GOLDEN HORSESHOES MURDERS

Lamb of God, you take away the sins of the world,
Have mercy on him.
Lamb of God, you take away the sins of the world,
Grant him peace.

Nora told Danny that she had not seen his letters, and she would pray for him. Her words were answered by Danny spitting at her, and she realized that this man had been reduced to the level of a suffering animal.

The detectives hustled him out of the room and took him in the back to a cell. They didn't much care as to what drove him to do what he did. Their concern was with the victim, and he would now face the consequences.

Nora asked Matt what would happen to Danny now, and he said that a good lawyer would probably get him off with lifetime confinement to a mental hospital for the criminally insane. Visions of the trapped men in *One Flew Over the Cuckoo's Nest* flashed through Nora's mind. She couldn't help feeling sorry for Danny, but then there was the matter of the helpless girl just walking down the street and having her life beaten out of her. "Please get me out of here, Matt," Nora tearfully said.

Later in the day, they were able to confirm the identity of the murdered girl when Deanna Vega contacted them and said she had been frantically looking for her roommate Amy Parker, who never came home last night. Once again, they would be making the trip to the Cook County Morgue so that Deanna could identify one of the many bodies that end up in this sad place every day.

Deanna told her that Amy had come to Chicago from Iowa, but she had no clue as to who her parents were. She said that Amy was a kind girl who had found work at the downtown Chicago Public Library. They used to go dancing at a local club every so often. Amy went to church once a while at the Baptist church down the street, but other than that, she didn't know much about her. She paid her rent every month and cleaned up her part of the apartment, and Deanna said that was all she was concerned about. One detail they might find interesting is that Amy was an expert in tatting.

"What the heck is tatting?" asked Gus.

Deanna said she didn't know too much about it herself, but Amy said it was a kind of crochet, a method for making lace with knots and loops using a small handheld machine. Deanna showed them an example of Amy's pretty decorative work on a pillow that sat on the living room couch. Matt thought that it would take a lot of patience and discipline to create such art.

"To each his own" was all Matt could say at the moment. The world was full of things he knew nothing about, and people did take up hobbies that seemed strange to him, but Amy must have spent many hours of her short life perfecting this skill. Now they had to prepare a case against Danny Moody and see if they could find Amy Parker's family and those things he thought he would know how to do.

Fiona Finnegan from the castle gave Nora a call and said they had received clearance from the Buildings Department that they could have another go at the start of construction for the Duffy Medical Research Center on 1 September. She said the document from Lucy Sullivan and Aloysius Stec signing off on the identity of the bones in the bone pit had been properly recorded. Tia Taylor's and Jake Madden's bones had been moved to a funeral home, and they were waiting to hear if the families wanted to give them a proper burial.

Nora thought that was the best news she could have hoped for, but she now hoped that the Irish winter would hold off long enough for them to at least get the foundations laid, the outer walls built, and a roof over it all. Nora contacted Kitty and Maryann and asked them to once again send invitations to everyone who had been invited to the disastrous last construction attempt, making sure that the letters to out-of-Ireland guests were mailed immediately. She also asked them to send out the usual e-mail reminders to Irish cities' and villages' news outlets, asking them to highlight this story. Nora also asked them to tell Mrs. O'Hara about it so she could start ordering whatever she would need to prepare her delicious treats for the day. She told Kitty that she would contact the garda and Chief Herlihy herself to be prepared for a busy day. Nora said she would be back in Ireland a few days before September 1.

Nora followed her usual procedure and contacted the various security people who would be needed for 1 September, and she also called Sneem's mayor so the town would be prepared for an onslaught of visitors.

CHAPTER

38

Monday, August 5
Chicago, Illinois; 8:00 a.m., CDT

The summer seemed to speed by quicker each year, and it was now time for the Duffy children who were still in school to get ready for another year. Siobhan and Kevin would be leaving this week for Notre Dame, and high schoolers Brian, Molly, and Caitlan would be starting school next week. Kevin, a Notre Dame freshman, had been hopeful that his small stature and red hair would make him competitive for the position of Notre Dame Leprechaun mascot, but he'd discovered there were too many others at the university that looked like him too. He was put on the waiting list, but the lucky leprechaun always had such a good time at the football games Kevin doubted that the person chosen for this coveted position would miss any.

Doctor Duffy had season tickets for the ND football games, but he often had to miss them because of his busy schedule. Jim, the oldest boy in the family, liked to use them, but his fiancé, Trish, had graduated from Northwestern, and he often found himself attending their games as well. The family had season tickets for the Bears, and they hoped that this season would be a winning one for them.

Nora was happy to see that the garden she and Tommy had planted, with the help of their housekeeper Jesse, was blooming so abundantly with many varieties of flowers that looked so pretty. The tomatoes, cucumbers, and squash plants were producing more vegetables than they could use.

Nora gathered a bouquet and some of the extra vegetables and took them down the street to St. Mary's rectory for Father Ahearn and Monsignor Callahan. Their housekeeper Annabeth was delighted with the flowers and happy for the vegetables and said she would use them for tonight's dinner. Nora told the two priests that once again they were going to attempt to start construction of the Duffy Medical Research Center on September 1, and she invited them both to come. Father Ahearn said he'd love it. Monsignor Callahan was going through a bad time with his arthritis, but he said that if Father Ahearn was willing to get him there in his wheelchair, he too would be happy to come. Nora said she would hire someone to help them during the whole trip, and they were both thrilled.

Nora had set up a meeting today with Gloryann Graber, the administrator for the Duffy Foundation—US, and with Dan Buck, the CFO. She had appointed these two people to run her charitable foundation right after she found out about her inheritance, and she could tell after reviewing the latest detailed report that Glory had everything well in hand. So far, they had given out 5.1 million dollars to 1,125 people. They had saved homes from mortgage foreclosures, financed peoples' dreams, helped students attend colleges, and more.

One of the requirements to be a recipient of these funds was to provide a picture of themselves doing some type of charitable work, and Glory had filled every square inch of space on the walls of their office with these pictures and had to resort to huge albums to hold the rest. One of Nora's favorite photos showed her smiling young nieces Beth and Maeve organizing their grandparents' books and sewing materials. Their sweet request for one thousand dollars had helped their parents to return to the scene of their honeymoon on Mackinac Island for their anniversary, and they immediately knew what their charitable work would be and had done it so well.

For those with a hope of repaying the loans with low rates, Nora had requested that they gradually start to do that a little at a time as a way to replenish the fund. After Dan and Gloryann had done such a good job in Chicago, Nora had started a Duffy Foundation—Ireland, and they too were helping many people. Nora thought that Uncle Cy would be happy to know that good deeds around the world were happening because of his generosity. His astute business acumen would also be glad to know that when the requests came from people they didn't know, thorough background checks were done on them before the people received any funds.

There was another monthly family birthday party in the evening, this time for five people, at Aunt Betty Gear's house in Oak Park. Nora and Tommy met most of her family, and they had a great time visiting and enjoying everyone's favorite hors d'oeuvres, Aunt Betty's creative dishes, and a precarious-looking ten-layer chocolate cake. The singing and dancing went on for hours, and Nora reminded everyone that they were all invited to Ireland for the construction opening of the Duffy Medical Research Center on September 1.

When they got home, Nora sent texts to her former Irish dancing "best buds" and said whoever was available should come to the Conrad Hilton hotel downtown for a reunion on Saturday night, August 17. Nineteen "girls" responded right away that they would love to come. Nora told them all to bring their old hard shoes, and if they could still fit into their old costumes to bring them, or something similar, as well. Nora asked Kitty to finalize arrangements with the hotel for a room with a dance floor, and she looked forward to seeing her old friends.

Nora received a call from her friend Cathy O'Mara, saying that the orphan girl they hoped to adopt, Peggy, had left St. Brigid's Orphanage and had come to live with them, and all seemed well so far. Nora said she was thrilled for them, and she hoped that they would come to Chicago to visit them since one of her father's best friends in Chicago was a renowned plastic surgeon who specialized in fixing burns. Usually, they would have to wait a long time to get in to see him, but she was sure that her dad could pave the way for a quick appointment, if they were interested. Nora told her that she had looked carefully at the scars the last time she saw Peggy, and she was sure that Doctor Miller could help.

Cathy found some bandages that made the scars practically disappear, and Peggy anxiously agreed to the trip. Adam had to stay behind in Ireland, but Cathy and Peggy traveled to Chicago to see Nora, who had set up an appointment with plastic surgeon Dr. Paul Miller.

Cathy and Peggy stayed overnight at Nora and Tommy Barry's, but the next day, they went to visit Nora's parents' house, and they met Nora's younger siblings Molly and Caitlan, who were fourteen. They were in the midst of practicing their Irish dancing, and they gave Peggy a hug and asked her to join them. Peggy discovered that she liked it a lot and with some training would probably be good at it. She was encouraged because if the girls noticed her facial scar, they had not said anything, and they seemed to accept her like an old friend.

That afternoon, they all visited the Art Institute and toured the Thorne Rooms exhibit, which contained tiny dioramas of famous external and interior architectural designs over the centuries. Peggy especially loved the art deco designs of the 1930s and said she would love to have that kind of furniture one day that looked so elegant.

The next day, Nora took Cathy and Peggy to the office of Dr. Paul Miller. He examined the burns on her face and her back as well as the cigarette burns on her arms. He made no comments as to why the burns were there, but Nora could see that he was furious that a young girl had experienced such misery. Doctor Miller explained that he thought they could make a big difference in the appearance of the scars, but it would take time, patience, and courage. He could do the initial surgeries in Chicago as early as the day after tomorrow, and he was acquainted with an excellent plastic surgeon in Cork, Doctor Niall O'Connor, and he thought he could do the needed follow up work. Doctor Miller prepared a full report and said he would make it available to Doctor O'Connor via the Internet.

Monday, August 12

Nora and Cathy O'Mara and Peggy O'Reilly met Dr. Paul Miller at Holy Savior's burn unit, and he prepared the girl for what she might expect during surgery. They would work on the face burn first and do the back afterward. The cigarette burns on her arms would require less attention, but they would get to those eventually. He would be taking skin from her thigh to put over the burns since it was the type of skin that would approximate color and type. He told her to be prepared for quite a bit of pain, but he was hopeful that it would not be the kind that would require extensive drugs to combat. Peggy smiled at him and said that anything he could do would be appreciated.

The surgery took several hours, and then Peggy had to spend time in the recovery room. The burns were covered with skin-colored bandages that would be sufficient for now. Peggy said the pain in her thigh area was worse than that on her face and back, but it was bearable. They were able to return to Nora's house the next morning.

Molly and Caitlan made it their mission to keep up Peggy's spirits, and they listened to music and played card games with her to help her stay still. Cathy O'Mara started to pack for their trip back to Ireland, and the Duffy family had a goodbye party for them on Saturday night.

On Sunday morning, Jim drove them all out to O'Hare, and Cathy and Peggy thanked them profusely for their help. Nora reminded them that they were due to attend the groundbreaking ceremony for the Duffy Medical Research Center on September 1, and they said they would plan on being there.

Saturday, August 17

Nora gathered with her former Irish dancing friends at the Conrad Hilton, and they spent several hours catching up on each other's news, sharing photos of families and boyfriends and husbands, and then Nora said it was time for them to go down memory lane. She had made arrangements for a video presentation of their glory days, and they clapped and laughed as they saw their younger selves doing so well at the World's Oireachtas competition. "We were pretty good, weren't we?" was a question that needed no more answer than seeing Maryellen Flynn hoisting the beautiful crystal trophy inscribed with "First Place" above their heads.

Then the music decibels increased, and the ladies were told to put on their hard shoes to try and recreate what they had just seen on the silver screen. Some of them did well, but others who had not kept their bodies in tip-top shape fell on the floor laughing. Nora took pity on them, and her sisters and their friends from the Trinity Irish Dancers burst onto the floor and put them all to shame. The older gals clapped and kept time with the music and said they could not believe they were ever that good.

The dancing was followed by the feasting, at least a young women's version of a feast, which consisted of salads, chicken strips, and a vegetable medley. The evening had been a catharsis for all of them, and they promised to keep in touch more often. Nora was so glad she had paid attention to her inner promptings that had resulted in getting them all together.

CHAPTER

39

Sunday, August 18
Chicago, Illinois; 1:00 p.m., CDT

Nora had an appointment at the hospital to meet with the parents of a five-year-old girl Fatima Gomez. The initial tests they had done on Fatima told her that it was very likely that she had a brain tumor. The beautiful little girl with the piercing dark eyes sitting on her mother's lap tried to smile at Nora, but her expression was one of pain. Nora shook hands with Fatima's father, Pedro, and her mother, Amelia. Both of them were holding back tears, which was understandable.

After a quick glance at Fatima, Nora noticed that the father's face was covered in sweat and he was coughing almost constantly. He was pulling on his long hair, jumping around in his chair, and could not seem to keep his eyes focused. Nora was immediately concerned that his physical appearance meant that he was suffering from some rather serious illness, rather than just being upset about his daughter's plight.

She pulled out a face mask and gave other masks to the parents and Fatima. She asked Pedro how long he had been sick. "We went to visit my relatives in Patagonia in South America, and we just got back day before yesterday. Maybe they had the flu, and we didn't realize it, but I've been getting sicker and sicker ever since. I am so weak, I can't eat, and I have a lot of pain in my stomach. I have had loose bowels, and I've been vomiting. This morning, I threw up some blood, and now I am really feeling sick. I don't want to give what I have to my family."

Nora asked Maria if she had any symptoms, and she replied that she was all right so far, but she had been getting more concerned about her husband. Nora asked Pedro more questions about where they had gone on their trip and if they had been bitten by any insects or animals. Her mind began to scroll through the cornucopia of infectious diseases that had similar symptoms of fever or chills, weakness, and abdominal pain:

Influenza was familiar since most people had contracted some version of it at least once in their lives. Sepsis was less familiar but could occur easily. Tuberculosis used to be a common killer, and this disease that destroyed people's lungs was a frequent theme in the operas of the nineteenth century. In *La Bohème*, Giselda tried to gasp out her last breaths while singing so beautifully. Nora had seen cases of TB, and it was highly unlikely that anyone so affected would have the strength to talk, let alone sing.

Nora had spent part of her residency in medical school studying exotic diseases, and she began to experience the first frisson of fear that Pedro might be suffering from something much more serious. The granddaddy of them all was *Yersinia Pestis*—in more common terms, the Black Death or the Plague.

In its early stages, this ancient and terrible enemy mimics many of the same symptoms of the flu, such as fever, chills, extreme weakness, abdominal pain, diarrhea, and vomiting. Then the patient develops bleeding from the mouth, nose, or rectum. If the patient has the bubonic version, the person develops bleeding under the skin or dark bumps or buboes—thus, the term Black Death. If he has the pneumatic version, a sneeze could send millions of infected droplets through the air, and anyone near him could also be infected.

The Plague acts virulently and quickly. Nora recalled a dramatic novel that she'd read some years ago about a young boy who had brought a sick squirrel home and been bitten by its fleas. He got extremely sick in a short period of time, but his disease went untreated. He developed the pneumatic type, and within a short time, he had infected his family, who infected many more people, and an entire city had been decimated before they were able to get it under control.

Nora had never seen an actual case of the Plague, but she began to think about the tests and protocols that would fall quickly into place at the hospital if Pedro did have it. He could be dead long before his little girl, unless he had also passed it on to her and his wife.

Nora asked for more background on their recent trip. Pedro said that his mother in South America had asked him to get rid of the rats in her backyard shed that were acting strangely. He had tried to catch them with a trap, but one particularly big fellow had bitten him several times. Nora put on a second pair of gloves and anxiously examined the teeth marks from the nasty bites. She was a trained professional, but she was beginning to feel some panic as old pictures of people infected with the Black Death flashed through her mind. She recalled that the Plague had killed at least one third of everyone in Europe in the 1400s.

We know now that the animals themselves don't cause the disease, but the fleas that inhabit their pelts bite the people and spread the contagion. Without the knowledge of the true enemy, the panicked medieval population had tried out many possible cures, but none of them worked. It was strange but true that these tiny little creatures could destroy us so easily when we are so much bigger and stronger than they are.

Nora called the receptionist Gail and asked her to find several doctors right away and tell them to get up to her room immediately, being sure to bring breathing masks with them. Gail called Sister Cecilia Clark, the hospital administrator; Dr. Will Stone, the infectious disease director; Dr. Hal Fong, the head of ER; and Mrs. Mary Conlon, the head of nursing and stressed that it was a real emergency. Nora might be wrong, but she knew that early detection and treatment were the best protection against the spread of any infectious disease.

At first, Will thought she was playing a joke on him, but when he heard the urgency in her voice, he threw down the phone, grabbed the materials she had asked for, and ran up the stairs to Nora's room.

OMG, he thought to himself, *I certainly hope that Nora is overreacting. What would we do if she's right?*

Pedro was put in isolation and a battery of tests were done. Anxious hours were spent wondering if they were sufficiently prepared to treat plague cases. Mercifully for all, they discovered that Pedro had a case of tuberculosis, and not the Plague. They thought that Pedro would have to spend a few days in the hospital but then could continue his treatments at home.

The hospital had had a good scare and a reminder that they needed to provide regular training to all medical personnel about their infectious disease protocols. Someday, there might occur a really serious unknown disease somewhere in the world that could make its way to Chicago, and they needed to be prepared in the best ways possible when and if that should occur. They appointed a panel of appropriate people to investigate their current protocols and to make recommendations for the future.

When Nora arrived home that night, she had a new story to tell Tommy about the interesting things that could happen to you out of the blue. She reflected that the old saying "You don't know what you don't know" was certainly applicable to today's events. She would call her old friend Dr. Estelle Glover in the morning at the Centers for Disease Control and Prevention to see if she had suggestions for them.

CHAPTER

40

Wednesday, August 21
Sneem, Ireland; 6:00 p.m., IST

Fiona Finnegan had called Nora and asked if it would be possible for her to come back to Ireland to sign the final papers for the Buildings Department so that everything would be in order for them to be ready for the construction dig for the medical research center to begin on 1 September. Nora asked if she could do this via fax or phone, but Fiona said there was a time crunch and it would be best if she could do it in person. Nora agreed, and she once again met up with her Aer Lingus friends and arrived back at the castle, to the delight of the staff and the pets.

She met up with Fiona and signed the needed documentation and they had a relaxing evening at Dan Murphy's Bar. Nora was also glad to be back in Ireland, where she had another meeting to talk about excavating the collapsed part of the old castle.

The next day, Nora went to Killlarney for meetings first with Alice McGillicuddy, the archaeologist, and then with Lucy Sullivan, the coroner. Both meetings were successful, and all seemed to be moving along well.

The weather had suddenly turned chilly and rainy, and the visibility got worse as she neared the coast and Duffy Hall Castle. She was anxious to get home to one of Mrs. O'Hara's tasty dinners, her Aran Island sweater, and a blanket. She steered her Ford Escape into its usual place but didn't see that any of the lights had been lit yet, in the parking lot or at the house, which was odd.

She tiptoed as best she could in her Louboutin heels through heavy puddles and made it to the side door of the house and its portico shelter. Nora pressed the Door Open button on her phone and pushed her way past the wind and rain into the hallway. She could hear Liam the wolfhound and Bran the Irish setter, whining for her. She gave each of them a tousle, but even before she turned on the hall light, she realized that one of the dogs had had an accident on the entrance flagstones, another odd thing which almost never happened. Biddy usually took them for a walk several times during the day. Other than the breathing of the dogs, it was so very quiet. Where was everyone?

Six months ago, she wouldn't have been concerned, but after the frightening events they'd gone through at the castle last year plus the discovery of the recent murders, Nora had learned to be extra vigilant about unusual events. Tommy had insisted that she purchase several guns and learn how to use them just in case. She had taken some shooting lessons from her friends at the Chicago Police Department, Lt. Matthew Braxton and his soon-to-be bride, Laura Belsky. It was Laura who had saved them all from the deranged killer on the roof of the castle last year because of her prowess as a marksman.

Nora still didn't feel comfortable holding a gun, but after she'd called out several times without receiving a response, she took the concealed handgun out of the beautiful lily bouquet on the hall credenza and began to walk quietly through the house, her heart in her mouth. There certainly were a lot of dark corners in this big old place she had come to call home. She heard some sounds from behind the dining room door and pointed the gun at it but had to laugh when it turned out to be just Tinker Bell, the kitten who was big enough now to walk down the stairs and go where she wished.

Nora, followed by her party of animal friends, walked quietly through the Great Hall, while trying to keep her wet hair out of her face. She thought she heard sounds of laughter coming from the kitchen, and she headed in that direction.

The entire household staff appeared to be having a grand time. When Mrs. O'Hara saw Nora standing in the hallway with water dripping down her chin and the gun wobbling in her hand, she stopped in midlaugh and ran to her with a towel.

"Oh, Miss Nora, I'm so sorry. Did we scare you? We've been having a birthday and engagement party for Biddy O'Halloran and didn't realize how late it was. Let me wipe the water off of you, you poor dear, so. Look at the time, Biddy. The lights aren't on and the dogs haven't been walked."

Everyone else in the large room apologized for scaring Nora, but she proceeded to wish all happiness to Biddy, admired her ring, and said she would like to hear more about the engagement after Biddy had walked the dogs. Bran never minded the rain, but Nora reminded Biddy that Liam hated to be wet, so she should stay under the portico. John Denning, one of the porters, told Nora he would take care of turning on all the lights, and he would clean up after the dog accident in the front hall.

Nora told Mrs. O'Hara that she would go upstairs and change into her comfortable clothes, and she would come back down for a bite to eat. On the way out, she replaced the gun in its usual spot and thanked God she had not had to use it.

Nora decided she would call her parents and Doctor Whiteside at the clinic after she'd had some dinner. She heard her phone ringing with the fast version of the Irish jig and saw that it was from Chief Brennan. He said that he had a call telling him that they should quickly come to the hospital to talk to Doctor Allenby, who was very close to death. He asked Nora to meet him there, and she agreed.

When they arrived, the professor told them in a halting whisper that he knew that he didn't have long to live, so he wanted to let them know that he was the one who had killed the two young girls on the beach and at the golf course. Nora shivered as she heard this and could hardly believe it. He also wanted Nora to know that he had been the one responsible for painting the golden horseshoes and sprinkling them with the lamb's blood on the castle's doors.

Chief Brennan was more inured to the capabilities of human nature, and he could well believe it. He had brought along his recording machine and told the sick man that he was going to turn it on. Doctor Allenby said that he had spent his whole life caring for young people, and now he realized that he was responsible for depriving four of them of their very lives. He didn't want to go into the next world with that on his conscience, and he wanted to alleviate the cares of their families.

He explained that a sort of horrible trance had consumed him when he encountered Dotty Dillon leaving her workplace. He had given her a ride close to her home, and then he tried to kiss her. When she refused and hit him with her big purse, he had lost all control and made her go unconscious with a drug-filled handkerchief he had brought along. He drove to the Coral Beach where it was raining so hard and dragged her body near the rhododendron bushes, found a large piece of driftwood, and bashed it over her forehead.

Rather than killing her, that seemed to awaken her, so he had no choice. He had brought along a large screwdriver, and he drove it with all his might into her back. Then he took off all her clothes and drew the golden horseshoes on her breasts. He meant the drawing as a warning to other women who would refuse to submit to men when they had such needs. He'd run through the wind and rain to get back to his car, so it had been him that Nora saw from the castle's window.

He went back home and tried to sleep, but he was still under the influence of his violent impulses. The next afternoon, he had been driving past the seniors' home, where he saw Annie Matthews taking out the garbage. He didn't know her, but she looked so pretty and likeable, and he'd thrown caution to the winds. He forced her to get into his car and had tied her hands behind her back. She had cried and whimpered all the way to the golf course, and she had tried to get him to change his mind. She told him he looked like a nice man who was just confused. She told him she was supposed to be playing a Mozart piece in a recital tomorrow, and she begged him for her life.

He did almost relent then, but he had made up his mind that he was going to rape her. When he got her down near the bunker, he found that his old nemesis was back, and he couldn't get his body to do what it needed to in order to accomplish a rape. He was embarrassed and tried not to look into her eyes as he bashed her over the head. He thought she was probably dead, but he stabbed her with the screwdriver just to be sure. He took off all her clothes and drew the golden horseshoes again and dumped her into the bunker.

Chief Brennan asked Doctor Allenby what the significance of the golden horseshoes was, and he responded that Dotty had screamed at him that he would never have any luck in this life. He still had his briefcase with him, and there were permanent markers in there. She was dead by the time he decided to do the drawing, but he childishly had wanted to respond to her that she was the one who wouldn't be having any luck ever again, so he had crossed out the traditional good luck symbol with the jagged red X. He just repeated the same process for Annie. As to their clothing, he said that he'd been wary of discarding it anywhere, so it was still in a big trash bag in the basement of his home.

By the time Doctor Allenby had finished with his confession, he had started to lapse into a coma. Chief Brennan said he thought the murderer might have been him all along, and he was glad that at least the two families would have some closure on these cases.

Nora's usual inclination was to extend mercy to people for their misdeeds, but this time, she found herself thinking that Doctor Allenby should receive an extremely cold welcome in the next world when he died. She disliked the concept of hell with no possible redemption, but he would be a good candidate for it. The doctor had opened himself up to evil and it had spilled out to encompass four young people, their families, and their communities. The doctor had wanted to project an image of being so academic and erudite, but in reality, he was as big a monster as any other serial killer. Nora could not stop crying as she thought about his victims and the tragedies that a diseased human mind could inflict on the rest of society.

Her mind was never very linear though, and Nora thought that perhaps impotence might be another problem that they could add to their list of topics at the new medical research center. Later that night, they received a call from the hospital saying that Doctor Allenby had died at 2:02 a.m.

CHAPTER

41

Thursday, August 22
Sneem, Ireland; 9:00 a.m., IST

M r. Gainer and Alice McGillicuddy had drawn up detailed plans to begin the excavation of the caved in part of the old castle. They thought that roof stress must have caused the roof to collapse hundreds of years ago. They weren't sure how long the planning and the excavation would take, but the first step was to have a team pick up all the loose bricks from the ground and move them to a safe distance in well-marked piles for the reconstruction.

The section that appeared to be most damaged was on the west side of the castle, and they started there and moved out. Then they erected metal scaffolding and used several cranes so they could safely start to remove the topmost bricks and gradually work their way down. A team of experts waited at the bottom and marked the bricks and catalogued their progress. It was painstaking work, but the team diligently worked until it was dusk.

They thought that another two days of work would enable them to remove enough bricks so that they might be able to enter the interior of the old castle and begin the project of shoring up the walls from the inside. Unfortunately, a sudden rainstorm came up during the night, but they had prepared for that eventuality and covered up the excavation site with huge blue tarpaulins. Nora was anxious to not destroy anything in there that had been hidden for four centuries.

It took several days to shore up the walls before they felt it was safe enough to cautiously enter the opening. They turned on their laser lamps and were able to see a large brown desk that appeared to have collapsed on one side. At its foot was a human skeleton that still had the remains of leather clothing stuck to it. It appeared that the man—they assumed it was a man—had died as a result of a huge ceiling stone that had fallen on his head since the skull was in several pieces next to the stone. The man would have had no chance to escape its deadly effects.

Everyone held their breath, and Nora uttered her usual prayer, "May the angels lead you into paradise." She very much wanted to examine the man right away, but Alice told her it was important to exercise restraint and patience. She insisted that photos be taken from every angle to document their progress so far, and she entered copious notes on her computer.

Alice carefully just looked at the skeleton and its surroundings to see what that could tell her. The brown leather clothing still appeared to be unmarked, and it was clear from the size of the skeleton that this man would have been tall and thin. On his feet were leather shoes that were stitched together by hand. In his hand, they could see a large yellow feathered quill, so he must have been in the process of writing something at the desk when disaster struck.

After Alice was satisfied that they had learned all they could from visual evidence, she said it would be safe to lower the skeleton so that it was flat on the flagstone floor and then carefully turn him over after they had installed protective coverings. It was creepy to hear the sounds of his bones clacking against each other.

Mr. Skeleton had a silver chain around his neck that held a silver and enamel crucifix that was still shiny, so he must have been the master carpenter who had built the altar and the chests in the hidden chapel. His leather vest had been well made and had two pockets. In the right-hand pocket, they found a white opal ring for a lady, wrapped in a cloisonné box. In the left pocket, they found a folded piece of paper that was very brittle. Alice was reluctant to open the paper, but it came apart easily, and they were all curious to see if they could read its contents.

They held their breaths, but Alice realized the ink had turned brown and the writing was hard to make out. The words were in the old Irish, and only she could decipher them. She began to read the letter slowly and translated some of the old Irish as best she could:

Sneem
30 September, 1666

My darling Meg,

I've finally managed to get back to our castle after encountering many dangers in London where I posed under the name of Erasmus Longbow. I was supposed to be an industrious Dutch farmer, so it was a good thing that my old nurse, Greta, taught me to speak her language so well. Suspicion went hand in hand with the London fogs, and the police were stopping people everywhere.

I had gone to London to acquire some more treasures for us after our friend, Dan Black, sent me a note saying that the Great Plague there seemed to be coming to an end after it had killed thousands of people. No sooner had I landed there than a tremendous fire broke out. Of course, the fire was blamed on the Catholics and the Jesuits. It was a terrible thing and most of the city was destroyed. I managed to escape by the skin of my teeth. Michael O'Flaherty picked me up in his boat and we got back to our shores as fast as we could.

I've managed to add to our wealth pretty well again, and I've stored it all in the chests in the chapel. You recall that in our younger days I worked as a carpenter for the Globe Theatre before those dour and dutiful Puritans tore it down in 1644. At the time, the theatre people couldn't pay me, but Dan said they had smuggled out a copy of Mr. Shakespeare's First Folio and gave it to me. I'm not exactly sure what that means, but they say the Bard will become popular again, and it could be worth something in the future. I've hidden it at the bottom of the book chest.

I am going to have to stay home for some time now, since our old castle needs a lot of work. Last night I thought I heard some of the stones in the great hall making a loud cracking noise, so I have to make sure they are stabilized.

Please leave your father's farm as soon as you receive this note that I'll post to you tomorrow and head back to me. I can't wait to see you and Brigid. I've made arrangements for Father O'Sullivan to say Mass for us next weekend. I think he'll be pleasantly surprised at the beautiful altar we've created for our small but hardy group.

I bid you a fond farewell and can't wait until you are in my arms once more. I have a surprise waiting for you.

Prayers to St. Patrick for your safety!

With love from your own,
Billy Fitzpatrick

So, a very revealing document that answered a few of their questions. Billy Fitzpatrick must be the one responsible for putting all the treasures into the hidden room, and he was likely the ancestor of Bridie, the castle's good ghost, as well as her father, Rupert Fitzpatrick, who appeared to have been as bad as could be. Nora couldn't help wondering whatever happened to Meg and Brigid and how terrified they must have been when they had no word from Billy. The opal ring in Billy's pocket was probably the surprise he had mentioned, but Meg had never had a chance to see it.

They also found skeletons of two large dogs and a cat not far from Billy, and Nora hoped the animals hadn't suffered too much as they died. She was anxious to find what other things lay under the section that had thoroughly collapsed. So far, it appeared that anything at the edges of the collapse had been thoroughly destroyed, but some furniture and other things in the middle might still be salvageable.

They were surprised that some of the things they were able to see untouched were a whole set of Worcester blue china and pottery pitchers and bowls. A set of silverware in the Sheffield pattern appeared to be fine, although in need of a thorough polishing. Shelves, dressers, chairs, and clocks also appeared to have just moderate scuffing, which could have been from just use over time. They even found some bottles that still contained medicines and soaps.

However, the closer they got to the edges of the cratered ruins, the impact of the falling roof had destroyed everything. They would have to carefully install scaffolding over these areas so they wouldn't collapse before they tried to remove anything.

Over the years, plants had crept into the ruins and they were blooming nicely and covered much of what they could see. Insects and mice had found homes among the grass and creeping plants, and they skittered away as the excavators moved some of the grass. New forms of life had found ways to flourish among the remains of the old.

They were thrilled with their finds so far and looked forward to moving all these things to Alice's laboratory so that they could be appropriately cleaned and catalogued. Nora thought that once all the investigations had been completed and photographed, she would ask Father Lanigan from the village to say a Mass for Billy and then move him to the family cemetery next to her uncle Cyrus and aunt Emily. He had done his best to keep the faith of the community safe and growing, and he deserved a founder's honors.

Mr. Gainer and Alice told Nora that she still had a decision to make about the disposition of the old bricks that were being saved. Should they just remove everything, or should they reconstruct the old section with modern construction methods? Nora didn't hesitate.

She said she would like to have the old section reconstructed as it might have appeared more than three centuries ago, and she would like a doorway to be made between the old and newer sections of the castle.

There were still more questions to be answered that would take more research. If Billy wrote his letter more than three and a half centuries ago, but the newer part of the castle appeared to be no more than two centuries old, who had built the newer section that Nora and Tommy now called home? Alice said she would help them with that query also.

CHAPTER

42

Thursday, August 22
Sneem, Ireland; 10:00 a.m., IST

Nora had talked to various people at Duffy Medical as to what they needed to do to prepare for their company to be publicly traded on the New York Stock Exchange. They discussed the many meetings this would likely entail, and CEO John O'Malley said it would be good if they had a base of operations in New York.

Nora thought about that recommendation and decided that she and Tommy should buy a condominium that was centrally located in New York. She contacted her cousin Ted O'Loughlin, and he said he knew of several places that would fit the bill for what she was looking for.

She asked Tommy if he would be willing to make the trip to New York to work with Ted and send her pictures of likely places. He agreed and left the next day. Ted showed Tommy pictures of six different condos, and when they went to see them, Tommy was dazzled by the many styles of architecture to be found in the giant city. He sent Nora many pictures of each place and made sure to title them so she wouldn't get confused. By the end of the day, he thought the rehabbed condo that overlooked St. Patrick's Cathedral with the large room big enough for a boardroom table would be ideal. Nora agreed that this place seemed to be the best, and she told Tommy to give a down payment to Ted.

Nora heard from Chief Brennan, who said that they had gone to Doctor Allenby's house and did a thorough search. They found the big black trash bag hidden behind a pile of bricks in the basement. It contained a receipt from a car rental agency for a black Mercedes S-Class car, a long screwdriver, the two murdered girls' clothes, and Dotty's black purse.

Dotty Dillon's family wanted nothing to do with the clothes, and they had asked the funeral home to send her remains to the local cemetery. Annie Matthews's parents had a funeral Mass said for her before her burial in St. Mary's churchyard. They said they would burn her clothes and sprinkle the ashes over the patch of ocean that Annie particularly loved. They had a recording of her playing Mozart's *Lacrimosa*, and they would listen to it as the ashes floated out over the waves. The chief had learned not to be too sentimental about his work long ago, but he said the response of the Matthews's family pierced even his thick skin.

Nora met with Tim Taylor, the veterinarian at the castle, and asked him how things were going for him and for the animals. Tim said that he and Betsy had attended a first meeting of Gamblers Anonymous, and he had been frightened to hear the stories of people who had lost everything due to their gambling addiction. He thought that he would never want to gamble again, but Betsy told him that he must continue to attend the meetings to make sure that was the case. They were scheduled to attend another meeting tomorrow night.

Tim and Betsy had scheduled their wedding for a year from now, and she was happy to wear a pretty engagement ring they had found at a resale shop. She also told Tim she thought she could be perfectly happy living in the apartment over the stables when the time came. They had also thought about how they could repay Nora's generosity and were making monthly payments toward that goal. Nora thought she would tell them later that they wouldn't have to do that forever, but she was glad to hear that Tim realized that would be a good thing to do.

Nora was also happy to hear that Chief Brennan had investigated the "Joe" who had gotten Tim mixed up with gambling. The garda found a number of violations that the smarmy man was involved with, and he was currently in jail awaiting a trial.

The animals were all doing pretty well. The bog ponies had contracted some kind of respiratory illness, but he had been giving them antibiotics, and they were showing a positive reaction to the medication. Flossie, Jack Boyle's dog, continued to show good progress after the vicious kicking she'd received, but he thought it likely that her left hind leg, which had already been a problem, would continue to bother her even more now.

Tim said that they were all looking forward to the end of summer party that was going to be happening on the castle grounds in a few days, so that would be good timing. Everyone had been preparing their own specialties for it, and so far, it looked as though the weather was going to cooperate. Betsy had told him she'd heard that so many people from the Ring of Kerry towns were planning to attend. She had started making jewelry and planned to have a booth near the stables. Nora thought that all sounded wonderful, but she hoped that no violent events would be occurring to mar everyone's good time.

Nora was anxious to see the condo that Tommy had picked out for them in New York, and she decided to travel there for a few days to check it out. Her father had traveled to New York yesterday for a convention of cardiologists, so the timing seemed serendipitous.

CHAPTER

43

Nora's only other trip to New York City had been when she was about three years old and her parents had made the long car trip to visit her father's aunt Hattie in Connecticut. She remembered the trip as being a lot about smells. Aunt Hattie had smiled at her a lot, but she kept wanting Nora to sit on her lap, and the old woman smelled as though she had poured a whole box of old talcum powder on herself.

When they stopped in New York City on the way back, her parents tried to point out various important buildings to her, but she was not interested after she smelled the garbage in the many alleys. She recalled sitting in the big park and throwing seeds to the pigeons, and they had a nice smell. She loved watching their shiny feathers and how they bobbed their heads up and down, and that was fun. Grownups were always in a hurry though, and she had been sorry to leave Joe and Josephine, as she had named the two prettiest birds.

As they were about to walk to their car for the trip home, two things happened to her that had remained important for her all her life. They passed a pawnbroker's store, and Doctor Duffy told her they knew it was that kind of store because it had a hanging ornament of three balls outside the building. Nora spotted a small violin in the window and refused to move. She had seen her neighbor Mr. Brown playing a violin, and she had been fascinated about how just a few strings could make so many nice sounds. Nora said she would like to try out the violin in the store window.

Eileen Duffy was reluctant to go into the seedy looking store, but Doctor Duffy said it wasn't often that Nora really wanted something, so they should take a look at the instrument. The proprietor said he thought their daughter looked awfully small to play the violin, but if they wanted it, it was a good quality instrument, and he would sell it to them for an attractive price. Nora loved the smell of the old instrument and the oil needed for the strings. They had found a talented teacher for her, Nora was determined to learn how to play well, and she had used that violin until she was a teenager.

Many years later, Nora had seen the very depressing but important movie with such excellent actors called *The Pawnbroker*. It was a mix of flashbacks to the Holocaust and visions of how the main character had suffered so much but survived to become a mean-spirited pawnbroker. She realized now where the merchandise in these shops came from and the broken dreams each item represented. She had no way of knowing who the original owner of her little violin had been, but she hoped that her long and happy use of it had provided some redemptive value for the person who had pawned this item so long ago.

They also passed a used bookstore, and the smell of all those books was addictive. Eileen Duffy had found a good quality illustrated book for her little girl of *Grimms' Fairy Tales*, and three-year-old Nora had learned to read as she made her way through the fascinating tales in the car all the way home. She noticed that people and animals in fairy tales seemed to come in threes or sevens, like dwarves and pigs and bears, and she had done a paper about that in high school. She always looked for these old bookstores when she traveled, and they had become places she loved to visit all her life.

Nora probably would not get to do much sightseeing on this trip, but she hoped to do that soon. The One World Trade Center building had replaced the horribly lost Twin Towers, and Nora hoped to get to that memorial before she had to go home.

Even if one had never been to New York City, if you read books, saw movies or plays, or watched television, you probably knew a lot about it already. History buffs remembered that those old Dutch traders bought Manhattan Island from the Lenape Indians for about twenty-four dollars' worth of trinkets. New York City was our nation's first capital for some years. Many people whose families had lived in the US for a long time could probably trace at least one ancestor who had come to the US via ship and was then processed through Ellis Island to make their fortunes—or not—in their new home.

Sometimes, they were given names quite different from their birth names. Just about every person in the world recognized the Statue of Liberty in New York Harbor as symbolic of our country. So many famous names came to mind when you thought of New York like Vanderbilt, Rockefeller, Roosevelt, Ruth, Macy, Trump and many more. You might not be able to pinpoint on a map where 34th Street; Fifth Avenue; Wall Street; Broadway; Central Park; the Hudson River; or the many museums, hotels, and sports stadiums were, but the names were familiar.

Nora smiled as she recalled the parade of famous movie stars that had sung and danced and talked their way through the hundreds of movies that had New York City as their backdrop. She thought of the many famous faces who played the characters on the other side of society as gangsters and their molls and the lawyers and policemen who opposed them. Movies had portrayed just about every facet of life in the city's many famous neighborhoods.

She hummed the song of the three famous sailors in Leonard Bernstein's *On the Town* as they sang about their favorite city:

> New York, New York, a wonderful town
> The Bronx is up and the Battery's down
> The people ride in a hole in the ground
> New York, New York, it's a wonderful town!

As she passed the Empire State Building and looked up, Nora could almost see Fay Wray screaming her lungs out when *King Kong* gently placed her on the building's top to spare her from harm as he battled the old planes and their machine guns. As the giant gorilla lay dying after falling from the peak, Carl Denham uttered one of the great movie lines, "It was beauty killed the beast." The Empire State Building was also the backdrop for Cary Grant and Deborah Kerr's *An Affair to Remember*. Nora thought that the handsome-but-self-absorbed Cary took too much time to realize why Deborah had not been able to meet him at the top. The ending was somewhat happy, but the matter of her wheelchair remained to be solved at a later date.

Nora thought that she probably was related to some of the charming-but-tough Irish policemen and politicians who had clawed their way up the ladder of New York society, but it was just as likely that one of her distant relatives had run a speakeasy.

She was able to get a taxi quickly at the airport and was astounded at the traffic that made Chicago streets seem mild. Her driver today was not the usual friendly sort she encountered in other cities, so she didn't attempt to have a conversation with him, but Hormuz was efficient and got her to her new address on Fifth Avenue at a pace that felt just short of being at the Indianapolis 500. Nora gave him a generous tip, and then Hormuz flashed her a big smile. Money is the universal language that unlocks the key to the heart's emotions.

Nora alighted from the cab and thought that Tommy had done very well indeed as to the location of the condo. She could see St. Patrick's Cathedral just a short way down the street, so future visitors could just ask for the Cathedral and cab drivers would have no trouble finding it. She stared at the famous old church building and could almost picture Fred Astaire and Judy Garland walking in their finery in *Easter Parade*. Nora wanted to see the inside of the Cathedral but decided to get settled in her apartment first.

Hormuz brought her suitcases up to the front of the building, and she bade him goodbye and good luck. She looked at the tented entrance of the building and was happy to see a doorman dressed in the black and gold livery of a toy soldier, including a proper top hat. Nora introduced herself to him, and he said his name was James, and he walked her into the lobby and introduced her to the security person for the morning, Rajah. He was a very tall dark-skinned man with the stiffest posture Nora had even seen. He said he knew she was coming today, and he hoped that she would be happy in her new home. So far, events were all going very smoothly.

Rajah gestured to a young man named Drexel, who put Nora's suitcases in an elevator and accompanied her to the tenth floor. He opened her room with his passkey, brought in the suitcases, and said he hoped Nora would spend many happy days with them. Nora looked out the window and was astounded at the height of the buildings and the little people she could see coming and going on the streets below.

She spent some time unpacking clothes and looking around the apartment. She thought this would be a perfect place to hold meetings for the Duffy Medical Board since the living room/dining room area was lengthy and could accommodate a table that would fit fifteen people on each side. There were three bedrooms and three bathrooms and a fully stocked kitchen. She wondered where the television was and found it nestled within a stylish buffet.

Nora thought that the white and chrome furniture was not the style she usually preferred, but it all looked very glamorous. She decided one of the first things she would do would be to order several unglitzy but comfortable armchairs for them. She was sure that the nighttime views of the New York skyline from the floor-to-ceiling windows would be spectacular.

Tommy was in Hawaii for a conference, and she called him to tell him that, once again, his genius was confirmed, and she loved the apartment. Tommy said he was in between sessions, and things seemed to be going well. He hadn't had a chance to see much of the beach yet, but he had been reminded of *The Brady Bunch* episodes about Hawaii that Nora and her family enjoyed so much. He hoped that he would not find anything like the little statuette that had brought the Brady boys such bad luck.

He was glad that Nora liked the apartment, and he agreed that they would need some comfortable furniture for it. Tommy said he hoped that they could both visit Hawaii on a vacation soon since the weather was glorious. He said he would see her in a few days, and he hoped this traveling would stop soon.

Nora tried out the condo's bed and thought the mattress was adequate, but she might have to replace that also. She took a nap and then had a call from her dad that his session was over for now, and he asked her if she would she like to come to lunch. She quickly agreed and dressed in a green daytime dress and started to leave her apartment.

As she was closing her door, an excitable corgi dog came running over to her barking and jumping on her legs. Nora thought the dog was adorable, and she did not mind at all, but her neighbor across the hall kept calling the dog and apologizing to Nora for her pet's boisterous behavior. "I'm so sorry, Miss. I hope Nula didn't tear your dress," intoned the tall woman across from her.

Nora explained to her that she was used to Irish wolfhounds, so a little corgi was no problem for her. Nora knelt down to pet the sweet dog, and Nula reciprocated with many kisses.

The two women shared some more conversation and then introduced themselves to each other. Nora pulled out photos of Liam the wolfhound, Bran the Irish setter in Ireland, and her other Chicago dogs. Margaret Kenmare was impressed that Nora could handle these dogs when she was so small. Margaret was another person who thought that Liam looked so huge that he could hardly be real, but Nora assured her that he was very real and very loving.

Nora told Margaret that Kenmare was one of the bigger towns on the Ring of Kerry tour in southwestern Ireland, so she had a famous surname. Margaret was surprised at that and said she would like to hear more about that another time, but she was on her way to meet her husband for lunch at the cardiologists' convention. Nora said that was a coincidence since her father was there as well. They traveled downstairs in the elevator, and Nula now made it clear that she wanted Nora to hold her, which she happily did. Margaret left the dog with the dog walker in the lobby of the hotel, but Nula barked out her displeasure with this arrangement. The two women proceeded to walk to the nearby hotel.

They met their men for lunch and had a delightful conversation. The cardiologists shared a little of what they had heard, and it did seem as though some improvements in technique seemed to be on the horizon. The two men got deeper into their medical conversation, so Nora and Margaret chatted some more.

Nora had become quite a good judge of character by now, and the more she heard Margaret speak about her interesting career in finance, she found herself wondering if this New Yorker would make a good addition to the Duffy Medical Board. In the past, the Irish Board members had expressed fears about Americans wanting to control their board, but she doubted whether Margaret wanted to control anything. She was so knowledgeable about finance and was an expert in international relations, and if Margaret was involved with something, Nora was sure that she wanted it to be as sound and perfect as possible.

Margaret was tall and slim, with short dark hair, and attractive in a no-nonsense way. She said she liked stylish shoes that accommodated her love for walking, but nothing would induce her to wear high heels. She was a New Yorker through and through, with the distinctive accent to match. She had grown up riding horses on her family's estate near Oyster Bay, and they were neighbors of the Teddy Roosevelt branch. When other children were playing hopscotch, Margaret was analyzing the movement of the stock market and keeping track of its progress. She had learned how to invest from her grandfather, and by the time she graduated from high school, she was already worth her first million dollars. She had to use her grandfather's services to invest for her since she was supposed to be at least twenty-one. Margaret could have gone anywhere to college, but she never liked being far away from New York, so she went to Columbia. She was like the proverbial New Yorker who thought of "west" as anything west of the Hudson River.

She was considered an expert on the New York Stock Exchange by the time she graduated from college and had become a consultant to several firms. She had met Martin at Columbia, but it had taken all his considerable charm to get her to marry him since she was so dedicated to her work. She had been horrified by the 9/11 damage that was done to her city, and she still found it painful to look at the space where the Twin Towers had been. She would have likely been in one of the towers, but Martin had talked her into flying to Mexico for a few days at the time.

Margaret said she relished a good cleaning lady and paid her more than she was worth since she did not like to spend time on anything that distracted her from concentrating on the flow of business. She said she was traditionally Catholic but only attended church on holidays. She thought she had family in Belfast but had never bothered to find them.

Nora asked her if she was familiar with Duffy Medical in Ireland, and Margaret said she had heard of them but since they weren't traded on the NYSE, she hadn't paid them too much attention. She had heard about her uncle Cyrus's death, and she had heard about Nora, her castle, and her fortune, but her knowledge was sketchy.

Michael Duffy and Eoghan Kenmare said they had to get back to their conference, so they bid them a fond farewell for now. Nora and Margaret walked the short way back to their hotel, and Nora thanked Margaret for a good time today. Margaret picked up Nula from the dog walker and went back to her apartment.

Nora went back to the condo with business on her mind. She knew that old Doctor Cadbury from the Duffy Medical Board was going to be retiring soon because of ill health, and she began to think that Margaret would make a good addition to their board. She called John O'Malley, Duncan Lloyd, and Fiona Finnegan and asked them what they would think if she recommended Margaret for membership on the board. She felt they needed an international membership, and Margaret would be a good start. They asked her to forward more particulars about Margaret to them and said they would talk it over and get back to her.

Margaret and Eoghan were having people over that evening and invited Nora and Michael to join them. Nora was impressed by her adroit handling of the people and the dinner. Nora steered the conversation to topics about the NYSE and once again Margaret handled it all with ease.

Nula the corgi contented herself with sitting on Nora's lap for a good petting, and Margaret said she had a new best friend. Nora told her more about Duffy Medical. Margaret said she was generally familiar with the company but was not so aware of where their scope of influence was. Nora found it interesting to meet other New Yorkers and found them to be just as she would have suspected, brusque, smart, and funny. She felt quite at home by the time the evening was over. The other women were dying to ask her more about her castle and her money, but they made an attempt to be polite and did not.

The next day, she heard from John O'Malley that the board would be willing to consider having Margaret join them, but they would want to meet her first. Fiona had her background checked out, and she appeared to be squeaky clean, except that she was a fan of Manchester United football, which choice was not popular with most Irishmen.

Nora called Margaret and Eoghan and asked them to come over to her condo that evening. They talked about a variety of subjects at first, and then Nora asked Margaret if she would consider becoming part of the board of Duffy Medical since they were looking for a more diverse membership. She told her that "more diverse" would mean anyone nonmale and non-Irish, so it would be something of a challenge. Nora said as the chairman of the board she had some influence, and she had given a heads up to the officers of the company, who were willing to hear what Margaret would have to say. That would involve her traveling to Sneem to meet them at their board meeting in a few days.

Margaret was intrigued and asked specific questions to see what they had in mind and then said she would consider it. Nora said she would sweeten the pot by giving her a good bonus. Eoghan said he also would be able to come for a few days.

Nora told her all about the postponement of the beginning of the medical research center and that now they were going to do it again on September 1. If it would be acceptable to them, Nora invited Margaret and Eoghan to this event, and they were happy to accept. She called Kitty at the castle and asked her to order plane tickets for herself and Margaret and Eoghan Kenmare of New York for August 27. Tommy would be meeting them there after his trip to Hawaii.

CHAPTER

44

Tuesday, August 27
In Flight to Ireland; 4:00 p.m., IST

Nora, Margaret, and Eoghan traveled to Ireland for the board meeting and the second attempt to begin construction of the Duffy Medical Research Center. Nora greeted her Aer Lingus friends and introduced them to her fellow travelers. The stewardesses in their green and blue suits paid extra attention to them since Nora was a very frequent traveler. The Kenmares were pleasantly surprised at their airline food. Margaret and Eoghan were looking forward to the trip since they had traveled to many countries but had never been to Ireland. Nora had provided Margaret with folders of information about Duffy Medical and a report that had recently been published about their balance sheet, and Nora saw her scribbling many notes on it.

Old Tim McMahon picked them up in Dublin, stowed their luggage in the boot, and asked them to look at the tasty treats Mrs. O'Hara had prepared for their four-hour trip to Sneem. Margaret and Eoghan delighted in the scenic countryside, and Nora was impressed that Margaret had taken the time to look up the financials for the state of the economy in Ireland. She said she knew that Ireland had benefitted from being a member of the European Union, and they soon saw a roadside sign that bore that out, saying that this highway had been built with funds from that source. Nora wondered what Margaret really thought of this much smaller country, and she was anxious to talk to her when they got to the castle.

Tim stopped the car at Tipperary so they could all stretch their legs and take a walk around. Eoghan said that the world was familiar with the name of this town since it had been popularized in the "It's a Long Way to Tipperary" song of World War I, but he thought of it as being a popular destination even today. The group partook of some of Mrs. O'Hara's treats, and then Tim said they should get back in the car so they could get to Sneem before it got dark.

As they approached the last stretch of roadway leading up to the castle, Nora thought she saw a smile on Margaret's face, and she was glad she was enjoying herself. She doubted whether this controlled woman let that happen very often.

Nora was glad that they were approaching her home away from home at Sneem, but it was going to take a long time before she would feel really comfortable knowing that neither Uncle Cyrus nor Aunt Vinnie were going to be able to give her a hug.

When they had negotiated the winding road leading up to the castle steps, Nora saw Liam and Bran waiting for her, and she braced herself for their enthusiastic greetings. After enduring many lickings and barkings, the dogs finally pulled away from her and let her breathe, and she petted their beautiful heads and sang them the special song she had created for them, "Good Morning, Glories."

Margaret had seen pictures of wolfhounds before, but the size of Liam was so amazing she could hardly believe it. The huge dog seemed much too big for little Nora with his extra tall height. No wonder Nora had no trouble controlling Nula, her tiny corgi. Bran the Irish setter was more reserved in his greeting, and he appealed more to Margaret.

The Kenmares recognized Nora's husband, Tommy, from his pictures. He and Nora embraced, and he gave her and Margaret bouquets of yellow daisies, the castle's symbolic flowers. Tommy shook hands with the guests and attempted to quiet down the excited dogs.

Mr. O'Keefe the butler and Mrs. Doyle the housekeeper strode in through the chaos and welcomed Nora and Tommy home and bid the others a thousand welcomes. Mrs. O'Hara the cook stood at the top of the stairs and asked them all to come in and get settled and said she had dinner almost ready.

Nora was happy to greet Father Ahearn, Monsignor Callahan, Gloryann Graber, and Dan Buck and his wife, Amy, who had come earlier today. The Kenmares greeted them and thought that Nora was an expert in finding a host of good friends. The younger Duffy and Barry siblings were unable to be here because they were already in school, but a few of Nora's siblings were able to come and they exchanged hugs.

Margaret kept looking around and writing notes in her diary. When Nora had called this a castle, she thought she might have been exaggerating, but the term castle was the only word that aptly described the tall limestone building with its crenelated top and its antique furnishings.

Nora had had an elevator installed a few months ago to accommodate older visitors, and Mrs. Doyle showed them to it. She led them to their rooms and said if they wanted to freshen up, they should do so, and then dinner would be served in forty-five minutes. She asked them to be on time since one of the dishes was a soufflé, which would collapse if left to stand too long, which would make Mrs. O'Hara very unhappy. Eoghan Kenmare just kept looking around in wonder and thought this would be a fun place to retire to.

The dinner guests saw the appealing table with its white lace tablecloth and Belleek china and Waterford glassware and silverware and were stunned by its beauty. The Kenmares had a discerning palette and had heard that Ireland was scenic, but its cooking was predictable. Mrs. O'Hara had chosen a wine that perfectly complemented the flaky filet of sole with a spicy sauce they could not quite identify, and the potato and vegetable soufflé was fragrant and fluffy. The baked apples came from an orchard on the castle's grounds. The rolls were homemade, and Nora introduced Eoghan to the brown bread she loved. When dinner was over, the Kenmares thought that whoever had said Irish food was boring had never visited Duffy Hall Castle.

The castle's food would not quite fit at a New York restaurant, but it was delicious in its own unique way, and both of them were hungry for more. Mrs. O'Hara's strawberry and golden raisin bread pudding with a lemon drizzle was "to die for," and like nothing they'd ever tasted before. Eoghan almost never ate dessert but he found himself asking for a second helping.

Everyone seemed quite comfortable, and the conversation flowed easily among the group. Margaret found it interesting that Nora and Tommy had left the gray bricked castle walls unadorned for the most part, but the atmosphere somehow appeared homey. Nora explained to them that they had made few changes to how the castle had been when Nora inherited it, but they had the circlet of spears that adorned the walls in the great hall removed and put into storage. This type of arrangement of various implements of war appeared to be popular in the old castles, but Nora refused to think more about what they had been used for.

The guests admired the large photographs of Cyrus Duffy, his wife Emily, and his sister Lavinia, and Nora and Tommy relayed a little about them. They also told them a little more about Duffy Medical and how the plans to construct the medical research center had come about. Nora thought it only fair to tell the Kenmares and the others about the recent murders that had happened not far from here and told them what they knew so far.

Nora got out her violin and played "The Wearing of the Green" as the Kenmares glanced through the many old books on the library shelves. By 10:00 p.m., Tommy told them he thought they should head upstairs to get some rest since they had arranged for some sightseeing for them tomorrow. Bran had taken a liking to Eoghan Kenmare and accompanied him to the stairway. Nora told them they would find fragrant products in the bathrooms and bedrooms that had been developed by her aunt Vinnie, and she hoped they would enjoy them.

She relayed a little about Aunt Lavinia's history and how she had started a perfume business with her friend from university, all unknown to her family. Today Carol Cleary's, Vinnie's name for her company, is a multimillion-dollar business. It all started with four perfumes named for seasonal feelings, Springy, Summery, Harvesty, and Shivery. Margaret found it hard to believe that the famous perfume line had started life in this out of the way place, which held more secrets than anyone knew! The reference to millions of dollars also caught Margaret's attention, and she said she would like to hear more about it later. Nora whispered to her that now that Vinnie was dead, Nora was also the chairman of the board for Carol Cleary's, and Margaret simply smiled and shook her head.

Nora told them they would start the day tomorrow fairly early, but they would let them sleep so they could get over their jet lag. The castle had the gift of restful sleep, but if they slept too long, she would send the dogs in to get them up. The Kenmares were beginning to think that there could be someplace worthwhile other than New York after all.

Nora and Tommy were glad to lay down on their beautiful bed and admired the ceaseless motion of the stars and the roar of the ocean waves. Tommy tried to tell Nora more about Hawaii, but as he reached over to give her a kiss, he noticed that she was already in the land of dreams.

Wednesday, August 28

Margaret Kenmare took Nora aside a day before the start of the board meeting and said she had carefully examined all the materials she had been given about Duffy Medical. She knew they were looking for information they could use to set up a meeting with the New York Stock Exchange and Securities and Exchange Commission representatives to talk about an IPO and when that might take place. Margaret wanted to warn Nora that she planned to tell the board they were not yet ready.

Margaret said they were doing an excellent job within their current sphere of influence, but as far as being an international firm, they had several drawbacks. They were too insular and too impressed with themselves. She would put this in more tactful language and knew this would not go over with them well, but they had hired her to tell them the truth and not to pat them on the back.

"Is there any hope for the future?" asked Nora as she contemplated what the serious woman across from her had just said.

"Of course, there is," responded Margaret, "and I have a number of suggestions, but I am going to tell them that they should wait for at least another six months before requesting the IPO. There's a lot more work to do."

Nora thought Margaret was probably right, but she knew the board members would likely not see it that way. Their bottom line was profitable, and they would not take kindly to a woman—and a non-Irish woman at that—telling them that they should delay their plans.

"I hate to put a damper on the excitement over the start of the medical research center, Nora," said Margaret, "but I believe that is the best recommendation I can give them. This is not a reflection on you as the chairman of the board, but I do not believe the NYSE will approve of the board's application at this time."

Nora said she knew Margaret was right, but she said she would ask the board to schedule that discussion for the end of the meeting so the rest of the meeting would not be too stressful.

When the board meeting was held two days later, the agenda had discussions about a few other problems, reports from Duffy Foundation—Ireland and US, setting the date for their Christmas Ball, and then the discussion about the IPO. Nora tried not to be too upset about what Margaret intended to tell them, but she was concerned.

She would update the board on the treasures that had been found in the castle and the preliminary planning for what was to become of them. She'd also have Chief Brennan attend so he could give them a report on the garda progress in discovering who had killed Jack Boyle since that had happened on the grounds of the castle, their company's headquarters, and they still did not know who had killed him.

Nora spent a few minutes talking to Fiona Finnegan, who said that she was impressed by Margaret Kenmare and thought she would make a good addition to their board. They needed a woman and a non-Irish member who was an expert in international finance, and Margaret seemed to fit that bill perfectly. Fiona said they should have Margaret talk to the board at their meeting tomorrow and see what the members' reaction would be.

Friday, August 30

Nora woke up with a premonition that everything was going to be fine at the board meeting. This was no guarantee of success, but she thought that she and the other officers were prepared for every eventuality, and she was sure that Margaret Kenmare would be a pleasant surprise to them. She had not been for a run to the Coral Beach since she had found Dotty Dillon's body under the rhododendrons, so she called Chief Herlihy and told him of her plans. He was not best pleased to get her phone call at 5:00 a.m., but he said he would send Johnny Moreland to meet her and accompany her. Nora explained that it was just going to be her since Tommy said he was going to stay in bed for a while.

Nora prepared for the day and got the dogs ready. She noticed that Tinker Bell was growing fast and could now climb out of her habitat by herself, so she picked her up as they all ran down the filigree staircase and put her in the kitchen where she felt more comfortable. Mrs. O'Hara would give her some treats as soon as she appeared in her kitchen.

Johnny appeared looking as though he wished he were still in bed, but he greeted Nora with a smile. She warned him that once the dogs got into their running mode, they set quite a pace. They skipped down the twenty-eight steps out the front door and began to run west. Nora saluted Uncle Cy's famous silver leprechaun statue that she had nicknamed Barney, but he was not shining very much today since the sky was overcast. The temperature was encouraging though, so she did not worry too much about rain. Her board members were used to the changeable weather on the Kerry coast.

Johnny was a young man, but he only ran once in a while. He was panting by the time they spotted the abandoned building, but Nora assured him they were almost there. She was happy to see that the first steps toward the construction of the lighthouse memorial for Jack Boyle had taken place. Nora had instructed Mr. Carmody to make sure that the foundation stones were sturdy so the lighthouse would stand for a long time on this spot. The place they had decided on appeared to be ideal too since it was on the rise of land next to the beach so its LED lantern would be seen for a long distance.

Johnny was glad when they finally stopped running, and he told Nora that he would stand by the wall with the dogs while she said good morning to her friends. Nora told him that she would appreciate his watching for any danger to her, but keeping Liam and Bran tied up was not going to work. She took back their leashes and led them close to the pounding waves and unstrapped their leashes and gave them a drink of the bottled water she had brought along and some treats. The dogs joyously greeted the ocean and barked out their happiness as they ran back and forth, trying to catch the incoming waves and the annoying seagulls.

Nora greeted some of the early bird-watchers, and a few of them gathered around her to welcome her back and tell her how happy they thought Jack would be about the lighthouse. She told them that she was hopeful it would be completed well before winter, and there would also be a patio area with several picnic tables and benches and a water fountain. She thanked them for any donations they had made and told them that she had asked Father Lanigan to come and bless the lighthouse when it was finally completed, and she hoped they would come for that.

Nora got out the blanket she had brought along and sat down to wait for the sun to appear over the hill and the thatched cottages. She thanked God for the new day and asked his blessings on her efforts today to move Duffy Medical forward with a few good pushes. The board members had worked hard for so many years, but it was time for them to move well into the twenty-first century. She felt happy and confident, and that was usually a sign of a good day ahead.

She mentally reviewed the agenda she would present to the board later this morning, and she thought they would be happy about the almost all good news at the soundness of their company's finances and future. When it came to the discussion about the NYSE and the IPO, she was concerned about it, but she had confidence in Margaret and her abilities.

The stars gradually disappeared, and the sun rose in glorious color. Nora had paid for a cell phone tower to be constructed in an out of the way place on the castle's estate, so there was no problem with using cell phones on the beach now. She called Johnny and said he should join her so that they could start the trip back to the castle. The dogs were disappointed to leave the water and some of their canine friends they had encountered, but they answered Nora's call and submitted to having their leashes put on again. She gave them treats, and they started the trip back to the castle. All had been peaceful.

Nora's sister Siobhan said she wanted to go into Dublin to meet with the director of the Abbey Theatre, who had potentially offered her a position with the company. Nora was hesitant to have her go into Dublin alone, but Maureen said she would go with her to act as chaperone. Nora and Siobhan both rolled their eyes at that, but it would be good for both of them to have a companion.

Nora wished Siobhan good luck and said she knew she would be a big hit. She had been preparing for this since she was five years old. She was auditioning for a part as one of the village girls in *The Playboy of the Western World* by John Millington Synge that had premiered at the Abbey Theatre many years ago, and she was so excited. Nora asked Tim McMahon to drive the girls there, which would take about four hours and wait to give them a ride back home. She gave Tim a generous number of euros so he could do some shopping while he was waiting.

Nora had debated about what to wear today but decided that her old and comfortable black suit with her black-and-white high heels would heighten her image to the board as business like but nonthreatening. She discovered that a little more sleep had restored Tommy's good humor. After they both got showered and dressed, they skipped down the stairs to see what delicious repast Mrs. O'Hara had prepared for them today.

Nora was happy to see that Margaret and Eoghan Kenmare were already seated at the dining table, and Margaret had chosen a similar outfit to Nora's with a green blouse under her black suit. She looked every inch of the financial genius that she was, and that added to Nora's confident mood.

The other guests gradually wandered in for the breakfast feast that Mrs. O'Hara had prepared for them, assisted by her helpers

Biddy and Johnny. Nora bid them farewell and said that she would be gone for a few hours for the board meeting, so Tommy would be in charge of being their tour guide today.

She was also looking forward to seeing the former officials of Duffy Medical who had had to resign last year due to the misplaced trust they had given to their wives' false story about Nora and Aunt Lavinia. Fred Carroll had been the chief accountant and Ben Jordan the treasurer, and they had been two of Uncle Cyrus's first hires. The board thought they had to fire them last year, but a number of members said they missed their wise counsel and expertise, especially with these discussions coming up about the New York Stock Exchange. The two men had apologized to her and to the board many times for their foolish mistakes, and they were anxious to help them now.

Fred Carroll's wife, Valerie, could have been accused of criminal behavior, and Ellen Jordan had helped her along the way, but Nora had been anxious to stave off bad publicity, and she felt sorry for the men who had helped Duffy Medical from the beginning. Valerie had learned a little humility by being sentenced to working at a pensioners' home. Once she started using her considerable talents in a better way, she could be a big help to them. Nora knew that she would delight in giving her advice about better ways to decorate everything. Ellen Jordan would fall into line with whatever Valerie recommended.

Nora, Margaret, and the other officers headed to the great hall where the secretary Mary Kenton handed them agendas and led them to their places at the long and highly polished table. As usual, Doctor Cadbury was already there, and Nora was sorry that he would be retiring but his ill health kept getting worse. The other members kept arriving, and at the stroke of 10:00 a.m., CEO John O'Malley promptly called the board to order. He welcomed Margaret Kenmare and said they would be hearing from her later. Nora thought she heard a few sighs from the older members, but she kept hoping all would be well.

Secretary Mary had forwarded the minutes of the last meeting, and she asked for a formal approval, which was quick in coming. Then they began the discussions of the items on the agenda. They began with a few problems that had arisen in a few countries, and after some discussion, they decided they were not that serious, so they would ask the CEOs in those locations to handle things themselves and submit a report at the next board meeting.

Most of the items on the agenda were informational for the members. They heard reports on the Duffy Foundation—Ireland and US, Nora told them about the treasures that had been found under the collapsed part of the old castle, and the preliminary planning that was being done about them. She told them they were still finding out if the treasures could be fully claimed by the castle. Nora had asked Chief Brennan to attend so he could tell them more about looking for the killer of Jack Boyle, but all he could tell them was that they were still pursuing the investigation with vigor. He assured them that some of his best men were still at the castle on a full-time basis to ensure their safety. There was some discussion about the best date for the Duffy Medical Christmas Ball, but they settled pretty easily on Saturday, November 30.

John O'Malley suggested they take a short break and when they returned, they would be discussing the plan for meeting with members of the New York Stock Exchange and the possibility of an initial public offering for Duffy Medical. Mary Kenton and her assistant tidied up the table and put out new water bottles for everyone. Nora saw some heated conversations going on in the hallways.

When everyone returned, John O'Malley introduced Margaret Kenmare, and she was greeted with restrained applause. Most of their members were younger, but a few of the older ones were still uncomfortable with the idea of a woman being in their midst other than in a subservient role.

Margaret had dealt with men like this all of her professional life, and she didn't let that bother her at all. She first got their attention by talking about Duffy Medical in a way that indicated to them that she knew more about the company than they did and that they had nothing to fear from her. She told them they had a meeting set up with members of the NYSE in the near future, and they should still hold that meeting, but it was her strong recommendation that they delay trying for the IPO at least six months so they could do more preparation and planning.

By the time she was finished, even the grumpiest of the group had to admit that she would make a good addition to their midst and seemed to know what she was talking about. Fred Carroll and Ben Jordan, the recently reinstated members, were the men who knew the most about financial affairs, and they said they thought Margaret's conservative approach was correct. A motion was made to have Margaret Kenmare become a member of their board and to have her meet with Fred and Ben on a regular basis. All hands were raised with aye, and Nora breathed easier.

Any spouses who had been patiently waiting for the meeting's end were then invited in for one of Mrs. O'Hara's brunch buffets. Eoghan Kenmare joined Margaret, but Tommy was acting as the tour guide today for the rest of their guests. Nora and Margaret exchanged a few smiles at the happy end to their perceived problems, and they dug into the delicious food and drinks.

Tommy suggested that they should all take a ride to Bunnyconnellan in Cork for the magnificent view of the ocean and their delicious food. Those with more energy could hike on some of the trails, while the others could go shopping or just sit and commune with nature. When everyone returned home to the castle, they were tired but energized by their engaging experiences.

Siobhan and Maureen arrived back from Dublin, and her huge smile told Nora all that she needed to know. Siobhan had been hired for one season and would have a small part in the play she had auditioned for! Nora wasn't sure how her parents would react to this news, but this profession of acting had been in Siobhan's blood since she was a little girl, and now she'd be able to see if she really wanted to make this her life's work. All in all, this had been a good day for the Duffys!

On Saturday, Nora and Tommy had final meetings with everyone who would be involved with the construction dig on Sunday and all seemed well. They gave Mrs. O'Hara and her crew a rest and imported food from the Two Squares Pub for dinner, and everyone had a relaxing evening. The sunset was gorgeous, and Nora felt as though it symbolized a happy day for tomorrow.

CHAPTER

45

Sunday, September 1
Sneem, Ireland; 6:00 a.m. IST

Today turned out to be an even better day weather-wise than the first time they had attempted to start the construction for the Duffy Medical Center. Nary a cloud appeared in the sky as Nora, and Tommy took the dogs for a run. Afterward, they again looked at the security arrangements, checked out the bathroom facilities and anything else they could think of that could go wrong, and everything seemed to be in order.

They made sure that all the sleepy heads at the castle were up and they directed Father Ahearn and Monsignor Callahan to the chapel that sat on the grounds of the estate. The two priests were amazed at the beauty of the lake and its multibirded population and waved to the red deer who seemed pretty tame. The chapel was small but beautifully appointed, and the two priests said a quick Mass for them while Nora accompanied them on the small pipe organ. The Kenmares were among the handful in the congregation, and Margaret automatically estimated the worth of this attractive building with its dark-hued stained-glass windows.

They passed the stone tower that had acted as Uncle Cyrus's astronomical observatory. Nora had the building restored and made sure there were no locks on the ground floor doors and phone capabilities were installed so future stargazers would have no security concerns. Nora told Margaret and Eoghan she hoped to show them the building later today.

Tommy led them to a front row seat facing the space, where the audience would be seated for the groundbreaking ceremony, and he gave them the brochure that portrayed the limestone foundation topped by two stories of glass and steel, where scientists and doctors would be researching rare diseases and hoping to develop cures for them.

Waiters were passing out Mrs. O'Hara's breakfast sandwiches and juices. They could see that the parking lot was getting crowded, and the two thousand seats were being rapidly filled.

John O'Malley, Duffy Medical CEO, and Duncan Lloyd, Chief Solicitor and their wives welcomed the Kenmares. Fiona Finnegan, Nora's personal solicitor, made it a point to sit next to Margaret Kenmare. They had discovered several shared interests, and it was a novel feeling for Margaret to feel as though she had made a good friend in this place so far from home.

While they were enjoying the festivities for the construction start, Nora also dedicated a white garden filled with the most beautiful white flowers she could find to the memory of Aunt Lavinia Duffy and placed a plaque on its wall. When the old part of the castle was finally rebuilt, Nora planned to dedicate it to Lavinia's long-dead fiancé, Mortimer O'Brien, as a place where people could come to study the amazing variety of Irish architecture, one of Mort's passions. Nora never forgot the debt she owed to Aunt Vinnie, and she planned to do whatever she could to keep both their memories alive.

Gradually, all the board members and their wives appeared, and Nora was happy to greet Ben Jordan and Fred Carroll. They greeted Nora with grateful hugs. Next to them stood their wives who had largely been responsible for the debacle that had led to their husbands being fired.

Valerie Carroll couldn't help herself. She said she admired Nora's green and blue outfit, but she somehow made it seem as though such a grudging admission was being dragged from her. Pride like Valerie's doesn't disappear overnight. Ellen Jordan nodded to Nora and gave her an awkward smile.

Nora saw her old friends from the estate and the town and greeted them all warmly. She was happy to see that it appeared that Lucy Sullivan, the coroner, was being escorted by the usually distant master coroner Aloysius Stec, while Gemma Doherty was on the arm of his assistant Paul McShane, who had been a widower for some time now. Nora thought these were interesting developments, and she hoped that things would continue happily for them.

Once again, the signal was given for the powerful tractors to begin removing the dirt from around the perimeter of the new building's footprint and a large section in the middle, and Nora had fingers crossed. This time, all went well and by the end of the morning it was easy to imagine how large this new building was going to be.

A few brief speeches were made by members of the board, Doctor McGarry from the castle, and Nora. Then the crowd was entertained by the children from the orphanage, and everyone again sang Ireland's stirring anthem. A barbecue lunch was served, and a huge cake that had been sculpted to look like the new building was cut and served. Nora thought the day had gone better than they had expected.

Tim Taylor was suddenly at her side, and he asked her to accompany him to the terrace where they could talk privately. He said that he was concerned about one of Nora's relatives who was out in the stable with the horses. Nora could tell by his demeanor that something was really amiss, so she asked Tommy to take care of the guests and said she had to attend to something.

Aunt Janet's youngest daughter was Carrie, and she was about the same age as the Duffy twins. She had accompanied her mother from Sonoma to the celebration today. Carrie had long blond curly hair and dressed like a rock star. When they were younger, the girls had so much fun together, but the twins noticed that Carrie seemed to have changed considerably when they had last seen her in California. She was only fifteen but wore provocative clothing, smoked when she thought her mother wasn't around, and told Molly and Caitlan she knew where she could get some weed.

The girls were shocked at first, and Caitlan didn't know what to say, but Molly had no trouble challenging her immediately since she was the president of the Say No to Drugs organization at her high school. She told their cousin that she was beautiful and smart, and there should be no need for her to use anything like a mind-altering drug. Carrie turned her back on them and left the twins in a huff.

Tim said that Carrie had gone out to the stables and saddled up Star, the beautiful white horse with a black star on her head that used to belong to Aunt Lavinia. Carrie had her own horse in California and was a frequent competitor in dressage. When Star did not respond fast enough to Carrie's commands, she had hit the horse in the side with pointed spurs that made bloody marks on the poor horse's side. Nora went out to see for herself and examined the horse. She was horrified to see that Tim was so right, and Star was whinnying in distress. Nora asked Tim to take good care of the injured horse right away.

She sent word to the house that Carrie Kelly should come out to the stables. The girl sulkily arrived and asked what the problem was. Nora told her in no uncertain terms that she could ride the horses after she had asked permission, but she was never to use pointed spurs. Rounded spurs just let the horse know what you want, but sharp pointed spurs could cause painful injuries. Nora asked her how the nonapproved spurs had come to be used on this horse that had belonged to her aunt and was so special to everyone at the castle. Carrie said she used pointed spurs all the time back home, and she found some at the back of the stable. Nora repeated that this would not be acceptable at her stables, but Carrie said she could not understand why there was all this excitement over just a horse.

Nora noticed the girl's dilated pupils and nervous motions and realized that Carrie was using drugs. She told her that no drugs were tolerated at Duffy Hall, and cousin or no, she would have to ask her family to leave, which would make her sad since her mother was especially loved. Carrie was sent back to the house for now and asked to stay in the game room.

Nora talked to Aunt Janet that night about Carrie and told her she was very worried about her. Aunt Janet said she had noticed how nervous Carrie had been lately, and she had wondered if drugs were involved, but Carrie had assured her they were not.

Nora responded to her sweet aunt, "Please get your beautiful daughter into treatment as soon as you get home. I know it feels uncomfortable that you can't believe her promises, and she will try to make you feel guilty because you don't. Above all, do not think you can handle this by yourselves. It becomes almost impossible to get people to just stop once they become addicted, which happens quicker than they think. They become good actors and will look you in the eye and lie convincingly. They will cheat, steal, assault, and even kill to get more money to buy drugs.

"Carrie needs to be on antidrug shots and be part of a drug rehab program right away. Young people are especially at risk for a drug overdose which can lead to mental problems or even death."

Aunt Janet tearfully thanked Nora for the advice and said she never thought that her beautiful daughter would do anything so foolish. Nora assured her that regardless of the family's demographics, the reliance on opioids was all too common and dangerous. Nora felt as sorry as possible for Carrie's dear parents and knew they were all going to have a hard road ahead.

For the most part, today had gone very well. Maybe they should add drug addiction to the list of diseases they were going to research at the new building. It seemed to be a very needy and timely topic.

Mr. Carmody said he estimated that the timing for the under-roof construction of the new building would be approximately 1 December, if the coming winter was mild "and the creek didn't rise." It would take another three to four months to complete the interior facilities, especially the protected safe room. Nora thanked him for his persistence, and said she appreciated anything he could do to get it finished quickly, but more importantly, she wanted the building to be constructed very well.

CHAPTER

46

Sunday, September 1
Sneem, Ireland; 9:00 p.m., IST

Nora and Tommy were happy to greet Adam and Cathy O'Mara and Peggy O'Reilly later that night and caught up on their news. When they had returned to their home in Ireland from Chicago, Peggy had joyfully picked out furniture for her bedroom that resembled the 1930s styles she had seen at Chicago's Art Institute. Peggy proudly showed them a picture of the long silvery drapes on the windows, the dark blue velvet headboard on the bed, and the intricately carved bookcase filled with books. It was the bedroom of a much older person, but Peggy's past experiences had hurried along her maturation.

They often met Mr. O'Mara for lunch, and Peggy had started school at St. Michael's. She was pleasantly surprised that most of the kids were nice to her, and she reciprocated. Of course, there were two girls who made some unpleasant comments about her bandages, but when the teachers became aware of it, the girls and the parents were called in and told that it had to stop immediately.

Peggy renewed plans with the O'Maras and gradually began to feel comfortable with them. They brought her back to the orphanage every few weeks to see the nuns and the other children. The O'Maras went to the local Irish dancing teacher and made plans for Peggy to begin lessons.

The O'Maras took her to see Doctor O'Connor in Cork, and he said the surgeries on her face and her back appeared to be healing well and he would watch them carefully. Doctor O'Connor heard Peggy's full story and also asked the O'Maras to visit his friend Doctor Mary Donovan, a psychotherapist.

Doctor Donovan assured Peggy that none of the events in her past were her fault, and unfortunately, she was hardly alone. She told her about the many thousands of children who were caught up in the web of the international sex trade, which Peggy had never heard about. She realized that things could have been even worse for her.

Peggy's new parents had been telling her that amazing grace was not just a song but a real gift to us from God and that we just have to be willing to accept it. She realized that, had she persisted in her foolish self-martyrdom, she could have brushed aside the salvation that was dangling right in front of her. She thanked God for the O'Maras and Nora Duffy and realized she was praying. It was a relief and a challenge, and she thought that she would very much like to be adopted by this wonderful couple.

She talked to the O'Maras about it when they got home, and they all had a good cry and rejoiced that this day had come about. They also realized that the path ahead would not always be strewn with roses since the next time they went to Cork, Peggy saw someone who reminded her of the man who had burned her face and back. She had a panic attack that night, but the O'Maras had learned some coping skills from Doctor Donovan, and the little family held hands and took strength from each other. They told Peggy to remember the days she had spent in the chapel talking to Mary, Our Mother, and she recalled them and was comforted.

Adam O'Mara told Nora they had one big hurdle to get over. They knew that Peggy's birth father was around somewhere, and they would need his sign off for them to officially adopt Peggy. Nora promised him she would find out more and let him know.

Nora had to do more about the treasures they had found at the castle, and she usually subscribed to the theory that a simple solution to a complicated problem was often the best. Duffy Hall Castle was not only their home but also the business headquarters for an international firm. Soon, it would also be the headquarters for a medical research facility that would house visiting scientists and doctors who would need quiet for their important work.

She was convinced that guarding the treasures from loss or theft would take too much time and effort as well as disturbing the peace of Duffy Hall Castle and the surrounding estate. She asked Fiona to get in touch with various institutions that were used to securing famous works of art and public visits to see if they would be willing to accept their treasures on an "on loan from" basis.

She thought the Vatican might like to have the cloth pieces, Chicago's Art Institute would probably like to display the famous paintings, and Trinity College in Dublin might like most of the books they had found. She thought the *King of Ireland* foul paper play by Shakespeare should be housed at Trinity College but produced as a play first by the Abbey Theatre in Dublin. She was still debating about where to house the Shakespeare First Folio. She had been thinking it might be fitting to keep it at the reconstruction of the Globe Theatre in London, but she wondered if they had sufficient security. A lot more research would be needed.

Before any of that happened, she'd been thinking that when the old part of the castle was reconstructed, they could portray Billy Fitzpatrick working at his desk with his two dogs and cat twirling around his feet and surrounded by his digital treasures. She recalled the movie producer she had met in California, Robert Durkin, and she thought he could recommend people to her that could make the treasures come alive via the gift of film and technology. That way, they would still have a digital reminder of the treasures but not have to worry about any of them being lost or stolen.

The first thing that put a crimp in her plans was that Fiona Finnegan had discovered that big institutions had a bunch of hoops that you had to jump through before they would accept more treasures. There were reams of paperwork, international rules that needed to be applied, security concerns, and curators and specialists that needed to observe and approve of the donated items. Then there were the schedules of the institutions that had to accommodate any new treasures. Most of them had their agendas planned for years into the future, so it was iffy as to when their treasures might be shown, no matter how valuable they were.

Word had gotten out in the literary community about the lost First Folio and the foul paper *King of Ireland* play, and the experts were surprised and willing to fight each other to acquire them. Nora thought about Billy Fitzpatrick and what he might think about all this.

Tommy and Nora and their guests would be leaving in the morning to return to the US, so Nora encouraged them to get to bed since they would be leaving very early. Everyone thanked them for the wonderful time they'd had, and they gradually headed upstairs to bed.

Nora and Tommy were going to New York in the morning to the condo they had purchased, and she had also discovered a man she thought might be Peggy O'Reilly's birth father and invited him to meet her there. She would do as much as she could to ensure that he would agree to the O'Maras' adoption of Peggy.

CHAPTER

47

Monday, September 2
In flight to New York

Tim McMahon chauffeured Nora and Tommy and their guests to Dublin Airport, and they headed to their respective gates after getting checked in. The flight to New York City was one of the best they'd had, and Nora and Tommy thanked their friendly stewardess Mary Lou for the attentive service.

Nora had brought along the mail that Mary Ann had passed on to her and perused the various envelopes after the plane took off. There were the usual bills, thank you notes, requests for money, and a few other letters she couldn't easily categorize. After going through most of them, she opened an envelope bordered with roses and lilies. At first, she thought it might be a wedding invitation, but it was a handwritten note of two pages with a date of two days ago and a signature of "One Who Cares."

A quick reading revealed that the gist of the note was that Nora might think that her husband, Tommy, was so squeaky clean, but he had been having an affair with an attractive woman for many months. The author of the note said that she (Nora assumed it was a woman) wanted to warn her about it, but she also wanted one hundred thousand dollars or she would take the story to *The Irish Times*, *The Daily Mirror*, and the *Chicago Tribune*. Nora was instructed to put the money into a brown envelope and leave it in the lockers at LaGuardia Airport storage. The directions said that it had to be there within two days.

At first, the note seemed like it was completely made up, rather like something out of a bad play. Nora's usual reaction to stress was to pause and decide what the best course of action should be. A number of questions swirled around in her mind immediately.

Could it be true about Tommy? Nora doubted it, mainly because she thought if it were true, she would have felt it. Tommy was a wealthy, virile, and attractive man, and many women could be after him, but she'd never detected a lack of interest by him in her or any of her endeavors.

Nora had always taken the advice of Fr. Thomas Merton, the famous Trappist monk, to have a sense of balance and not swerve too far in either direction when trying to make good decisions. She knew that she was not the most attractive woman since she was so short and had such curly hair. On the other hand, she took good care of herself and seemed to be attractive in the ways that appealed to Tommy.

Should she tell Tommy about the letter? He was soundly snoozing in the seat beside him, but she thought that she didn't have a choice. Grandma Peg's advice around such things was to think of the worst-case scenario and then have a plan. Nora allowed her mind to consider what would happen if she did find out it was true. *Would she still love him? Yes. Could she deal with the bad publicity? Yes.* But she wouldn't like it one bit. She thought of a number of other "what ifs" but decided to wait until she could get Tommy's attention. Was she being disloyal to him to even consider that it could be true? Probably, but she still had to know.

Once Tommy woke up, Nora relayed the news about receiving the letter and said she assumed it was all made up, but she had to know the truth before she could proceed with how to respond. Tommy was horrified to hear about the letter and asked to read it. He immediately responded, "This is a total fabrication, my love, and we can only respond to the blackmailer in a confident and unified manner. There are other attractive women in the world, but you're the only one I'm interested in. Also, if the time ever did come when I wouldn't feel that way, I would tell you about it, so stop worrying, please! Let's get that out of the way first.

"We knew when you first acquired all this money that there were going to be people who would try to drive us apart, but we won't let them do it, right? What we do have to solve is what to do about the blackmail demands since you know it would not end with one payment. If the blackmailer gives the story to the press, we'll just have to deal with the results. Those scandal rags lie every day, and I think most people realize that."

Tommy assured her he loved her more than ever, and he told her to call her friend Lt. Matt Braxton in Chicago and ask his advice as to who to deal with at the New York PD. She reached Matt immediately, described her latest problem, and he told her to contact Lt. Michael Lombardo at the NYPD. She gave the lieutenant a call, and he asked them to come and talk to him at his office. He gave them the address, and after they landed, they stopped there before even going to the condo.

Lieutenant Lombardo told them that the New York PD solves thousands of crimes every year, and he thought they should be able to resolve this one pretty easily. He wrote down all her information and said that he would assign a detail to watch the lockers at LaGuardia. They would have someone pose as Nora and put a package in the storage lockers at the airport, but they would have plenty of people watching in various spots.

Lieutenant Lombardo called them the next day and said that, fortunately, the man behind all this was one of those "stupid criminals" who didn't realize what a foolish plan this was to try to carry off in their fair city. As soon as the man tried to open the locker, the hidden police grabbed him and the package, a photographer took his photo, and the whole affair was wrapped up faster than you could say *Breakfast at Tiffany's*.

Nora and Tommy were pleased and surprised at this happy result and thanked the New York policemen profusely. This seemed like an excellent omen as their introduction to New York. Would that all their problems would be solved so easily!

Nora and Tommy stayed at their new condo for the first time and were so tired, they slept better than they had for a long time. In the morning, Tommy left early so that he could attend a meeting at his law firm's office in the city. He hoped that he would be back to the apartment in time for her party tonight, and he wished her good luck with the meeting with the members of the NYSE and with Peggy O'Reilly's father.

Nora wondered how the meeting would go this morning with Seamus O'Reilly, Peggy O'Reilly's birth father. She had done a gene-alogical and background check on Peggy after finding a letter in the meager suitcase that the sweet girl had brought with her to the orphanage. She found a Seamus O'Reilly who lived in New York and could potentially be her father. Nora had invited Seamus to her new "digs," the magnificent condo just down the street from St. Patrick's Cathedral, but she didn't tell him why she had invited him to meet with her today.

Seamus and his lawyer Josh McIntyre were cleared by security at the front desk and came to Nora's front door. They were shown in by Nora's assistant Tess McNamara. The men both took a deep breath as they glanced around the huge living quarters in the sea-of-white and silver condo that overlooked the Hudson River. The one noticeable color was the shiny ebony black concert grand piano in front of the floor to ceiling windows. They could only imagine how much the square footage of this huge space in downtown New York would cost. Tess explained that Nora Duffy was hosting a large party tonight in the main room, so they would be meeting her in her study.

Tess guided them around the corner to an equally spectacular, although somewhat smaller room that overlooked the steeple of St. Patrick's Cathedral. Nora Duffy stood up to welcome them and intro-duced them to her solicitor from Duffy Medical, Fiona Finnegan. Both women were dressed in elegant casual clothes, and they also exuded an aura of self-confidence. Seamus recognized Fiona's Dublin brogue immediately. The fact that Nora introduced her as her solici-tor rather than her lawyer told him they were well prepared for some-thing to do with Ireland.

Nora asked the men to be seated at a nearby glass and silver table and said she hoped they did not mind having an early breakfast since she had to prepare for a Duffy Medical meeting and party later tonight. Seamus was dying to ask Nora why she had asked him to come there, but he resisted the impulse to ask. He first thought that she wanted to hire him for some job, but after seeing Fiona Finnegan there, he felt that was probably not the case.

Nora started right in. "I've had a background check done on you, Mr. O'Reilly, so I know your basic information. Do you have a family?"

If Seamus was surprised by this question, he tried not to show it. "Yes, I was a widower with a daughter when I met my wife, Veronica Burton, after I came here from Ireland. We just celebrated our third anniversary, and my daughter Chelsea is ten years old. We live in Tribeca, and I sell real estate in Manhattan. Veronica runs a downtown boutique. Our daughter attends a charter school for gifted learners."

"Do you have family still in Ireland?"

"My parents are dead, but I have a brother who lives in Belfast."

Tess came in and served them ice water with lemon and a ham and cheese quiche with a salad. A baguette and butter sat on an adjoining crystal plate. They chitchatted about the weather and New York until they finished the delicious meal. Then Nora got right down to business.

"Seamus, I told you I'd done a thorough background check on you. I would have felt better as you were telling me about your history if you had mentioned that you have another ten-year-old daughter. I don't know what assumption you made as to why I invited you here, but it involves a ten-year-old girl in Dublin and her dead mother. There is some evidence that you used to visit a prostitute Clare Clark, who got pregnant and had your twin girls.

"You said you were a widower, but I could find no evidence of your marriage in Ireland. I do not know why you left Dublin and came to New York, but you evidently left one of the twins behind. The mother is long dead, and the little girl has suffered terribly. Can you tell me why you decided to come to New York with only one of the girls?"

Seamus was uncomfortable now, but he responded, "I loved Clare at first, but she couldn't stop using drugs. I told her I was going to take the girls and move to New York to be with my brother, but she begged me to leave the 'runt' with her. I did that, and later, I tried to find them, but they had moved. I came to New York five years ago with my daughter Chelsea, and later, I married Veronica. She and Chelsea seemed to bond well, and we live happily enough.

"I sometimes think about Clare and how easy she was to get along with and regret that things weren't different for us. I told Veronica I was a widower since it made my history sound better, and I didn't mention Peggy."

Nora recounted Clare and Peggy's story from the little that she had been able to glean from Sister Mary Ann and the Dublin Garda. She did not pull any punches when describing what Peggy had gone through. "A neighbor alerted the Dublin police about a terrible smell coming from Clare's shabby apartment. They found Peggy sitting next to her mother who had been stabbed to death. The child was filthy, her clothes were in tatters, and she was playing with a sex toy. Rats had started to chew on the mother's flesh, and the child was crying hysterically. Lieutenant O'Shea said it was a pitiful sight that broke his heart. The police knew about Uncle Cyrus's orphanage, and they brought Peggy there with only a small suitcase of meager belongings. She's been messed up physically and mentally ever since."

Nora told Seamus that her only interest in finding him was to ensure that he would not stand in the way of Peggy's being adopted by a wonderful couple, the O'Maras in Ireland. "I would say that the O'Maras would fit in the category of happily married, fairly well off financially but not wealthy. They have a cute little home and a nice SUV. They know all about Peggy's history and seem committed to helping her in any way they can. They have also taken her to a burn specialist who has started the process of fixing the deep burns on her face and back that were inflicted on her by one of Clare's men.

"Adam O'Mara is a successful Volvo car dealer, and Cathy O'Mara is a schoolteacher and part-time nurse. They have also adopted a golden retriever puppy that seems to have helped Peggy's ability to relate to humans as well as dogs. One reason they went to Chicago was to see one of my father's friends, a renowned plastic surgeon Dr. Paul Miller, who made a good start on fixing the burn scars. Another plastic surgeon in Cork has been doing follow up work on her.

"Peggy has been with the O'Maras for a number of months now, and the adoption proceedings could be finalized next month. I don't think I'll tell her about you and her sister just yet since she's had so much to get adjusted to already. That might just confuse her, but at some point, we'll tell her about you and Chelsea, and then depending on both sides, perhaps there could be some relationship there. I think she would be happy to know that she has a sister."

Nora showed him a picture of Peggy, the O'Maras, the home they live in, and Peggy's bedroom. He commented that Peggy looked so much like Chelsea, although skinnier. Peggy's bedroom looked fancy in an old-fashioned way. Nora said that was because Peggy had bypassed most of the things that children like and had gone right to an early adulthood. Peggy had seen pictures of art deco furnishings and decor, and the O'Maras helped her to purchase them. "It's a beautiful and restful room, and one that will be comfortable for her for many years to come.

"I've brought along a legal document that says you relinquish parental rights to Peggy, and I am hopeful you will sign it. That means that you will have no monetary obligations toward Peggy, but perhaps things can change between you at a later date."

Andrew looked over the agreement, and they gave Seamus some time to glance through it. "Did they ever find out who killed Clare?"

"The police looked for a suspect, but they had no real clues since the neighbors said there were a variety of men who visited the apartment."

"Can you give me more time to think about this?" queried Seamus. "Of course, I've thought about the two of them vaguely for all these years, but to know that Clare died in such terrible circumstances and Peggy has suffered so terribly is quite a shock. When I left them, it seemed as though Clare had a plan in mind for how to support herself. She was so proud, and she would not accept my help. She had started a laundry and ironing business that seemed as though it was working well. I gave her the equivalent of one thousand dollars when I left, and I bought the baby some clothes and food. I'm happy that there's a nice couple willing to be her parents, but I would like to see the girl."

300

"Apparently, an autopsy showed a high concentration of drugs in Clare's system, so she likely wasn't thinking clearly for some time. Does your wife know about Clare and Peggy?" inquired Nora. "I think most women would find it hard to adjust to that knowledge. I'd really like you to sign the document today since I'm going home to Chicago in a few days and then I'm headed back to Dublin to help with the adoption.

"Frankly, I don't care if any of this makes you uncomfortable," said Nora. "My main concern is that there will not be any hurdles in the way of the adoption proceedings. Every child with a missing parent dreams that she has a loving father somewhere, but when Peggy discovers that you abandoned her and her mother to such a desperate fate, I would think it would take her quite a while before she'd want to see you. I think she would be happy to know that she has a twin."

Seamus answered that his wife ran with a sophisticated crowd, and she would probably not take kindly to knowing about his relationship with a woman like Clare and that there was another child. His daughter's friends had high opinions of themselves, and Chelsea would probably not like it either.

Andrew, the lawyer, told Seamus that he should sign the document so his other daughter might have a happy future to look forward to. "Eventually, your wife and daughter might accept that there is a former lady friend and a sister to deal with," Andrew advised.

Nora thanked Seamus for signing the document and told him that she would keep him updated about Peggy and her new life. Seamus and Andrew left the beautiful condo, but Peggy's father was conflicted between emotions of relief and guilt. Nora called Adam and Cathy O'Mara and relayed the good news to them that she had Seamus's signed release, and she would get it to them as soon as possible.

CHAPTER

48

Nora and Tess McNamara had spent the day preparing for the meeting of the Duffy Medical personnel with representatives from the New York Stock Exchange. Margaret Kenmare had warned them that the NYSE would likely not approve of their application yet, but they wanted to still go ahead with the meeting.

Everything in the room was shiny and welcoming, but Nora was nervous about the decisions that might be made here today about the possibility of Duffy Medical, Ltd. becoming publicly traded on the NYSE. She had studied the complex and confusing rules around such a venture, but she would defer to the financial acumen of her board members.

When the NYSE members arrived for the meeting, they were pleased to see Margaret Kenmare there, who was well known to them. Nora greeted them and they were then introduced to the other officers and members of the Duffy Medical Board who were present. The NYSE representatives listened carefully to the presentation that John O'Malley gave in his well-elucidated Irish accent, and then they asked Margaret Kenmare for her opinion.

She told them she thought another six months of preparation and planning would be helpful, and they said that was their opinion as well. They said they probably would have turned down the proposal all together, but having Margaret Kenmare involved gave them more confidence that they could make this work. They assigned one of their members Mr. Claude Deakins to work with Margaret and said they would be happy to meet with them again in six months or so. They thanked Nora for her hospitality and left. The Duffy Medical board members breathed a sigh of relief that there was more hope for them now in a few months, but they knew they would have to work hard to make it all come together by next spring.

Later that evening, Nora had invited some people to join them for a party. Austin Tennill the artist and Robert Durkin the movie producer that they had met at Aunt Janet's in California and their partners were invited to the party. Also invited were members of the St. Patrick's Cathedral staff since they were planning a fundraiser for New York's Catholic Charities and the many people it helped to support. Nora had asked Austin Tennill to do some quick sketches of the various people at the party, and Nora requested that Robert Durkin film various sequences for a future documentary.

Tommy called and said that several problems had come up, and he was stuck at the office, so he would probably not get back to the apartment until much later. He apologized but said they were in the middle of some tense negotiations. Nora thanked him for the call and said to be careful if he would be coming back so late.

When Robert arrived, she was again struck by the fact that he seemed so familiar to her. The food and drinks were provided by the famous 21 Club, and everything looked fantastic and tasted better. The party was a huge success, and guests from the Metropolitan Opera entertained them. The children from the Catholic Charities Orphanage sang their hearts out and everyone was impressed by them as they sang "God Bless America," the old Frank Sinatra hit, "New York, New York," and a number of other lovely songs.

After everyone had left, the professional cleaners came in and returned the apartment to pristine shape, Nora said goodnight to Tess, and she sat down and kicked off her high heels. She played a little music on her violin and was just getting sleepy when she heard a knock on her door. That was very strange since no one was supposed to be able to come up to the apartment unless they had checked in with security who would have called her.

Nora had been the victim of too many surprise attacks recently, so she had a few minutes to think about what she would do if the knocker was also an attacker. The first thing she did was to open her bedroom door and release the twin Doberman dogs Rover and Spot, who were on loan from the NYPD. She had requested them as an added measure of security, but she had not needed them earlier. The dogs had been so quiet during the party, and she doubted that anyone even knew they were there. Nora had been spoiling them and they were devoted to her, but the sleek and powerful Dobermans were most decidedly undevoted to anyone she would designate as an enemy. She picked up her hand dog whistle and put it in her pocket.

She called Lieutenant Lombardo of the NYPD and asked him to come over to the apartment right away, and she also alerted her friend Lt. Matt Braxton from Chicago who was visiting nearby. She also pushed the ON switch on her recording equipment.

Nora then opened the front door a crack to see who had been knocking. The hallway was dark except for some diffused light from a hallway sconce. Robert Durkin's face looked ethereal as he greeted her with a forced smile and said he had left his book in the living room and asked if he might retrieve it.

Nora knew this was a lie since the cleaners had not found anything like a book, and she tried to prepare for what might happen next. She murmured the prayer to St. Michael the Archangel, patron of police and firemen and asked him for his assistance.

The movie producer started to back away when he saw the two dogs with the very formidable teeth that were on full display, but Nora invited him to come in. The dogs were quietly but intently growling, and it was clear they were not a fan of Robert Durkin. As she had been looking at the small view of his face in the doorway, she suddenly recognized why Robert seemed familiar to her.

"Please come in, Mr. Durkin. The apartment has already been thoroughly cleaned, and there was no book found. I've had the strongest feeling for some time now that you remind me of someone, and I've just realized who that is. You must be related to my good friend who grew vegetables on my estate in Ireland, Mr. Jack Boyle. Won't you please tell me what that story is?" Nora made sure to leave the door open a crack so that Lieutenant Lombardo could get in when he arrived.

"You're a smart lass," Robert Durkin said as he abandoned all pretense of having an English accent and reverted back to a thick Irish brogue. "I saw you staring at me several times during the party, and I knew you were about to figure out that I look a lot like my Uncle Jack Boyle. Long ago, Jack's brother Ian O'Boylan helped out the IRA in Belfast by blowing up a British fort. After that, Jack said he wanted nothing to do with any of them. All he really wanted was to be a farmer and live in peace. The only way he could do that was to change his name and run away and hide out in that piss-hole village of yours for so long.

"When he left Belfast, Jack took money and a record of the family's activities there. We'd been looking for him off and on for years, and I finally tracked him down. After I killed him, I found everything hidden under the floorboards of his cottage. I know you thought of him as just a nice old guy, but believe me, he could shoot the eyes out of a sparrow, and he did that many times before he got 'religion.'"

Nora noticed that Robert Durkin's jacket was missing a middle button, and she was sure that the garda would confirm that the gold button they'd found tightly clutched in Jack Boyle's dead hand would match perfectly. Nora responded, "Your sweet uncle wrote his killer's name in his own blood, Mr. Durkin. Are you 'Bill C.?'"

The man menacing her replied that his real name was William Connelly, which his uncle knew. "And now it looks as though I'm going to have to kill you too," said Robert Durkin as he started to pull out a gun.

Several things happened concurrently. The tall woman dressed in the black coat with the stringy black hair and wearing the pink pom-pom hat burst through the door and shot the gun out of Robert's hand. The Dobermans also leapt for both of Robert Durkin's arms, and he screamed in terror and pain.

"Bitsy, it's Laura underneath this goofy disguise," shouted out the woman in the pink hat. Pick up that gun that he had and make sure he can't get to it." Laura Belsky then removed her ugly wig and the pink hat, and her beautiful face was revealed.

"Thanks, Laura dear," Nora screamed out. "I don't know why you've been wearing that outfit and following me around, but once again you've saved my life. You really are like Annie Oakley."

Laura promised to tell her more about it all, but just then, Lieutenant Lombardo and several officers from the NYPD burst through the door. Lt. Matt Braxton from Chicago was close behind.

Robert Durkin tried to say that Nora was making up the whole story, but she assured him that she had turned on the recording machine and all that he had said was captured on there. Durkin was struggling to get the dogs off of him, but she advised him to stay quiet. "Mr. Durkin, stop struggling or these handsome lads may chomp down through both your wrist arteries. If that happens you would bleed to death very quickly."

Durkin realized that he had no choice, and Nora gave a signal to the dogs who let go of the frightened man's arms and trotted meekly over to her side. Durkin screamed at Nora and said she shouldn't quit her day job to try to be a detective. He had been behind the attempts on her life for months now, and she never even suspected him. He had thrown in the golden horseshoes at Jack Boyle's cottage after he heard about the girl being found on the Coral Beach.

He tried to spit at her, but the NYPD team said that they would take Durkin to their headquarters, where he would be charged with the attempted murder of Nora. They would contact Chief Brennan and the Irish Garda, who would pursue the charges against him for the murder of Jack Boyle in Sneem, and anything else they could find.

The detectives left with the snarling Robert Durkin, who was demanding to be taken to a hospital to have his bleeding hand attended to. Nora thanked the policemen for their timely help, and finally, Nora, Laura, and Matt Braxton were left alone.

"Holy Cow, Bitsy," Matt uttered a Chicago expletive as he sat down with a thud. "Between the vicious people you attract and these vicious dogs, I was scared to death there for a few minutes."

"You and me both, Matt," Nora laughed. "How can you call these sweet boys vicious?" she said as she petted the now very sleepy

Dobermans and gave them treats. They sat one on each side of her like black and tan marble statues.

"Okay, Laura," inquired Nora, "what's the story about that strange getup you've been wearing, and why have I been seeing you so often in different places?"

Laura laughed and began to relate the background of her outfit and her involvement. "Your dear husband, Tommy, worries about you so much, and he asked me to keep an eye on you when he couldn't be around. After those first murders happened, he knew you would not be able to resist trying to solve the puzzle, so he asked me to shadow you and wear something you wouldn't recognize. It was not always easy to keep track of you and then disappear quickly.

"When I resigned from the Chicago PD, it was just a case of going on leave, so I still had my gun. He talked to California and New York and got me clearance to have my gun there as well. And a good thing too.

"When Tommy heard you were going to have this big gathering at your New York apartment, he rented out the apartment next door, and we made arrangements for me to stay there and listen in on the party with this sophisticated recording equipment he had installed. He asked me to stay on duty for several hours afterward until I was sure you were asleep. Tommy had a feeling that the killer would use the party as an opportunity to try to finish his dirty work. I put on my disguise in case I needed it.

"As soon as I heard that Robert Durkin came back to your apartment, I listened to his confession, and then I pulled out my gun and was ready for him. I'm glad that it worked out well.

"By the way, I am supposed to be preparing for our wedding in two weeks," Laura said as she reached for Matt's hands.

"Can we go home now, please?" Matt inquired sounding so relieved. "New York is a fantastic place, but it's better to deal with the devil we know."

"I guess we've about rounded up all the bad guys now," said Nora, "so let's finish everything up here and get out of Dodge."

Nora pulled out her phone and called Sergeant Rodriguez, the dog handler from the NYPD, and asked him to pick up Rover and

Spot. He arrived shortly, Nora gave both the dogs an ear tousle and a hug and more treats, and then all was quiet. She thanked Sergeant Rodriguez profusely and said she hoped she could work with him again soon.

Tommy came jogging down the hallway after his long day and said he had seen the police leaving. Had something happened? Nora, Matt, and Laura just laughed at that, and Nora said she would give him a quick update. Nora said she was pretty tired out now and would like to go to bed. Laura said there was a huge bedroom in the apartment next door, so she and Matt left. Nora told them she would have Kitty make reservations for them on the flight home tomorrow, and then they said a very good night to these dear friends.

Nora and Tommy talked about their "interesting" evening and she thanked him for getting Laura involved in her protection. They both enjoyed a good laugh at the outlandish outfit that the lovely Laura had worn during her sleuthing escapades.

Nora called her brother Jim and asked him to pick them up at O'Hare tomorrow afternoon. He also said that he had gone to see Connie Carroll that afternoon, and she had walked through her house without a walker for the first time, so things were definitely looking up.

In the morning, Nora and Tommy and Laura and Matt attended an early morning Mass at St. Patrick's Cathedral, and Nora found herself feeling emotionally drained. She usually felt uplifted by the building's beauty and incredible architecture, but all she could do today was thank God that she and her friends were still alive. Listening to the magnificent pipe organ and the choir was a first step in renewing her energy, and she rather numbly sang along. Her spirit was usually pretty resilient, but she asked St. Patrick to help her get past this latest violence. She posed a question to God: What was the use of her having all this money when it did not seem like there was anything substantial that she could do to obtain "peace on earth"?

She tried to remember the advice she gave others when they were feeling down, and she recalled the words of the song, "Pick yourself up, dust yourself off, and start all over again." They said goodbye to St. Patrick's pastor, who thanked Nora and Tommy once again for their generosity. He told them that many people would have a place to stay and food to eat because of them, and Nora felt a little better.

The four friends had a quick breakfast at Fitzpatrick's—Manhattan, part of an Irish hotel chain, and then they headed out to LaGuardia for the trip home. As they traveled through the busy streets, Nora thought of the song that epitomized New York for her, *42nd Street*:

> Come and meet
> Those dancing feet
> On the avenue I'm taking you to
> Forty-Second Street.
> Hear the beat
> Of dancing feet
> It's the song I love the melody of
> Forty-Second Street.

New York is the city that never sleeps with millions of feet walking, running, and dancing, and anything good or bad was possible here. She hoped to spend more time here when there was time as they continued to plan for the Duffy Medical, Ltd. IPO. She told her family that they would be able to use the condo if it was available when they needed it.

CHAPTER

49

Sunday, September 8
Chicago, Illinois; 10:00 a.m., CDT

Ralph and Hitch, the Duffy Hall Castle ghosts, had been asked by Angel Christopher to look out for the Duffy family's welfare in Chicago for a few weeks before they were sent back to Ireland. They had been hanging around Doctor Duffy's home and noticed a lot of activity there, so they perched themselves on the roof for a better vantage point. They saw the family arrive with fall flowers and other paraphernalia and smiled when they saw the toddler Dylan being given many hugs by everyone. Ralph said he thought he looked like him when he was a wee one. Hitch said that would be impossible since Dylan was so good looking.

As people settled down for a lunch, the ghosts realized that Dylan was heading over to the area where construction was being done in the backyard and they watched him closely to see what he would do. The ghosts spotted a board studded with many old nails and, of course, that was where Dylan was heading.

Both ghosts immediately swooped down and pushed the little guy onto the ground and away from the board. The little boy started to cry and had a few scrapes on his hands, but at least he was saved from the painful injuries that could have happened to him if he had fallen on the protruding nails. Dylan's parents quickly ran over to him and picked him up and said they had not realized that the board was even there.

Bridie, the former good ghost of the castle and now a member of the angelic choir, saw it all too, and she was amazed at how quickly her two old pals had acted to prevent serious injury to the little boy. She noticed that Ralph and Hitch were still smiling and seemed to have enjoyed doing something good without wanting to counter it with something bad. She would be giving a full report about it to Angel Christopher.

Saturday, September 14

The day for Matt Braxton and Laura Belsky's wedding finally arrived, and the temperate weather cooperated. Laura was a parishioner at one of those enormous Polish churches whose tall spires pierce the Chicago skyline all over the city. It was inspiring to think that these huge and beautiful churches had been built by thousands of laborers who appreciated their new home and thanked God for it by erecting these magnificent edifices and accompanying schools.

Laura had asked Nora to be a bridesmaid, but she said she knew that Laura had sisters, cousins, and friends who would be more appropriate for this, and she would be honored just to be there. Laura's parents were so happy that this day had arrived for their little girl. Mr. Belsky was a big man with a hearty laugh and a full head of white hair, and he said it was about time that Laura got with the program and gave them grandchildren while they could still spoil them. Nora could see that Laura had come by her beauty naturally since her mother looked gorgeous in her blue chiffon dress, and her silvery blond hair had been woven into an intricate pattern.

The many bridesmaids were dressed in champagne pink with seed pearls and held large bouquets of pink and white roses. The groomsmen were in gray tuxes with pink cummerbunds. Nora counted ten junior bridesmaids and four little boys, and she thought it was one of the more elegant weddings she had been to anywhere.

The stars of the show lived up to the many expectations. Laura was so pretty she would look good in a paper sack, but her elegant white silk wedding dress, decorated with thousands of seed pearls, had an exceptionally long train that rustled when she walked down the long aisle. Her grandmother had created the veil out of a gossamer material that shone under the lights. The wedding planner had told her to wear a poker face during this walk, but Laura paid no attention to her and was smiling from ear to ear. Matt was dressed in his formal policeman's uniform and looked like the cat that swallowed the canary all during the mass. Father Chiomsky had a booming voice that carried well in the enormous church, and his final words of encouragement to them would be remembered as long as they lived.

The dinner was held in the church hall, and everyone enjoyed the Polish sausage, sauerkraut, and pierogis, as well as the beef, pork, and chicken. The magnificent cake decorated with roses and lilies of the valley was cut, and then the dancing started and went on until midnight. Nora and Tommy had given the couple a generous gift toward a house, and Nora reminded herself that she might not still be alive if it were not for these two dear friends.

Matt and Laura said their preference for a honeymoon was to go to Yellowstone National Park and hike as many trails as they could and take a thousand pictures. They had been warned to take clothes appropriate for all seasons since in the fall it could be pleasantly warm or even snowing, but they couldn't wait to see the animals and the geysers. Their grandparents had instilled in them that there were so many beautiful places in this country there was no need to travel elsewhere.

It had been a perfect day for them, without a hint of murder or mayhem, and that was the best gift they could have hoped for.

CHAPTER

50

Sneem, Ireland, and Chicago, Illinois

The signed document by Seamus O'Reilly relinquishing his parental rights for Peggy O'Reilly had been received and recorded, and Peggy's adoption by the O'Maras was steadily moving forward and should be finalized before Christmas.

The Duffy Medical Research Center building was well underway and under roof, but there was much more that needed to be finished. They would work on the interior during the winter, and the attractive building should be ready by the spring. They had commitments from ten doctors so far, who said they would be involved in pursuing research at the facility. It would also provide work opportunities for about twenty local people. At Christmastime, there would be a tall Christmas tree shining behind the glassed-in walls and giant shining stars would appear on its roof.

Love seemed to be in the air in both countries. Tommy's sister Lucy Barry and fiancé, Kevin, planned to marry in April at the castle. Nora's brother Jim and his fiancée Trish were preparing for their wedding next May, and his slightly younger brother Jim had formally proposed to Sally Doerr, and they set their wedding for next June. Enda Feeney's Bill Callahan presented her with an impressive diamond, but they didn't want to wait too long, so they set their wedding date for Valentine's Day. Nora offered to let them stay at her New York condo for their honeymoon, and they had gratefully accepted. Tim Taylor and Betsy Reilly had been faithfully attending the Gamblers Anonymous meetings, and they also set their wedding date for next May. The coroners Aloysius Stec and Lucy Sullivan seemed to be an item, as did Gemma Doherty and Paul McShane.

Nora hosted a baby shower for Pam and Allen Pepper at her home and was excited that so many of Pam's family and friends were able to attend. Nora bought them a crib, and Tommy gave them a generous check.

Margaret and Eoghan Kenmare looked at one of the homes near Killarney that Aunt Vinnie's fiancé, Mortimer O'Brien, had built many years ago that was for sale. They said that Mort was ahead of his time since the flow of the rooms and the charming exterior would fit nicely into the pages of a modern architectural magazine. They bought the vacation house and had some of it restored and thanked Nora for her help. Eoghan said he had not realized until they came to Ireland how much they had been missing out of life. He had enjoyed fishing as a young boy, and he planned to take that up again on the lake across from their new home.

Margaret only liked fish when it appeared nicely cooked on her plate, but she did like sitting on the shore with a book or a financial prospectus while her husband pursued his hobby. She was still getting used to being away from New York for any length of time, but now she would be close to Sneem when it was time for the Board of Directors' meetings. She was surprised at how much she enjoyed furnishing and decorating the house, and she was beginning to learn about antiques and where to find them in Ireland and England. She had also been contacted by some of the locals who had heard about her and asked her to act as their financial advisor. Margaret and Eoghan both had something to look forward to when their busy lives allowed them some free time to explore the many Killarney attractions. Nora gave them a guidebook that also exposed her to information about so many other notable places in Ireland they could visit.

Nora's and Tommy's families were always so busy during the holidays, and they had many activities planned between now and New Year's Day. They were looking forward to a fall trip to Maine to visit one of Doctor Duffy's former interns Ben Durant, who now ran a successful farm-to-table restaurant with his wife. They planned to do some sightseeing in the surrounding states and spending time on the huge beach while enjoying the Northeast's famous multicolored trees. They thought they might also host a big Halloween party at their home.

Nora loved all the holiday traditions and family gatherings at home, but she would have to go back to Sneem for the Duffy Medical Board meeting and Christmas Ball on November 30, which should be fun. She was also looking forward to seeing how the store on the Duffy estate was doing now that it would be open.

The past year would be memorable for them for so many reasons, but Nora and Tommy were scheduled for a visit with Dr. Phyllis Bateman, her friend and obstetrician at Holy Savior, this week. Nora thought that she might be pregnant, and that would be thrilling! Like all new moms, she had a few concerns about her health and having to limit her vigorous lifestyle, but her mother had had ten babies and had few problems, so she hoped it would be the same for her.

She knew she should probably wait for confirmation before telling her family, but she was too excited. She couldn't wait to share the good news with her mother just to see the look of joy on her face. Her brother Kevin provided the succinct response of the entire family to the news by exclaiming, "Holy Cow, Bitsy, we never know what exciting surprises to expect from you. Here we go again!"

Nora had become more mindful of the sunrises and sunsets in Chicago since she had become so familiar with them in Sneem. She and Tommy climbed up to the third-floor balcony of their home, held hands, and watched the sun slowly go down behind the small woods to the west of their home amidst an orange and pink sky. They remembered Father Joseph's words from the wedding in California and knew that they were going to need the help of many hands as they proceeded through this next adventure.

As Dickens powerfully reminded us, it always seems to be "the best and worst of times," but when they reflected on the many people who had supported them during the past year, Nora and Tommy vowed to face whatever the future held for them with hope and joy!

EPILOGUE

Nora and Tommy were thrilled beyond words that her pregnancy test was positive! This is the kind of happiness that no amount of money can buy! They entrusted themselves and their coming baby to God's hands and talked about future plans at the house. As she usually did, Nora mentally arranged the new furniture in the bedroom next to theirs that would be needed for either Baby Emily Lavinia or Conor Cyrus. They decided they did not want to know the gender of the baby ahead of time and were content to wait for the big day. They were delighted to anticipate all the planning that would be done for their new little one's arrival.

After living in Dublin for a few months and working at the Abbey Theatre, Siobhan Duffy decided that while she loved the company there, she missed her family and her friends too much. The theater would always be in her blood, but she had contacted a friend in Chicago and was told that they could find a place for her in the Shakespeare festival's upcoming season. She would continue to visit Ireland frequently and would keep in touch with her old acting companions, but she was glad to be going home.

The new lighthouse dedicated to Jack Boyle at the Coral Beach in Sneem that would be surrounded by a small park was well on its way to completion. Bill Callahan had finished the painting of Jack and his collie Flossie at its base. Jack's story had been picked up by many news outlets and churches throughout Ireland, and they thought it likely that the lighthouse would be a popular tourist destination.

Robert Durkin was in jail awaiting trial for the murder of Jack Boyle and the attempted murder of Nora, but one of the good things he had done earlier was to contact a friend Paul Kane, who made documentaries. Nora had seen some of Paul's work and agreed that it was artful and lyrical, and she engaged him to make the movie about Duffy Hall Castle and its founders. He gave her a proposal, and she agreed with his timetable. He said he would start to shoot footage next month, would continue through the winter months, and it should be finished by the spring.

Adam and Cathy O'Mara thought that their new daughter, Peggy O'Reilly, was now confident enough in herself and her new family to hear the news that her birth father and twin sister were alive and lived in New York City. Peggy had learned a lot from the various doctors that had helped her to get to this point, but she said she was ambivalent about wanting to see them. She knew that she had been abandoned by this man, and whatever his reasons were, his leaving had contributed to the death of her mother and her mental and emotional trauma. It was exciting though to think that she had a twin, and she thought of the happy Duffy twins and how close they were. She supposed that this girl that lived in New York might not want anything to do with her, but she used her newfound interest in prayer to ask God for his help.

Nora told Peggy that she should take a few more months to get used to the idea, and she would keep in touch with Seamus O'Reilly. They kept in close contact with the psychotherapist Mary Donovan, and she advised patience.

Fiona Finnegan discovered that it would take many months to sort out which museums and academic institutions would be interested in the Duffy Hall Castle treasures. A museum in Dublin said they would be willing to accept the lot of them and hold them in their secure vaults for a fee, and they would assess which objects they would be interested in featuring. Before any of that happened, numerous conservationists, historians, and photographers prodded and investigated it all. Filmmakers then made digital copies of every item, and those would be shown in the special area of the old castle that was being prepared for this.

Angel Christopher had received Bridie's positive report about the castle's ghosts Ralph and Hitch and had summoned them into his presence. He told them that he was pleased to hear of how they had saved

Dylan Duffy from serious injury, apparently with no thought of recompense, and he thought it was high time for them to join the angelic ranks. He agreed with them that their screechy voices would not blend well with the angelic choir, but he had a better idea for them.

Word had reached him of a pair of twins at St. Brigid's Orphanage in Ireland that were driving the teachers crazy with their mischief. Christopher told Ralph and Hitch that they would now be guardian angels, and their first assignment would be to keep these twins out of trouble. The ghosts thought it ironic that they would be given this task when that had been their specialty for so long, but they said they would give it a try. They asked Christopher to thank God for his faith in them. Hitch asked if he could have an occasional Guinness, and Christopher said he would see what he could do. Angel Bridie applauded and said she was so happy that her old friends were joining the band of angels that keep watch over those in their charge.

Ralph and Hitch looked especially proud that Angel Christopher had given them each two garda stars to wear on their new angel uniforms. They made them feel more official and confident about their new roles.

Nora was about to close up her computer on New Year's Eve when she was delighted and surprised to see a message from Michael Chow. Michael was a former classmate from medical school, but she had lost track of him after he went back to his home in Wuhan, China to practice his microbiology specialty.

Michael's message was brief:

> Bitsy, Krakatoa!! I'll be shot if they see me sending a message so this will be quick. A new and terrible virus is loose in my city and thousands of people are sick and dying, including my grandparents. I've been trying to figure out how to stop it night and day in our lab, but it's too elusive. We know it's a coronavirus, like SARS or MERS, but it's even worse and much more contagious than the flu. I'm so sick, and I know I'm not going to

make it. God help us all if it gets out into the world. You're the smartest person I know other than me. Protect yourself and your big family. Thinking of you and our happy days in school. Pray for me. I'm so scared, Number Two Son.

Nora read through the pensive note a second time with horrified fascination and shivered with apprehension. Dear sweet Michael, so brilliant and so funny, not much bigger than she was, and happiest when he was eating a bowl of fruit loops with hot chocolate that he said helped him think.

Krakatoa, the huge Indonesian volcano that erupted in 1883 with the loudest sound in recorded history that was heard three thousand miles away had been their code word for the worst possible thing that could happen to them. In their school days, that might have been the cancellation of days off for a month, but he really was now experiencing the worst. He was still trying to keep a sense of humor as he was dying. They used to laugh at the quirky Charlie Chan movies, and Michael would say that he was like Charlie's number two son.

Everyone at the medical school had pleaded with him to stay in the US after graduation, but Wuhan lured him with a big title and a big bonus, and besides, his grandparents were still there. Now, those elders that he loved so much must be dead already.

They used to banter back and forth about who was the smartest, but she always knew it was him. If Michael couldn't figure out how to stop this terrible virus, she doubted she could do much, but she could at least alert the CDC. They might know about it already, but she vowed that she would call the CDC and talk to her friend Estelle in the morning and ask for her advice. Estelle had helped Holy Savior Hospital to update their infectious disease protocols after their recent Plague scare, so they should be well prepared for a new challenge.

Nora thought about sending Michael a response, but if someone was watching him, she didn't want to add to his troubles. Her tears started to flow as she thought about the stress he had been going through. He might already be dead after his body had been invaded by a deadly entity, billions of times smaller than he was, but oh so effective in its quest to survive and flourish. She murmured a prayer for her friend and all those who had been infected by this new virus.

She also recalled the note she had received yesterday from Father Joseph, the California priest, saying that one of his fellow priests had just died in China from a terrible flu that killed him in days. Visions of the 1918 worldwide flu that killed twenty-five million people flashed through her mind, but she thought that this new enemy couldn't be that serious. A worldwide pandemic made for good movies, but a real one was unthinkable. After all, it would be the year 2020 tomorrow, and we live in the strongest country in the world with the best medical resources possible. Surely, our scientists and doctors would find a cure for this disease if it made its way to the US?

Nora put her hands over her stomach in a protective gesture and asked for help for her developing baby and the world. She didn't know much about coronaviruses other than they originated in animals and were then passed on to humans, but she thought she'd better learn fast. She didn't need one of her *fairy fey* moments to tell her that 2020 was likely going to be a year of impossible challenges. To echo Michael's words, God help us all!

ABOUT THE AUTHOR

Babs is from Chicago and enjoys reading mystery stories in general and particularly those that take place in Ireland and England. *The Golden Horseshoes Murders* is set mostly in Sneem, Ireland, the home of Babs' great grandfather, and in an area of Chicago where many of the inhabitants claim Irish descent. This book is a sequel to *Murder at Duffy Hall Castle*, and many of the same characters are back as well as some new and interesting people. All of the people in the book are fictional, as are many of the places and events.

Babs has always been a lifelong learner, and she finds that writing books is an excellent way to learn more about the world, her family, and herself. She has been a musician since she was four years old as well as an amateur astronomer. Like many others addicted to reading, she has been known to read the back of the cereal box if a book isn't handy. She has been a book club member most of her adult life and has learned as much from the other members as from the books themselves.

She has a large family and her greatest joy is when she can spend time with them. If she can't actually give them a hug, she is grateful that they can communicate via social media platforms. Babs has a circle of close friends who have supported each other in good times and bad for many years and are more like adopted sisters. They've encouraged her to continue writing every step of the way.

When Babs concluded writing this book, the worldwide coronavirus pandemic was still ongoing. It seems to be lessening its grip somewhat, but hot spots continue to crop up, and the future is uncertain. It is a cautionary tale that the efforts of every scientist and doctor in the world seem to be unable to defeat this tiny but virulent enemy. Babs applauds the efforts of everyone who has provided their help during these dark days.

As Charles Dickens reminded us, it always seems to be the best and worst of times, but Babs believes in the power of Paul's words: "If God is for us, who can be against us?" This past year saw the death after a long illness of Babs' beloved husband, Don Croker, her Renaissance man. He remains a hero to his family and friends, and this book is lovingly dedicated to him.

9 781648 019005